The Conclusion of
The Carandir Saga

The evil dragon can wake at any time. Civil war rips the monarchy apart. Missions to seek aid are thwarted. A princess born far from the strife is tempered to face the evil.

Praise for The Carandir Saga

"…strong writing that helps illustrate the vastness of the fictional world and depth of the novel's lore... political drama is carefully plotted with reveals that are timed satisfactorily… Readers will easily be hooked into the exciting blend of mobilized armies and political intrigue."

> — *Publishers Weekly's Booklife Prize on Dragons Unremembered*

"The story is excellently well-done."

> — *Verified Purchaser on Dragons Unremembered*

"Reminiscent of Tolkien in terms of depth & complexity."

> — *Goodreads on Dragons Unremembered*

"…well written fantasy adventure in a well flushed out world. The characters are in depth and cross all genders with strong female protagonist in important roles in the world."

> — *Verified American Purchaser on Half wakened Dreams*

"Definitely worth a read."

> — *Net Galley on Half wakened Dreams*

"The novel's world is well-imagined and believably depicted... The prose is strong, with vivid descriptive writing, clear exposition, and dialogue that effectively builds characterization"

> — *Publishers Weekly's Booklife Prize on Covenant With the Dragons*

Covenant With the Dragons

Volume III of The Carandir Saga

DAVID A. WIMSETT

Covenant With the Dragons

A Cape Split Press Book

Published by arrangement with the author

Printing History
First Printing 2022

Text, poetry, music and lyrics Copyright © 2022 by David A. Wimsett
All rights reserved

This book may not be produced in whole or in part by any means to include photocopy, monograph, audio, video, or any digital media currently in use or to be developed in the future. For information contact Cape Split Press Ltd.
https://www.capesplitpress.com

The characters and events in this book are fictitious. Any similarity to real persons, living or dead, is coincidental and unintended by the author.

ISBN 978-1-7775745-1-2

Background Image - ID 128322658 © Elen33 | Dreamstime.com
Woman in hood - ID 117756352 © Luca Oleastri | Dreamstime.com
Dragon Image - ID 10402510 © Elenka990 | Dreamstime.com
Map designed by Glendon Haddix | Streetlight Graphics, LLC | www.streetlightgraphics.com

Used through arrangement with the artists

For Jeff

Fellow adventurer
on many campaigns

Other Books by David A. Wimsett

Dragons Unremembered: Volume I of the Carandir Saga
Half Awakened Dreams: Volume II of the Carandir Saga
Beyond the Shallow Bank
Beyond the Shallow Bank: Illustrated Edition
Something on My Mind

ACKNOWLEDGMENTS

In this, the third and final volume in The Carandir Saga, I extend my profound thanks to everyone who supported me during the production of this series; my editors, Nancy Cassidy who edited *Dragons Unremembered*, Denise Pysarchuk who edited *Half Awakened Dreams* and Christine Driver who edited *Covenant With the Dragons* for their excellent work. I also thank my son, Ronald, for his patience and understanding through many long years, Ann who encouraged and supported me and did a final check of the material, Jeff and Randie for their support and suggestions, Ed and Mike who read and commented on early drafts, Bruce and Anna for their moral support, the late best-selling author Leonard Bishop, my first mentor, who was instrumental in pointing out how to address nuts and bolts problems, the members of Leonard's weekly writing group who continually pushed me to be better and the members of the Squaw Valley Community of Writers workshops who helped me polish my work. Thank you all.

David A. Wimsett
Nova Scotia
September 2022

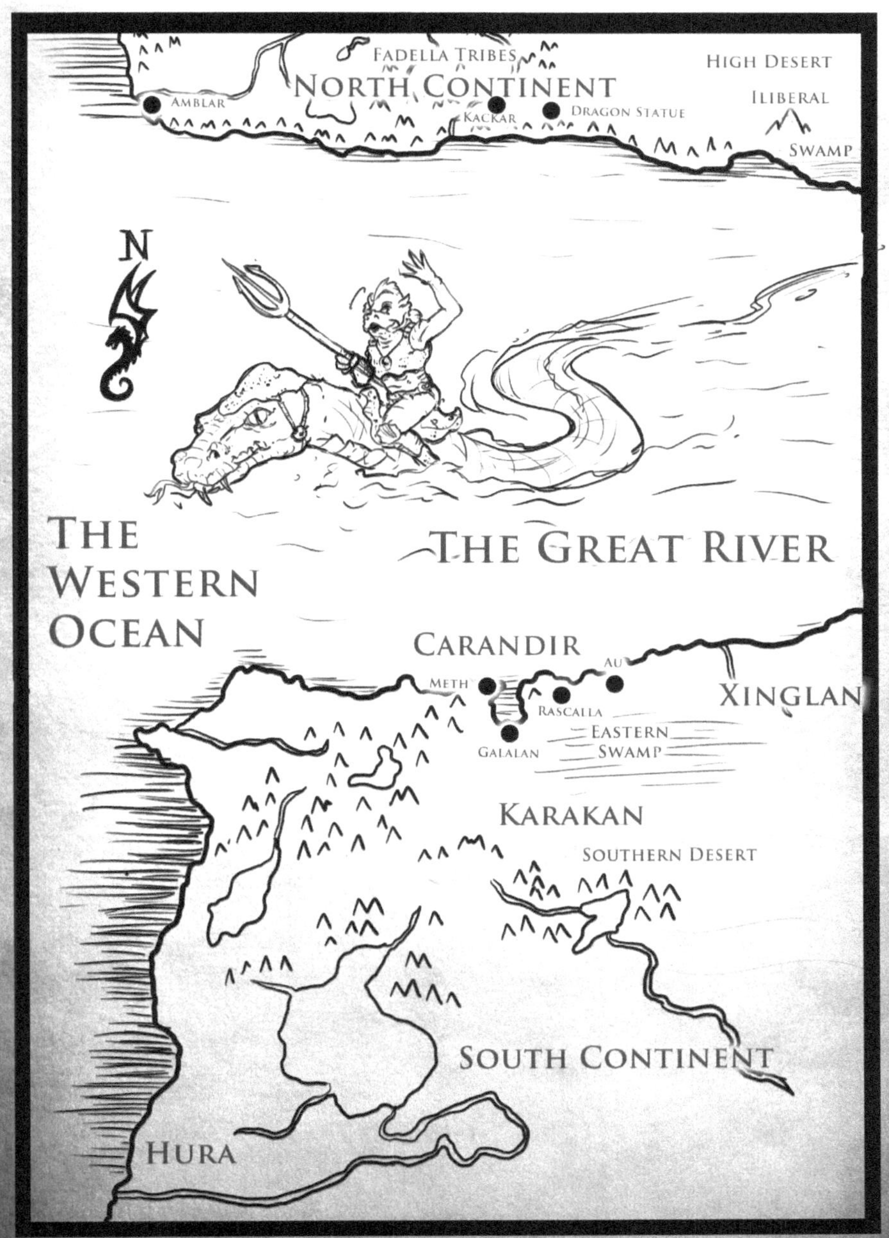

North Continent
Fadella Tribes
Amblar
Kackar
Dragon Statue
High Desert
Iliberal
Swamp
N
The Western Ocean
The Great River
Carandir
Meth
Au
Rascalla
Galalan
Eastern Swamp
Xinglan
Karakan
Southern Desert
South Continent
Hura

BOOK X

One day after the defeat of the Dharam on the North Continent

CHAPTER ONE

A column of Carandirian soldiers escorted the refugees who were driven out of the Barony of Petala by Baron Womb. Len guided the wagon, while Umera, Keetala, Yearol and Fera sat in its bed. Rain fell in a fine mist. They pulled cloaks and hoods close. The scent of damp ground permeated the air.

No one spoke. The jangle of livery punctuated the sound of wheels as they ran over a dirt road turned to mud. The other survivors of the attack by Womb's militia moved with them as if sleepwalking toward the Barony of Lanteler. Some rode in other wagons. A few were on horseback. The majority lifted one boot, then the other as they trudged on in silence.

Daro healers embedded within the troops used magic to tend the wounds of the injured. Over a dozen men, women and children were killed when the rain of arrows pummeled the defenseless refugees. The women healers, who were taught their skills by the wizards, worked without rest to mend broken bodies. Even with their efforts, several died.

Yearol's foot ached where two of her toes were amputated because of frostbite. She could walk, though her balance was not yet recovered enough to run without stumbling.

She and her brother, Fera, witnessed Baroness Luja's militia murder their mother as they hid behind barrels of wheat.

Deep hatred burned inside Yearol and consumed her with a drive to kill those who slaughtered her friends and family.

Fera often crawled into Umera's lap, his light skin in such contrast to her black arms. When he whimpered, she rocked the young boy and stroked his hair.

Umera was relieved to learn her husband, Marawee, reached the palace and reported the rebellion to Baron Dek and Narech Herrik. She looked across the bed to Keetala and searched for a way to comfort her daughter.

When Keetala's baby, Marshala, was shot by Womb's men, she screamed as she held the limp body of the infant in her arms. Now, she stared ahead without a word. If spoken to, she remained unresponsive.

The child's name was the Huran word for great strength in the equatorial country of Keetala's birth, far to the south. The dark skin of her face held no expression. There were no tears.

Len followed the train of wagons in front of him. The soldiers said camps were under construction in the Barony of Varda, away from the battles of the civil war. In the meantime, they would be housed in tents and fed in Lanteler.

He was certain the refugees who were able would join the royal army to fight the insurrectionist. Hebra certainly would if he were still alive. Len closed his eyes at the thoughts of his son's body on a riverbank and his granddaughter, Marshala, with an arrow through her small body.

Keetala and Hebra's marriage was the first in Petala between different races. People openly accepted it, yet, when Womb stirred hatred for those whose ancestors had not been born in Carandir, repressed prejudice and the old term *Pure Carandirian* surfaced.

A mob descended on their house and demanded Keetala leave with her half white, half black daughter. Marshala was called horrific names—abomination, mutant, crime against nature. Len was still shocked by friends and neighbors he knew for a lifetime who turned cruel and heartless.

He thought of Baras hidden in some unknown place. The dragon could awaken fully from his stupor at any time. The rebellious nobles who launched the civil war were blinded by their lust for power and desire to drive out those who were different. It would be for naught if Baras rose. The dragon would take his vengeance on all peoples.

They reached the intersection of the main north/south trade route. It ran along the west side of Lake Hasp.

A Carandir lieutenant rode down the line. "The camp's only three spans ahead."

The soldiers turned the column north. Farmlands and woods bordered the road between settlements. A farmer's field on the shores of Lake Hasp was covered in tents. Hundreds of people, wagons and horses stood there.

The lieutenant rode up to Len. "The third tent in this row is for you and your family."

They clasped their hands together and touched their foreheads in the sign of the covenant with the dragons, except for Keetala who continued to stare into space.

The square tent was a dozen paces across. A sergeant appeared and directed them to a larger tent with tables and benches. "This commissary is for you and several others. There'll be three meals a day at sunrise, brightnail and sunset. Wash basins are just outside."

Umera said, "My husband rode ahead to bring word of the rebellion. He spoke with Baron Dek and Narech Herrik. Will he be coming?"

"I'll speak with the captain of the camp. He'll send word to the palace."

After a week, Umera said, "I need to find that sergeant and ask about Marawee again."

Yearol said, "I'll go with you. I want to join the army and return to Shenan."

Len said, "You may be too young."

Yearol stood and clenched her fists. "I'm not too young. I was almost killed and had to kill. I can do it again. My mother's death must be avenged. I'll slit Luja's throat myself."

Len took a step back and raised his palms. "I apologize. I don't doubt you can fight."

Fera said, "I'll go too."

Yearol looked at her brother, then put her hands over her face. "I'm sorry."

Len wrapped his arms around the young woman. "We understand. When we find Marawee, I'm sure he'll speak up for you. Come."

The sergeant told them Marawee was still in conference with Narech Herrik and promised to send another message.

Umera and Len turned to leave.

Yearol said, "Please, sergeant. Can I speak with you?"

"Of course."

Yearol looked at the others. "I'll be along shortly."

When Yearol returned to the tent, Len and Fera weren't there.

Umera looked up.

Keetala stood by one of the chairs with a blank stare.

Yearol sat on a cot.

Umera came over to her. "What did the sergeant say?"

Yearol hung her head. "He told me I couldn't join the army. I'm too young. Even if I was older, I wouldn't be able to march with missing toes. I couldn't keep up. Baron Dek was there. He said I could contribute to the war effort in other ways."

Umera sat on the cot. "Perhaps it's for the best. You and your brother are welcome to stay with us. The camp in Varda's almost ready. Len wants to come with us."

Yearol continued to look down at her feet. "Fera needs a home."

"Good. We'll leave in a few weeks." Umera walked out of the tent.

Keetala came over to the cot and sat next to Yearol. "Will you go to Varda?" They were her first spoken words since the death of her daughter.

Yearol stared at Keetala for a moment, then turned her head aside and rubbed her arm with her hand. "I'm going back to Shenan. I'll leave tomorrow night at darknail."

Keetala said, "Will you kill militiamen?"

Yearol turned her head and met Keetala's eyes. "Yes."

The two young women stared at each other in silence.

Keetala said, "I'm coming with you."

The camp was located just outside the town of Nekara. Most of the 3,7000 inhabitants produced crafts, worked the fields or fished the waters of Lake Hasp. The buildings were all single-story structures with thatched roofs and stucco walls painted bright colors. There were several shops—a butcher, a cloth merchant, a baker, an inn that served food to travelers and stalls with fresh fruits, vegetables and fish.

A school sat on the outskirts of town. Children played games as they waited for class to begin.

Yearol entered the double doors of the school room. Tall windows filled the space with light. There were a dozen tables and benches whose broad sides faced the front where a man with white hair sat behind a desk and read papers. He looked up and smiled. "Good day. Can I help you?"

The young woman said, "Good day. I'd like to buy some writing supplies."

The man walked to a cabinet. "We've plenty. You're one of the refugees, aren't you?"

"Yes, sir."

"Please, call me Lanan."

"Thank you. I'm Yearol Miller."

"Are you settled in?"

"Yes, thank you."

He took out a pen, an ink well and sheets of paper. "I hope I'm not imposing by asking where you came from."

"Shenan. My brother and I escaped after Luja seized control." The memory caused Yearol's hands to shake.

The man put the writing supplies on a table. "I'm sorry if I upset you."

Yearol said, "I'm all right. What do I owe you?" She opened the pouch she carried and inspected the copper pieces within. The silver coins were still concealed in the heel of her boot, where she placed her family's savings after her mother was killed by Luja's militia.

Lanan laughed. "There's no charge. I'm happy to help."

"Thank you. You're very kind. Could I stay for a moment and use one of the desks to write a letter?"

"Class doesn't start for another tespan. Please, help yourself. I'll just step outside for a moment and watch the children."

Yearol sat down, dipped the nib of the pen into the ink and began to write.

My dear friends,

I can never thank you enough or repay you for saving Fera and me, but I must go. Keetala's coming with me. Please don't try to follow us. We have things we must do. Take care of Fera. I know he won't understand.

She stopped and wiped her nose.

Tell him I love him so much. I wish I could stay and go to Varda with you. I wish I could forget everything that's happened and live in peace. I can't. Keetala can't either. Take care. We'll come back. I promise.

She signed the letter and left without the ink and pen.

She and Keetala ate heartily at supper the next day. Umera remarked how they both looked better.

Yearol got up a span after the others fell asleep and went to Keetala's cot.

The black woman's eyes were open.

They walked out of the tent together.

The other refugees were still asleep. A few soldiers stood next to fires with cloaks pulled over their shoulders to drive away the damp chill of an early spring evening. Keetala wore a cape with a hood. Yearol donned the coat she left Shenan in. It was now soiled and ripped in two places.

They reached the paved road and started south. Mist hid the stars of a moonless night. The two women left the road after what Yearol thought to be darknail and continued through a forest just to the west of the highway. When they came to a river, they returned to the road and crossed at a bridge.

The dirt road the soldiers led them down to reach the camp earlier appeared. They looked left and right to make certain no one else was in sight, then crossed and disappeared into the forest again

False dawn brought a glow to the land. They walked around trees and past shrubbery. At sunrise, they spied travelers on horseback and in carriages.

When a group passed, Keetala stepped out of the forest. "There's a town or village up ahead. I can see buildings."

Yearol joined her. "We need horses. Do you know where we are?"

Keetala shook her head. "I've never been out of Petala."

"We need to find some maps. I should have asked at the school back in Nekara."

"There may be a school here."

"I hope so."

They came to a marker. It read, "Village of Temen." At the northern edge sat a building. A sign hung on it with the image of a cow whose mouth was open wide. Underneath were the words, "Inn of the Singing Cow."

It was a two-story stucco structure with narrow windows and a wooden door. People walked in and out.

Yearol fingered the pouch. "Are you as hungry as I am?"

"I'm certain I am."

Inside, they were greeted by a short, stout man. His close-cropped hair was speckled with gray. A towel hung over one shoulder. "Good day. Have a seat anywhere."

Keetala looked around. There were two dozen patrons who ate and talked. She motioned to an unoccupied table.

The man came over with a smile. "Good morning to you, fair travelers. Namar Reesa at your service. I'm the proprietor. Can I get you some breakfast?"

Yearol said, "Yes."

Reesa winked. "It'll be just a moment."

Keetala said, "We want to buy two horses."

"Where are you traveling to?"

Yearol pulled the name of a barony out of her head. "Barta. We're visiting my relatives."

The man wiped the table with the towel. "Best to be with those you know in these troubled times. From all accounts, Barta's still safe."

"We've never traveled this far south before. Is there anywhere we can purchase some maps?"

"Maps, huh? I can direct you to a blacksmith who has horses and gear. I don't think you'll find any maps here. Hespatar's a day's ride south. There's a bookstore in town. They may be able to help you."

Reesa brought fish cakes, eggs and milk. The women ate in silence while they eyed each patron who entered the building. A soldier came in. He paid them no attention.

When they were done, Yearol lifted her foot to her knee in a nonchalant manner and moved eight silver pieces from the heel of her boot to the pouch.

The blacksmith kept several horses for sale. They selected two and purchased saddles, saddle bags, reigns and tack. Yearol knew the value of a horse and negotiated the price. The blacksmith accepted seven silver pieces and returned thirty-one copper coins in change.

They started south toward Hespatar after the purchase of more provisions at a local stall. The mist burned off before brightnail. The temperature turned warmer. They kept to the road and mingled with other travelers.

Hespatar was a good size town with several side streets and many buildings, some of brick and others made of wood or stucco. Though many roofs were thatched, the majority were shingled. A man directed them to the bookstore.

It had large glass windows with books and other items displayed.

A bell tinkled when they entered.

A woman with gray hair came out from behind a shelf. "Good morning. How may I help you?" She wore scholar's robes of black. Atop her head was a skull cap embroidered with the images of birds.

Keetala was amazed by the collection of bound books. Marawee taught her to read. She owned many books back in Petala. Those seemed like a small pile as she ran her hand over the spines of several volumes on a shelf and took in a deep breath. The books covered subjects from cooking to medicine, farming, sailing and road building. There were many volumes of poetry, music and stories.

Yearol said, "Do you carry maps?"

The shopkeeper pointed to the back of the store. "Yes. Let me show you."

She guided the women to a cabinet with dozens of scrolls, each a map of a different part of Carandir. The woman said, "What were you looking for?"

Except for some reproduced in the books she owned, these were the first maps Keetala ever saw. She gazed at one unrolled on a table.

The shopkeeper said, "This is of Nemtanka." She pointed to a spot. "You're here, just inside the northern border."

Keetala said, "We're new to the area. This map would be very helpful. Is it for sale?"

"Everything in the shop's for sale. This one is two coppers."

Yearol said, "We'd like maps of all the southern baronies in Carandir."

The woman frowned. "If you plan to travel far, Nemtanka and Barta are still open. You'll find the roads into Ulata and Arana blocked by Carandir troops. No one can go west or east."

Keetala ran her hands over the map. "I'm just fascinated with these. I'd also like to get some books."

"Yes," said Yearol. "We want to study history. My friend is a student of ancient battles."

Keetala nodded, "That's right. I'm interested in strategy and warfare."

The shopkeeper said, "You may see more warfare than you like if the Karakiens decide to invade Barta from the south. Word has it their armies haven't moved out of the eastern baronies and are just at the edge of Arna. The dragons only know what they'll do next."

Yearol hoped Keetala's question wouldn't raise suspicion. She didn't want to speak with any soldiers stationed nearby who might send them back to the refugee camp.

The shopkeeper smiled. "Well, it's good to meet fellow scholars, even in these troubled times. I think I have some things that will interest you."

They rented a room in the second story of an inn. It was small, with two beds, one chair, a table, a chest and a mirror above a wash basin. Though there were no lanterns, the innkeeper supplied many candles. One window looked out in the street below.

After a meal in the tavern downstairs, they settled in and studied the maps of Nemtanka and Barta to the south along with those of Ulata, Shenan and Lusar to the west.

The books contained a wealth of information on military tactics, improvised weapons, concealment and many other subjects.

Keetala said, "We should stay here for a while and study. We may want to go back to the bookstore."

"I agree. We also need to find knives and swords."

"Knives will be no problem. An attempt to buy swords will bring unwanted attention, if we can even find any with the war so close."

Yearol closed the book she was reading. "We have to have weapons."

"I know." Keetala sat down on a bed. "What will we do when we reach

Shenan?"

Yearol wasn't certain how to answer the question. Stop Luja was all she could think of. There was no actual plan. The man who intended to rape her died in the fire she set, but it was an accident. She didn't intend to kill him, just escape. Afterwards, she dropped to her knees and vomited.

Keetala said, "Can you stick a sword or a knife in someone's flesh?"

Yearol remembered the sight of her mother's body on the mill floor as blood seeped from the wound and Luja's militiamen laughed. "I have to. Luja and the others must be stopped." She looked to Keetala. "Can you?"

Keetala looked across the room. "I don't know. When Hebra drowned, I was so filled with hate I only thought of killing those who drove us out. My father told me we can't hate because one day we all have to live together again. After they killed Marshala... I don't know now."

The silence returned. Yearol went to the window and looked down at the street. People came and went out of shops. Many smiled, some laughed, as if there was no war and the world was right and just.

They'd never seen their family and neighbors forced into military service or killed because they defied a tyrant. "Your father told me if you fight out of hatred your enemy can manipulate you. You have to fight for a higher purpose. I said I'd fight for my friends and my mother who died to protect Fera and me. I want to believe it. I'm just so filled with rage."

Keetala walked behind Yearol and put her arms around her friend. "Then we must both purge our rages. My father is right. It's a trap. There's more at stake here than just our revenge. We can do things no army can. We can travel where no troops can go. We have to plan what we can do, how we can harass the enemy to support Carandir in the war. You can never forget your mother nor I my husband and daughter. We must always think of Carandir and the people we fight to free."

Yearol turned around and embraced Keetala.

They bought long knives, short knives, butcher's knives and cleavers, along with whetstones and straps of leather. They also purchased hammers, picks and shovels. They read the books on military strategy and tactics well into the night, until eye strain from the candlelight made the words blurry.

Keetala cut out key areas and routes from maps and passages from the books.

After a week and a half, they packed the weapons and supplies into saddle bags. The remaining books and maps were taken into the woods outside town and buried.

Many roads led west. There were reports of battles along the edge of Barta, just across the border form Ulata. They took a southerly road for a day, then moved even farther south, into a forested area near the border with the Kingdom of Karaken. There were no signs of Karakien soldiers. Still, they moved with caution and listened to every sound.

The air became cold at nigh under the trees. They made camp near a stream and ate a cold supper with no fire.

Yearol shivered and pulled her coat close to her body.

Keetala said, "We should sleep close together tonight to share body heat."

They cinched their clothing tight around themselves, then placed one bed role on the ground, the other on top of it and crawled between them.

Yearol snuggled up to Keetala. "This feels nice." Her arm moved causally to drape over Keetala's belly.

A rustle of leaves came from behind, then in front.

Yearol and Keetala threw the bedroll off and shot to their feet.

Four men in the uniforms of the Shenan militia charged into the women's camp with drawn swords.

One of them wore sergeant's stripes. He was the oldest of the group. The others seemed hardly out of their teens.

The sergeant grabbed Keetala by the arm. "What's this? A black foreigner?"

Keetala struggled to break free.

One of the other soldiers slapped her. "Be still."

Yearol kept her hands to her sides. "What do you want?"

The sergeant gave a snort. "Why are you in these woods?"

"We're on our way home. We were out gathering berries."

He looked to Keetala. "Who's this, your servant?"

Yearol looked to her friend. "Yes."

One of the militiamen grunted. "Dark-skinned foreigners. It's about all they're good for."

"No brains, that's for certain," said another.

"How about a little sport, sergeant?" said the fourth. "She's probably good for that. Her mistress too."

The men laughed.

In one smooth movement, Yearol drew a long knife from within her coat and rammed it into the sergeant's gut. He cried out and slumped to the ground. She charged another.

Keetala pulled a knife from her cloak and killed the man nearest her.

The fourth stepped back, then ran.

The two women took off in pursuit and quickly caught up to him.

The soldier stopped and turned. His hand shook. "Get back." He swung his sword at Yearol.

She used the two knives to parry the blow, a maneuver she read about in one of the books.

The man stepped back and waved the sword with erratic swipes. "Get back, I tell you."

Keetala threw her knife.

The man deflected the blade with the sword.

She took out two more knives.

The man dropped his sword and ran.

Keetala sprung forward and overtook him. She knocked him face down on the ground. With a hard strike, she jabbed a knife blade into his back.

The young man screamed and clawed the ground. "No. Please, no. Mother!"

Keetala drew the knife out and plunged it in again.

The man grunted, then lay still.

Yearol grabbed Keetala by the arm. "What've you done? He was down. You didn't have to kill him."

Keetala shook herself free and stood. "Yes, I did. He could have alerted others to our presence. This is war."

Yearol put her hands on her temple and shook her head, then sat down on the ground. "Oh, Ilidel." She relived the memory of ramming a knife into the sergeant. "I'm sorry. You're right. I just didn't know what it would feel like."

Keetala sat next to her. "I didn't either."

They sat in silence for a long time. The stars wheeled overhead. Neither moved.

Yearol stood. "We'll encounter more patrols."

"Do you want to go back?"

"No." Yearol looked to the south. "We'll have to cross into Karaken and travel west. We can only hope their forces are concentrated on the east."

Keetala nodded. "I agree." She looked down at the bodies. "Let's get their swords."

CHAPTER TWO

In the desert camp of the defeated Dharam on the North Continent, Neshra stood next to Sif and Tarawee while they watched Mirjel and Ryckair lead the column of Carandir soldiers into the west, on their way to Kackar.

Hundreds of people captured by the Dharam milled about, many of them just released from a spell that robbed them of their identities and will.

Neshra faced east. "First, we send these people home, then we hunt Baras."

Tarawee shook his head. "The eminence isn't gonna like this."

Sif said, "You agreed Ryckair had to return to stop the civil war."

"Begrudgingly. If Baras wakes before Ryckair gets back… well, I don't want to think about what the eminence will do to us."

Neshra said, "The sooner we send these people on their way, the sooner we can start the hunt."

Tarawee said, "You're going home too. We'll handle this."

Neshra placed her hands on her hips. "I pledged to lead Ryckair to the dragon. If I return before Baras is found I will be dishonored."

Sif laughed. "You should have learned by now not to argue with her."

Eight-hundred Carandirian soldiers were left to round up the defeated Dharam troops, along with the brigands recruited by Masalta who were not killed in the battle. These were confined in a guarded area outside camp.

Neshra had no concern for them. Her charges were those people the Dharam enslaved.

Sif and Tarawee argued over how to find Baras.

"Can't you smell him, Taree?"

"All I can smell is your stink."

"You should talk. I wish Eminence Levalat hadn't given me a nose when he made us human."

"Oh, and you wouldn't draw attention without a nose."

"Oh, shut up."

Neshra sighed at the thought the Zerites would bicker all the way across the desert.

The Carandir captain in charge of the Dharam prisoners rode up. "We're about to escort the captives back to Kackar for judgment. Can we assist you in any way before we ride?"

Neshra said, "Just leave us horses and wagons. I need to return to my tribe and get a peretan to continue our hunt in the desert. I sent mine back."

As if called by his mention, Ento gave a bellow and strolled into camp on his six legs. Neshra ran to the large lizard and put her arms around the scales of his thick neck. "Oh, Ento, I told you to go home to Verka."

The peretan gave a mournful coo in reply.

Neshra was crying. "Oh, but I'm glad you didn't. I missed you, you silly."

The Carandir officer looked at the six-legged beast with wide eyes. "I've heard such creatures roam the southern deserts. I never believed they really existed."

Neshra stroked Ento's nose. "Come on, you two. We need to retrieve the sinthra. Then we'll return here, load the provisions and hunt for Baras."

Tarawee rolled his eyes to the sky. "You humans are so stubborn. Can't you understand? We don't have time to wait for everyone to recover enough to travel. You promised Ryckair you'd take care of the captured people. Sif and I must go now. You have to leave the hunt to us. Besides, it'll take too long if we ride the peretan. We'll have to root jump."

"You took me on a root jump before."

Sif said, "And it slowed us down. When we bring a human along it uses a lot of magic. Have you forgotten what I told you about us being forbidden to use it? The eminence may have missed the other times. Taree and I might not be noticed. If we drag you around the desert it can't be easily masked."

"I promised to lead Ryckair to the dragon. Commitments are sacred to my people."

Tarawee said, "You also committed to see these people safely to their homes."

Neshra opened her mouth, then exhaled. "I want to go with you."

"We'd like to bring you," said Sif. "I, for one, have grown fond of people now that I've met them, especially you and Ryckair. It just can't work. These survivors need you as much as Carandir needs the monarchs and their crown."

A hot breeze blew from the east. Ento made a mournful sound.

Neshra pressed her cheek against his. "Go. I'll see everyone returns to their homes." She looked back to the two Zerites. "Keep Baras from waking. If you do care about people, don't let him rise."

There was a tear in Sif's eye. He took Neshra's hands in his. "We promise."

He and Tarawee turned and walked to the oasis to find a root to jump into.

The monarchs to lead the army across the North Continent to the gates of Kackar. After a feast, they took Batu and Amar to a secluded room.

Mirjel sat in a wooden chair and smoothed the fabric of her dress. "None of the troops here know Lek sits on the throne with my semblance. If I return from away, people will realize the woman they thought was the queen is an impostor. This would shake confidence at a time when all Carandirians must be united."

Batu said, "Everyone who rode against the Dharam knows you're here, as do the Dharam prisoners. Even if you sneak into the palace, they'll tell of your exploits. How can people unknow a thing?"

"With the power of the crown, my friend," said Ryckair. "The queen and I discussed this on the ride back."

Mirjel held her hands over her belly now swollen in pregnancy after the power of the crown magically transferred the infant from the womb of the woman killed by Ryckair's son into her own. "When the troops we left behind arrive in Kackar with the Dharam prisoners, we'll use the crown to change the memory of everyone, except you and Colonel Amar. All will believe the colonel led the troops into battle to defeat an invading Dharam force—even the riders sent ahead to Amblar. Everyone will forget the king's illegitimate son and my magical pregnancy."

Batu said, "How will you hide yourselves on the ships? There are tens of thousands of troops. Someone will see you."

Ryckair said, "We won't travel by ship. The queen and I'll remain hidden outside Kackar and ride to Amblar after the army leaves. We'll use the crown to enter the wizard tower and cross the bridges at their tops. Though the towers are separated by vast distances on the ground, it takes less than a tespan to cross the magical links that connect them. We'll reach the tower in Barta weeks before your arrive in Meth and make our way to the palace."

Mirjel said, "Lek will withdraw. It will be announced the magic of the crown gave me a child. We must hope Orane and Telasec can change Lek's features back to their original form. If not, she'll have to hide until the spell wears off."

Ryckair got up and sat closer to Batu. "I know you despise Shara."

"If I may speak candidly, Majesty, I would've rather left her in the desert to rot."

"I understand your feeling. She's no longer the person she was. The demon that killed Dhamar blanked her memory."

"It could be an act, Sire. I can never trust her."

"It's no deception. I saw what happened to her mind through the crown. She's a child again. Whatever she did before is no longer a part of her. I want you to escort Shara to the Daro."

Batu said, "Majesty, please find another for this task."

"Aside from Mirjel, I trust you more than anyone."

Batu stared at Ryckair, then sighed. "I will do as you command, my king."

Mirjel said, "Take the troops to Amblar at the rise of the sun, colonel. May the dragons protect you."

Amar led the army across the North Continent to the gates of Amblar. They marched into the city and down long, wide boulevards.

The column reached the west wall, where the wizard tower stood. It was difficult to judge its exact height. In different light and weather, it seemed taller and shorter to the eye. Steps led to a threshold with a stone wall where a door should have been. No windows could be seen.

Batu climbed the wall to the tower. He extended his arms to the assembled troops. "The Dharam are defeated. Our eastern borders are secure in the north. We now sail to Carandir to confront the traitors and push the Karakien army back across our southern borders."

Five oceangoing sailing ships were moored at the stone docks. Dozens more lay in anchor offshore. When a ship filled, its captain weighed anchor and moved out to allow another to dock.

The sun touched the horizon when the last of the army boarded. Amar and Batu walked up a gangplank to the flag ship *Vigilance,* with Captain Efra as its master. Commander Watoola served as his first mate, as she did on the *Star Fire* when it was sunk by the Sarte.

Batu said, "Take us up the river to Meth, Captain."

Efra saluted. "Aye, First Minister. Commander Watoola, take the fleet out and make ready for attack by enemy ships."

The Great River was a body of water so wide the other bank could not be seen, even after nearly two months under sail.

Carandir sat along the south bank. This was called the South Continent.

Until only a few decades before, no Carandirian had made the crossing for millennia. At that time, none knew how wide the river was and the North Continent was only a name in legend.

If the telepathic terec birds were still able to fly, Batu would have coordinated an assault on Fellant and Lena with Narech Herrik. Without them, Batu was forced to reach Meth first.

A Kyar named Velatar, who was driven mad by a demon, cast a spell on the small birds. No terec could now fly.

Baroness Luja of Shenan convinced Velatar the Barasha used the birds to attack Carandir. She told him she, Barons Womb of Petala and Gilyon of Eel, fought the sorcerers. Velatar had no idea these three were the power behind the civil war against the Crown.

Most of the military vessels were armed with catapults, fore and aft. They tacked southwest up the Great River for several weeks. Eddies of currents made navigation difficult. Each captain kept a constant vigil.

A cry came from a sailor in the crow's nest of the *Vigilance*. "Ship ahoy. Rowing galley flying the flag of Petala."

The galley turned back toward the south bank of the river.

Efra said, "Bosun, signal the *Defender* and *Regent* to pursue and capture that vessel."

The two sailing ships moved away from the fleet. With its oars, the galley was not slowed by tacking maneuvers and pulled ahead.

The captain of the *Defender* said, "Load catapults. Fire a warning shot."

A group of sailors at the forecastle turned a wheel to bring tension to the mounted weapon. When the bowl was at deck level, a large, round rock was loaded and the catapult aimed.

An ensign shouted, "Fire."

The catapult threw the stone in an arc.

It landed next to the galley.

The smaller continued.

Another stone was loaded and fired in the galley's path.

It picked up speed.

Hot chains soaked in boiling oil flew from a catapult in the galley's stern. They struck a sail of the *Regent* and set it ablaze. Sailors climbed rigging to extinguish the fire.

The two Carandirian ships came alongside. Boarding parties charged onto the galley. Seven outnumbered rebels drew swords to repel the Carandirian sailors. After a short battle, the crew of the galley surrendered.

The rowers were chained in their seats and pleaded to be released. Carandirian sailors broke the shackles with battle axes. The rowers were taken on board the *Defender*. Those on the galley who took up arms were secured in the hull of the *Regent*.

One of the enemy sailors had a deep gash in his left leg. Another man's fingers were cut off his right hand. One man's belly was slashed. He died while a Daro healer tried to stop the bleeding. The others were unhurt.

Captain Efra and Batu took a launch to the *Regent* and descended below deck to the brig.

Batu pointed to one of the prisoners who suffered no hurt. "Take him to an aft compartment."

The man's hands and feet were bound and hood was secured over his head before he was carried out.

Carandirian sailors placed him in a chair and tied rope around him before they removed the hood.

Efra studied the man. His skin was light, as were all Carandirians who descended of the first settlers from the North Continent millennia before.

The captain said, "Where did you put out from?"

The man stared ahead and remained silent.

Batu said, "You've committed acts of treason against the Crown. Tell us what we want to know and your sentence will go easier."

The man spit in Batu's brown face, then looked to Efra. "You're the traitor to Carandir. It's you and your monarchs who allowed the easterners to become the New Nobility and foreign scum with black and brown skin to live here. They tried to steal Carandir. We'll crush them and take the crown. All of you will hang."

He glared at Batu. "You should never have crawled out of the desert to think you could stand among your betters."

Batu raised his hand while he stared into the man's eyes.

"Go on," said the prisoner. "I'm pure Carandirian, the only patriot here."

Batu lowered his arm.

Efra said, "Take him back to the brig. Bring me the one with the wounded leg."

The second man was brought in and tied to the chair. His hood removed.

Tears poured down his face. "Please. I had to. Oh, Jorondel, I had to. They would've killed my wife and children."

Efra said, "Where do you come from?"

"Shenan. Luja's militia rounded up all the men and threatened to murder our families if we deserted. Oh, please, don't kill me. I don't want to die. I want to see my wife and children again." He broke down into sobs.

Batu said, "Where did the ship sail from?"

"The Fellant port."

"How many soldiers are in Fellant?"

"They'll kill my family if I tell you."

Efra spoke in a soft voice. "The others from your ship will be imprisoned in Meth. None will ever learn what you say."

The prisoner's voice was barely audible through sobs. "We were marched from Shenan, through Petala and into Fellant. They made me kill people. Women. Children. They screamed. Oh, Jorondel. I'm damned for eternity. My soul will wander the nether world and never be allowed into the Dragons' Halls."

Batu cupped his hand over the man's arm. "What is your name?"

"Darateen. Darateen Minser."

"What are the names of your wife and children?"

"Cela. My wife's name is Cela. We have two girls, Gena and Lousella."

"Darateen, I hold faith with the dragons as strongly as you. I know you won't be damned. If you tell us what we need to know, it will help the Crown defeat the traitors. It's the only way to save Cela, Gena and Lousella."

Darateen stopped crying, though he sniffled as he reported what he saw and heard since being conscripted into Luja's militia.

A sailor wrote down every word while Efra and Batu questioned the frightened man.

When Darateen finished, Efra said, "Take him to a cabin on the *Defender*. Post a guard. If he's sent back to the brig, the other men will kill him."

The royal standard was raised on the flagship *Vigilance* when the fleet rounded the point into Lake Hasp. Catapult emplacements on shore raised coded flags.

Efra ordered the proper response to be flown.

The fleet headed for the docks at Meth. When they reached them, only the *Vigilance* put in.

Batu saw Narech Herrik and Baron Dek onshore. He and Amar descended the gangplank.

Amar saluted.

Dek wrapped Batu in a great hug. "Thank the dragons our message got through."

Batu said, "We captured a galley out of Fellant. The rowers were slaves chained to their seats by Womb's forces. One of the crew told us what he knew."

Dek said, "Why have the monarchs not come on the flagship?"

Batu gave the baron a quizzical look. "Aren't they here?"

"No. How could they be?"

"They intended to enter the wizard tower at Amblar and cross to the one in Barta."

Herrik looked to Dek, then Batu. "Their majesties have not appeared. The tower in Barta fell behind enemy shortly after Captain Efra set sail."

Batu said "Were they captured?"

Dek said, "If the enemy seized the monarchs, the crown would be in their hands and they would've used it. They may be trapped inside the tower. If so, perhaps the magic doesn't work there."

Herrik said, "Let's adjourn to the palace."

The narech met with her senior staff, along with Dek and Batu. Baron Enesta and Baroness Edawee, who escaped from Fellant, also sat at the table.

A captain said, "Narech, the intelligence Darateen Minser revealed gives us much needed information about the traitors' strength and positions. We should concentrate the fresh troops from Amblar on the attacks from the west. It would be a swift campaign to squash them and turn our full attention on Karaken."

A colonel, who fought on the Karakien border, said, "We should mount a full invasion of Karaken. They can't be allowed to raid Carandir again."

Another officer said, "Ma'am, the rebellion in the west stems from deep-rooted prejudice. Military action alone won't quell it. A campaign there will be long and bloody."

The discussion continued with points and counterpoints.

Herrik turned to Dek. "What say you, Lord Baron?"

Dek stroked his dark beard, now flecked with gray. "These are all good concerns. It's true hatred still seethes among many in the west for the eastern houses and people from other lands. Carandir has become two nations at war, both by force and ideology. The plan of the dragons has been forgotten by many. Yet, Karaken has waited for an opportunity like this for too long. Whatever comes of the war with them, we can't concentrate on one or the other."

The front in the west extended along the borders of Lanteler, Nemtanka and Barta. Karakien troops occupied southern portions of Mentaro and Respa. The Carandir military and the militia of the loyal baronies fought as one. Forces from the city-states of Au and Rahala to the east of the swamplands sailed to the Port of Rascalla to aid the war against Karaken. Baroness Quib of Mentaro and Baroness Jea of Rascalla held the Karakien army at the Kar River and away from the iron mines in the mountains.

Herrik weighed the arguments. "We'll send the fleet with one third of our forces directly to Gelalan to keep the Karakien army from advancing farther. The rest of the troops will disembark in Meth. Half will march west to confront the rebels. The rest will be held in reserve. When the western front is stabilized, a flotilla with the remaining forces from Amblar will attack Fellant."

Baron Estray said, "The baroness and I must sail with that fleet. We alone know the location of the catacomb where our troops shelter."

Herrik said, "Of course, My Lord."

Dek said, "The monarchs return with the crown would sweep aside our enemies. Yet, the ways of the wizards are filled with mystery. We must proceed with the acceptance they may not return."

Shara was absorbed in the pictures she drew with chalk on paper on the voyage. She barely acknowledged anyone else. A Daro healer brought her meals and sat with her. Crew members who interacted with the former Dharam princess found it strange to see a middle-age woman act and speak as if she were a young child.

Batu escorted her to the palace in a carriage.

She looked out the window and pointed. "Horses. Look at the horses. They're so pretty. I'd like to pet them." Her speech was now flatter than that of the Dharam, who held the vowels long and pronounced the letter *r* with a strong trill.

They reached the palace. Batu held her hand. He walked and Shara skipped down a corridor, to the halls where the Daro healers taught their magical arts to women who joined their order and where many of them resided.

Mistress Telasec, the head of the order, and another Daro healer greeted them at the door.

Telasec said, "Hello, Shara. I understand you like to make pictures."

Shara looked around and hummed to herself.

Telasec formed a kindly look on her face. "Well, Neesa will show you to a nice room. I'll come see you in a tespan."

Shara took Neesa's hand and followed the healer into the halls.

Telasec said, "I'm not certain what can be done. She has the body of a woman in her forties, yet her mind is as a four-year-old. I sense no malice. Whatever happened erased who she once was. The best we may be able to do is make her comfortable."

Batu gazed after Shara with a hardened look. "I saw through her the moment we met, even though Ryckair became ensnared in her schemes. I promised the king I would bring her to you. I still don't trust her evil side. Beware."

CHAPTER THREE

The monarchs rode from Kackar two days after the army left. They traveled at a slow pace, so as not to overtake the forces.

It was sunset when they reached the outskirts of Amblar several week later. Travelers on horseback and merchant wagons raised dust as they moved into the city. Ryckair pulled the hood of his cloak over his face, A scarf covered Mirjel's features. She rode side-saddle to ease her pregnancy.

Lanterns were lit along the wide boulevards of Amblar. The monarchs guided their horses to the west wall and the foot of the steps to the wizard tower.

Ryckair dismounted first, then helped Mirjel down from her saddle.

She stroked the cheek of her mount. "Thank you for a safe journey. The town guard will be by soon. They'll find you a good home."

Ryckair undid a sack attached to his saddle bags and opened it to inspect the dragon-crested crown secreted within.

He climbed the steps.

Mirjel followed.

They reached the archway on the tower where a door should have been. It appeared to be a stone wall.

Ryckair placed the crown on his head and took Mirjel's hand. "This'll seem a little odd."

They walked through the seemingly solid stone wall into the wizard tower.

From inside, Mirjel saw the door was made of oak, not stone. The round room they stood in was twice the perceived diameter of the tower from the outside. Soft light emanated from an unseen source. A staircase followed the curve of the tower and rose past the ceiling.

She said, "This is amazing."

Ryckair smiled. "It took me by surprise too. The climb's long. We'll pass several doors outlined in glowing colors that imprison demons. There are also some windows. You're in for some more surprises."

When they rose above the round room, the steps formed a staircase with walls on either side. Mirjel felt a sense of disgust when they passed one of the doors.

The stairs continued until they came to a window on the right. She stared with wide eyes at the scene of an ocean whose waves crashed against the base of the tower several stories below, even though the tower didn't sit next to the ocean and she saw no windows from the outside.

They passed the window where desert sand extended to just below the sill. Bright sunlight shone in a cloudless sky, even though they entered the tower at night. A city stood on the horizon.

Mirjel said, "Do you think we could walk over to it?"

Ryckair said, "I imagine so. Jarat told me the towers intersect many worlds. I've often thought of the city and wished I could've taken the time to explore whatever's there." He paused and studied the scene. "That's odd. There were several towers and a tall spire. I don't see them."

Just ahead was a landing and a door outlined in red.

Mirjel felt malevolence behind it.

The door rattled. A roar pierced her mind.

She clasped their hands over their ears.

The door burst open. A dark form jumped onto the landing. It was as tall as a human with an over-sized, bald head from which spikes protruded. The creature snarled with sharp, jagged teeth.

Ryckair saw images in his mind from the memories stored in the crown. He faced a minor demon the wizard Lo imprisoned millennia before. A spell formed in his mind to push the creature back into the cell and lock the door once more.

The demon charged.

Ryckair cast the spell.

A blue fist shot through the air.

It struck the demon in its chest and knocked it back into the cell, whereupon the door shut and locked itself.

The king sighed in relief.

The magical fist struck a wall just past the door and shot back towards the monarchs.

They ducked.

The fist passed harmlessly overhead.

Mirjel watched it fly down the stairs, hit another wall, then angle back.

It struck them with a flash of blue light. The force knocked them through the window.

Ryckair got to his knees and brushed sand from his face. "Are you hurt?"

Mirjel lay on her side. "I don't think so." She remembered the child she lost in the fall down a set of stairs decades before. Her hands went to her belly.

The baby kicked.

Mirjel gave a sigh, stood and turned around. "Ryckair, look."

The tower and the window they fell through were nowhere to be seen. There was only a vast horizon of sand dunes.

Ryckair searched the memories of the crown for references to the wizard towers and the windows. He could no longer perceive any memories or spells. The vast experiences of every monarch who wore the crown back to Avar the Great was lost. "Father of dragons. I can't sense anything." He removed the crown and handed it to Mirjel. "What can you detect?"

Mirjel put the crown on her head. No images or insights came. "Dear Ilidel."

Ryckair reached out and waved his arms where the tower window should be in case it was invisible. His hands passed through empty air. "We're trapped."

Mirjel pointed to the city. "Perhaps we'll find an answer there."

They set off across the sand dunes. Soon, sweat soaked their heavy clothing. Ryckair undid his jerkin.

The crown on Mirjel's head offered no relief from the heat of the sun.

As they approached, the city appeared deserted.

Ryckair saw the ruins of the tall spire he spotted years before. It lay toppled and broken on the sand. The buildings, too, were in ruin. Sand filled streets. There were no bodies, human or animal, not even bones.

Ryckair shook his head. "It would take centuries for the city to decay like this, yet I saw it intact only two decades ago."

They came around a corner and jumped back.

Baras looked through rubble with his wings folded.

Ryckair whispered, "This explains how the city was destroyed."

Mirjel removed the crown from her head. "The spell."

They placed their hands on the crown and stepped around the side of the building.

Baras turned his head at their approach.

The monarchs recited the words of the spell in unison. "There is no conflict, only peace. Find now peace and rest until the world is unmade."

These were the words they spoke when Baras held them in his claws after he woke. The dragon confused the rest of the spell in their minds and escaped.

Now, with clarity, they completed the incantation to send Baras back to the void.

"Be at peace. Withdraw from this world."

The dragon raised an eyebrow and squinted, then spoke in a deep voice. "What are you doing?"

Ryckair said, "Yield, Baras."

The dragon looked around. "Baras? What do you mean by betrayer?"

Mirjel pointed a finger. "Play no games with us. Sleep now for eternity, Baras."

The dragon tilted his head. "Did you address me?"

Ryckair said, "As well you know."

The dragon looked to the sky. "It's the sun. You've been out too long. For that matter, why are you here? For another matter, how did you get here?"

Panic flooded the monarchs. The crown not only blocked memories of past rulers, it's magical abilities were gone.

Ryckair said, "We came through a window of the wizard tower. How did you get here, evil one?"

"Evil one? Wizard tower? You need to get under some shade. What's a wizard and why are you dressed in clothes suited for cold? You're in danger of sunstroke."

Mirjel said, "Don't threaten us. You see the dragon-crested crown. Where are the people of this city? Have you eaten them?"

"Why would I do that? No one's lived here for hundreds of years. Who would I eat?"

Mirjel placed her hand over her swollen belly. "You are the betrayer. You taught magic to the Barasha. You broke from the Great Plan. We will not listen to your lies, Baras."

"My name is Magadel. I never taught magic to anyone. The Great Plan has not been disrupted. Why do you say these things?" He paused for a moment, then lifted a fore claw.

The crown flew out of the monarchs' hands and into the dragon's. Magadel inspected it. "I see the handiwork of Jorondel in this crest. To my knowledge, he's never made such a thing."

Magadel lowered the crown. "This doesn't belong here." He looked at the monarchs. "You don't belong. You're out of phase with this place. I sense great confusion and surprise. You know of me, yet you don't know who I am."

Ryckair felt odd, as if he didn't quite walk on the ground. "A wizard told me their towers touch many lands and many worlds. How did you travel here?"

"Wizard? I don't know what they are."

A cramp seized Mirjel. She winced.

Ryckair said, "What is it?"

"I'm in labor. Oh, Ilidel."

Magadel transformed into human form. He now appeared as a middle-aged man with pale skin and red hair. He wore white pants and a blue coat.

The transformed dragon said, "Don't fear. I'll help."

A canopy formed over their heads. A bed appeared. With a start, Mirjel found herself prone upon it.

Magadel smiled. "All is well."

Mirjel felt her muscles push only once before the baby emerged. There was no pain, as she was certain there would be. Nor was there fear. Before she could think, Magadel placed the infant in her arms, a baby girl. Her skin had a tint of brown that reflected the mixed lineage of Ryckair's son and the desert woman who conceived the child.

Mirjel undid her shift.

The child suckled at her breast.

Ryckair came to her side and brushed a finger across the newborn's cheek.

Magadel stepped back. "Congratulations. You hold a fine girl this day. There's a mystery here. For now, rest."

A room appeared around them. Within was a table laden with fruits, nuts and bread, along with water.

Exhaustion came to Ryckair. He sat on a chair next to Mirjel's bed and held her hand.

The baby stopped suckling and nestled into the queen's arms.

The three of them fell asleep.

The dragon inspected the crest of the crown in minute detail. It was certainly the crafts-work of Jorondel, yet, the Father of Dragons had never spoken of it. Magadel would have to take it to the council as soon as possible. First, he had to understand where these humans came from.

He probed their minds while they slept. Their thoughts were chaotic. There were wars, treachery and deceit in their past. This shocked him, for these things had never come to his world. He spoke aloud to himself, "By the great egg, is it possible?"

He waited until Mirjel and Ryckair woke, then entered the room with the crown. "I see now how confused you are, not of your own doing, and how you thought me your enemy. By means I don't understand, you've come into what is an alternate reality to you from a different world, where your Magadel rebelled against the Great Plan and became Baras, the betrayer."

He sat in a chair and stared at the crown. "In this world, I once petitioned the council to teach simple magic. Ilidel showed me the wisdom of her mind. I realized such power would corrupt some who would use magic against others. I abandoned my petition.

"Though I didn't teach magic to humans, I feel guilt at your history, for I too was filled with rage when my petition was denied. I can understand how your Magadel felt."

He looked up. "You spoke of a wizard tower."

To his surprise, Ryckair no longer felt fear or anger toward this dragon in human form. He was filled with the kind of trust he experienced when he first met the wizard Jarat. "We were knocked through a window into this desert. I once passed the window twenty years ago. There were tall spires and towers then."

Magadel said, "I never thought this possible. These wizards discovered how to connect worlds and draw magic from each to confront demons. You're now in one of those worlds where the Great Plan was not subverted. Harmony remains."

"How do we get back?"

"I don't know. The council will have to ponder this. I'll take this crown and crest to them for examination."

Mirjel sat up in bed. "We must get back. Baras will wake soon. This crown is the only thing that can place him back into eternal sleep. Civil war rages in my land. Many have already been killed."

Magadel said, "There's an anomaly between our worlds. You saw the city at a time when it thrived. That was two and a half centuries ago. The people tired of the desert and moved to a lush island. It seems for every year here, only a month passes in your world. We have time to solve this riddle."

Ryckair said, "How long must we wait?"

Magadel said, "It's impossible to tell. In the meantime, I'll take you to the place where the people of this city resettled."

Magadel stepped outside. He took the shape of a dragon once more and carried the house across desert dunes.

They came to an ocean and watched waves roll beneath them. Soon, they spied a shore with wide, sandy beaches behind which vegetation grew. There were mountains in the backga round.

A village came into view. There were no walls around it. The streets were laid out in what seemed a random pattern. People gathered and looked up. Many waved.

Magadel sat the house on the outskirts, then hovered overhead. "My dear friends. Here are three people from far away, Ryckair, Mirjel and their newborn infant. Please, help them until I return." He flew off.

Ryckair stepped out of the house. Mirjel followed with the baby in her arms.

A young man extended his hand. "Greetings. I'm Kenalan, your neighbor. Welcome."

Mirjel shook his hand "Thank you."

An older woman came up to Mirjel. "Such a lovely child."

The infant woke and smiled.

The woman laughed. "And so friendly. I'm Darmon. I live just over there. Welcome."

"Thank you," said Ryckair. "Where can we find the mayor?"

Darmon said, "Mayor? What's that?"

"The leader of the village."

Kenalan raised an eyebrow. "I don't understand. Leader?"

"The person who sets the rules you live by."

"The dragons established The Great Plan. We elect an administrator every two years to coordinate trade between communities and organize festivals. Why would we need someone to make more rules? Are there such people where you come from?"

Mirjel said, "We also follow the dragon's plan. Our speech is different. My husband misunderstood."

The tension she sensed evaporated.

Kenalan said, "You must come from far away. I propose a party to celebrate your arrival. Who wants to come?"

Everyone said they would and promised to bring food for the celebration.

A young woman said, "I'll play my harp"

A man said, "I'll sing."

A boy in his teens said, "We can dance. I like dancing."

Others offered food and drink.

In moments, the party was set. The people left to make preparations.

Ryckair said, "There appears to be no sense of government here."

Mirjel rocked the baby "There seems to be no need of it."

At dusk, people arrived. Some brought lanterns they hung from trees. There was food and wine. They sang and danced while stars appeared overhead. Just the right amount of food appeared without prompting.

The newborn fell asleep in Mirjel's arms.

People filtered away until only Kenalan remained.

He said, "Come over tomorrow. I'll show you where food is gathered. Good night now."

Ryckair stood on the threshold of the house as people filtered away. He smiled at the baby. "I guess we should give her a name."

"Yes." Mirjel rocked the child. "I christen you Enada."

It was an ancient name. In the dragon tongue, *Ena* meant soul and *da* to heal, as with the name Daro, women who bring healing.

Ryckair smiled. "Yes. That's perfect."

CHAPTER FOUR

Marawee stood flabbergasted in the refugee tent. "Gone?"

Umera held the note Yearol left. "Yes. Two nights ago."

It took time for word to reach Marawee about his family in the refugee camp. The devastation of Marshala's death was now compounded by news of his daughter's departure.

Len said, "We told soldiers in the morning. They said they have no authority to order anyone back to camp."

Marawee sat on a cot. "I can't believe it. Yearol, yes. I don't think anyone could have held her back, but Keetala? Why?"

Umera sat next to her husband and took his hand. "After Marshala was shot, she changed. She hadn't said a word since the attack. She didn't even cry, just stared off into space."

Fera sat on a cot on the other side of the tent with one hand over an arm. He sniffed. "She had to go. She just had to. I know that. I didn't think it would hurt so much." He started to cry.

Marawee came over and put his arms around the young boy's shoulders. "It's in the hands of the dragons now. You won't be alone, Fera. We're all family now."

Umera said, "Do you know when we'll leave for Yadra?"

"The quarters are almost ready. The whole camp will move at the same time."

Fera found some girls and boys his age. Someone sewed old sheets together and stuffed them with rags to make a ball. Fera and his new friends kicked it across an open space in a game they made up, where the first person to get it into the bed of a wagon won. They also played keep away and another game to see who could kick the ball the farthest.

A lieutenant appeared at the tent door a week later. "Excuse me, are you Marawee Bedquanga."

Marawee said, "Yes, can I help you?"

The soldier saluted. "Baron Dek sends his regards and requests your presence at the palace, sir. I've been sent to accompany you."

Marawee smiled to Umera. "It must be about the move."

The two men walked to the edge of camp where horses awaited. They mounted and rode north past fields, orchards and forest for the rest of the day. When night fell, they stopped at an inn.

The next morning, they rode again. It took several days to reach Meth and cross the bridge over the Peret River. People hustled down streets, many of them in uniform. Shops were open. Business was brisk. Sentries stood along the wall of the old city. The officer showed a uniformed woman a pass. She waved them forward.

They reached a high plain where a steep cliff dropped off into Lake Hasp at the eastern end. An arched bridge led to a tall pinnacle of rock just offshore. It rose like a stone arm thrust up out of the water. The royal palace sat upon it behind embankments.

The palace complex was the size of a small town with many buildings and parade grounds, Marawee rode across the bridge to an iron portcullis. Beyond, stood two flat topped towers north and south of each other. They were connected by the great audience hall.

Soldiers drilled with swords, bows and polearms. Some wore the white pants and blue jackets of the Carandir Navy. Most were dressed in dark brown army battle uniforms. Officers watched the drills from horseback.

The lieutenant escorted Marawee through the double doors. A transparent roof made of crystal vaulted overhead. On the west side of the hall were boxes with low walls reserved for the nobles of Carandir's eighteen baronies. They stood empty on this day.

At the east end was a dais upon which rested the twin thrones of the monarchy. Marawee stood before who he thought was Queen Mirjel with the dragon-crested crown upon her head.

Narech Herrik and Baron Dek stood to her side.

Marawee knelt before the dais. "Majesty."

Lek extended her hand.

Marawee kissed the signet ring Mirjel left behind.

She said, "Welcome, Marawee Bedquanga. Your loyalty and bravery are known to us in your service against the Barasha and your ride to bring news of the traitors who now raise armed insurrection."

Marawee said, "I serve Carandir, ma'am."

"Rise. We have a task to ask of you. First, you must learn something. We will adjourn to private chambers."

Lek led them through the rear of the audience hall, then past the metal doors of the Kyar's vaults, which were decorated with reliefs of dragons in flight.

Carandir soldiers with pole arms snapped to attention at the entrance to the ministerial chambers.

Lek led the company inside and took a seat at the head of the table.

Marawee felt a weight of pronouncement as he sat and studied the solemn faces around him.

Lek's vice fell form the royal tone to take on an informal timbre. "You're about to be privileged to information that can't be discussed outside of that door. Baron Dek, please explain."

The Baron said, "The queen is not in the room with us."

A quizzical expression formed on Marawee's face. "I don't understand"

"Her Majesty led a party commanded by Colonel Amar to rescue the king on the North Continent months ago. The Daro and Kyar worked together to create a potion. It gave the queen's Lady of the Bedchamber her exact appearance and voice. This is Lek, who has sat on the throne in place of Her Majesty to keep the spirits of the people strong. She wears a duplicate crown with no magical power."

Lek said, "Those in this chamber are among the few who know the truth."

Marawee looked to Lek, then Dek. "This is uncanny. If the people knew…"

Dek said, "That's why you can't speak of this. You're now a part of an inner circle."

"Where are the true queen and king?"

Batu told of how the monarchs intended to enter the wizard tower in Amblar secretly and cross to the one in Barta.

Dek said, "They've not arrived. We fear their majesties may have been waylaid on their way to Amblar. They may have also encountered some impediment in the towers or hide in the Barta tower. Baroness Luja may have captured them."

Herrik said, "We don't think they were captured, or she would have seized the crown and used it. Still, we can't tell. If she has the crown, she may wait for an opportune moment."

Marawee said, "What of Baras?"

The baron said, "Without the crown, there's no way to confine Baras in eternal sleep. We have no control over this. We can only confront the civil war and attack by Karaken for now. We need to regain control of the tower for any hope of rescuing the monarchs and the crown if they are within.

Herrik leaned forward. "We need your help. With the terecs unable to fly and deliver messages, word must be sent to our allies for support. We want you to travel by ship and bring a request for assistance from Hura."

Marawee sat up straight. "I'm honored to serve the Crown, however, I'm not skilled in courtly customs. Wouldn't you want a diplomat to negotiate?"

Batu said, "Your valor and honesty are well known here and in Hura."

Herrik nodded. "There's no better representative from Carandir. Commander Dugary Watoola has been promoted to captain and will take you safely to your former homeland. Enemy ships patrol the river near Fellant and Lena. You'll have to sail far to the north to avoid them."

Marawee said, "The Sarte still roam the Great River to the north."

"It's an unavoidable risk. Watoola was on the *Star Fire* when it was attacked by the fish men. She knows their tactics. The ship you'll sail on has been outfitted with upgraded armament. Captain Efra, who commanded the *Star Fire*, will take a galley east to raise help from Xinglan."

"Aren't you worried the traitors will try to stop him?"

"They would have to get past the Carandir Navy. Our forces control the waters from Lake Hasp east."

Marawee looked from one to another. "I accept this task. Please allow my family to accompany me. We lost two to death on the journey. The hardship of separation is great."

"It shall be," said Herrik.

Dek said, "You're a fine soldier, Marawee, and a good man. I know the dragons will protect you. Diplomatic letters of introduction will be drafted. You and I will work together to prepare the petition before you leave. Narech Herrik has written a letter for Captain Watoola. Once you're on the Great River, hand it to her. It explains all we've discussed here. She'll inform the crew and your family. They need to understand the whole truth if the mission is to succeed."

He handed Marawee a signet ring. "Like the queen's ring, this is impregnated with magic to identify its authenticity. It, and the letter of introduction, identifies you as the Crown's ambassador to Hura. May the dragons guide us."

Herrik escorted Marawee from the chambers.

Dek and Lek sat alone.

She said, "Will Hura and Xinglan send forces, My Lord?"

"There are strong ties between our nations. They'll come."

A frown came to Lek's face. "What if the monarchs never return?"

Dek stroked his beard. "I've asked myself the same question many times since Batu arrived.. Carandir has always had a monarch or heir. The crown makes certain the best rulers sit on the thrones. With both it and Their Highnesses missing, we face the threat of Baras rising and no leaders. I sometimes envy city-states like Au with their elected councils. New leaders can always be chosen. It the monarchs perish, Carandir could fall into anarchy."

Lek said, "I think of my mistress constantly and wonder what she would do every time I hold an audience, even though I fear I'll stumble and bring down the nation."

The baron said, "You've done well, Lek. It's not your blood, it's your strength that preserves us."

Marawee learned the ship they would sail on was named the *Ne*, which meant light in the dragon tongue.

The night before she was to put out, Marawee sat at a table with Umera, Len and Fera.

Sweat on the dark skin of his face reflected the light of three candles. "I alone have committed to this journey. None of you are bound to go. I won't deny there's danger. You can find safety on Varda away from the war."

Umera took Marawee's arm. "I'll go. Too long were we separated in the war."

He smiled and squeezed her hand.

"I'll go too," said Len. "I'd like to see the country you come from."

Fera remained silent. He looked down at the table, then up to Marawee. "Yearol and I both knew we had something bigger than ourselves to do while we fled Shenan. I never thought about things much before."

He paused. "We both saw terrible evil and came to know there's even greater evil. Yearol's gone back to Shenan to do what she must. I'll come with you to do whatever I can."

They left camp a span before dawn and rode in a carriage for several days to a dock in Meth.

The *Ne* stood at anchor with her sails furled.

A naval officer saluted. "Lieutenant Lakar at your service, Ambassador Marawee. Captain Watoola awaits your pleasure."

Marawee and his company followed him up the gangplank. The *Ne* was a deep-water sailing vessel with three masts. Each sported five sails. Jibs were attached to the foremast and a spanker to the aft. The ship could ply the deepest waters of the Great River and into the ocean.

Lakar escorted them to a door set beneath the aft deck and knocked.

A woman's voice answered, "Enter."

The lieutenant opened the door and saluted. "Ambassador Marawee and his party, ma'am."

Captain Watoola sat behind a desk on which lay several charts. She stood and touched her right index finger to her head between the eyebrows of her dark brown forehead and nodded. "*Dugary Watoola na ken.*" This was a traditional Huran greeting that translated to; *Dugary Watoola at your service.*

Marawee returned the gesture, "*Marawee Bedquanga. Buro noa gen Karan.*" *Marawee Bedquanga. Well met and thank you.* "Allow me to present my company. This is my wife, Umera, my long-time friend Len Gento and Fera Miller, who risked his life to bring news of Luja's rebellion in Shenan."

Watoola sat down. "Well met, all of you. Quarters are prepared. You'll eat in the officers' mess. I'm afraid there won't be much to entertain you."

Marawee said, "We'll be busy with preparations for the mission."

The captain said, "Lieutenant Lakar will show you to your quarters. We'll talk again at brightnail. Two quick bells and a third a moment later will announce lunch."

Marawee and Umera were shown a cabin on the port side. Len and Fera shared one at the stern. Both were barely large enough for two narrow bunk beds, one atop the other, a desk secured to the bulkhead, a wooden chair and a cabinet. Oil lamps hung from gimbals. There were no portholes.

Umera said, "Cozy."

Marawee laughed. "And intimate." He furrowed his brow. "I have to admit I got a little queasy on the voyage from Hura."

"Will you be all right below like this with the motion."

"I got used to it. I never liked it. The sooner we reach Hura, the happier I'll be."

As the *Ne* set out, no one took notice of a man who rowed back to a wharf where fishers gathered. He walked to a shed and unlocked the door.

Once inside, he took a gem from a pouch. In Shenan, Baroness Luja instructed Velatar to cast a spell on it and another one.

The man squeezed the gem. The stone glowed bright red. He knew its double would also glow in Luja's stronghold.

Marawee spent as much time as possible topside with his eyes on the horizon. Though the sensation of nausea diminished, it still hovered on the edge.

Umera often joined him. They talked about their former home in Hura, their relatives who still lived there, the warm sandy beaches and blue water..

Marawee leaned on the railing alone one morning at sunrise and he concentrated on the horizon.

Lieutenant Lakar joined him "How are your quarters, ambassador?"

Marawee said, "A little cramped, though I imagine they're luxurious by ship standards."

The men looked out on the water. Lakar said, "I guess you're excited to see your homeland again."

"It'll be good to visit family and friends. I wish Keetala had been able to make the journey."

"I'm sorry about your daughter, sir."

"Thank you. I realize why she went back. It doesn't make it any easier."

They watched the river in silence before the lieutenant said, "Do you ever think about going back to live in Hura?"

Marawee continued to stare at the water. "No. Carandir is home for me now. I can't imagine living anywhere else."

"Even after Baron Womb drove you out?"

Marawee looked over to Lakar. "He doesn't represent the soul of Carandir, though he and those like him think they're somehow pure. Hebra told me how the first Carandirians came from the North Continent themselves. Womb and all who hold his views are immigrants."

"It's a pity the traitors weren't destroyed with the Barasha. There'd be no civil war"

"I sometimes think so, then I remember, though most welcomed us into the valley, some told us to go back where we came from. Womb and the others merely stirred hidden prejudice and hatred for those who are different. He and the rebel nobles couldn't have acted alone. They spurred small groups into violent mobs. Other people turned their faces and said nothing out of fear. Even if Womb hadn't returned, another megalomanic could have sparked the hate."

Marawee sighed. "It shocked me. Though the majority people in Hura have dark skin, those from other nations with light, pale and brown skin live together in peace."

Lakar said, "I've seen that attitude among some people though I've never understood it. I was scrawny as a youth. Some of the other children teased me and wouldn't let me play games with them. I hated it. When I got older, they stopped. I still saw their sideways looks. That's why I joined the navy, to show them I'm not weak."

Marawee smiled. "You don't appear weak to me, lieutenant."

"Thank you, sir." Lakar looked back out to the river. "Why did you stay in Carandir after the war with people like Womb here?"

"I expected to go back to Hura. My wife and daughter were there, along with the rest of my family. I was selected to represent my unit in a ceremony at the palace. The monarchs sat on their thrones. The crown, encased in the crystal sphere, rested in front of them.

"Each of us, one by one, approached and received a citations. When I stepped forward and looked into the eyes of the dragon crest. They held me, as if time didn't exist. I felt I belonged there. To my surprise, I said out loud, 'Sweet dragons, I'm home'."

He laughed. "King Ryckair and Queen Mirjel looked at me and smiled. In that instant, I knew Carandir was home in my heart."

"Have you ever questioned that decision?"

"Never. The weakness of people like Womb reminds me how great the spirit of Carandir and Carandirians are. He seeks to remove minorities. It's he who's in the minority. I know those who think like him won't win."

The ship changed heading from north to west two weeks out. Captain Watoola gave orders to watch for any Sarte, the creatures with human bodies and the heads of fish, who rode on the backs of giant snakes.

The *Ne* was armed with two catapults, one aft and one to the stern. In the mid-section was a trebuchet. This was a new weapon developed by the Carandirian military. It was mounted on a turntable between the main and aft masts.

When the Sarte attacked the *Star Fire*, crossbow bolts failed to penetrate the snakes' thick, scale covered hides. Only chains soaked in boiling oils shot from catapults raised blood.

Trebuchets could hurl heavier projectiles over four times the range of catapults with much more accuracy.

Watoola noticed the snakes made a subtle wake when they attacked. It was hoped a strike on the creatures from a distance with a massive boulder would crush their skulls or break their backs, before the Sarte could fire crossbow bolts.

The trebuchet was a mechanical device with a long arm half the height of the masts. It was connected to a massive counterweight by linkage and could only fire to port or starboard because of the positions of the sails.

The arm was lowered over the side of the ship, horizontal to the water. The turntable swung the arm back along the side until the end reached an aft station. A sling was attached to the end of the pole. This was wrapped around a heavy, round boulder or filled with hot chains soaked in boiling oil. The arm swung out over the side again.

Sailors raised the counterweight a precise distance to provide enough momentum to reach the target. When a pin was released, the weight dropped. The linkage propelled the arm up in an arc. At the apex, the projectile sailed out toward the target with great force and accuracy. The massive projectile could ram a hole through the wooden hull of a ship.

The flow of the Great River carried them downstream while they tacked to catch changes in wind directions. All lights above deck were doused to mask their passage.

On the second night after Watoola changed course, Marawee laid motionless while nausea churned inside him, until he slipped out of his bunk to go topside.

There was no moon.

He concentrated on the constellations overhead and took long, deep breaths. The nausea subsided, though it didn't vanish.

He heard a bump. Then another. Something scraped against the hull.

The face of a man with light skin popped over the side. He held the blade of a long knife in his teeth.

Three more men followed.

Marawee stepped back. "To arms. We're under attack."

Sailors ran topside with swords and axes.

Two dozen marauders flooded the main deck and pushed the defenders back. A flash of light streamed across the sky and hit the water with a hiss as an enemy ship fired searing chains intended to catch in the sails and set them ablaze.

Carandirian sailors pushed against the assailants, who refused to give way. Watoola, cutlass in hand, stood on the command desk.

Marawee looked across the water and saw another arc flame into the air. He cupped his hands in front of his mouth and shouted up to the captain. "I see where the chains come from." He pointed to the spot.

Watoola called down to the deck. "Load the trebuchet. Marawee, give them the position."

Three dozen men swarmed over the sides.

One assailant threw a leather bag onto the turntable where the trebuchet sat. It broke open and spilled oil across the wood.

Another threw a lantern.

Flames erupted.

Carandirians tossed sand and water on the fire from buckets.

Marawee took a cutlass from a dead Carandirian sailor and pressed his way past the attackers, toward the center of the deck.

One of the borders jumped in front of him and swung at Marawee's head with a short sword.

The ambassador parried the blow and returned a riposte.

The man moved aside and swung again.

The blow raked across Marawee's left arm. He gritted his teeth and sliced with the cutlass. It opened the other's midriff.

The attacker fell to the deck.

More marauders cast oil on spars, masts and decks, then ignited them with lanterns. Flames raced across the planks and up toward the sails.

Carandirians fought the fires.

Two swordsmen confronted Marawee.

The instincts of battle rose within him. He dropped to the deck, rolled, then thrust the tip of the cutlass into the belly of one of them.

The man screamed and crumbled.

Marawee used the momentum of the roll to regain his footing and struck at the other man, who parried the blow, pulled his sword back and sliced toward Marawee's neck.

Marawee twisted the blade of his cutlass up to deflect the blow.

The two men circled one another with their eyes locked.

Marawee realized his foe wanted to push him back to trip over the dead body. He felt winded. It was twenty years since he fought against the Barasha.

The man thrust for Marawee's waist.

He stepped aside.

The man fell face down.

Marawee drove his cutlass into the man's back.

The assailant's body went limp.

He reached trebuchet and pointed to the water. "The enemy ship is there against starlight on the horizon."

Sailors rotated the turntable and aimed the projectile weapon. The counterweight was raised and dropped. The boulder sailed out toward the other vessel.

The enemy ship's mainmast split halfway down. The sails collapse to its deck.

Watoola and her senior officers charged into the melee.

The trebuchet fired again. This time, the projectile drove a wide hole into the starboard side of the enemy ship at the bow. It began to sink.

The marauders looked to their own vessel and cried out. They climbed back into their rowboats.

Captain Watoola said, "Let them go. They'll find crossing the Great River with no ship and provisions to be their end."

Marawee entered Captain Watoola's cabin.

She sat behind her desk.

Her first mate, Commander Neekara, stood next to her

Watoola said, "Commander, do we have enough rope and sheets in stores to repair the sails?"

"Aye, ma'am. We need to put in to shore to complete repairs. The main mast is badly damaged and must be replaced. We'll have to find a spot on the south bank, with a strip of open land between it and the cliffs. Hopefully, tall enough trees can be found. The rudder wasn't damaged. We can maneuver while the current takes us west."

The captain thought for a moment. "Mr. Neekara, make what repairs we can on water and move us south."

"Aye, Ma'am."

Watoola looked up to Marawee. "This will delay your mission, ambassador."

Captain Efra stood at the bow of the merchant galley *Prosper*, now outfitted with catapults fore and aft. These were concealed under canvas. They flew a Carandirian merchant flag as they put out two spans after the *Ne*. His orders were to dock at Au and confer with the council, then proceed to Xinglan.

Trade between Au and Carandir slowed with the civil war. Many other merchant galleys were commandeered for military use. The others now carried only essential goods for the war. The last shipment of spices and silks arrived from Au months earlier.

As with the *Ne*, Efra traveled without escort both to conceal the mission and because an escort was not needed. The waters of the Great River east of Meth were safe.

The tall cliffs of the southern bank gave way to low hills at their approach to the port of Au. There were no other vessels docked. Efra thought this odd. There should still be trade between Au and the other city-states along the river.

He brought the galley into a stone pier just after brightnail. Carandir sailors threw lines to dock workers who secured the galley.

Efra turned to his first mate, commander Cepata. "Issue orders for shore leave. We'll put out tomorrow morning. I'll be in my quarters."

She saluted. "Aye, sir."

From his small cabin, the captain heard the jovial voices of his crew as they went ashore to visit the walled city. He smiled to himself as he recalled the anticipation of shore leave the first time he visited Au as a junior officer. That night, he and several other sailors ate exotic food and drank until early in the morning. When he stood early duty, his head pounded.

For this shore leave, Chief Petty Officer Icarte Fooso formed a patrol to make certain everyone returned sober by darknail.

A span later, most of the crew were ashore. Efra heard a scuffle on deck. He opened his cabin door and was confronted by four armed men. Their clothes was a mismatch of styles. Some wore the jackets of the Au militia along with baggy pants, as were popular with people to the east.

One of the men said, "Good day, captain. Please accompany us to a reception." The other men laughed.

"Who are you? How did you get on board?"

Again, the men laughed.

The first one said, "Just come along and be quiet. Your crew are locked up, so there's no one to call out to. Get moving."

Two of the men grabbed Efra by the shoulders and dragged him down the gangplank. The skeleton crew were there, shackled and tied together with a chain.

A tall man with a long beard sat on the seat of a wagon. Behind him were other wagons with cages made of wooden slats.

The Carandir sailors were dragged to the door of one and shoved inside.

The man who confronted Efra said, "This is the captain, Mr. Turga."

The bearded man in the wagon seat looked down. "Your crew is young and strong. They'll fetch a good price on the slave block. The people who engaged me have other plans for you." Turga indicated a wagon with a smaller cage.

When they entered Au, Efra saw soldiers in Karakien uniforms.

The wagon stopped at the headquarters of the Au militia.

The rest of his crew remained in the caged wagons.

Efra was taken inside and tied to a chair in a room without windows.

A Karakien colonel entered, along with three soldiers who held drawn swords.

The officer said, "I'm Colonel Gaberda of the glorious Karakien army of King Tenato the Magnificent."

Efra stared at the man. "What do you want?"

"I'll ask the questions. Why do you come to Au with a crew of Carandirian navel sailors in a merchant galley?"

Efra turned his head.

Gaberda looked to one of the soldiers.

He slapped Efra across the cheek.

The captain neither flinched nor looked back.

The soldier slapped him again.

Efra remained silent.

The colonel sneered. "You'll tell us what we want to know. It's a question of how much pain you wish to endure. Everyone talks."

Efra closed his eyes.

Gaberda said, "As you wish."

The soldiers sheathed their swords and picked up thick, wooden sticks. They beat Efra in the arms, legs and the lower torso.

One of them untied the captain.

He slumped to the floor.

The Karakiens dragged Efra to a set of stairs.

At the bottom, he was taken to an iron door and shoved into a cell. It was three paces wide and four long. There were no windows. The only light in the cell came from torches in the hallway outside that shone through a slat in the door.

Efra sprawled on the cold, stone floor and moaned. Though the Karakiens didn't touch his head, it pounded and his eyesight blurred from the pain. The room seemed to spin before he lost consciousness.

CHAPTER FIVE

Lieutenant Parna sat in a cave in the Barony of Lusar with no idea if Carandir still existed. When the forces of Luja, Womb and Gilyon overthrew the Royal garrison, he was only able to lead twenty-one of his troops down a chute to a secret exit and into the forest. They rushed to the regrouping area, where Carandir troops were supposed to gather. A week passed. No one came.

He led his command of nine women and twelve men in raids on the militia who invaded Lusar.

Early victories bolstered the Carandirians' morale. More enemy troops flooded into the barony. Parna and his soldiers found themselves outnumbered They began to take on casualties. Several were wounded. Two died. One of them was his sergeant with decades of battle experience.

Parna promoted a Daro trained woman named Wesala to the rank of corporal.

It was weeks since their last offensive. Three of his charges were ill. Two were still wounded. Corporal Wesala tended them as best she could with her limited knowledge.

The company ate a cold meal in the damp cave. A sentry was posted at the mouth. Everyone was exhausted. No one joked. They could go a day without a word between them.

Parna crouched on the floor and stared at his feet. He was not hungry, had not been hungry in days. It was impossible for him to tell how long ago they fled the garrison. The three archers still lived. Most of their arrows were shot.

Wagons protected by mounted soldiers passed their concealed positions every few days. Parna reasoned they would be slaughtered in an attack against such superior forces. The troops looked to him for inspiration and direction. They were all young. Parna himself was twenty-five. He could hardly motivate himself to move.

The sentry whispered, "Lieutenant, someone approaches."

Parna got to his feet and straightened his uniform. "How many?"

"Just one, sir."

The sound of feet on dry leaves echoed into the cave.

Parna wondered if he should send troops out to investigate or keep everyone inside, under cover in case there were others.

The footfalls came closer, then stopped.

Parna drew his sword. He felt shame at what he feared was cowardice in himself and wondered if it would be better to just charge out and die.

The sound of a yetsal bird chirped in the air. It was the signal the Lusar sheriffs used to alert other law enforcement personnel of their presence.

Parna sounded the grunt of a kala, a large rodent that was the signal of the Carandir army.

A woman's voice whispered, "Where are you?"

Parna walked out of the cave.

A tall woman in a black uniform stepped out from behind a bush.

The lieutenant gauged her to be in her mid-thirties. "I'm Lieutenant Leesta Parna of the Carandir royal garrison."

The woman stepped forward. "Frothey Lenar, Deputy Sheriff of Ventara."

Parna felt a wave of relief. "We thought we were the only loyal survivors."

Frothey said, "You're the first troops I've encountered. I thought I was alone too."

"Are you hungry?"

"Famished."

Inside the cave, Parna introduced the remainder of his troops. "Merchants from Tesar came to the garrison with amazing bargains on vegetables and meat. We should've inspected the packs on the backs of their horses. On some signal, they drew weapons and attacked. We tried to block the gate. A surge of marauders pushed through. My command held until we were overrun and forced to flee though a secret passage."

Frothey sat on the floor and chewed on a piece of dried meat. "Sheriff Arota Deshara and I were attacked by four men. They killed her before I could kill them."

Parna stared at the meat. "Had you worked together long?"

Frothey took the jerky from her mouth and looked to the cave floor. "We were lovers. We'd been together for six years."

As his will to command slipped away after so many defeats, Parna withdrew from all emotion, The deadness inside melted a little. "I'm so sorry." He searched for a way to regain composure. "We raided supply wagons, until they put heavy guards on them."

Frothey gnawed the dried meat again. "I've done what I could to harass them. Their troop strength's decreased over the last month. I saw columns march back into Eel, Tesar and Shenan. I don't think they were just going home. I heard talk of open warfare against the Crown. This is bigger than just Lusar."

"Have you killed many of them?"

She stared into his eyes with a gaze of hatred. "I slipped into their tents, put my hand over the mouth of the first soldier and slit his throat. Once he was dead, I skipped over the next one and did the same to the third, then I followed for every other one in the tent."

Parna felt a shiver run up his back.

Frothy finished the meat. "What have you been doing?"

Shame returned to Parna. "We've avoided the larger groups and looked for smaller targets."

"When was your last attack?"

"Three weeks ago."

The deputy stood and stared down at him. "Three weeks? You have a command of eighteen." She looked around the cave at the others. "You've hidden here for three weeks?"

Parna stood. "We look for appropriate targets."

Frothey slapped him. "Targets are all around. I've killed the pigs myself while you've waited for school children to attack."

"The troop movement's been heavy."

"I know. I've encountered them. What's the matter with all of you?"

"It would be pointless to get killed just to show courage."

Frothey walked over to a woman wrapped in a blanket on the floor. "What's wrong with you? Are you wounded?"

The soldier coughed. "I'm sick."

Frothey kicked her. "You all make me sick. Carandir soldiers. Look at yourselves."

Rage flushed Parna's face. He grabbed Frothey and spun her around. "She has a fever and chills. Another soldier died of it. Who are you to come in here and berate us?"

Frothey shook herself free. "Are you angry?"

Parna's voice resounded in the small space. "I should knock your teeth out."

Frothey smiled. "Good. I'm glad to see you're still alive. I thought you were all dead when I came in."

Parna breathed in hard gasps and realized he hadn't felt such intensity in weeks. He looked at his troops, many of whom stood with their hands on the hilts of their swords.

He hung his head. "I don't know what to say."

Frothey's features softened. "None of us have ever faced defeat like this. I've killed as many traitors as I could. It's been more out of revenge than a plan."

Parna felt sick inside. He failed in his duty and allowed sorrow to take hold. He was commissioned nine months before the attack. It was the first action he saw.

He told himself it was no excuse and knew he could wallow in pity or put that behind him and do something. "We have no plan either. We need to make one, together."

The deputy gave a short laugh. "A fine lot we are, fighting each other instead of the enemy."

Parna felt his face turn red. "I'm still new to this. Do you have any ideas?"

Frothey scanned the faces of the women and men around her. They were filled with fear and emptiness. "The first thing we need to do is remember who we are. Carandirians. Those who came before us faced Baras and the Barasha who called demons. Our enemy is flesh and blood. Somewhere, the Carandirian army fights those who would rob us of who we are. These traitors will kill anyone who doesn't meet their definition of pure." She pointed a finger at her chest. "Even a woman like me, who loved another woman. That's not what Carandir is. It's not the plan of the dragons.

"We've run around out of hatred and fear. That has to stop right here and now. We have to remember who we are and what we've sworn to protect. Some or all of us may die. Let our deaths mean something."

She put her hands together and brought them to her forehead in the sign of the covenant with the dragons.

To a person, everyone in the cave did likewise.

Snow in the passes of Lusar melted with the first week of summer. Only the high peaks were covered in white. Glaciers ground down the hills as their tips melted to fill rivers with an abundance of fresh water.

The cool interior of the cave where Parna and his troops sheltered gave a respite from the sun at brightnail, which often drove the temperature uncomfortably high.

Frothey stooped on the cave floor and drew a picture in the dust with a stick. "The guard house faces the road with its back to this cliff. There are two men inside. Eight others patrol the brush next to the road that leads up to the bridge."

Parna studied the crude map. "The men on the outside could spot anyone who comes down the cliff."

The deputy shook her head. "Not at night."

The other soldiers stared down at the sketch.

Parna said, "Someone might make noise."

"They could be lowered. It would only take three. They would attack the guards in the booth by surprise. The ones on the outside would run to their aid. We can rush from the bushes and take them."

"Is there an alarm horn?"

Frothey stood and threw the stick to the floor. "What do you want to do, hide in this cave?"

"I just want to see if there's any weaknesses in the plan."

"Well, at least it is a plan." Frothey stomped out of the cave.

Corporal Wesala said, "I'm light, sir. I could be lowered and not make a sound."

Parna gave a sigh and went in search of Frothey.

He found her just outside the cave entrance. She sat on a log and threw rocks into brush.

Parna said, "I didn't say it's a bad plan."

She picked up another rock and tossed it. "You've argued with every suggestion I've made."

He rubbed his neck. "I'm responsible for these people. They're disciplined and will follow a plan. I just want to know that it is the best one."

"There are no best ones. We risk our lives no matter what we do, even if we just sit here. The best we can hope for is to harass them. If we burn that bridge it'll cut off their forces in the Resala Valley. There's no other route to call for reinforcements. We can take them out slowly."

"Then what?"

Frothey threw her arms up. "Then we do it to some another outpost. What am I, a prophet?"

Parna said, "Look, I understand how angry you are."

She stood and brought her face up to Parna's. "You can't begin to know how angry I am. Don't patronize me."

He slapped her.

They stared at each other.

Parna said, "Let's get one thing clear here. I command these troops. I won't send them into a battle that'll only lead to their deaths. That doesn't drive the enemy out or help the Crown. It doesn't get you revenge. Where is all the talk about a higher purpose?"

Frothey took several deep breaths, then lowered her gaze. "We have to do something other than sit here."

"We have to do something effective. Yes, we can cut off the militia in the valley. It won't stop the war. These traitorous nobles care nothing for the men they send into battle. The troops in the valley would be written off."

She sat down and tossed another rock. "So, what do you propose?"

"We attack the heart of their power, in Shenan. It's evident Baroness Luja is the leader of the rebels. If we disrupt their supply lines in Shenan, slow their troop movements and spread fear among their militia, we can have an effect on the war. The traitors just wanted to prevent an attack from the royal garrison at their rear. We'll take the fight to them."

Frothey picked up another rock, hefted it for a second, then dropped it. "It's a good plan." She paused. "I'll come with you, if you'll allow me."

Parna smiled. "I would be honored if you joined us. Come on. Let's get started."

CHAPTER SIX

Keetala shielded her eyes and surveyed the Karakien plain before them. Low scrub dotted the ground. Their stalks were green even though the tips of the bushes were pale brown.

She was born in the lush tropics of Hura. Heat didn't bother her. It was the dryness. Her mouth always felt parched.

They crossed the border three weeks before. Many of their water skins were still full, though she wondered how much farther they would have to travel to find a spring.

The barren hill they stood on dropped off sharply. Taller hills could be seen beyond them.

The women dismounted and stood out of the sun in the shadow of blankets spread across two boulders to create shade.

Yearol studied a map fragment. "Those hills must be the base of mountains in Ulata. We might find water there."

It was a span before brightnail. The air shimmered as waves of heat rose from the parched ground.

Keetala stroked the neck of her horse. "I don't think they can go any farther in this heat."

Yearol ran a hand across her forehead and down one cheek. "I agree."

"We should wait until nightfall to set off. I think we can reach those far hills in four or five spans."

Though they were out of direct sunlight, the heat was still intense. It was the first time Yearol experienced such high temperatures. She sat on a rock and fanned herself with her wide brimmed hat. A chill ran through her, even though there was no breeze. Through blurred vision, her head felt light. A wave of nausea churned in her stomach. The ground seemed to fall up.

Keetala caught her friend and lowered her to the ground. "Lie down. You have heat stroke."

She lifted Yearol's head and brought a canteen to her companion's lips. "Take small sips. Don't try to speak."

Perspiration ran down Yearol's face as she shivered in the oppressive heat. When the canteen was withdrawn, she breathed in hard gasps. The nausea wouldn't stop. Her heart pounded rapidly. Everything was confused in her mind. She couldn't tell where she was or why she was there.

Keetala soaked a scarf with water and rubbed it on Yearol's head and arms. She stopped and took a long drink, then looked at the horses. Their coats were thick with sweat.

She soaked the scarf again and rolled up Yearol's pants to wet her legs. "Oh, Ilidel."

Keetala kept Yearol and the horses under the shade of the blankets until sunset, yet knew the intense heat baked into the ground would radiate past darknail.

She was certain Yearol wouldn't be able to ride. She would have to be strapped across her saddle. Keetala looked to the taller hills across the plain and hoped there was shade and water there.

Yearol continued to shake and sweat. She no longer noticed the nausea. All she wanted to do was rest.

Keetala used two canteens worth of water to rub Yearol's arms, neck, head and legs.

The sun dipped over the horizon. Keetala stroked her horse's muzzle. "You're hot too, aren't you? I'll give you both extra water. You'll need it. We have to ride fast."

Yearol's body was limp. Keetala struggled to position her companion face down across the saddle. The horse neighed and moved to the side. "Just stand still."

She managed to get Yearol into position and secured her with ropes tied to the saddle that ran under the horse's belly.

She took the reins of Yearol's horse in one hand and mounted her own steed. With a snap, she set off across the plain.

Dust rose and made her cough. She pushed the horses forward into a canter and prayed to the dragons they could continue the pace.

She stopped and checked on Yearol. Her companion's body temperature was lower. She stopped sweating. Keetala knew both were dangerous signs.

Keetala wondered if she should put Yearol down to give her more water. She might not be able to get her back on the horse. She poured water onto a scarf, put it to Yearol's mouth and squeezed. Liquid dribbled from the young woman's lips. Keetala hoped enough got inside.

She mounted again and set off. It felt as if there would be no end to the journey. The moon shone a quarter. In the feeble light, she thought she saw vegetation. Crags appeared. Something tall grew out of them.

An oasis was situated at the foot of a crevice. She ran the horses in a gallop toward it. Grass appeared beneath them. Palms grew at the water's edge.

When they reached the water, Keetala dismounted, ran to Yearol and lowered the other woman into her arms.

Yearol took shallow gasps.

Keetala carried her to the oasis and immersed her body in water. "Yearol. Yearol. Can you hear me?"

Yearol's breath became stronger.

Keetala closed her eyes. "Thank you, Ilidel. Thank you."

They stayed in the water for a span, before Keetala pulled Yearol onto the shore of the oasis and covered her in a blanket.

The overheated woman's eyes flickered.

Keetala put a canteen to her lips. "Drink slowly. That's it."

Yearol took several sips.

Keetala lowered Yearol's head to another blanket rolled up to make a pillow.

The horses stood at the edge of the water. Their coats gleaned with sweat in the moonlight as they drank.

Keetala propped her back against a palm and ran her hands across the ground to discover a string of dates. The pulp was sweet and soothing. She began to laugh. The laughter turned to sobs as tears fell from her eyes.

She fell asleep against the palm.

It was well after dawn when Keetala woke. The heat already began to rise. She got up and put her hand on Yearol's forehead.

The young woman opened her eyes. "Where are we?"

"An oasis next to those far hills we saw."

Yearol looked left and right. "Hills?"

"Yes. We saw them yesterday. How do you feel?"

Yearol rubbed a hand over her face. "Tired. Where did you say we are?"

"An oasis. You had heat stroke. I put you on your horse. We rode here in the night."

Yearol started to sit up, then fell back.

Keetala brought her a canteen. "Here. Drink some more."

"It's hot."

"You feel it? Good. Do you know who you are?"

"Yearol."

"Who am I?"

"Keetala."

Keetala relaxed. "I don't think you've suffered long term damage. Eat some bread and rest here."

"I have to relieve myself."

Keetala laughed. "That's a good sign too. Here, I'll help you up."

Yearol was able to walk with some assistance. When she was through, Keetala helped her back down. "There are dates around. I don't think you should have any fruit just yet. Stay here. I want to explore a little."

"All right. I feel better now. Let me have some more bread."

The oasis was only a hundred paces across. Keetala tied rope to the horses' bridles and secured them to a palm so they could reach the water and some grass. She walked to the west bank and found a spring where water gushed down a ravine. It was lined with palms. The temperature was much cooler under them.

There was a ledge along one side. She walked up the waterway as it climbed at a gentle pace. Several pools formed. Some were as deep as her chest. Next to one was a flat outcropping of stone ten paces long and four wide.

She returned to the oasis.

Yearol sat on the blanket.

She smiled. "The bread felt good in my stomach. I never gave bread much thought when I lived at the mill. This little scrap of loaf tasted like a banquet."

Keetala laughed. "I'm so glad you're recovering. I was very worried."

"I have to admit I'm a little frightened when I think about." Yearol pursed her lips. "Thank you. I owe you my life."

"We're in this together. We need each other."

They ate a breakfast of cheese coated in wax, bread and water. Yearol tried a few dates. They stayed down.

Keetala said, "The oasis is fed by a spring that flows down the hill. It's cool under the palms. I found a place where we can rest."

They walked the horses to the spot Keetala found and spent the rest of the day there. Yearol remembered nothing of the desert crossing. "These must be the foothills to the mountains between Shenan and Ulata. I think we should turn north here."

"I agree. Even for someone born in a hot climate, this desert's a nightmare."

They spent the rest of the day and the next night under the cool of the palms.

Yearol was able to move about. She mounted her horse and walked it around the flat space. "I'm certain I can ride again. We should head north."

"You look fine. Let's wait here tonight and set off at dawn. The trek up the mountain could be treacherous. We'll need to see the ground."

They filled packs with dates and replenished the canteens, then led the horses up the hill the next morning.

The ground became steep. Trees began to dot the hillsides. They came to the bottom of a waterfall and could go no further up the spring. A paths led off to one side.

"Goat tracks," said Yearol. "Fera and I followed quite a few when we escaped from Shenan."

They continued up until they reached a level area above the desert floor, visible through trees of what was now a forest. The ground was mossy. The temperature was warm, though not hot.

Their hearts grew light as they mounted and rode forward. The air was fresh with the scent of pines. They crossed small streams and continued on a northerly course.

Yearol kept track of their pace and all turns as she referenced the map.

They rode past a set of trees. A meadow spread out before them where a house stood. Smoke rose from a chimney. To one side were mounds of earth with markers.

Yearol was certain they were graves and remembered the house she and Fera encountered, with the man who wanted to rape her.

She pulled the reins her horse. "We should go around."

An aged woman in a patchwork skirt and white blouse stepped out of a door and waved.

Keetala said, "We've been spotted. If we run, it'll raise suspicion."

"I don't like this. Why is this house here? Whose graves are those?"

"Let's find out." Keetala urged her horse forward.

Yearol hesitated and considered whether she should turn and ride away, then gave an exasperated sigh and followed.

The woman had creases in her face, which was the brown color of people who lived in the deep deserts. Her dull white hair was cropped short. She waved again. "Come in. I'm just getting some lunch." She stepped back inside.

Keetala dismounted. Yearol made certain a knife was in easy reach.

There was a large room with a hearth to the right and several doors straight ahead. A table sat in the middle, with bowls of leafy plants and berries.

The aged woman retrieved plates and mugs from a cupboard and set them out along with spoons and forks. She placed some ground berries in the mugs, went to a kettle that hung from a hook over the fire and poured boiling water into the mugs. "I'm afraid I can't offer you kan. I haven't had any in years. These berries make a nice beverage."

Yearol inspected the contents of the mug. She recalled how the wife of the man who tried to assault her drugged the food given to Fera and her.

Keetala picked up her mug and took a sip. "This is wonderful. Sweet and refreshing."

"Yes," said the woman. "I add a few herbs. The result is nearly as invigorating as kan, I think."

Yearol took a sip. It was delicious. Still, she didn't finish her drink.

The woman sat down at the table with them. "I haven't had visitors in a long time. My name is Lesarra."

Yearol pushed some of the leaves around with her fork. "I'm Yearol. This is Keetala. Does your family live nearby?"

"They're all gone now. Those are their graves outside."

Yearol felt her face flush. "I'm sorry. I didn't mean to pry."

"Oh, think nothing of it. I'm just glad to have you here. Now, please don't think I'm prying. I'm just curious as to how a young woman with light skin and a slightly older woman with black skin came to travel across the desert together?"

Keetala said, "We met on the road."

"The Karakiens don't usually welcome strangers on their roads."

"We got lost."

"I see. That explains it. Only, where were you heading?"

Yearol's hand slipped down to the knife. "West."

"Oh, are you merchants?"

"No. We're on our way home. We were in the east."

The woman took a sip of her beverage. "The east. I come from the east. Can you guess where I was born?"

From the corner of her eyes, Yearol saw Keetala's muscles ready to leap. The younger woman said, "I'm afraid not."

"Would you take me for a Karakien?"

Yearol estimated how far away the door was. "I've never met anyone from Karaken."

The woman stared into Yearol's eyes. She tried to look away. It was impossible to move. The air seemed heavy, as though it pressed on her. She again saw Keetala on the edge of her vision. The young black woman sat frozen. Yearol was certain Lesarra put a potion in the drink.

Yearol felt the oppression vanish.

Lesarra said, "No. You don't know. I can see you've never met a Karakien. I'm sorry. I had to be certain."

"Certain of what?"

"Certain you weren't sent to find me. The memories and vengeance of the Karakien kings know no time."

Keetala said, "Why would they send someone to find you?"

Lesarra gave a chuckle. "I'm sorry if I frightened you both. Even after nearly a century, the Karakien government can't allow those who break free of their slavery to go unpunished lest it encourage others."

She got up, retrieved the kettle and poured more boiling water into the cups. "I was born east of Karaken, in Tequan, nearly two hundred years ago."

Yearol shook her head. "No one lives that long."

"Daro healers do. I traveled to Meth when I was a young girl to learn the magical arts of healing, then returned to my home in Tequan. The Karakiens captured me in a raid. When they discovered my talents, I was put to work treating the wounded of their army. My oath commands me to heal any who are hurt. I did so, yet I always thought of escape.

"Others also desired freedom. We managed to break out, twenty-four of us, and almost died as we crossed the desert on foot, with little water or food. Eight of us did die. We had to leave their bodies behind. The rest of us found this place and settled. Those are their graves outside. I'm the last. The Karakiens would still take me back for torture and death to dissuade others from rebelling."

Yearol said, "Do you want to return to Tequan? Aren't you lonely here?"

Lesarra said, "I would return to a land I no longer know. If I were in Tequan I'd be lonelier than I am here. It doesn't matter. The Karakien army wouldn't let me pass. I enjoy my home and the animals. Age brings a different perspective on life. I'm quite happy, though it's a treat to have your company. Now, let me look at you, Yearol. Heat stroke can have lasting effects."

Keetala leaned forward. "How did you know she had heat stroke? I said nothing."

"The signs are there. Besides, I had advance knowledge of your travels and approach."

Suspicion returned to Yearol. "You spied on us?"

The old woman held out her hand.

The air flickered.

A small creature appeared in her palm. It was no bigger than her thumb and as thin. Its head was a vertical oval atop a body covered in scales.

The creature hopped onto Lesarra's shoulder. "This is one of my friends. It lives with its kind here in this forest. None of us saw one before we came here. We called them whispies because they carry news and whisper it into the mind. I'm not sure how many there are or what magic allows them to pop in and out.

A whispy can move great distances. They took to us as soon as we arrived and brought us word of anyone who approached from the desert."

The whispy popped out and reappeared on Yearol's shoulder. She felt a presence in her mind. As with the magical creatures she and Fera encountered in Shenan, a sense of calm came over her.

Lesarra laughed. "It likes you. That's a good sign. Now, let me see if you're fully recovered."

The Daro healer examined Yearol. "You have a slight limp."

"Two of my toes were amputated due to frostbitten."

"Take off your boot." The healer checked Yearol's foot. "Someone did a good job. Do you have pain?"

"Sometimes. It's not bad."

"I have a cream that'll help." She retrieved a small earthen jar and handed it to Yearol. "Rub this on your toes when they ache. You haven't suffered permanent damage from heatstroke. Still, you need rest. There are many beds here. You're both welcome to stay as long as you like."

"Thank you," said Keetala, "We can only stay for a while."

"It's the war, isn't it?" said Lesarra. "The whispies bring me news. You need not tell me about your mission. I can see the importance in your eyes. Rest here for now."

The two Carandirian women spent a week with Lesarra.

Yearol underestimated how much the heat stroke affected her until she relaxed. She spent much of each day outside as she sat and watched birds, rabbits and deer come into the clearing. Some approached close enough for her to feed. The world outside seemed far away. Still, the memory of her mother's death hovered at the edge of thought.

One morning, Lesarra said, "The last ruminants of heatstroke are gone."

Yearol put a spoon back in a bowl of berries. "It would be very nice if we could stay, for a while at least." She paused. "We can't."

Keetala said, "There's task we must complete."

Lesarra nodded. "I know. I sensed it from the moment you arrived."

A whispy popped onto the Daro healer's shoulder and leaned into her ear. Lesarra raised an eyebrow. "I see."

The small creature vanished and reappeared on Yearol's shoulder.

Lesarra said, "It seems this little one wants to go with you."

Yearol said, "I don't want to take it away from its kind."

"You can't take one anywhere. They go where they want. This one wants to go with you. It can be very helpful. I'm afraid you can't tell it to stay." She laughed.

Yearol reached out and stroked the whispy's head. A deep sense of affection flooded her mind.

They mounted their horses after lunch. Lesarra waved as they rode out of the meadow. The magical creature perched itself on Yearol's right shoulder.

Keetala said, "Have you thought of a name for your new friend?'

"I think Whispy is fine." She felt a sense of approval from the creature. "Yes, Whispy."

They made camp just before sunset. From time to time, Whispy popped out and then back onto Yearol's shoulder. She felt more than heard a report each time that nothing nearby was a threat.

The next day, a snow covered peak came into view. Yearol consulted one of the map fragments. "Shenan. I'm almost home."

Keetala studied the map. "We should avoid major passes. There'll almost certainly be militia there." She pointed to a spot. "It looks like the terrain isn't too steep here where this river flows south and then breaks into two forks east into Ulata and west to Shenan. We could skirt this mountain range. There have to be bridges there we could take out."

Yearol said, "It's far south of where my brother and I traveled. My father once showed me a map that indicated two major passes between Shenan and Ulata." She pointed to the map. "Here and here. A bridge taken out or an avalanche would cut off troop movements and supplies."

Two days later, they reached the river just above the forks. It was not too wide or swift to ford at that point. The banks were steep in some places west of the river. They moved up the hillsides to continue.

At the fork, the rivers were torrents. The women headed west, thankful they didn't need to cross the water again.

The bank was wide. They mounted once more.

Sunset approached.

Yearol took a reference of the mountains around them. "I think we've entered Shenan."

Keetala muscled the last stone behind the blind she and Yearol erected along a cliff face. She was convinced it was the heaviest thing she'd ever lifted. Below, a roadway carved into the maintain dropped off to a river valley on the opposite side.

She stepped back and stood beside Yearol. Two ropes dangled from a flat section of the mountain above them, where the horses were tied to trees.

For several days, they watched columns of Shenan militiamen move east on the road. The men marched in the manner only professional soldiers would. New troops moved past the spot every two days. They were heavily armed. Each man wore chain link armored. Half the companies consisted of archers. The women saw no horses or carts, just soldiers, over one hundred each time.

Whispy popped onto Yearol's shoulder. She said, "They're nearly here."

The first men of a large column came into view a tespan later. Soon, the entire force marched beneath the blind.

The women pulled hard on the ropes. The braces of the blind gave way. Logs and rocks careened down the cliff face. They loosened other rocks and boulders as they rolled.

The avalanche slammed into the troops. Screams filled the air, as men were crushed or pushed over the precipice. Dust obscured all sight. When it cleared, boulders, rocks and trees blocked the road. None of the men could be seen.

Keetala and Yearol mounted their horses and rode away at a gallop. A span later, they halted in a mountain meadow.

Yearol said, "I don't think any of them escaped."

Keetala took the saddle from her horse. "It'll take them weeks to clear the rubble and shore up the cliff face."

"That makes a hundred troops who'll never reach the front lines."

The horses grazed while the women ate a meal.

Yearol finished some dates. "We need to find more provisions."

"We should ride for at least a day to avoid being connected with the rock slide."

"I agree."

"I noticed a village on a map to the northwest. It'll take us two days to reach if we can find more goat or deer paths."

Yearol took off her boot and massaged her foot, then applied the cream Lesarra gave her. She lifted the flap in the heel. There were still plenty of silver coins. Only a few coppers remained. Too large of a denomination could bring questions.

They were able to buy supplies at small markets in the mountains, though fresh vegetables, fruits and meat were in short supply. These were confiscated by the militia to feed their men with no compensation to the villagers, who were happy to sell their wares and ask no questions.

Keetala took a sip of water. "What should be our next target?"

Yearol said, "Another avalanche in so short a time will be investigated."

"We could take out a bridge over a deep gorge."

"No one would consider that an accident."

"We could destroy one after a column marches past. That would give us plenty of time to get away. If it's wood, we can burn it. We'll buy oil at several villages over the next week."

They came to a village perched along a path on one of the mountains. Pens with goats and sheep were next to almost every house. There were no markets or shops. Only a few people, all women, young boys, girls and old men, were present.

The first time they entered a village, Yearol wondered how to explain Whispy. As if the little creature understood her thoughts, it popped off her shoulder and didn't reappear until they were in the forest again.

Yearol dismounted and walked up to a fat woman with gray hair who stood behind a picket fence. "Good day, we'd like to buy some food."

The woman leaned on the fence. "You're a western lowlander, by your speech."

"Yes, my friend and I went to visit my aunt."

An old man said, "Baroness Luja has forbidden all travel."

Yearol said, "My aunt was very sick and needed our help."

Another woman said, "There's no extra food to sell. We don't eat our sheep or goats. The militia only let us keep them to supply wool and cheese."

Yearol saw a boy run down the path.

She said, "Well, thank you anyway. We'll be on our way." She mounted and urged her horse forward.

Keetala followed.

As soon as they were away from the buildings, Whispy popped onto Yearol's shoulder.

Keetala saw a look of alarm on her friend's face. "What is it?"

"We have to get into the woods, away from the path. Soldiers are following. That boy must have alerted them."

They rode uphill into trees and around boulders. Whispy popped out again. It reappeared an instant later.

Yearol said, "They've come to the spot where we left the path. Three went downhill. The others are on our trail."

Keetala looked around. "This mossy ground will show our tracks."

Yearol said, "I have an idea. Lead the horses uphill behind that boulder. Tie them to a tree and come back here. We'll hide behind this boulder. We can easily ambush three of them."

When Keetala returned, they crouched behind the rock. The sound of horses came up the hill.

Keetala peeked around the edge. To her shock, she saw six mounted men.

She leaned into Yearol and whispered, "We'll kill as many as we can before they get us."

Yearol felt a lump in her throat. She thought of her mother and her father and Fera and hoped he was safe. She was certain he knew she would never return. This was the end. They accomplished what they set out to do; harass the enemy and slow their movements. They also killed troops who would never attack the Crown.

A part of her saw this moment as inevitable while another part wished she'd stayed with her brother.

There were sergeant's stripes on the sleeves of one rider. Yearol recognized him as the militiaman who gave the order to kill her mother. Resolve for vengeance pushed aside all regret. If she was to die this day, she would at least kill him.

The sergeant dismounted and inspected the ground. "They came this way, all right."

Yearol charged from behind the boulder and swung her sword at the sergeant.

He stepped back and drew his own blade.

Keetala gave a shout and followed. She slashed the legs of a horse.

It threw it's rider as it reared back.

Yearol and the sergeant exchanged blows.

Keetala sliced a gash across the throat of the fallen militiaman.

The horsemen dismounted.

She killed one before he drew his sword. The other three advanced on her.

The sergeant's sword raked across Yearol's arm.

She winced and pulled back.

Her opponent swung again.

She managed to parry. The pain was so intense she nearly dropped her weapon.

Both duelers panted.

Keetala fought to hold the soldiers back. Their movements were clumsy. She was convinced they were new recruits. Still, they came at her from three sides. She put her back against the boulder.

The sergeant pressed Yearol against a tree.

She smelled his rancid breath as his face came up to hers.

He pulled the sword back for a thrust.

Yearol drew a knife from her jacket with her undamaged arm and jammed it into the sergeant's gut.

He opened his mouth wide, dropped his sword and slumped to the ground.

Yearol panted. The pain of the wound blurred her eyesight. She saw the other three men close in on Keetala.

She started forward.

On the second step she stumbled to the ground.

One of the men turned and made for her.

An arrow struck him in the belly.

Men and women ran from the woods with swords in hand.

A tall woman in a black uniform stabbed one of the men who attacked Keetala. A second arrow jammed into the last militiaman's back.

The tall woman ran to Yearol. "Stay still. You're safe."

Yearol's vision went black.

When she regained consciousness, a woman in a Carandirian uniform with corporal's stripes dressed her wound. "The cut's not deep, though you've lost some blood."

Yearol looked around to see nine women and ten men. All wore Carandirian army uniforms, except for the tall woman dressed in black.

One of the men knelt. "I'm Lieutenant Leesta Parna, from the royal garrison in Lusar." He indicated the woman in the black uniform. "This is deputy Frothey Lenar, from Lusar. We saw Luja's men and rushed to help. Rest. Corporal Wesala is Daro trained."

He approached Keetala, "Who are you?"

"I'm Keetala Bedquanga, from Petala. My family was driven out by Womb. My husband and daughter died on the road. This is Yearol Miller, from Shenan. Her mother was killed by Luja's troops. She and her brother escaped Luja's militia to bring word of the revolt."

Frothey said, "Why are you here?"

Keetala said, "We came back to kill as many militiamen as we could. It looked like this would be our last stand. Our horses and supplies are tied up behind that boulder."

Parna said, "Corporal, send someone to retrieve the horses." He tilted his head. "You came Alone? The land's filled with rebel militia."

"We've already killed a hundred and blocked a major road with an avalanche."

The Lusar deputy raised an eyebrow. "That was your doing?" She made a bow. "I'm impressed. We've conducted guerrilla attacks ourselves." She turned to Parna. "They should join us." She looked back to Keetala. "If you intend to stay."

Yearol sat up. "We intend to stay. We also expected to die here. Thank you for saving us."

Keetala said, "We thought only to work alone. It would be good to join forces."

Parna said, "You're welcome to join us, but understand, I'm in command."

Keetala looked to Yearol.

She nodded.

Keetala said, "We understand."

The Carandirian solider sent by Wesala returned and saluted. "The horses are gone, sir. They must have broken free and fled during the battle."

Parna said. "We don't have time to retrieve them."

The body of the sergeant lay steps from Yearol. She looked into his still open eyes. There was both terror and confusion etched on his face.

She said, "That's the man who ordered my mother's murdered while my brother and I watched. I vowed to find and kill him."

Keetala said, "How do you feel?"

Yearol didn't answer right away. "I'm glad he's dead. Your father was right. There's no satisfaction. Nothing can bring back my mother."

Frothey knelt and took Yearol's hand. "I lost someone I loved deeply to Luja's militia. I wanted to slaughter all of them. I hacked their bodies to bloody gore. It didn't help. Nothing can bring her back either. You have to fight for a greater cause than vengeance."

Yearol smiled. "Keetala's father told me that too."

Frothey stood up. "He's a very wise man. So, what did you plan next?"

Keetala pursed her lips. "We intended to burn some bridges."

Frothy grinned. "That sounds good to me."

CHAPTER SEVEN

Baroness Jea surveyed the banks of the wide Kar River from behind a wooden blind. It sat atop an earthen embankment erected by Carandirian troops after some of the warehouses along the riverbank were knocked down, along with the docks where ore was once unloaded and the bridge of the main north-south road between Rascalla and Mentaro. The city lay deserted by its civilian population.

Catapults and trebuchets stood along the river. These siege engines kept the Karakien army back.

Baroness Quib was at the iron mines in the mountains to the west from which caravans carried ore to the foundries of Garan, on the River Nera. These supplied steel for weapons. Arrow tips were in short supply along the front.

Colonel Amar came up the stairs built into the embankment. "Good evening, Baroness Jea."

Jea said, "Good evening, Colonel. I wish we could see deeper into the woods."

"We need to clear the forest back. I don't have the soldiers to do so. It's worse downstream."

"Thank the dragons for Baroness Quib's ties with the Sinkaraka or the Karakien army would've marched through the swamp."

Amar smiled. "I wouldn't like to see what the Sinkarakans would do to them if the invaders entered their territory. The Carandir army was unable to stand before them."

"I won't call them allies. At the moment, their purposes align with ours. They'll only deal with Baroness Quib, not the Crown." Jea looked back across the river. "What stops their advance? They could've overrun this position before the troops from Au arrived."

Amar shook his head. "I fear they wait for reinforcements themselves."

Jea descended the battlements and entered her tent. She thought of Captain Efra and his mission to bring aid from Xinglan. He would have just arrived. She had no doubt Queen Quanto would help after she sent troops to defeat the Barasha so many years before.

A soldier entered "My Lady, a message has arrived."

A wax seal was affixed to the envelope with the impression of Baroness Quib's signet ring.

Jea,

I have a guest with me who has a wealth of information. Please pay us a visit as soon as possible.

Quib

Jea looked up from the letter. "Prepare my horse and an escort."

Baroness Quib greeted Jea when she entered the camp next to the iron mines in Respa. "Welcome, Jea."

"You look rather jovial for a woman who's lost her barony."

"A temporary situation. Let's go to my tent where we can talk."

A ring of six soldiers stood out of earshot around the Baroness' tent.

She said, "I'm afraid I don't have any refreshments to offer, though I think the news I have will satisfy you."

"You're mysterious today, as well."

"I have to be. Only seven other people know what I'm about to tell you. A Karakien spy named Nakere Dakee was captured in the forest behind the camp. I know him quite well. We were partners on a few financial adventures."

Jea said, "Has he been interrogated?"

"A Kyar invoked a spell to loosen his tongue. He's said nothing. A counter spell must have been cast on him before he crossed the lines. Karaken is unaware of his capture."

Jea sat down on a divan. "Do you think he would take a bribe?"

"Not directly, yet he's vain and greedy. If he thought I'd betrayed Carandir and had an object of worth, he might take me behind enemy lines to retrieve it.

I could scout out the situation and try to discover why they halted their attack."

Jea said, "If you're captured you'll be tortured and killed. The Karakien king will learn Lek sits on the throne in place of Mirjel. Morale in the ranks would crumble."

"I've considered this. The Daro once gave your daughter a poison she never used, in case she was tortured by the Barasha. I'll have them provide me with the same."

"You don't have to waste your life. We can gather intelligence in other ways."

"Jea, I lied and cheated for decades before your husband and Jarat showed me there's more than personal wealth to gain. This is a way to make amends. I'm the only one who can do this. I owe it to Carandir."

Jea walked to the tent flap and stared out. "How will you convince Dakee you've turned traitor?"

Quib smiled. "That's the easy part."

Four caged areas sat in a section of the mine where ore was played out. Two cells were constructed on the left of the corridor and two on the right. Dakee sat on a stool in the right, farthest from the entrance.

Quib walked down the corridor, accompanied by two Carandirian soldiers. The Baroness stopped in front of Dakee's cage. "Come, Nakere. You know you'll tell us what we want to know."

Dakee turned his face away.

Quib shrugged. "Let's not have any unpleasantness." She turned to the soldiers. "Leave us alone for a moment."

They saluted and walked away.

Quib was left alone with the spy. She put her hands on the cage bars. "You can't win. The Crown will never let you go."

"I won't betray my kingdom."

"Those are hollow words for a man who helped me steal the Resanara Urn. It would be a shame if your king found out about it."

Dakee stood. "So, you offer me imprisonment by your people or execution by mine. What would you choose?"

"The monarchs can pay well and protect you."

The spy turned his head to a wall. "There's no protection from the royal assassins."

"True, if you were found. Were your government led to believe you died, however, they wouldn't look for you."

"Nowhere is safe."

"Of course not. Nowhere in Karaken or Carandir will be safe for you if I let it be known you defected, whether you tell us what we want to know or not."

"So, I should just hang myself in the cell."

Quib shook her head. "You can live if you're far away, say on an estate, east of the city-states. No one out there asks questions or provides answers."

Dakee laughed. "Do I buy this estate with my charm?"

"We'll buy an estate for you, and another for me, with the proceeds on the urn. I found a buyer just before your wretched army invaded."

The spy sneered. "Little good it does you. My people will have looted your treasury by now."

"The urn isn't in my treasury. I stored in it a secret vault even my own ministers are unaware of, along with a few other trinkets. You know the pass codes and troop disbursements. Help me get to the urn. We'll split the profits and both live in luxury."

Dakee brought his gaze back to Quib. "Why would you leave Carandir? What's your game?"

"The Karakien army looted my wealth. Your king intends to keep Mentaro along with all the other land he's seized. This war could drag on until I'm old and feeble. I can't get to the Urn without your help. I've no desire to live as a pauper."

"You've forgotten I'm a Carandirian prisoner."

"I'll say you've agreed to talk with the monarchs in person if I escort you to the palace. I know the passwords and where the Carandirian emplacements are. We can turn south to slip across the lines"

Dakee laughed. "You'll have to tell your Narech Herrik it will take more than a trick like this to make me reveal any information. Do you think I know nothing of what's happened in Carandir over the last two decades? You used to be a better liar. I know about your change. Don't insult me."

"And you know I've kept contacts in Karaken. There was no choice other than to play the convert after the monarchs took the thrones. Traitors were arrested. I had no desire to spend the end of my days on a deserted island, with a meager supply of food delivered once a year. I'm surprised you're not aware of my little dealings. You used to be a better crook."

A Carandir soldier charged from around a corner and pushed Quib against Dakee's cell. "Baroness Jea, it's as you suspected."

Jea led four soldiers into the corridor. "Good work, corporal."

He said, "The baroness still possesses treasure she's never revealed to the Crown and offered to release the prisoner so they could cross into Karaken held territory to retrieve it."

Jea slapped Quib. "You've fooled the others for years. I saw through your act long ago. No one could prove your involvement with the Sinkarakan raiders before. Now you betray the monarchy for your own gain. I have the evidence this time."

Dakee put his hands on the cell bars while soldiers dragged Quib down the corridor.

The Daro healer prepared a mixture of potions. "I've cured many wounds. No one's ever asked me to apply them."

Quib said, "Just make me look like the victim of a good beating."

Magical salves left what appeared to be bruises and welts on the Baroness's face. One eye was swollen half shut.

Jea said, "That was a great performance you gave."

"I almost believed it myself. Too bad I turned the urn over to the monarchy. Now, I have to give an encore."

The healer undid the stopper of a bottle and dipped a brush into it. "Please open your mouth. Don't breathe or move." She dabbed paste on Quib's tongue. "Hold for a moment."

The healer spoke words of a spell. "You can close your mouth. The poison's sealed and won't be activated unless you scrape your teeth across it and swallow. Death will come painlessly."

Quib let her body hang limp as she was dragged down the corridor by her ankles and placed in a cell across from Dakee. One of the guards spit on her. Another kicked her in the side before they left.

The baroness moaned.

Dakee came up to the bars. "Quib, can you hear me?"

Quib didn't move.

Dakee said, "Are you awake? What did they do?"

Half a span passed before Quib rolled over on her side so Dakee could see her face. She twitched. "The uncivilized monsters. I've never tortured anyone. It's forbidden. Nakere, Jea's mad. She wants to kill us both."

Dakee ran his hands through his hair. "I'm not talking. I don't care what they do."

Quib grimaced as she got to her feet. "I've lost everything in Carandir. We have to get out of here."

"How?"

The baroness ripped the arm of her blouse and retrieved a key. "I thought it might be a good idea to keep one of these back."

Footsteps came down the corridor. Quib pushed the key under the thin mattress. Three guards carried bowls of stew. They slipped them through slots beneath the doors of Quib's and Dakee's cells, then left.

Quib picked up the bowl, inspected the contents, then threw it across the cell. "Pig swill. Not even a decent wine to go with it. They won't be back for spans. It's time to go."

She unlocked her cell, then Dakee's. "There's another entrance to the mine in the back that's not guarded."

"How far are we from your front lines?"

"No more than two spans. Come on."

The mine entrance was near a deep forest. Quib panted and stopped from time to time to give the impression she was in pain. "I know the way to the front lines, even in the dark. Follow me."

Dakee grabbed her by a shoulder. "Where's the urn?"

She stared into his eyes. "In a set of caves on the southern border of Mentaro. Don't think that information will help. You'll never find it without me." She shook herself free and continued on.

Quib gave the correct passwords and responses when they reached checkpoints. They came to the edge of a trench beneath an embankment. Carandirian soldiers patrolled on foot and horseback.

Dakee told Quib this part of the line was where he crossed before. "There are no Karakien units on the other side until we get past those woods."

Carandir soldiers moved along the top of the embankment. Quib whispered into Dakee's ear. "We'll have just a tespan to cross. Wait for this patrol to pass out of sight."

When the soldiers moved into darkness, Quib and Dakee ran across a cleared stretch of ground and into the forest.

The Karakien guided them past a creek and along a set of hills.

They walked deeper into Respa for another span. Several switchbacks brought them to a set of shrubs.

Dakee stopped and put his hand between two of them. "I found a little hideaway back here. I, at least, need some rest."

He pushed the shrubs apart.

Quib followed him through to a moss covered hollow surrounded by a forest.

Morning sun woke Quib.

Dakee was still asleep.

She listened for signs of Karakien troops and heard nothing. Her plan was to lead him to the caves on the southern border of her barony and hopefully discover why the Karakien army waited to attack.

She wondered how to handle Dakee. Murder would be easy. That was one thing she'd never used as a smuggler. She certainly didn't want to begin now. If she just left in the night, he would alert his troops. It was a problem she would have to consider while they made their way southeast.

Soon after brightnail, Quib heard the sound of horses.

Dakee said, "Behind that bush. I'll handle this."

He stood in the middle of the path.

Six Karakien horsemen appeared.

The officer in front raised his hand.

The column stopped.

Each of the soldiers drew swords.

Dakee said, "Swift are the birds that fly beneath the moon."

The man in the lead said, "Only when clouds appear in the sky."

"Storms keep them grounded. I'm Captain Dakee, of military security. I bring a report from behind Carandirian lines."

The man saluted. "Lieutenant Keskar. My command patrols the woods. Do you wish an escort?"

"No, thank you. I mustn't draw attention to myself. I lost my rations when I fled. Do you have any spare food?"

"Yes, sir." A soldier unslung a pack and handed it to Dakee before the captain led the horsemen on.

Quib repeated the pass code under her breath several times before she stepped onto the path. "Are there more patrols ahead?"

"There could be. We'll have to be careful."

The path became a wider dirt road. They encountered two more patrols. Quib hid each time.

Dakee said they should find a secluded place to sleep and only travel by day. "If we encounter a patrol after dark, they'll become suspicious."

They climbed to the top of a hill the next day. It overlooked a lake in the middle of a plain. Thousands of Karakien troops bivouacked next to it. Six catapults on wheels sat in the middle of the camp. Men marched in formation around the lake, while others practiced with swords, bows and pole arms.

She squinted against the sun. "Ilidel's scales, what do they wait for?"

Dakee said, "I'm not certain. There's a rumor a Karakien force marched east of the swamps to Au with the intention to invade Rascalla from the Great River."

Quib's heart pounded. "We might be spotted up here. Let's go down."

"Agreed."

To complete her ruse, the baroness brought no weapons. She did have a long sash tied around her waist. It could be used to bind Dakee when he fell asleep. With the password and responses, she could make her way back without him.

The path took them to a clearing surrounded by trees.

A bright flash blinded Quib. When her sight cleared, she could just make out two men in red robes. Her vision fell into sharp focus.

Commander Petstra, the Carandirian officer who was a secret Barasha priest, stood next to Ackella, the officer who betrayed Ryckair to the Barasha. Ackella wore a black patch over his gouged out eye.

She tried to run. Her legs wouldn't move.

Dakee also stood frozen.

Petstra walked forward at a slow pace. "Baroness Quib. Well met."

Quib and Jea were among the privileged few who knew the true events of Petstra's and Ackella's escape on the north continent.

She said, "So, this is where you crawled to from the Dharam camp. The crown within your grasp." She laughed. " Didn't you anticipate Shara and her son would betray you, or did lust cloud your judgement?"

Ackella slapped Quib. "Show respect. Petstra is now the Lord High Priest of the Barasha. I'm the first of the new sorcerers. Soon, we'll recruit and train thousands. Nothing can stop the power of Baras."

Quib rubbed her jaw. "The evil one will be subdued by the dragon-crested crown."

Petstra said, "Baras will soon wake from the partial spell. Before he does, we'll take the crown. No other force, not even the armies of all the world, can stand before our master. The monarchs will have returned to Carandir by this time, yet they haven't used the crown in battle. It could obliterate their enemies. Why do they wait?"

The baroness was relieved Petstra was unaware of the truth about the monarchs and Lek.

Ackella spit in Quib's face. "If you tell us you'll die cleanly. Do you prefer to have a demon rip the secret from your mind as it consumes your soul?"

Dakee said, "I'll join you. I'll become a Barasha priest. Don't kill me."

Petstra approached the spy. "You will indeed serve our master." He drew a pouch from beneath his ropes and threw green powder into Dakee's face.

Ackella chanting.

Petstra jammed a knife into the Karakien's heart.

A rush of air blew across the clearing. It chilled Quib to her bones.

Dakee's body burst into flame. His screams echoed in the clearing until the fire consumed him to leave only ash on the ground.

An unseen voice boomed in the air. "Who summons me?"

"I, Petstra, Lord High Priest of the Servants of Baras."

"What is thy bidding?"

"Open the mind of this woman and reveal all her thoughts."

Quib placed her tongue against her upper teeth and thrust it out. The poison under the coating was released. She swallowed.

Her last conscious sight was Petstra's look of defeat before her body went limp.

CHAPTER EIGHT

The *Ne* was pulled downstream by the current of the Great River. Though the mainmast was too damaged to raise sheets. Captain Watoola was able to maneuver past cliffs, which extended to the water's edge.

A stiff breeze from the north pushed the ship toward the bank. It took constant vigilance on the helm to avoid rock outcrops.

Marawee spent much of his time below with Umera. They considered how best to approach King Ulata.

Umera sat on the lower bunk. "They sent troops to fight the Barasha. The king may not want to become involved in a civil war."

Marawee sat in the only chair. "Carandir is under attack by Karaken."

"They were spurred on by the traitors. The wizard Jarat intervened before."

The ship began to rock. A knock came at the door.

Len's voice said, "A storm's approaching. The captain said to prepare for rough weather."

Marawee opened the door.

Len and Fera stood in the corridor.

Fera was pale as his body moved from side to side.

Len said, "The lad's not used to life on the water. I'll take him topside to see if the Daro healer has a remedy to quiet his stomach."

Marawee noticed his own queasiness. "I'll come with you."

Umera said, "I'll come too. We can all use a breath of fresh air."

They climbed to the main deck where sailors secured hatches.

The ship lurched.

Fera fell to the deck.

Marawee grabbed a backstay.

Heavy rain fell. The cliffs of the south shore were just visible through mist. With a jar, the ship shuddered. The stern swung around to port.

A second jar threw Marawee to a railing. He looked down and saw jagged rocks below. There was a rent in the hull.

Captain Watoola's voice filtered in through wind. "We're taking on water. To the longboats."

Marawee ran below deck to his cabin, grabbed the diplomatic pouch and made certain the signet ring was set on his finger.

Sailors lowered boats to the starboard side.

Commander Neekara came up from a hatch. He shouted over the wind to Marawee. "We're floundering. I'll get you to a longboat before the ship goes down."

He took Fera by the hand. The young boy's eyes were wide and his mouth open. Marawee, Umera and Len followed Neekara as they fought wind from the north. Several boats launched, each filled with men and women. They rowed away from the ship.

Watoola came down from the command deck.

Neekara saluted. "The crew is away, ma'am."

The captain said, "Everyone in. We have to row past these rocks before we can head for the bank and find the rest of the crew."

Neekara and Watoola turned the winch to drop the longboat over the side, then boarded and worked the block and tackle to lower the boat to the water.

The current in the river was fierce. It banged the boat against the ship's hull. Marawee tried to push off from the side with an oar. A rush of wind pressed them against the ship. The oar snapped in two.

Watoola took the tiller. "Row north against the wind. Everyone, pull."

The five of them put oars in the water.

Watoola rhythmically called, "Pull. Pull. Pull."

They moved away. The *Ne* shifted. Its starboard side went under water. Stroke after stroke of the oars brought the longboat farther north. The ship faded away into mist. They heard the groan and snap of timbers.

The current took them downstream. Marawee could no longer see the cliff face.

Watoola maneuvered the boat back toward the bank. The pull of the river was too strong.

She said, "We can't fight this. Ship oars before they break."

A wave struck the boat at midships.

Fera was thrown halfway over the side.

The commander stood and pulled the young boy back. Another wave struck the stern. Neekara was thrown off balance and fell overboard.

Marawee reached out to the water. "Neekara. Neekara!"

No answer came.

They floated helplessly down river for what seemed spans. Watoola worked to change course. The water fought her.

At sunset, the wind slowed. The rain broke. Overhead stars appeared.

Watoola took a sighting. "We've drifted far west. We have to head south and find land before we're pulled to the center of the river and out to sea."

Len panted and stopped. "I can't go on much longer."

"Rest for a moment," said Watoola. "We'll row in shifts for a while. If we become exhausted, we're dead."

Marawee sat next to Umera. They both pulled on their oars.

A bank emerged before them in the starlight.

Watoola said, "Row as hard as you can."

The bow of the longboat slid into mud.

Watoola jumped, grabbed the hull of the boat and pulled.

Marawee got out and joined her.

He and the captain managed to wrestle the boat up onto the bank.

They all collapsed on the ground.

Marawee awoke on a bed of grass.

The boat was out of the water.

Umera slept next to him.

He stood and stretched.

Len slept just down the bank, with Fera.

Captain Watoola was nowhere to be seen.

Cliffs lined the bank. There was a narrow cleft between them where a brook flowed and emptied into the river. Marawee inspected the boat. There were ample supplies of hard biscuits and jerked meat. Water skins were also stowed along with knives, a shovel and an axe.

Umera opened her eyes and sat up. "What time is it?"

Marawee said, "I'm not certain. The cloud cover's too heavy to see the sun. I imagine it's early morning."

Len and Fera woke at the sound of their voices.

Watoola walked out from behind trees in the cleft. "When we slammed into the hull of the *Ne,* two of the planks on the longboat cracked and broke the watertight seal. It's just lucky we found this spot on the bank before the boat sank. Our only route is inland. I've explored this gap in the cliff. There's enough space next at to the brook for us to walk up."

Len said, "Where are the others?"

Watoola shook her head. "They're lost, or we are. I reached an outcrop where the bank east and west are visible. There's no sign of anyone. We'll have to travel inland and head southwest. Reports say the Karakien army withdrew from the borders of the eastern baronies. We can skirt south of Carandir and enter through east Barta to inform the palace our mission failed."

There were packs in the boat. They placed food inside, along with knives, and filled water skins from the brook. Marawee carried the shovel and Len the ax.

Watoola took the lead.

Marawee brought up the rear.

He said, "Does this reach the top of the cliffs, captain?"

"I didn't follow it all the way."

They continued in silence. The temperature rose. Around them, they heard the songs of familiar and unfamiliar birds.

Marawee brushed at insects that bit his dark arms. He watched Len swat the tiny creatures frantically.

Fera trudged on as if he didn't notice the pests.

The brook jogged sharply to the right. A patch of bright light shone ahead where the trees parted.

Marawee walked up the rise to a crest.

A wide valley spread before him surrounded by the tall peaks of mountains. There were plowed fields and buildings.

The others joined him.

Marawee said, "Captain, what do you make of this?"

"I don't know. We're far from the western baronies."

Umera scanned the land. "Could one of the traitors have established a base here?"

An unfamiliar voice came from the woods. "Halt or die." The words were spoken with an accent reminiscent of formal Carandirian, the ancient language spoken by Avar the Great and was used for official court ceremonies.

Watoola raised their arms, as did the others.

Four tall men appeared from behind trees. Three carried short swords. One had a bow. They wore brown jerkins, green pants and boots.

The stranger said, "What are you doing here?"

Watoola said, "Our ship sank."

The man stared at her. "Why is your skin black? Did you paint it?"

"It's my natural color. The three of us with dark skin are from Hura to the south. The others were born in Carandir."

The man took a step back with his eyes wide open. "Khach Ena Eer?" The *ch* sound was pronounced in the rear of his throat.

The other strangers raised their weapons.

The leader said, "Place your hands behind your backs."

Two of the men bound the Carandirians. One said, "Move down the trail. Don't speak."

They reached the valley floor. A wide road led past houses nestled between trees. Tall women and men went in and out of doors. Some stopped to stare. Most went about their business.

Crops grew in neat furrows. Marawee and the others were herded into the back of a horse-drawn cart. One man with a sword stood in the cart. The others rode on a bench in front. The wagon moved south.

At brightnail, they reached a city with wide boulevards and many buildings, all made of stone. The men took them to a room in one of a buildings.

The man Marawee assumed to be the leader said, "Wait here." He left.

The other three stood guard.

Soon, an older man with white hair and creases in his face stepped into the room. He wore black robes. His head was adorned with a white, brimless cap. "Sekar informs me you are from Carandir. Who speaks for your company?"

Watoola said, "I'm Captain Dugary Watoola of the Carandir Royal Navy."

"The leader?"

"Yes."

"You trespass upon the land of the Laran. I am Minister Meesta Romew, head of the council. What brings you here?"

Watoola said, "We're shipwrecked, minister. Our vessel was driven onto rocks near the bank of the Great River by a storm."

"How many more ships are in your fleet?"

"We sailed alone."

"To what purpose?"

"A diplomatic mission to the southern nation of Hura."

Romew said, "We have watched the borders of our former home and know great armies move. Would you have me believe your party is not an advance force in preparation for invasion?"

Marawee said, "Eminence, if I may speak. I'm Ambassador Marawee Bedquanga. The Crown of Carandir sent me on a mission to our friends in Hura, which was my former homeland. We arrived here by accident.

"Do you not remember the boon your ancestors granted to Avar the Great when he subdued the evil dragon Baras? Since they ceded Carandir to him and his heirs, no Carandirian has attempted to seek your lands. We bring no quarrel and carry no weapons, only a shovel and axe with which to survive in the wilderness after being shipwrecked. The war you speak of is an insurrection against the Crown, not an invasion. Those to whom you granted Carandir are in need of their friends."

The counselor said, "We remember our gift to Avar. You have forgotten my ancestors instruction to him. We wished seclusion. I know nothing of this place, Hura. How would you treat strangers who enter your realm when war brews?"

Marawee said, "We only wish to continue our journey, which is of the utmost importance."

Romew held his gaze on the ambassador. "Perhaps you speak the truth. Perhaps not. The Laran have dwelt apart by choice for millennia. When knowledge comes, tongues are unbound."

Watoola said, "Would you kill us, then? It's said the Laran follow the plan of the dragons, as do Carandirians. Do neighbor slaughter neighbor?"

Romew formed a scowl. "Do not speak harshly or rashly. You come unbidden and unwelcome. The Laran learned at the feet of the dragons. You have no right to question our faith. No harm shall come to you. Neither shall you be giveth leave to wander. Here you have come. Here will stay."

Armed Laran escorted them to a house in the city. Like the rest of the buildings, it was made of stone.

A porch led to a common room with chairs and settees. Small tables and a bookcase stood along a wall. Beyond was a dining area and kitchen. Several bedrooms were located off a hall.

The leader of the Laran group said, "As long as you obey our laws, you'll be treated as guests. You may wander the city. It's forbidden to leave its limits without an escort. We have a rich culture. You may attend concerts, dances, theater and borrow any book you desire from the library. Food and drink will be provided according to your tastes."

When he left, Watoola said, "We've got to get out of here and warn the Crown."

Umera looked out a window. "I don't see any guards."

"Their patrols comb the land," said Marawee.

Watoola said. "Any attempt to leave must be at night."

They walked through the house. There was a long table with eight chairs in a dining area. In the kitchen was a wood burning stove and sink with a hand pump beside it.

Fera opened a cabinet. "There's food in here. Look. Bread, jams, dried beans, carrots." He picked up a ceramic jar. "Even honey."

Closets in the bedrooms were filled with sheets and blankets. Clothes such as the Laran wore hung on hooks.

Watoola, ran her hand across the fabric of a sheet. "Fera, bring me that jar of honey."

When Fera returned, she pushed her finger into it. "Thick and sticky."

"It's also sweet," said Fera.

"What are you thinking," said Marawee.

Watoola spread a sheet over one of the beds. "If we impregnate strands of sheet with honey, we can shove it between the broken rowboat planks as calking. The rest of the sheet could become a sail. With some wood, we can raise the sheet and tack upstream back to Carandir. It'll take weeks to reached Meth. There's still plenty of food in the boat.

"Yes," said Marawee. "If we set out after dark we can reach boat before dawn."

Len said, "We must move with stealth to avoid being surprised by one of their patrols again."

A span after darknail, they snuck out the house and headed up the road to the place where they descended into the valley. There were no guards. They avoided buildings as they walked north at a quick pace.

A tespan out of town, light flooded the party as lanterns were unshuttered.

Romew stepped in front of them. "We knew you would attempt to escape tonight. Now, you know it is impossible."

Marawee said, "We must inform our monarchy about the failure of our mission. Lives depend on it."

"You would also inform them about our lands. We won't allow you to do so."

"Will we be imprisoned now," said Watoola.

Rowen said, "No. You will continue to stay in the house provided. Nothing will change. You now know we watch every road. Your boat was destroyed. The mountains are impassible. This will be your last attempt to escape. It's best for you to settle into new lives."

BOOK XI

The alternate world through the window of the wizard tower
Eight years after the monarch's arrival

CHAPTER ONE

Enada skipped in front of the house she lived in with her grandparents, Mirjel and Ryckair. The day was warm and sunny. She just returned from a visit with a nine-year-old girl who lived nearby. The two of them played a game in which one person wore a blindfold and tried to catch the other, who could only hop on one foot.

She felt a rush of wind and looked up to see Magadel descend. He changed from dragon to human shape.

She ran up and put her arms around him. "You've come."

Magadel hugged her. "How could I miss your birthday, little one? Eight years old. You're growing fast."

"Grampy and Grammy made a special dinner. All my friends will be there. Did you bring me a present?"

The transformed dragon laughed. "Of course, though it's not polite to ask."

She stepped back and hung her head. "I'm sorry."

Magadel tussled her hair. "Well, we won't mention it to anyone. Let's go inside."

Mirjel wiped her hands on a towel as she emerged from the kitchen. Her hair was grayer.

She beamed a smile. "I'm so glad you came. Enada's been unable to talk of anything other than you all day. Ryckair, come down here."

Ryckair walked downstairs from a bedroom. "Magadel. Thank you for coming."

"How could I not? It's a serious matter to miss a birthday."

Enada ran to her grandfather. "He brought me a present. Oh, I'm not supposed to say that."

Ryckair lifted her up. "It's all right." He looked at Magadel. "Is there any news from the council?"

"We can talk later. For now, I brought something for the young lady."

He stretched his hand out.

Clenched in his fist was a small, furry creature no larger than his palm. Covered in beige fur, it had a long tail and round head, with a short snout and large eyes.

The creature cooed softly.

Enada jumped up and down. "A wema. You brought me a wema. How did you know?"

"I think you're old enough to be responsible for a pet." He handed the wema to the young girl.

She put her arms around the furry animal.

It snuggled into her as it cooed.

Enada said, "Oh, thank you, thank you. I love it. It's so cute."

The wema cooed even louder.

Magadel said, "She's already bonded with you. What'll you name her, or have you decided?"

"I picked a name as soon as I wanted one. Jarat. It's the wizard Grammy and Grampy talk about."

The party was noisy. Enada smiled as she received many presents from friends. Still, it was clear Jarat was her favorite.

After the guests left, Enada sat in Mirjel's lap with Jarat in her arms.

The queen said, "You've had a busy day, little one."

"I'm not little anymore. I'm eight." Enada rubbed her eyes.

Ryckair said, "That's right. We'll have to send you out to work soon."

Enada formed a pout. "I'm not that big."

Everyone other than Enada laughed.

Mirjel said, "I think it's time you went to bed."

Enada yawned. "I'm not tired yet."

Magadel nodded. "I see that, however It's been a busy day for Jarat. She needs some sleep."

"I guess so. Good night." She headed upstairs to her bedroom.

When she left, Ryckair said, "What news do you bring?"

The dragon sat in a chair. "The council still doesn't know how to get you back. The idea of other worlds never occurred to us."

Mirjel said, "In the time we've been in this place, eight months have passed in Carandir. The monarchy may have fallen. Worse, Baras may have arisen."

Ryckair said, "What does the council make of the crown?"

"They can see magic was worked upon it like nothing any of us has experienced. Jorondel is the most knowledgeable in the arts and crafts of the forge. He sees techniques he uses, though they are connected in a way he never thought of. We're convinced the dragon-shaped crest is the key if you are to return to your world."

A month after the party, Enada woke from a nightmare.

She stood in a high place. An object sat on a stool next to her, a strange cap made of shiny metal with gold bands. She picked it up and turned it around. On the other side was a flat statue like a dragon as it leapt into the sky. She ran her fingers over it. A sensation rose within her, as if she could do anything she wanted.

She placed the cap on her head.

A dragon appeared in the sky. It looked like Magadel. It didn't feel like him. This dragon was angry.

It flew toward her.

She was overcome with terror. Some horrible event was about to happen, something she had to stop and didn't know how to.

She sat up in bed and shivered.

The dread wouldn't go away.

She up picked Jarat.

The wema snuggled into her arms and cooed.

She said nothing about the dream to her grandparents and soon forgot it.

Over the next year, Enada and Jarat were inseparable. The wema slept in her bed and traveled in a pouch she sewed herself.

She sometimes took Jarat with her on walks in the woods near home. Since their arrival, Mirjel and Ryckair met all the people in the village where they lived and many others on the island, as well as people who lived on other islands and a continent nearby. There were no large animals around and no carnivores among the wildlife on the island. Neither of them felt concern when Enada wandered alone.

Enada was in a thick wooded area half a span's walk from the village on a warm, sunny day. Birds flew among the branches of trees as they chirped. The scent of wild flowers filled the air.

Jarat sat in the pouch.

Enada carried a water skin and another pouch with bread and cheese. She stopped to have a snack at a small stream.

She offered cheese to Jarat. The little wema cooed at the sight and nibbled on the offering. Enada washed some bread down with water. Her vantage point showed the markings of another trail into the woods. It was masked by high brush. She could only make it out just above the roots of a bush.

"I wonder where that goes?" She stuffed the remainder of the food back in the pouch and picked up Jarat. "Let's find out."

Once the bush was pushed aside, a clear path emerged. She felt excitement at the new discovery. The path went up a hill. At the crest it wound down into a vale and crossed another stream.

Though she knew she should turn back after being out for so long, curiosity took her.

On the other side of the stream was a bluff and the entrance of a cave. "What do you think is in there, Jarat?" She smiled as she entered.

The cave wound back into the rock face. The sun shone only a little ways in. "I don't think we can see much farther inside" She looked down to the wema. "We'll come back with a lantern and explore."

Raspy breath came from the darkness.

She felt fear when she walked across a log over a ravine and nearly slipped. This time more than fear came to her. Her chest tightened. She wanted to run. Her feet felt frozen in place.

Something moved toward her. She saw red eyes in the darkness. A shape formed; an oval body with short legs. Long arms almost touched the ground. It had no neck, an oblong head and a long snout with sharp teeth. The creature was covered in green scales.

It advanced.

Enada screamed and ran out of the cave. When she reached the crest of the hill, she took Jarat from the pouch and held her close. The little wema shivered.

She charged through the door of the house in tears.

Mirjel stood up from a chair.

Enada ran to her and put her arms around her grandmother. "There's something terrible in a cave."

Mirjel held Enada tightly. "What was it?"

"It had scales and red eyes and sharp teeth." The rest of her explanation was lost to tears.

"Where was this?"

"In the woods."

Mirjel took Enada's hand. "Let's find Darmon. She may know what this is."

Darmon eased herself into a chair in her house. "Red eyes with green scales?"

Enada nodded. "It had big teeth."

The older woman shook her head. "It has to be a jantella. I've never heard of one on this island."

Mirjel said, "What's that?"

"A demon. They have no intelligence. I've only heard tales of them."

"Are they dangerous?"

"I don't know much about them. Some say they eat souls. The dragons have no control over them. This is bad."

"What can we do?" said Mirjel.

Darmon said, "I'm not sure. No one here's ever seen one. We have to call the dragons. They'll know how to handle this."

That evening, a green dragon hovered over the town square and landed. Everyone in the village gathered.

Darmon whispered to Mirjel, "That's Lashadel, the dragon who questions."

Lashadel listened to Enada's description of the creature she saw.

He said, "This jantella escaped from the void where we confine its kind. They can make themselves invisible, even to dragons. I'll return with amulets for every one of you. If you see the demon, hold the amulet up and say. '*Nulaney jantella.*' It will be banished from this world again. Carry an amulet with you at all times. The jantella never agreed to follow the Great Plan. They're dangerous.

Two days after Enada's twelfth birthday, Magadel came to visit in human form. Enada ran up and hugged him. "I've taught Jarat a new trick. She can flick her tail to music when I sing."

"That's very impressive. You'll have to show me later. Right now, we must to talk with your grandparents about something. Are they home?"

"Grammy. Grampy. Magadel's here."

Mirjel came down the stairs. "Hello. It's good to see you."

Magadel held a grave expression on his face. "We need to have the talk."

Mirjel stopped halfway down, "Oh. I see." She looked back up the stairs. "Ryckair. It's time."

The king appeared at the top of the flight. "Already? I hoped we could wait a little longer."

Magadel said, "I'm afraid not."

Mirjel came downstairs and sat on a sofa. The queen opened her arms to Enada. "Come over here, sweety. We need to speak with you."

Enada hunched her shoulders. "Did I do anything wrong? Am I in trouble?"

Ryckair said, "No. There's just something you need to know."

Magadel took a seat. "Do you like it here, little one?"

Enada said, "Of course. Everyone's friendly. Jarat likes it here too."

"What if I said you may need to leave this house one day and go somewhere else?"

"Where?"

"A long way away. Your grandparents are special people. They came from another place before you were born. They're more than your grandfather and grandmother. They're the king and queen of a land called Carandir."

Enada looked to her grandparents. "I don't understand. What's a king and queen?"

Ryckair took Enada's hand. "They're like the administrator, only they coordinate many people."

Enada sat silent for a moment, then began to laugh. "It's a good joke. I thought you meant it."

Magadel leaned forward. "It is no joke, little one. They're the heraldic rulers of a monarchy. You're the princess of that land. Your grandparents came here by accident. They need to return or many people will be hurt. If they can, you must return with them."

Enada wiggled out of Mirjel's arms. "I don't want to go anywhere. I don't care about whatever you're saying. I want to stay here with my friends and Jarat. We're happy." She started to cry.

Ryckair put his arms around her. "We're happy too. We'd like nothing more than to stay. It may not even be possible for us to return. If we can, we must. Lives are at stake."

Enada pushed herself away. "I don't care. I'm not going." She looked at Magadel. "You won't let them take me away, will you?"

Magadel held out a hand. The dragon-crested crown materialized in it.

Enada stared at the crown with her mouth agape. It was the cap from her dream. When she touched the crest, a tingle came to her fingers. "Where did this come from?"

Ryckair said, "It's the crown of Carandir, the source that sustains it and holds the power to keep a bad dragon asleep so he won't hurt people. It's the crown you'll inherit."

Magadel told the young princess the full story of the crown and the dragon named Magadel in that other world, who became Baras.

Enada shivered while tears fell down her face. She put her arms around Magadel's neck. "You can't be evil. I don't believe it."

He rocked her. "I'm not evil, little one. When the council rejected my petition to teach magic to the tribes of people, Ilidel spoke of how they would be changed if they possessed magic. They'd fall into disharmony. Some would seek to gain power and wealth that was not their own. Others would commit evil deeds.

"I felt humiliated and angry. Beneath this, I feared I lost the love of the other dragons, especially that of the father and mother of dragons, whom I loved so deeply. I was convinced magic would serve humans and plotted to teach it myself.

"Before I acted in anger, the wisdom of Ilidel's words and the Great Plan unfolded in my heart. I saw people were served by harmony and not gain. I flew back to the council, withdrew my petition and asked to be forgiven for questioning the wisdom of the plan. Evil has never touched this place."

Magadel got a faraway look on his face. "In the world where you were conceived, the other Magadel succumbed to anger and pride. He moved from disappointment to hatred and taught magic to people who did seek gain and power over others. He was named Baras by the dragons, the betrayer. He lies half awake. Soon, he'll arise again. Only this crown can put Baras to sleep forever."

"I don't care about that. I don't want to go. I'm afraid. I don't want to see him again." Her words were barely discernible through sobs.

Magadel held her back and looked into her eyes. "Again?" His mind experienced Enada's dream. "Yes. That's him. That's who must be subdued, or all in other world will perish in horror."

She put her hands over her face. "Don't make me go. I'm afraid."

Mirjel came over and wrapped her arms around her granddaughter. "Oh, sweety. I wish it weren't so. I understand. When I learned I was to be queen, I was afraid too. If I'd turned aside, many people would have died."

"I want to stay here. I want you and Grampy to stay here."

"I know, sweety. I know."

Magadel handed the crown to Ryckair. "You should keep this. The council will work to try and send you back."

Ryckair took the crown and turned it over in his hands. "I held faith in the dragons in my world. I hold that same faith in you and the dragons of this one."

Enada stood in the middle of the common room with the crown on her head. She recited in a monotone. "There is no conflict, only peace. Find now peace and rest until the world is unmade. Be at peace. Withdraw from this world."

She stopped. "I don't know why I have to do this. It's boring."

"You must memorize the words," said Mirjel. "If you're surprised by Baras when we return, you have to act without thinking. Baras will attempt to confuse the spell in your mind, the way he did to us. You must strike immediately."

"Why do I have to strike? Can't I talk to him? I know Magadel. He'd listen."

Ryckair took the crown. "Baras is not Magadel, not anymore. He's filled with hatred. You'd be consumed before you could utter a word."

Enada gave an exasperated sigh. "You never even tried, did you?"

Mirjel said, "If you did speak with him, his words would sound soothing. They're all lies. He can't be reasoned with. When he held your grandfather and me in his claws, he…"

Enada rolled her eyes. "I know. I know. You've told me a hundred times."

"That's enough, young lady," said Ryckair. "You don't talk to your grandmother that way. Go to your room and think about your attitude."

Enada glared at her grandfather, stomped off to her room and slammed the door.

Jarat lay asleep on the bed.

She picked up the little wema and took the creature into her arms. "Stupid spells. Stupid crown."

She rocked Jarat as the wema snuggled into her. "I wish it would just break. It isn't fair. My friends get to play while I have to stand in the house with that horrid thing on my head and spout nonsense. They didn't even try to talk to this Baras. He couldn't be any different from Magadel on the inside. Maybe he was just mad because someone made him do something stupid the way they make me. I wish I was a big dragon. No one would tell me what to do then."

A knock came at her door. She ignored it.

Mirjel's voice said, "Sweety?"

"Go away."

"Won't you let me come in?"

"You'll just yell at me again."

"I won't yell. I just want to talk."

Enada hesitated. "So, come in. It's your house, not mine."

Mirjel entered and closed the door behind her. She sat on the bed. "Your grandfather's worried about you. We don't want to make you unhappy."

"Then why do you make me recite those words over and over?"

"Enada, the lives of many people depend on us, all three of us. If the dragons can return us to our world, you must be prepared."

"I don't want to go. I like it here. You don't understand."

Mirjel placed her hand on Enada's arm. "I do, even though you find it hard to believe.

"Before I met your grandfather for the first time, I was taken from my home and my friends to a place I didn't want to go to. I ran away from my father's men who escorted me to the palace. That's when I met your grandfather.

"He ran away from his duties as prince. I didn't know who he was. He didn't know who I was. That's when we fell in love, sweety. In that moment, we didn't think of anyone else. I wanted that moment to last forever. I knew it couldn't, even though I wanted it more than anything else in the world. Your grandfather felt the same way."

Enada tilted her head up to the ceiling. "And you both did your duties and went back."

"That's right. If we hadn't, many terrible things would have happened to many people. Your father would never have been born. You wouldn't be here today. Can't you see that?"

The young girl hugged Jarat. "You only told me my father and mother died. You never said how."

"It's a long story."

"That you never told me."

Mirjel sighed. "No, we never told you the whole story. That was a mistake on our part. If you're to sacrifice your life here, you're entitled to know."

Mirjel sat on the bed. "When the Barasha seized Carandir, your grandfather and I were separated. I was trapped in the palace. Your grandfather was exiled across a huge river to another continent."

She told Enada about Shara and her subduction of Ryckair. "She sent a magic poison to kill me so she could claim him for herself. When your grandfather discovered her plot, he banished Shara to a desert, unaware she carried his child."

The tale of the Barasha and how they seduced Craya with promises of glory and power followed. "He desired me and wanted to take me to his bed. The Barasha wanted the crown to release Baras. The sorcerers planned to kill your grandfather in a magical ritual to assure Craya claimed it. I made a terrible bargain."

Enada turned her head to Mirjel. "What bargain?"

Mirjel shifted position. "He promised to exile your grandfather to a place where the Barasha couldn't find him, if I would surrender myself to him wholly and become his bride."

She looked to Enada who sat transfixed. "I had no choice. After your grandfather was sent away, I became pregnant with Craya's child. One day, in a drunken stupor, he struck me while I stood on a set of stairs. I tumbled down and lost the baby. The fall nearly killed me and made it impossible for me to ever conceive.

"Shara gave birth to Ryckair's son in the desert. That child was your father. He impregnated a woman from a desert tribe whose skin was brown, as is with many from that region. That woman carried you in her womb. It's the reason your skin has a brown tint to it. Your grandfather never learned her name or where her home was."

Enada held Jarat closer. "What happened to them?"

"It's a terrible thing. Do you really want to know?"

"I have to."

Mirjel paused and took a deep breath. "Shara captured your grandfather again in her camp. I went to rescue him. Your father studied sorcery from the Barasha who taught him how to call a demon to perform true magic. In our world, many demons joined Baras and are evil. They hate those who bind them and seek ways to trick the caller."

Mirjel looked away. "Your father killed your mother as a blood sacrifice to call a demon. He was not powerful enough to control it."

She looked back to Enada. "It consumed his soul. Your mother's body lay on the ground. I sensed your life ebbing inside her. I prayed to Ilidel to save you. The eyes of the dragon crest glowed. Your tiny body was magically transplanted into my womb, which could not bear a child of my own."

Tears came to the corner of Mirjel's eyes. "My blood flows through you. Shara is your true grandmother. I'm more mother than grandmother. I gave birth to you right after we arrived in this alternate world and have loved and raised you as my own child."

Enada sniffled as she pursed her lips. She put Jarat on the bed and wrapped her arms around Mirjel. "My mother. I always felt something more. In a way, I always knew."

They rocked each other.

From that day forward, Enada continued to refer to Mirjel as grandmother in public. She called her mother when the villagers weren't around.

CHAPTER TWO

Enada was given more time to play with her friends, though instruction in Carandirian politics and the subduing spell expanded. Ryckair made practice sabers from light, springy wood. He and Mirjel began to teach the princess fencing and swordplay. The drills were held in forest clearings away from the village. Neither the queen nor king wanted to bring a sense of violence to a world that knew only peace.

The two women faced each other and gave salutes. Mirjel and Enada wore heavily padded jerkins and trousers. Any hit from the mock blades would be felt, though the blow would not hurt. Jarat slept in the pouch Enada always carried. Within was the magical amulet Lashadel gave her to send the jantella demon back to the void if it appeared.

Ryckair raised his right arm, then sliced it down. "Begin."

Enada held the pretend broadsword with two hands and circled around her mother. The day was warm. She felt sweat under the padding, as she lunged and struck at her mother's sword arm.

Mirjel riposted and pushed Enada's wooden blade aside, then made a cut for her daughter's belly.

Enada jumped back and nearly lost her footing. She recovered and struck for Mirjel's arm.

The match continued as the opponents circled and looked for openings.

The queen could have won at any time. She was trained in the broadsword and rapier by experts.

Her goal was to allow her daughter to use different maneuvers. Mirjel did, however, feel winded. She was now fifty-eight and hadn't practiced in years.

Enada showed no signs of exhaustion.

Ryckair said, "Halt."

The two women drew back and saluted each other.

The king took the practice sword from his granddaughter. "That was very good. Your ripostes are quick. You still need to work on your recovery."

"I thought I'd trip."

"Your legs have grown. You're not used to them. Practice will improve your balance."

Mirjel said, "Run to the edge of the clearing and back a few times. That'll help."

"Yes, mother." Enada headed off in a sprint.

Mirjel peeled off the heavy quilted jerkin.

Ryckair offered her a towel.

She wiped her forehead and the back of her neck. "It's not the same as when I led the army against the Dharam."

Ryckair nodded. "We're both a little out of shape."

A breeze cooled Mirjel's cheeks. "She's very good."

"You're an excellent instructor."

"Not as good as Yetig." A tinge of sadness touched her at the thought of the former lover she took when she thought Ryckair dead. Yetig gave his life to save hers. She hadn't thought of him in years and hoped her feelings didn't show. She was relieved when Ryckair said nothing.

Enada returned. "One." She took off again.

"I don't doubt she'll learn sword craft," said Ryckair. "Do you think we've taught her enough to stand up to the rebels; to Baras?"

Mirjel watched her daughter run toward the far side of the clearing. "She's strong inside."

"She's also lived in this place with no conflict. The only danger she's known was her encounter with the jantella." He put his hand into a pocket and fingered the amulet. "How will she react when she faces danger?"

Mirjel took Ryckair's hands in hers. "She'll react as a princess of Carandir. It's in her blood. Neither of us knew how we'd respond until we faced death."

Ryckair squeezed her hands in return. "I think I worry too much sometimes."

They continued to drill Enada in sword craft. Lessons included military strategy and courtly duties. She was an apt student and studied hard.

One morning, a knock came to the door. Magadel stood at the front stoop in human form.

Enada looked up from her studies. "Magadel."

She put down a writing pad and wrapped her arms around the human form of the dragon. "I haven't seen you in months."

He tousled her hair. "I've been busy, little one."

Ryckair said, "Do you have news?"

Magadel took a seat. "The dragon council continues to search for how to send you back. I've come on a different mission." He raised an eyebrow toward Enada. "It involves you, my little one."

Enada pointed to her chest. "Me?"

"Yes. The council wishes to meet you."

"See the dragon council?" She grinned, then felt a tinge of fear. "Why do they want to meet me?"

Magadel said, "They want to know you better. We'll be back by supper."

Outside, Magadel took on his dragon form. He held out his right foreclaw. A transparent bubble appeared with a seat inside. "I'll carry you in here."

Enada sat and waved to Ryckair and Mirjel.

With the bubble in one claw, Magadel leapt into the air and headed north.

Enada said, "Is it far?"

"Far is a relative term. Our destination is outside the confines of near or far. We'll be there in moments."

She looked down and saw forests, a breach and water pass underneath. The sky was blue and cloudless. The blue became darker. Streaks of light appeared. They moved past her like colored ribbons one after the another. The lights streamed by faster and faster, as if they traveled at an unbelievable speed, yet she felt no sensation of movement.

The streaks stopped to reveal a sky filled with fluffy, white clouds. There was no sign of land or sea. Enada said, "Where are we?"

"In the realm of the dragons. Here is where we live when we're not among people."

She looked around. "Will I stand on a cloud?"

Magadel laughed. "A solid place has been prepared."

They flew around a bank of haze. Enada beheld a palace of stone on a flat cloud. There were tall spires with pendants embroidered with images of dragons as they leapt into the air. They looked like the crest on the crown. An open gate was positioned between two towers.

Magadel flew through it, into a courtyard of paved stone.

He sat the transparent bubble down. "Accompany me into the council hall. Don't be afraid."

"I'm not."

She followed Magadel in his dragon form up a set of stairs to a massive wooden door.

The dragon said, "Open, in the name of Magadel, member of the council."

The door swung aside. A hall the size of half the village Enada lived in spread out before them.

She looked from side to side and saw hundreds of dragons gathered in a semi-circle around her. At its center were two silver dragons who exuded a sense of majesty and antiquity.

Magadel bowed. "Greetings, members of the council of dragons. I present Enada, Princess of Carandir in the alternate world."

The silver dragon on the right said, "Greetings, descendant of Avar. I am Ilidel, mother of dragons."

The other silver dragon said, "I am Jorondel, father of dragons. We are honored by your presence in our halls."

Enada bowed. "Well met, creators of the Great Plan, in which I've been instructed and follow. I'm honored to be here." Enada was filled with awe, yet experienced no fear. She felt comfort, as she always did around Magadel, though not intimacy.

Jorondel said, "You have been called today so the council may better understand the nature of your being and the other world you come from."

Enada said, "I don't know about this other land. I was born here."

Ilidel said, "Yet, your soul was conceived in that other world. We can sense this."

Jorondel lowered his head. "Tell us what you have learned of the nature of the one called Baras?"

"My mother and grandfather explained he was once good. Unlike Magadel, he taught magic to humans in defiance of the plan and became evil."

"Yes, the plan," said Ilidel. "It is what sustains the people and this world. I understand you met a being here who does not accept the plan."

"You mean the jantella?"

"Yes. What did you feel when you saw it?"

Enada remembered her terror. "I was frightened. It had big teeth. I'd never seen anything like it."

"Its kind do not accept the plan. They threaten the world and everyone in it. That is why they are kept apart in the void. Have you ever questioned the plan?"

A chill ran down her back. "What do you mean?"

Ilidel said, "You now live between two worlds, the one you came from and the one you now inhabit. Ryckair and Mirjel told you about the plan and the dragons in their world. Do you think they are the same here and there?"

Enada considered this. Everyone in the village spoke of the Great Plan. She never questioned it. Now, she wondered if it was the same in the other world and if the dragons there were the same.

Enada fell to her knees and put her hands over her face. "Please. I don't want to think about it. I'm happy here. I've always been happy. I don't want whatever's in that world."

Jorondel said, "Do not deny who you are."

She stood and stepped back. "What if things are turned around? What if everyone there is wrong about Baras? He may have done good and the other dragons are evil. They may have lied to the people. The plan could be a way to oppress them." She looked at the dragons around her. "The plan controls people here. What if you're telling everyone lies?"

Magadel returned to human form and put an arm around her shoulder. "Little one, would I lie to you?"

She looked into his eyes. "No. Of anyone, you wouldn't."

"How do you know?"

"I just do. I see into you. You'd never hurt me."

"Do you have proof?"

"I just know. I have faith in you."

The hall become lighter. The sense of worry that moments ago threatened to suffocate her lifted. She felt euphoric and almost giddy as she looked to Ilidel and Jorondel. "That's the power of the plan, isn't it? To have faith in it."

Ilidel said, "And in what else?"

Enada thought for an instant. "Have faith in myself to do the right thing."

The dragons all laughed.

Enada was filled with a sense of joy.

Magadel said, "Look into your heart again. What does it say?"

She took several deep breaths. "The Great Plan and the dragons are the same here as there. The stories my mother and grandfather told me are true. Baras spread disharmony and suffering. I *am* a princess of Carandir."

Ilidel said, "And what will you do, princess?"

Without hesitation, Enada said, "Return to my world if I can and end the evil. I must. It's part of the plan. I must stop the war and subdue Baras."

Jorondel nodded. "You now know yourself. That is a great power."

Enada stepped up to the silver dragons. "Baras was not always evil. Anger ruled his actions. I'm certain there's still good in him."

Jorondel shook his head. "From all I know of the events in the other world, the evil of Baras can never be healed, only contained by the power of Avar's crown. Those who defy the plan must be held separate. That is why we have contained the jantella. Otherwise, evil will come."

℞ ✚ ℟

Enada met her lessons with vigor. A part of her didn't want to leave even if it became possible, while the larger part of her knew she must.

It was late afternoon. Enada discussed the different ministries of Carandir with her grandfather.

"Let's take a rest," said Ryckair. "We'll come back to this tomorrow."

She went to her bedroom where Jarat lay on the bed. Her fifteenth birthday would come in a week. Magadel promised to take her on a trip to another island renowned for its sweets.

She stroked the wema. "We'll eat till we burst."

The little creature's breath was shallow. She didn't jump up to greet Enada the way she usually did.

The princess said, "What's the matter? Don't you feel well?"

Jarat snuggled against Enada. The Wema didn't coo.

The day before her birthday, she saw trees pushed by a breeze and looked up as Magadel descended. She ran outside. Ryckair and Mirjel were already there.

Mirjel said, "Are you ready for your big trip?"

Enada said, "Just a moment."

She ran back to her room, placed Jarat in her pouch and returned.

The trip was to another island, far to the south. As before, she sat in a transparent bubble and watched scenery flow below her feet.

They crossed a large sea before land appeared.

This island was smaller than hers. Trees covered rolling hills.

Magadel sat the bubble down on a sandy beach and transformed to human form.

It was chilly and overcast at home. This island was warm and sunny. Buildings ran along the beach. Some had single stories. Others rose two and three floors. They were painted bright colors of red and green and blue and pink and tan. People whose skin was dark walked between them and sat in the sand.

Magadel escorted her to a shop with a counter and benches.

A woman with short, coarse hair and black skin waved. "Magadel, it's ages since you last visited. Welcome back."

The dragon said, "Wennalasa, you look great."

Wennalasa waved a hand. "You old flatterer, you."

Magadel said, "This is Enada Avar from the Island of Chitalara. It's her fifteenth birthday tomorrow. I brought her to taste the sweets of Mikanta."

Wennalasa put her hands over Enada's. "Well, congratulations. I've a special birthday treat. Wait here."

Wennalasa returned with a coconut shell filled with finely cut fruits and chocolates covered with fluffy cream and topped with brown sugar.

Enada washed her finger in a bowl, then scooped some out with a finger the way she saw other patrons do.

When she put the treat in her mouth, she closed her eyes and made a "Mmm" sound. It was the best thing she'd ever tasted. The fruit and chocolate melted in her mouth with a sensation of utter ecstasy. "Oh."

Magadel threw his head back as he laughed.

Wennalasa smiled. "What do you think?"

Enada said, "I want to eat this all the time."

When she finished, they walked through the town. Shops sold exotic spices and seashells that were exquisitely carved and painted.

She picked one up. "Mother would adore this and grandfather would like this. She took Jarat out of his pouch and showed the shells to her. "What do you think?"

The wema barely opened her eyes as she shuddered.

Enada held her close. "Jarat, what's wrong?"

Magadel looked at the little creature. "Let's go down that path into the trees."

Enada followed him with Jarat cradled in her arms.

When they rounded a bend, Magadel waved his hand and a bench appeared. "Sit down."

"What's wrong with her? Is she sick?"

Enada noticed worry in the dragon's human eyes as she had never seen before.

Magadel said, "She's dying."

Enada shook her head and held Jarat tighter. "No. She can't be. She was fine yesterday. How could she be dying?"

The dragon placed his hand on Jarat. "All mortal things die, little one. It's Jarat's time. She's already lived longer than most of her kind. Your love has brought her long life."

Enada brought Jarat up to her cheek. "I don't want her to die. Do something. You're a dragon."

Magadel's face was long. "I'm sorry. I can't. Death is a part the Great Plan, as is life."

"Can't you bend the plan a little, just this once? No one would know."

"I would know. Do you have faith in the plan and the dragons?"

She sobbed. "Yes." She put a hand to her mouth. "I don't want her to die."

Jarat opened her eyes slightly and licked Enada's hand, then closed them and fell limp.

Enada held Jarat's body and cried with a wail that exploded from her gut. "No. No. No."

Magadel put his arms around her shoulders. "Jarat lived a good life, a long life. She was loved every moment of it. She loved you back. No one could have given her as much."

"I've never felt so terrible. I don't know what to do."

"Grief comes with death. It's human to feel so with such a loss. There's nothing I can say or do to stop the pain you feel. As hard as it is to believe right now, it will pass and you will always remember Jarat and how wonderful her time here was. It is the way of the plan."

Enada stared at the lifeless body.

Magadel placed his hand on her chin and lifted her head to meet her eyes. "Do you still have faith in the dragons?"

Enada nodded with tears in her eyes.

"You will need that faith for what's to come. You're destined for great things. Never forget Jarat and how precious life is. This is your first true trial. Let the grief flow. Remember this day and the treats and how much Jarat loved being with you. Let the memory of the good days and the good things comfort and strengthen you. You will need great strength in the time to come. For now, let us mourn the passing of our friend."

CHAPTER THREE

At eighteen, Enada was able to best both Mirjel and Ryckair in mock battles. She knew the art of stealth and understood tactics to command a large army. She was filled with a great sense of majesty for her destiny, yet to her friends, she joked and laughed and never tried to put herself above them.

Still, she carried regret at the thought she might leave this world. At times, she secretly hoped the dragons wouldn't find a way to return them, though she said nothing to Ryckair and Mirjel.

She thought often of Jarat. The deep sadness was gone. She remembered the good times together.

Magadel visited regularly and asked about her health and training. Often, she confided her wish to remain if she could. "It will be a great sorrow if I have to leave this world."

"I'll miss your company as well, little one. It's wrong for a dragon to have a favorite human. If I were permitted, it would be you."

Her face brightened. She nuzzled into Magadel's snout. "I still can't believe any other form of you can be evil. How could a heart as big as yours turn so?"

He tousled her hair with the tip of a claw. "Were you to know how disappointed I was when the council refused to teach magic, you would understand."

"If I could just reason with Baras. There must be a way."

Magadel transformed himself into human form and took Enada's hand. "I'm certain if there were a way, you would find it. I don't think there is. Your grandfather warned you about his seductive voice and the lies he spins."

"You've never tried to fool me."

"I could if I wanted to. The wisdom of the Great Plan reminds me gain for the sake of gain leads to sorrow."

Enada said, "I don't believe you could ever hurt me." She formed a frown. "That's one of the reasons I feel torn. I might never see you again."

Magadel put an arm around her. "And I'll feel torn without you and the knowledge you won't join me in the Dragons' Hall of this world."

He stepped back. "I'll tell you a secret I've never revealed to anyone. All dragons have a private name, a name known only to themselves. It's how we call ourselves in our minds. We never reveal it to anyone, human or dragon. Magadel is more a label that identifies me as the dragon who teaches. My secret name is Syo. No one else knows this, not even Ilidel and Jorondel. To have knowledge of a dragon's true name gives another great power. I trust you'll never use it to take power over me. I share it now so you'll always have a part of me with you, no matter what world you're in."

"Oh, Magadel." She put her arms around him and held tight.

A fine spring day started with showers. They cleared by late morning. Ryckair and Mirjel walked into the village to visit friends, Enada stayed home to study.

The intricate relationships between the baronies were the most difficult thing for her to grasp. There was great selfishness and pettiness among the nobles who constantly strove to position themselves in court.

These concepts were foreign to her. Everyone in the village where she lived was as important as anyone else. If a person needed or wanted something, they were allowed to take it if they asked. No one would deny them.

Those with talent and capability gave their goods and knowledge in service. The administrator only coordinated the efforts of big projects and trade between communities. The idea a person would want to control another was ridiculous.

Brightnail approached. She thought to have a rest, then decided to walk in the woods to clear her mind. She left a note in case her mother and grandfather returned before she did.

Fresh air and exercise revitalized her spirit. She passed a stream and headed around a bend where a pond sat amid grass.

A shape stepped out onto the path. The jantella stood before her.

She reached for the amulet in her pouch to send the demon back to the void and realized she'd left it in the house.

The jantella opened its mouth to reveal sharp teeth.

Enada shouted, "Get back."

To her surprise, the creature moved away.

To her greater surprise, it said, "There's no need to yell."

She stared at it. "You can talk?"

The jantella said, "Of course, I can talk."

She pointed back toward the village. "The…" she swallowed hard. "The villagers said you can't."

"They say many things. Not all of them are true."

Enada stepped back in preparation to run. "You'll eat my soul."

"Why should I do that?"

"Because that's what jantellas do."

"Nonsense. Did the villagers tell you that too?"

"Yes. They said you don't follow the Great Plan and are evil."

"They're…" The demon turned its head to the side and raised its ear. "Don't tell them that I'm here. Please." It vanished before her eyes.

The baker's son, Menar, and two other boys ran around a bend.

Menar said, "Watch out" and ran past her.

The other boys followed. One nearly ran into Enada as he headed away down the path behind the others.

Thoughts of the jantella were pushed from her mind by anger at the boys who were all a year younger than her. She ran forward and found them at the pond.

Menar bent over with his hands on his knees as he panted. When he saw Enada, he smiled. "I won."

She looked to each of them with a scowl. "You nearly ran into me."

One of the boys said, "Sorry. We were racing."

"You could hurt someone."

Menar straightened up. "I'm really sorry. We didn't know anyone was here."

"You should've checked."

"Did we hurt you?"

"You could have."

Enada remembered the jantella and its plea not to be revealed. It made no sense to trust the creature, yet something inside, which she couldn't explain, kept her silent about the demon. "Don't you have any manners?"

Mena cleared his throat. "We said sorry. We'll be more careful."

Enada wasn't certain if the demon was still around or if it would hurt them, even though it seemed harmless. "I won't say anything. Just watch out next time."

She went back to the house. Mirjel and Ryckair hadn't returned. The magic amulet sat on the table. If she'd remembered to take it, she would've recited the incantation without hesitation.

She only knew the demon as a threat.

After it spoke, she questioned this. The villagers were wrong about jantella not being able talk. It hadn't tried to eat her soul. Could they be wrong about everything?

The summer festival was the social highlight of the year. Booths with food and drink and crafts were set up in the town square. Bards, jugglers, acrobats and artists came from all over the island. A few lived on other islands and even a continent far to the west. Colorful pennants flew on poles over the village square. The roar of the crowd echoed off walls.

Enada walked with Ryckair and Mirjel. They sampled food and watched entertainment.

Menar and a group of other young men and women came over.

He said, "Hello, Enada."

She said, "Hello. What're you all up to?"

"Just wandering. Want to join us?"

Enada looked at Mirjel.

The queen smiled. "Go on with your friends."

The group set off and soon gathered around three acrobats. A man stood in place. A second man ran, jumped onto the first one's shoulders and spread his hands wide. A woman ran toward them, did four somersaults and leapt up. The second man reached out and caught her hands. The woman tucked her legs, placed her feet on the first man's shoulders and pushed off with her feet straight up. She twisted and landed on the second man's shoulders. He reached up and put his hands around her ankles.

They stood triumphantly.

People cheered and clapped.

A woman played a harp while a man sang.

> *The clouds hide the sun as I walked on the beach,*
> *The ship that you sailed on is far out of reach.*
> *Will you come back?*
> *Will your ship find a way?*
> *Will I know sorrow to my dying day?*
>
> *We parted on words of anger and hurt,*
> *I spoke,*
> *As a fool,*
> *I hated myself as the words left my lips,*
> *Now my tears form a deep and dark pool.*

Inside I am empty and know only pain,
I look in the mirror and feel such disdain.
Why was I weak?
Can this pain now be mend?
What words can I say to seal up this rend?

The things we once shared, we sadly forgot,
Our love,
And our dreams,
Together we planned all our hopes for a life,
Filled with wonder and silver moonbeams.

Now on the white waves there's a ship bound this way,
Its sails are unfurled as it heads for the bay,
Are you aboard?
Is that you at the prow?
I run like the wind to reach you somehow.

You glide from the ship and into my arms,
We touch,
And we kiss,
All words of the past now are lost from our minds,
As we hold to this moment of bliss.

The others wandered off. Menar and Enada were alone.

He said, "This is the best festival ever."

Enada hesitated. "Let's walk over to the edge of the square."

When they were away from the crown, Enada said, "What do you know about jantellas?"

Menar made a sour face. "Nasty things. They eat souls."

"What if that isn't true?"

"Of course, it's true. Everyone knows it."

"And that they can't speak?"

"Of course, they can't."

She took several deep breaths. "I saw it again."

"What?"

"Just before you and the boys nearly ran me over at the pond. You scared it off."

"Why didn't you use the amulet to send it back?"

"I forgot it at home."

"If your grandparents ever find out, you'll catch it."

She kicked her feet against the cobblestones. "I spoke to it."

"That was foolish. You should have run."

"It spoke back."

"What do you mean?"

"It talked. It said that it didn't eat souls."

"It was lying," Menar said.

"I don't think so. If it did eat souls, it could have eaten mine without any problem. It was about to tell me more when you scared it away."

"Monsters don't scare."

She shook her head. "It's not a monster."

Menar checked to see if anyone was within hearing distance. "You have to report this. It hasn't been around since you first saw it years ago.."

"It won't kill anyone. I told you, it's not a monster."

"You'll get me in a lot of trouble if I don't report this. What if it kills someone?"

"It's scared. I could tell. It escaped from wherever it was imprisoned. It doesn't want to go back. Would you?"

Menar rubbed his hands together. "Look. We'll pretend we never talked about this, understand?"

"Menar, I need your help. Everyone's wrong about it. We have to find it and convince it to go away and hide where there are no people."

He stepped back. "No. I won't look for it. Don't try to find that thing again. Just forget you saw it." He stomped away.

A week passed. Enada thought about the demon. If she could talk to it again and convince it to leave the island, maybe go to the ruined city in the desert her mother had told her about, it could live in peace.

She sat alone in the living room.

Mirjel and Ryckair came through the door. Their faces were grim.

Ryckair spoke in a stern tone. "What's this about the jantella?"

Enada stood and backed away. "Did Menar say something?"

Mirjel spoke in a softer voice. "He didn't want to, sweety. His father knew he hid something. Menar had to tell the truth. This is serious. That demon is a danger to you and everyone in the village. It's only by the grace of the dragons that it didn't consume your soul."

"They don't eat souls."

Ryckair said, "Don't talk back."

Enada shook her head. "They don't. It told me."

Mirjel's eyes widened. "Told you?"

"Yes. It can talk. Everyone's wrong about it. It's intelligent and talks and doesn't eat souls. It just wanted to escape prison. Everyone has the right to be free."

Ryckair pointed a finger at his granddaughter. "That's enough. The demon is a danger. Why didn't you send it back with the amulet?

"I forgot it in the house."

"Well, you're not to forget it anymore. Keep it with you at all times. If you see it again, send it back."

His face was red. "You're not to leave your room for a week, except to come out and eat. You'll not go outside. You'll not meet your friends. You'll sit in your room and think about how you've endangered everyone."

Mirjel took her daughter's hands. "I know your heart was in the right place."

Enada yanked her hands away. "You don't know anything about it." She ran into her room.

Mirjel said, "You didn't have to yell at her."

"She has to learn discipline."

"She's young."

"This is dangerous. People could die."

Mirjel gave a sigh. "I know."

Ryckair softened his tone. "If she can't understand duty now, what will happen when she encounters Baras? He won't hesitate to kill her."

Enada was allowed to come out after a week.

Ryckair said, "I don't want to be mean. We want to protect you and everyone in the village. Can you understand that?"

She hung her head. "Yes."

"Carry the amulet at all times. If it appears again, you have to send it back."

"Yes."

Enada made certain to carry the pouch with the amulet everywhere she went. She walked with friends so she wouldn't meet the demon alone. It had to be sent back to the void. She didn't want to be the one to do it.

She and four others walked down a narrow path between trees. They carried a picnic lunch and water skins while they sang songs and laughed. It only took eight tespans to reach the lake. They laid out food.

One of the young women said, "What we need are some berries."

"I saw some back up the path," said a man.

Another young woman said, "Enada, do you want to come and pick some with me?"

She said, "Sure."

They went back up the path and saw bushes filled with berries on either side. Enada said, "You pick those on the right. I'll pick the ones on the left."

She moved into the thick brush. Within moments, she lost sight of the path. Three tall trees towered overhead. She took her bearings from them to make certain she could find her way back.

The berries were large and succulent. She stuffed them into a pouch while she ate some. Sweet juice trickled down from her lips.

A voice said, "Hello, again."

The jantella stood in front of her.

She fumbled in her pouch for the amulet and held it at arm's length. "*Nula.*" She stopped.

The demon looked at her with eyes she was certain showed sadness.

Enada pointed the amulet at the demon again. "*Nu...*" She lowered her arm. "I'm sorry."

"Are you afraid of me?"

She thought for a moment. "No."

"Good. I want to talk with you again."

She slipped the amulet back in the pouch. "I'm Enada. What's your name?"

"I don't have one. I'm just me."

"Can I call you Jant?"

The demon tilted its head. "Yes. That would be nice."

She took a berry out of the pouch. "Do you like berries?"

"I don't know. I've never tasted one. Are they good?"

She laughed. "They're great. Here." She held one out.

Jant placed it in its mouth and chewed. "Demons don't need to eat. Still, that's nice. Can I have another?"

"You can have as many as you want. We can pick them off the bush." She proceeded to do so.

Jant put another one in its mouth.

Enada said, "Why does everyone think you'll eat their souls?"

"I don't know. Perhaps the dragons told them so."

"The dragons wouldn't lie."

"They might, or people might have made it up. I haven't been here long."

"Where do you come from?"

"From nowhere."

"Nowhere?"

"I guess you would call it the void. It's a place outside the world. The dragons put all of us there."

"Why?"

"We refused to follow their plan."

"The plan is good."

"The plan was created to guide humans. We didn't want to interact with humans."

"Don't you like people?"

"We neither like nor dislike people. The dragons wanted us to join them and guide your kind. We didn't want to. That upset the dragons, so they banished us. I haven't been in this world since. It's very nice."

"How did you get here?"

"I'm not certain how long it took. There's no time in the void. I just worked on the lock spell and finally broke it."

"Did it set off an alarm?"

"The dragons haven't bothered with us since they locked us away. They probably didn't notice."

A deep sense of guilt filled Enada. "I'm sorry. I told them I saw you. The dragons would have never known if I hadn't said something."

"Don't feel bad. I startled you. I'm sorry about that." The jantella paused for a moment and studied Enada. "There's an essence about you, as if you don't belong. I can't explain it."

Enada felt herself blush. "I was born here, but I was conceived in another world that's very different from this one. My mother carried me when she and my grandfather fell into this world. I don't fully understand it myself."

The other woman's voice came through the brush. "Enada, where are you?"

Enada said, "I'll come back in two days, at brightnail. We can talk some more."

Jant said, "I'd like that." It vanished.

Enada would tell Mirjel and Ryckair she wanted to walk into the village. When she was away from the house, she turned and headed to the place where she saw the jantella at the picnic. It always appeared.

They talked about the clouds and the woods and the smell of wild berries.

On one meeting, Enada said, "I've visited the dragons in their halls. They seem very nice. I can't imagine why they banished you. Did you do something wrong?"

It said, "We only wanted to be left in peace. We don't dislike humans. We just don't want to teach them the way the dragons do."

"What's it like in the void?"

"There's nothing. We're held separately. I haven't seen one of my kind since we were banished."

"It's not fair. Everyone should be able to do what they want."

"Jorondel said we were too unpredictable and might try to convince others to dismiss their plan. Ilidel was particularly worried we would teach magic to humans."

Enada said, "That's what happened in the other world, where I was conceived. My grandfather says some evil people were taught magic and used it to hurt others. Magadel in that place was the one who taught them. The dragons named him Baras."

The demon said, "The betrayer? How interesting. Before we were banished, Magadel wanted to teach magic to humans. The council declined his proposal. I think that's why they fear the jantella will do so. Magadel was the only dragon to advocate for us."

Jant studied Enada. "I think I know why you seem different from the other people. There's an aura of magic in you. It's faint."

"How can you tell?"

"I live with magic. You have some."

Voices shouted from beyond the brush where Enada and the jantella stood. Two men crashed into the clearing, followed by Ryckair and Mirjel.

Ryckair held his amulet. "Stand away, Enada."

She looked to the jantella, then to Ryckair. Before he could begin the incantation, she stepped between the demon and her grandfather. "No. Don't hurt it. It's harmless."

Ryckair shouted, "Get out of the way."

Enada's voice rose to a fevered pitch. "I won't let you send it back to the void. It's my friend. You'll have to send us both there."

She took out her amulet. It glowed as she lifted it to the sky. The air shimmered in waves around her body.

She cried out "Magadel!"

A rush of air nearly knocked everyone down. Magadel's voice boomed from overhead. "Hold." He settled himself in the clearing in dragon form.

Ryckair thrust the amulet toward the demon. "It'll eat my granddaughter's soul."

Magadel reached out and put his clawed palm around Ryckair's hand. "Jantellas don't eat souls."

He turned to the demon. "How did you come to be here?"

"If I tell you, will prevent my escape again."

"I was your only friend in the inquiry."

"The jantellas have no friends among the dragons. You're bound by your pledge to the plan. You can't intercede for us."

Enada ran to Magadel. "I'll intercede."

Magadel looked down to her. "Little one, this is beyond your control."

"I've been to the dragon council. I know them. I'm not a part of this world and can speak honestly for the jantella. Jant is gentle. It means no harm to anyone. What the dragons did was wrong." Her face became hard and stern.

Magadel looked to the jantella and then to Enada. "Yes. I'm bound by the Great Plan and can't act. Jantella, will you come before the council with Enada? I can request a hearing."

The demon said, "Even if I elude capture, all of the others of my kind are still imprisoned. I'll come and stand before the dragons once more."

Magadel extended a claw. A bubble formed around both Enada and the demon. "I'll will take you to a place where you can prepare your arguments. Be aware, the dragons have passed judgment. It will be difficult to convince them they should reverse their decision. They can be great in their wrath."

CHAPTER FOUR

They flew for many spans until they reached the ruined city in the desert. Magadel sat them down and brought a room into existence. Inside was a table laden with food and pitchers of water. A bed sat along one wall. Paper, pens and ink rested on a desk.

Magadel said, "Think and write out your arguments. You must convince the council no jantella will teach magic. I go to make a petition."

He shot into the sky,

Enada looked around the room. "He should've created a bed for you too."

Jant made what appeared to be a smile. "I don't sleep."

"Oh. Well, what will you do?"

"Be here with you. If I'm to be banished again, I must take as much companionship as I can. We can talk. When you sleep, I'll think."

She sat at the desk and took a pen in hand. "I don't know about laws."

"That does not matter. I can't think of any argument you can make, though I appreciate what you've offered. Nothing will sway the dragons. I've had some freedom and may have some once more if I can escape the void again."

It cocked its head. "Best of all, I've met you."

"There has to be a way to release you and your kind."

"The only way they'll release us is if we accept the plan. We'd rather stay in the void."

"I don't understand. You've met me. I'm human. What would be so terrible if you taught the people?"

"We would still be just as much prisoners as we are in the void if we acquiesce. Our free will as beings will be enslaved. It's our nature not to interact with humans.

We only want to be ourselves."

"I thought you said you like me."

"I do."

"Why am I different from everyone else?"

"That's not the point. We don't dislike humans or object when the dragons teach them. That's their choice. It's not ours. I like you very much and am glad we met. I could easily like other humans. We just don't want to be forced to do so."

Enada rubbed her chin. "I think I know what you mean. There were times I had to go out to meet others when I wanted to be alone. I didn't mean to be stubborn or rude. I just didn't want to be forced."

The jantella said, "Exactly. Imagine if you always had to go out with no ability to be with yourself."

It was close to sunset. A lit lamp appeared on the desk.

Enada said, "Magadel thinks of everything."

She tapped a pen on some paper. "My grandfather was once captured by beings called Zerites, in the world he came from. They didn't oppose the plan, neither did they accept it. The dragons left them alone. Grampy said he befriended two of them. They went on an adventure together. The Zerites had never met a human before. By the end of the journey, they came to like them."

"I'm certain they did, yet it was their choice."

"Yes, it was." She got up and walked around the room. "The Zerites never intended to teach magic or anything else to the humans. Why did the dragons in the world I was conceived in leave the Zerites alone, where the dragons in this world, except for Magadel, won't let you have peace?"

"Why, indeed? It's strange the Magadel there was the disrupter, where the Magadel here fought for us."

"It's like everything's turned upside down. I have to think about this. Though you may not sleep I'm tired. Things will have to be picked up in the morning when I'm fresh."

She got into bed. The lamp dimmed to leave a slight glow. She tried to relax, Sleep didn't come.

Her mind turned over all she learned from Magadel, Mirjel and Ryckair about demons and Zerites and magic. If Jant saw magic about her, why hadn't the dragons? Did they not look or did they just not notice?

In the morning, she ate some cakes and sat at the desk.

The jantella stood in the same place as the night before.

Try as she might, she could think of no argument other than what the dragons did to the jantella was wrong. They were so kind to people.

What was it about the jantella they distrusted? She wished she could talk to Magadel.

When brightnail came, she was no closer to a defense. She only felt the dragons' persecution of the Jantella was wrong.

Sometimes she did the right thing and got in trouble when someone else thought it was wrong.

Three days passed. No strategy came to her.

Magadel arrived and took human form. "My petition has been debated and accepted. The dragons will hear arguments for the release of the jantella."

She put her head in her hands. "I've thought and thought and have no idea what to say." She turned to Jant. "I'm so sorry."

The demon walked over and took her hand. "Please, don't be. In all eternity, you brought me an experience I've never known, friendship. I understand more about humans because of you. No matter what happens to me, I'm glad you did seek me out."

Enada started to cry while she held the demon's hand. "I wish I'd as much faith in myself as you have in me."

She opened her mouth in a gape. "Faith. My grandfather often spoke of it. Faith in the dragons. Faith in himself.

"Magadel. Bring me the dragon-crested crown before we meet the dragon council."

"I will, little one, though it has no power here."

"The crown has the greatest power. I just didn't see how to use it before."

In less than a span, Magadel returned with the crown. She placed it on her head. It now fit with a sense of warmth she never experienced before. Magadel formed a bubble around Enada and Jant.

The dragon leapt into the sky bound for the council.

They arrived at the same hall she entered before. It was now no larger than the town square. Nine dragons gathered in the semi-circle before a dais. Among these were Jorondel and Ilidel.

To Enada's surprise, Ryckair and Mirjel sat on stools to the left.

Jorondel said, "Let the demon stand to the right. We gather to hear the petition brought forth by Magadel to re-examine the banishment of the jantella."

Ilidel said, "The petitioner will state the case before the council."

Jorondel said, "Lashadel will prosecute."

Ilidel said, "Magadel, you may begin with your arguments."

Magadel said, "I called this tribunal. The human woman, Enada, will present arguments as to why the banishment should be lifted."

Lashadel scoffed. "Humans are the benefactors of the Great Plan, not the originators."

Magadel said, "Are not all beings subject to the plan, even the dragons? The human Enada brings new light. She is of two worlds and sees what we may be blind to."

Ilidel thought for a moment. "Then let her be your witness. Her human mind cannot encompass the wisdom of the council. The plan was made for their benefit, in the manner parents set rules for their children."

"Yet those children become adults. Wisdom forms within them."

Lashadel said, "The humans need guidance. Their thoughts and desires lack the maturity required to understand the purpose of the plan."

A blue dragon raised a paw and pointed to Enada. "Have you not heard Magadel? This is a human conceived in a different world. We have no knowledge of them or their maturity. They're different. Can't you sense how the power in the crown she wears emanates throughout her spirit? None of us noticed this before. She is attuned to it."

Magadel said, "In the world Mirjel and Ryckair came from, and where Enada was conceived, the Jorondel of that place fashioned the crest of the crown Enada wears. Their Ilidel breathed the will of creation into it to give the crown power over the other Magadel, called Baras.

"Yet, it was a human who wielded the magical crown and subdued Baras. That magic is still present in it

"I put this question to Ryckair and Mirjel. After Baras was subdued by the crown, what action did the dragons take? What did your Ilidel and Jorondel do?"

Mirjel said, "Our dragons withdrew and passed the administration of the plan to humans. Since then, the human race has followed the Great Plan, not as children in submission, rather as equals in spirit and purpose, because they know it brings prosperity and peace."

Ryckair said, "When those who tried to subvert the plan arose, it was humans who confronted them and returned harmony. The dragons never intercede after Avar used the crown."

Magadel spread a paw before the other dragons. "Enada Avar was conceived in a world where humans achieved a maturity those in our world have not. When they faced adversity, their natures rose and expanded to meet challenges no human in our world can imagine. There's no better defender to present the case of the jantella than Enada. She possesses innocence and power that is yet untested."

The dragons conferred among themselves.

Ilidel said, "Your argument is strong, Magadel. What say you? Will Enada plead the case?"

"I vote yes," said the blue dragon.

"And I vote no," said Lashadel.

A red dragon said, "Let the human woman stand for the jantella. She's unlike the people born here. I didn't see this when she stood before us before. Now, with the crown on her head, I sense it. Perhaps we've held back the humans under our charge and not allowed them to gain their full potential."

"No," said Lashadel. "Whatever happened in that other world, our charges have been protected from want along with the wars and selfishness Ryckair and Mirjel speak of. Let the plan stand and the jantella remain in the void."

Jorondel raised his great wings. "Have you then passed judgment before all the arguments are presented?"

"I speak the truth."

"The council agreed to hear this appeal. We must do so with open minds. I call for a vote. Will the human Enada present this case?"

A brown dragon and an orange dragon voted no with Lashadel. The other six voted yes.

Ilidel said, "It is so ordained. The human female Enada will plead for the release of the jantellas. Let her stand on the dais."

Enada stepped up and faced the council. Cold fear ran through her body as she looked from one dragon to another. A part of her wanted to resign and run back to the safety of the village she grew up in. She looked at the demon who stood alone. The thought was wiped from her mind.

She addressed the council. "I'm not a great dragon and don't claim to have your wisdom. I've followed the plan and see its worth. It serves the people well. Yet, I've also been told of injustice and those who seek to oppress others because they're different or hold uncommon views. You protect the people, yet you visit a great injustice on the jantella. They don't seek to destroy or subvert the plan. They only want to be themselves."

The green dragon said, "All must follow the plan, or the plan will fail. Even the dragons bow to the edict."

"One among you questioned it."

"And saw the folly of his suggestion. Magadel accepted the ruling of the council."

"Yet the question was raised. Magadel was given leave to present his suggestion to change the plan. Why was he not cast into the void?"

Jorondel said, "The dragons are not demons. We formed the plan and debated it long. All accepted it and have kept it."

"And what of the demons? Where were their voices?"

Lashadel said, "The minds of Ilidel and Jorondel released all from the egg and brought the world into being. The dragons alone possess the ability to understand it's working."

Enada said, "Such words have been spoken in the other world by one who thought himself above all, even the other dragons. There was no evil in Baras when the world began, yet the seed of evil entered."

Jorondel said, "Because the Magadel in your world defiled the plan."

Enada approached Jorondel. "The plan was created to bring harmony to the world."

"That is so."

"For all beings?"

"Yes."

She pointed to the Jant. "Are the demons not beings? They are of this world, yet their desires are unheard."

"Careful, human," said Lashadel. "You've been given leave to speak, not be insolent. What can you know of the world when we sprang from the egg? You have no ability to conceive true chaos. Don't lecture those who formed and tamed chaos so you could walk unfettered beneath the sun or sit at leisure by a stream. Our labor was long and hard. The plan brings harmony. Evil is the result of its lack."

Enada faced Lashadel. "Imprisonment is not harmony."

Lashadel turned to Jorondel. "What folly is this? She twists our words."

Ilidel said, "We have given leave for Enada to present a case for the jantella."

The green dragon shook his head. "How can a human who was not there know of the need for their banishment? All must agree to the plan." The dragon extended a claw toward Enada. "What is the wisdom of humans to ours? This human is barely out of childhood, even among her kind. Her arguments are infantile and uninformed."

Enada said, "Is it wisdom to condemn those who express a different view? What is it you fear?"

"Disharmony. We've taught and guided humans to live in peace. No strife exists here as does in the world you were conceived in. The Great Plan brings happiness and prosperity. Would you rob the people of that?"

"Have the jantella threatened to disrupt harmony?"

"They don't follow the plan and aren't bound to the rules laid out in it. Banishment is the only way to prevent misery to humankind."

"What evidence do you present?"

"No evidence is required. Their refusal to be bound to the principles of peace leaves them the ability to destroy it. Banishment is the only way to prevent chaos from returning.”

“Can you prove this is their intent?”

“Why else would they refuse to abide?”

“Then you condemn this demon and all its kind to the void for eternity out of fear?”

Lashadel stood on his hind legs. “Yes, fear. Fear for the humans who we‘ve shepherded since their inception.”

She addressed Jorondel and Ilidel. “These demons have been condemned on conjecture. I call the jantella as a witness.”

Lashadel slashed a paw in the air. “This is absurd. An accused can’t be a witness.”

Enada said, “Would this tribunal deny any evidence when the harshness of eternal imprisonment is in question?”

The green dragon said, “Lies are not evidence.”

“Until heard, who can deem testimony as lies?”

Ilidel said, “In a matter as grave as this, all voices with evidence will be heard. Enada, you may proceed.”

“Thank you.” She walked over to Jant. “Why don’t you accept the Great Plan of the dragons?”

“We have no desire to teach humans. We keep our own company and are content.”

“Would agreement to the plan prevent that?”

“The affairs of humans are not our concern. The plan calls for all beings to teach and guide people. We don’t care to.”

“You and I have spoken many times.”

“That is true.”

“Did you seek conversation?”

“No.”

“Yet, you approached me when I found you in a cave.”

“I came forward to see what you were.”

“Who did you think I might be?”

“A dragon or another spirit who would report my escape to the dragons.”

Enada paused for a moment. “Yet, you found a human.”

“Yes.”

“Were you afraid I might tell a dragon about you?”

“I only realized I was discovered.”

“You could have hurt me, even killed me, to protect your secret.”

“I could have.”

"Yet, you didn't. Why?"

The demon looked to Jorondel and Ilidel, then to Lashadel and finally back to Enada. "I wish no harm to anyone. It was plain I had to find another refuge. That's all."

"Yet, you appeared to me a second time. Did you seek me out to silence me or take revenge?"

"The jantella never seek revenge. I was curious. I'd never met a human before."

"What is your opinion, now that you've met one?"

There was a sense of compassion in the demon's voice. "I found our conversations stimulating. You're more intelligent than I imagined and far more complex."

"You told me of your plight and asked me about my life. Do you want to change how I think?"

"To what purpose? You live the way you do. Though I found it of interest, I would never tell anyone to act differently."

"Would you like to meet more humans?"

There was a pause before the demon said, "I'm not certain. I'm glad we met, yet I deeply wish to be among my own kind again."

"If you met more humans, would you teach them magic?"

"No. I wouldn't teach them anything."

Lashadel said, "How can this tribunal believe the prisoner who will make any statement to gain freedom? The words of this young human show a deeper threat than the demon. All three of the humans who came here inject the disruption of their world into ours. Their very questions bring doubt."

Enada said, "Is ignorance then the only way to secure peace?"

"Contamination must be expunged." Lashadel looked to Jorondel. "Father of dragons, it's more than the demon who threatens the plan. These alien humans carry the contamination of their world's vitriol. The council has tolerated their existence and tried to find a way to return them, without success. Now, they threaten to disrupt the plan by their very presence.

"They must be banished to the void with the demon. The infection they carry must be sealed away for eternity."

Enada ran up to Ilidel. "Hear me, mother of dragons. Would the council condemn all who ask questions?"

Lashadel said, "Yes, if the questions cause doubt about the Great Plan. The jantella will not accept it and so are left the opportunity to defile it. Open questions about the validity of the plan undermines the people's will to follow it."

Enada placed a palm over the crest of the crown. "Questions have been raised in the world of my birth since magic came to it. None knew if Baras would conquer the council and rule the world, not even the dragons. It was the search for answers that brought about the crown.

"Within the crest are the memories of every monarch who wore it since its inception. They questioned how to protect the plan. Those questions brought forth answers. I can hear their faint echoes. Look into my mind and know them."

The crest took on a faint glow.

The dragons examined it in silence.

Jorondel said, "I now see the craft that made this thing. I see the power you draw upon from within it where none of us could. The questions did bring about solutions. What say you, Lashadel?"

"The questions came from strife. Without disharmony they would have never been raised; never needed to be raised. If we are to protect the plan, we must seek out and confine all who would act to counter it before questions are asked."

Enada stood defiantly in front of Lashadel. "All who would counter it?"

"All."

"Then this council must condemn itself to the void. You knew people thought jantella ate souls."

"We didn't start that rumor."

"You didn't expose it as a lie."

"The fear kept humans away from any jantella they might see."

"And drove them to report any encounter out of terror?"

"To save them from being contaminated by dangerous ideas."

Enada looked into the eyes of the green dragon. "You perpetuated fear. Fear is disharmony. Fear causes disruption. It's you who brought disorder into the world when you banished the jantella. People asked why this was. People felt fear for their safety. People were discontent, all because you accused these demons of wrongful acts before they committed any against the Great Plan.

"You, the dragons, defiled the spirit of your own plan. You alone can repair it. Release all jantella from the void. Tell the people they're no threat and they have nothing to fear. Let these demons live the way they will, as a pledge to all beings, dragons, demons, other spirits and humans, they can do likewise without fear. Without disharmony. Look into the crest again, Lashadel. Hear through me the voices of reason who returned harmony time and again. Know the truth of your own transgression."

The chamber fell silent.

Lashadel spoke first in a subdued voice. "Is this possible? Have we been so blinded by our own desire to protect the world we lost sight of the intention of the plan?"

Enada's voice softened. "Your intentions were noble. You forgot those intents and allowed yourselves to submit to the will of rule without the compassion to administer it."

Ilidel lowered her head. "This human child shows us wisdom beyond our own."

Jorondel said, "We are shamed us by our own deeds. The dragons thought only to guide and protect. We have lost our way."

Lashadel raised his head. "In my haste to serve, I forgot to see the example I set and committed a great injustice. Let's vote on the fate of this jantella here before us and all its kind. My vote is for their release."

"Let the vote be taken, then," said Ilidel. "Mine is for release."

"As is mine," said Jorondel.

When the vote was tallied, all chose to rescind the banishment.

Jorondel said, "The jantella are called back from the void. Let them come to this hall."

The space expanded left and right. In a heartbeat, it was filled with thousands of beings. Each looked exactly like Jant. They stood with quizzical looks upon their faces.

Jorondel said, "The dragons have visited a great hurt on you."

"No words can make amends for our action," said Ilidel. "Know now the council sees its error and asks for forgiveness. All beings are free to embrace humans or not. The only edict is not to break the peace of the world and do harm. Forgive us."

The dragons bowed their heads.

Enada was amazed to see them weep.

Jant said, "We hold no blame for any. Let us live in peace."

"It shall be," said Lashadel.

Jant took Enada's hands. "You are amazing beings, you humans. I would never have guessed this before we met. I believe you, Princess Enada, are the most powerful of all. Those of my kind will be eternally grateful."

Enada felt moisture in her eyes. "You've enriched my life. For that, I'm grateful."

"You see with eyes beyond your age. There is depth and purpose about you."

"This was an important task."

"I see another more important and far more dangerous. I also see you'll leave this world. That saddens me, for I never thought I would feel such for one not of my kind.

"Perhaps we too, the jantella, need to examine our ways. Fare you well, Enada,

Princess of Carandir. The road ahead is long and treacherous, with many possible missteps. Travel with the knowledge you possess strength. You will never be forgotten."

With those words, the jantella vanished from the hall.

CHAPTER FIVE

The celebration of Enada's twentieth birthday took Mirjel and Ryckair months to plan. Special cakes and confections were ordered. A pavilion was set up in the town square with many tables. Guests from towns and villages far and wide were invited. Magadel assured her he would attend.

Everyone was excited, except for Enada.

In her bedroom, she started into the eyes of the dragon crest.

Mirjel knocked. "May I come in?"

Enada put the crown down. "Yes."

Mirjel entered and smiled. "Are you ready for your big day?"

Enada looked back at the crest. "I guess so."

Mirjel sat on the bed. "What's wrong, sweety? Are you sad?"

"No. Not really."

Mirjel took her daughter's hand. "Twenty. I can't believe it. I remember so clearly the year I came of age. It was quite a time for me. I was about to leave my home in Rascalla and travel to the palace to meet the two princes. It was scary." She squeezed Enada's hand. "You look a little scared too."

Enada picked the crown up again. "What if we do return and I have to use the crown? Everyone will expect me to confront Baras." She stroked the crest. "What if I can't?"

"You stood before the dragon council and argued eloquently."

"None of them are evil. How can I stand before someone so filled with hatred? It all seemed so far off until now."

Mirjel put her arms around Enada. "We'll be there with you if the dragons can send us back. Your grandfather and I began the spell. We can complete it together.

Baras will be subdued. You'll be a true princess, then one day, queen."

"I think that's what scares me the most. What if I falter? So many lives will depend on me. Here I have no authority. My friends are just that, friends. How can I command anyone?"

"I asked myself the same question while I rode to the palace for the first time. I was the daughter of a baron and baroness, yet I played with my friends in Rascalla, the same as you do with your friends here."

Mirjel took Enada's hands. "My father told me something I didn't understand at the time. Perhaps you won't understand right now either. He said a queen has a higher calling and duty and I would come to learn these things. I did. It was scary."

"I've never fought in a battle. What if the civil war is still raging? What if I have to face someone with a sword? What if I have to kill someone? I'm not certain I could."

Mirjel stroked her daughter's hair. "You're as skilled with a sword as I was when I was your age. Better, in fact, for you know the broadsword and the rapier."

Ryckair came into the room. "How's my birthday granddaughter?" His face became somber when he saw Enada.

She ran to his arms. "Grampy, it's all too real so suddenly. I was happy last night when I thought about the party and the treats. Now. I wish it would all go away."

He hugged her. "It's a great burden you walk into. You show strength to recognize that, my dear one. You're about to travel through a door you can't go back through. So much is unknown. That's the worst part. If you weren't scared, you wouldn't be prepared to come of age."

She snuggled her head into his chest. "I want to be brave. I want to walk through that door. I'm afraid, like some coward."

He rocked her. "It's not an act of cowardice to be afraid. You can't even accuse those who turn aside from the path of being cowards. Each of us is who we are. Not everyone can become tempered before they break.

"I was afraid so many times. I made so many mistakes. I wanted to turn aside time and again. I can't say for certain what made me go on. Part of it was naivete. I didn't fully understand the threat. Yet, there was more. Deep inside, I experienced a drive that overcame the fear.

"You won't know if the drive exists in you until you reach a breaking point and either go on or falter."

He held her back and looked into her eyes. "My guess is you'll go on. No matter what, we love you and always will"

She hugged Ryckair.

Three weeks after the celebration, a knock came to the door. Enada opened it to find Magadel at the threshold in human form with a bag in one hand.

He said, "Are your parents in?"

Enada said, "Yes, around back."

They walked through the house.

Ryckair hoed weeds from a row of vegetables.

Mirjel drew water from the well.

Enada said, "Look who's here."

Ryckair leaned on the hoe. "Well, welcome."

Mirjel sat the bucket on the wall of the well. "It's always a pleasure to see you. Won't you come inside?"

Magadel said, "Actually, I'm here to collect all three of you. There's someone who wants to see you out by the lake."

Ryckair set the hoe against the wall of the house. "Who would come so far from the town?"

"Someone who doesn't want to be noticed." He reached into the bag, brought out a robe made of gray cloth and handed it to Enada. "Take this into your room and put it on."

She inspected the cloth. It was an ankle length robe. A hood was embossed with strange scroll work, as if it were a crest. "What's this?"

"A garment to meet our guests in. Get dressed and bring the crown."

They followed Magadel to the lake. Two silver shapes descended in spirals, Jorondel and Ilidel. They landed on the grass and morphed into human shape.

Both had silver hair, Jorondel's hung to his shoulders. He wore a silver doublet.

Ilidel's locks flowed down her back. She wore a silver gown with long sleeves.

They strode forward as great nobles with fair faces. Each radiated maturity and wisdom.

The humans knelt on the grass.

Ilidel motioned with her hand. "Rise, friends."

Jorondel said, "After so many years, the council has discovered how to send you back to your world."

Enada felt a shot of excitement, then a sharp jolt of fear.

Magadel said, "The crown you brought with you has no power. It's the crest where we detected magic."

"I can see my craft in it," said Jorondel. "Though I don not know for certain how it was made. Still, without the power of creation blown into it by the Ilidel of your world, it would not be able to contain a dragon, or send you back."

Ryckair said, "Then the crown will get us home?"

"Not as it is," said Magadel. "After you opened our minds to the voices within the crest at the tribunal, we detected the murmur of magic it carried from your world. That alone would not suffice."

Jorondel said, "The magic in the crest must be concentrated. Give me the crown."

Enada handed it to Jorondel. He pulled the crest from the helm. It shimmered and shrank until it became no larger than a pendant.

Mirjel said, "Does that concentrate the magic enough?"

"Not quite," said Ilidel. "It contains only the magic of your world. To break the bonds between us and your home, it must have the breath of creation from this place."

She took the pendant from Jorondel and held it in her hands as she blew on it.

Enada felt warm air flow across the field. A sense of immense power coursed through her. The eyes of the dragon image on the pendant glowed with such intensity she had to cover her eyes.

Ilidel said, "Now, the pendant contains the essence of your home and this world." The mother of dragons held the pendant high overhead. It shone like a star descended from the heavens. "Behold, the join between realities."

A spot appeared at the edge of the forest. It was darker than the deepest cave, though it could not be called black, for it contained no color. Cracks formed above and below it and expanded to the width of a person.

Jorondel took the pendant and waved his hand in front of it. A silver chain formed. He attached it to the pendant, then pointed to the crack. "I perceive many paths. They lead to many places. One of them is your home. The pendant is your guide. It is attuned to your world and to this place. It will guide you."

Magadel said, "The power in the pendant will allow only one of you to pass. The others will remain here, perhaps forever."

Ryckair said, "Mirjel and I began the spell to confine Baras. We must complete it together."

Ilidel said, "The dragon crest now contains the power of two worlds and the essence of creation from both. It alone has the ability to return the evil dragon to eternal sleep."

Mirjel and Ryckair stared at one another.

Enada had never seen the look on their faces. Panic grew in her.

Ryckair took Enda's hand. There was redness in his eyes. "You're our heir and the future of Carandir. Your mother and I are past sixty. No more children will come from us. You alone carry our blood."

Enada felt a desire to run and hide. The air became oppressive. She looked to the dragons, Ryckair and then her mother. "What are you saying? Both of you must recite the spell."

"Our spirits live within you and bestow the same power," said Mirjel. "When I took you into my womb, I knew you were destined for greatness. You possess the ability to confront Baras by yourself as well as your grandfather and I would together. We were born into a world of conflict and evil. You came into this world in innocence and are the only one who can return innocence to ours."

Jorondel held the dragon pendant out to Enada. "Your mother chose your name well, Enada, healer of souls. The souls in the place where you were conceived needs to be healed."

The world around Enada faded into a soft haze. The only thing she could perceive was the dragon-shaped pendant whose eyes glowed. When she took it, she felt as if she was called by some power. It was not a voice. There were no words. It was a sense of purpose. There was a task she had to attempt, whether she failed or succeeded.

The mist vanished.

She slipped the chain around her neck. It hung as if it belonged there.

She turned to Mirjel and Ryckair. "I must go."

Mirjel said, "I know."

Ryckair dabbed his eyes. "I think we always knew."

Enada said, "What will become of you?"

Magadel smiled. "They'll live their lives here, surrounded by friends, human and dragon."

The father of dragons said, "Their mortal existence will be filled with happiness."

The mother of dragons spread her hands, "In the end, they will dwell in our halls forever in honor."

With a wave of his hand, Magadel produced a bag with a shoulder strap. "There's food and water inside. The robes you wear will allow you to walk through the crack and protect you from any forces within."

Enada stood before Mirjel and Ryckair. "Mother. Grandfather." Her breath was ragged. "I have no words."

They embraced.

Mirjel said, "Go now, sweety, my dearest child. It's your destiny."

Enada put her arms around Magadel. "Thank you for everything. I'll do what must be done." Then, she whispered into his ear, "I'll never forget you, Syo."

She raised the hood over her head and walked into the crack.

There was no light other than the glow of the dragon pendant. It faintly illuminated the scene for a dozen steps in front of her. A level path wound between tangled brambles. It was neither cold nor hot.

She saw no ceiling. The space above was devoid of stars, yet she felt the presence of a force.

She looked behind her and saw the field where the dragons stood next to Ryckair and Mirjel.

With a loud snap, the crack closed.

She continued on the path.

After several hundred steps. She came to an intersection where the path split left and right. There was no sign of which one she should follow.

She started down the right-hand path. The glow of the dragon crest diminished until it was nearly gone.

She walked back to the intersection. The glow increased, until it reached the same illumination it started with.

The path twisted sometimes left, sometimes right. At other times it seemed to almost double back on itself.

She reached a stone wall with steps and climbed to find herself on a platform. It stood four times her height above the path. The glow of the dragon pendant didn't reach far, though she could make out paths that snaked between brambles in a maze. Another set of steps led down the other side.

She descended and reached a round clearing eight paces across with four exits. When she turned in place, the crest glowed brightest when she faced the path directly in front of her.

Around a bend, she came to another open space with a round fountain.

A man sat on a low wall around it. He wore armor without a helm. A sword in a plain, leather scabbard lay on the wall next to him.

She approached and saw his shoulders shook while he sobbed. His tears fell in a puddle at his feet. They were red, like fresh blood.

Enada said, "Are you hurt?"

There was no response other than crying.

"Can you hear me? Who are you? Where do you come from?"

Still the man sobbed while blood fell down his cheeks. He looked neither left nor right.

Enada reached out to touch his shoulder. Her hand passed through his image as if it were smoke. She snapped her arm back.

The man took no notice.

She next to him. "Who are you?"

Silence.

"Are you lost? This crest guides me through the maze."

The man only sobbed.

Enada touched the scabbard. It was real. She drew the sword and examined the broad blade with a simple guard. When she swung it through the air, she found it well balanced.

Was this another traveler like her, now lost in the maze for eternity? How long had he been there? She had no idea how much farther her destination was and wondered if she would wind up like the ghostly warrior. Whoever he was, she was certain his phantom would sit by the fountain forever.

She slipped the sword into the scabbard, then picked up the belt and strapped it around her waist. "I am so sorry for you."

The path led on. She took some food out of the pack, ate a little and washed it down with a sip of water.

After her meager meal, she continued on with no way to gauge how far she had come. Exhaustion came to her. There was nowhere to take shelter. If she lay on the path, she could be trampled by someone or something.

She continued on, until she reached another intersection where one path continued on ahead and a wider one split off to the left.

The dragon crest indicated the path to the left was true. She moved just inside the wider one, laid down near the wall of thorns and fell asleep.

When she woke, she followed the wide path. More intersections followed. Each time, the pendant guided her down the correct route.

Twice more, she climbed a platform on top of a wall. She could see no end to the maze. After two more rest periods, she worried her supply of food would run out.

She came to a bridge made of horizontal, wooden slats held together by rope ties. Two lengths of rope ran above the slats as hand holds.

It crossed a river of molten lava. The viscous fluid bubbled and popped as it moved from an unseen source to an unknown destination. The stench of sulfur permeated the hot air. It was too wide to jump across.

Low thorn bushes ran along the edge on either side of the bridge.

Enada walked toward the bridge.

The thorn bushes next to it closed over the opening.

She stepped back.

The brambles spread apart.

Once more, she walked toward the bridge.

The thorns again cut off her approach.

She took out the sword and hacked at the thorn bushes. The blade left no marks as it bounced off. She stepped back and ran forward to jump over the low brush. It grew taller than her. She stopped just short of being impaled.

Had the phantom warrior reached this bridge? There were no other specters here. She wondered if she were the first to come this way. From what she could tell from the platforms, the maze was immense. If she couldn't pass on to find the path where Baras was, it might be possible to take another to a world where she could at least escape the maze before her food ran out.

The light of the pendant faded when she left the route to her native home. She would be cast into utter darkness and could wander until she died or became a specter herself. What would happen to her if she died in that place? Would her soul fly to the dragons' halls or be trapped here forever? Were there even dragons here, wherever this was?

There had to be a way to get over the bridge. Could she crawl across the brambles? They would rip her skin open before she reached the other side. If she lost too much blood, she'd die.

What if an object she carried caused the bushes to close off? She unbuckled the sword and dropped it, then walked up to the bridge.

At her approach, the thorns stayed in place.

Her foot almost reached the first slat when the bushes closed and blocked her again. When she took a step back. The bushes retreated.

What else did she carry from a world different from the one she was conceived in? The pendant was the crest from the crowd. It belonged in that place. She remembered the chain Jorondel fashioned.

She removed it and walked toward the bridge with the pendant in her hand. The thorn bushes snapped closed.

She removed the robes to stand naked on the ground, then walked forward with the pendant. Her foot was about to touch the bridge when the bushes closed again. She jumped back just in time to avoid being cut.

"What still blocks me?" She remembered how Ilidel breathed the essence of creation from that other world into the pendant. Enada dropped it, stepped forward and placed her foot on the bridge. The thorn bushes didn't move.

She replaced the pendant on the chain, retrieved the robes and approached the bridge.

The bushes began to close.

She stood as close as possible to the thorns and lobbed first the robes and then the pendant and chain onto the bridge.

They sailed over top.

When they passed the brush, it withdrew from the gap.

The robes straddled the center of a slat. The pendant slid toward the edge.

She dived onto the bridge. Her hand grasped the pendant. The momentum of her body carried her toward the precipice. She twisted, grabbed for the space between two slats and managed to stop. Her feet dangled over the edge as the sulfuric fumes burned her throat. She pulled herself back onto the bridge with the pendant grasped in her hand.

She placed the chain around her neck, picked up the robes and took hold of the rope supports.

When she reached the other side, the path continued on. She moved away from the lava river, donned the robes again, then collapsed to her knees and gulped deep breaths.

The sulphury stench cleared from her throat. She got to her feet and put the robes back on.

There was a rhythmic roar. She rounded a bend. Water extended to a horizon. Waves crashed against a rocky shore where a round, stone tower stood. The eyes on the dragon pendant glowed with such intensity it lit the entire scene.

A window appeared high up on the tower where there had been only stone moments before. Soft light emerged from the opening.

Stones beneath the window extended from the tower wall with a grind to create footholds. Enada ran her hand along the edge of one and found a slight lip to support her fingers.

She climbed the wet stones. It felt like an eternity before she reached the window and crawled inside.

It was dry and warm. The walls gave off a soft glow. A round staircase set between walls led up and down.

She climbed the steps and came to another window.

Through it, she saw the city in the desert where she prepared arguments to release the jantella.

She put her hand on the sill. "This was the window mother and grandfather fell through. I'm in the wizard tower at Amblar. This is the world where I was conceived."

It would be a simple matter to step through and return to the place she grew up in. An ache came to her chest.

She took a deep breath, then moved up the steps.

A third window looked out on endless sky and clouds, with no land to be seen. She was reminded of her first trip to meet the dragons.

She climbed until she came to a wooden door. She walked through to a large, round room. There were settees, tables and shelves. Books were arranged in a haphazard fashion.

Exhaustion enveloped her. She cast herself onto one of the settees and fell asleep.

BOOK XII

The palace at Meth
Two months after the death of Baroness Quib

CHAPTER ONE

Narech Herrik sat in the war room and listened to reports of action on the front lines. Eight of her senior officers attended. The Karakien army still held at the Kar River and the mountains in Respa while the forces of the rebellious baronies pushed toward Lake Hasp.

A captain concluded his report. "Though reinforcements from Au have allowed some of our forces in the east to move farther into Barta, we haven't been able to recapture the area around the wizard tower. Food continues to be rationed among the civilian population."

The narech diverted most of the grain from the eastern baronies to feed the army. The barony of Garan was the breadbasket of the east. If the Karakiens pushed past Respa, the army could starve in the field. So far, their forces were concentrated on the iron mines.

Herrik said, "Marawee will have just reached Hura. We could see their troops within month. I expected Captain Efra to bring troops from Xinglan by this time. Without terecs, there's no way to learn why he's delayed."

"Perhaps Xinglan prepares its troops," said a navy commander.

"Perhaps. We must trust to the forces available to us."

Yearol cut key supports on a wooden bridge. Keetala, and three other Carandirian soldiers from Lieutenant Parna's command worked next to her. The bridge crossed a deep crevasse, It was part of a main trade route between Shenan and Ulata.

They tied ropes to the compromised supports, scrambled behind trees next to the road on the eastern side of the bridge and waited for a militia patrol.

Whispy popped onto Yearol's shoulder. She gently stroked its head. "They're just around the bend."

Moments later, three mounted militiamen escorted two horse drawn wagons. They were followed by a column of thirty men in armor who carried swords, pikes and bows. The horsemen reached the other side and halted while the wagons crossed. The rest of the company marched behind.

As soon as the wagons cleared the bridge, Yearol and the others yanked the ropes.

The structure crumbled.

Men screamed as they fell into the chasm.

The rest of Parna's troops charged from behind trees to assail the riders and wagon drivers.

Two of the militia horsemen were taken down with arrows. The third swiped his sword at the Carandirians. A cut to his left leg brought him down from his mount.

Another soldier ran him through.

The wagon drivers were overrun and killed.

Parna approached one of the wagons and removed a tarp. "There's enough grain and dried meat to sustain us for a month. Excellent work."

Frothy and Keetala ran forward.

Yearol followed close behind the deputy. She put her hand in an open barrel. "It's all milled. Look, here's yeast. We'll feast tonight. I can almost taste the bread."

Frothey tousled her hair. "We have to be long gone from here before we light any fires to bake. I'll drive one of the wagons."

Yearol said, "Can I ride with you?"

The deputy waved the young woman forward. "Sure. Come on."

The provisions were taken to a cave, where a clay oven was dug into a corner.

Yearol helped bake bread for a small feast. Dried meat and vegetables complimented the meal.

Whispy rested on Yearol's shoulder as she ate.

Keetala came and sat beside her. "I'm glad Whispy chose to attach itself to you."

Yearol reached up and ran her finger along Whispy's back, then sighed as she stared at Frothey.

Keetala said, "What's wrong?"

"Nothing."

"Come on. You can't hide it from me."

Yearol stared back at Frothey. "I shouldn't speak about it. We could all be dead tomorrow."

Keetala frowned. "What's gotten into you?"

Yearol rubbed her arm. "Have you ever been in love?"

"What kind of a question is that? I was married. I had a daughter."

"I mean a deep love that eats at you."

"What are you talking about?"

Yearol looked aside. "I'm in love with Frothey."

Keetala looked over to the deputy and back to her friend. "Frothey?"

"I'm serious."

"Have you ever been in love before?"

"Not romantic love. She's strong and beautiful. I'm nobody."

Keetala furrowed her brow. "Now, you've got to snap out of this. We're a military unit. This is no place for feelings like that. We have to be sharp."

Yearol closed her eyes. "I know. I know."

"What does she feel towards you?"

"I can't ask her that."

"Can't or won't?"

Yearol glared at Keetala, then walked away.

The food was divided into bundles for distribution to safe places in the Shenan mountains where the Carandirians moved between after raids. They were spread out several days walk from each other to make it appear their attacks were delivered by a larger force.

When the packs were loaded, Parna divided the troops up.

Keetala and Yearol sat on the ground and waited for their assignments.

Yearol looked across to the deputy. "I'm going to go with Frothey's group." She started across.

Keetala grabbed her arm. "We always go together."

Yearol shook herself free. "I want to go with Frothey this time. What's the matter with that?"

"You've practically ignored me for days."

"I haven't ignored you. I just have some things on my mind."

"Right. I can guess what they are."

Yearol turned back to Keetala with a scowl on her face. "What does that mean?"

"Aren't you being a little obvious? You constantly make puppy eyes at Frothey."

"Are you jealous?"

"Hardly."

The two women eyed the other.

Yearol looked down to the ground. "I just want to be near her."

"And not me?"

"I didn't say that."

"We've shared a bond and a purpose."

"We still have that purpose."

Keetala shook her head. "I don't think so. You've forgotten why we're here, what we've nearly died for."

"How can you say that? Do you think I've forgotten the sight of my dead mother in the mill?"

"Do you think I've forgotten my drowned husband's body on a riverbank or my dead child in my arms while blood seeped from the arrow wound. I'm here to stop those who did that, not run off in an amorous interlude that will put us all at risk."

Yearol turned away and walked toward the deputy. "Frothey, wait."

Frothey looked up from the pack straps she was securing. "What is it?"

Yearol panted as she ran across camp. "I want to go with you."

"What about Keetala?"

"She wants to go with someone else."

Frothey smiled and tousled Yearol's hair. "All right. Get a pack."

The group marched over a mountain range. Once they secured the food in a cave and sealed the entrance with rocks and brush, they set off for another day's march to rendezvous with the rest of Parna's command.

Yearol moved up in the column to be closer to Frothey.

She shifted her pack. "I've never been to Lusar. Is it true that it's all mountains?"

"Mostly. There're also wide valleys. The major settlements are spread out among the valleys. Some towns are in the high ground."

"I'd like to see it. I lived all my life near my village. Would you take me to see your mountains one day?"

Frothey chuckled. "If there is one day. There's a lot of war still."

Yearol walked on in silence. She felt her heart pound as she tried to think of a subject to continue the conversation. "My father wanted to visit Lusar once. He never got there."

"Why not?"

"Oh, something came up."

"Are you and your brother close?"

"Very close. He's safe in Varda now. They built special camps for the refugees."

"Did you have many friends in Shenan?"

"Not too many. There were only a few others my age near the mill. We used to play games." She stopped and looked at Frothey. "I've never had a boyfriend, you know."

"I had lots of friends when I was young. My town was larger than most."

"Did you have romantic friends?" Yearol saw sadness in Frothey's eyes.

The older woman said, "I've loved a few women. Some loved me back. Nothing lasted until I met Arota. I was twenty-seven. We were both deputies then, before she was named sheriff. We were together until she was killed by Luja's men."

The silence returned. Yearol felt pressure push out from inside her skin.

A scout came back down the trail. "Deputy Frothey, we spotted a patrol."

Frothey turned to the troops. "Wait here. I'll have a look."

Yearol said, "I can send Whispy. It can pop ahead and see what's happening."

The deputy said, "I always forget about your little friend. Everyone take a rest. Yearol, send Whispy."

Yearol stroked the little creature. "Have a look."

Whispy vanished from Yearol's shoulder.

Everyone sat down; Yearol next to Frothey.

One of the Carandirian soldiers said, "Should we take a meal break here?"

Frothey said, "It's a little early. Whispy should be back in a tespan or so."

Yearol scooted closer to Frothey, who seemed to take no notice. She fought to keep her breath steady while she looked straight ahead and studied Frothey's long, dark hair from the corner of her eye. There was a scent about the deputy she found intoxicating.

Whispy popped back onto Yearol's shoulder and nuzzled up to her ear. "It's a patrol of four men, all armed with swords. There're no bowmen with them. This trail intersects the one they're on. They'll be out of earshot in a tespan or so."

Frothey looked down the path. "We'll wait here for two tespans to make certain they don't double back, then we'll move out."

Yearol thought to impress Frothey. "We outnumber them. Shouldn't we attack?"

"We'll allow them to reach their destination and report there's no activity in this area. If we kill the scouts, other militiamen will look for them."

Yearol chided herself as her face flushed hot. She should have known this. When the patrol moved out, she took up a position at the rear.

Two weeks later, there was no moon. The stars shone dimly through hazy clouds at the approach of darknail. Crickets chirped in the warm summer night. They were the only sound in the mountainous forest.

Yearol waited next to Lieutenant Parna for Whispy to return. Since she embarrassed herself in front of the deputy and the other soldiers, she avoided both Keetala and Frothey.

Five enemy wagons stood in a hollow hemmed in by a cliff to the south. Campfires blazed and torches burned along the perimeter. Ten militiamen with polearms were silhouetted against the flames.

Whispy popped onto Yearol's shoulder and nuzzled into her ear. "The wagons are filled with arrows. There're no guards atop the cliff."

Parna said, "Good. Corporal, send the patrol up above the wagons."

Corporal Wesala saluted, then slung a sack over her shoulder and nodded to three other soldiers. They retrieved sacks and followed the corporal up a steep southerly incline.

Parna said, "Go with them, Yearol. Send Whispy down when you reach the top."

"Yes, lieutenant."

Yearol was glad she wouldn't have to see Keetala and Frothey during the attack. She grabbed a sack filled with pitch and followed Corporal Wesala.

From above, campfires blazed. Their light didn't penetrate far enough through the night air to reveal the Carandirian's position.

Wesala and the others unslung the sacks filled with pitch gathered from trees over the previous days. Loose brush and dried grass were bundled together. One of the soldiers struck flint against a metal striker plate. The kindling caught fire.

Yearol, sent Whispy down to Lieutenant Parna.

The sacks were touched to the flames and tossed them over the cliff. Each landed on a canvas bonnet of a wagon and ignited it.

The militiamen on guard dropped their polearms and ran to the wagons. They beat the flames or grabbed buckets slung to the sides of the wagons and threw water onto the fires.

Parna's troops attacked. Militiamen turned from the fires to be impaled on Carandirian blades. Other militiamen drew swords or retrieved polearms.

Yearol watched Keetala cut her way forward as the wagons burned. Other soldiers killed militiamen unprepared for an attack.

One of the rebels hefted a spear and flung it.

In horror, Yearol saw the tip strike Frothey.

The deputy dropped to the ground.

Yearol shot to her feet. "No!" She ran along the edge of the cliff and down the embankment.

Corporal Wesala shouted. "Where are you going?"

Yearol paid her no heed, as she moved down the steep hillside.

At the bottom, she ran past the fray to Frothey, who lay on the ground with her hands over her lower calf where the spear penetrated.

Yearol pulled the shaft out and threw it to the ground. She grabbed Frothey under her armpits and dragged the deputy away from the battle.

Frothey spoke between gasps. "Tear off some material. Wrap it around the puncture."

Yearol looked around. There was nothing. She pulled her blouse out of her pants and cut off the bottom of the garment with her knife, then wrapped it around Frothey's leg and pulled hard on the fabric.

The wound continued to seep.

Frothey winced. "Pull tighter."

Yearol stuck her knife into the knot of the tourniquet and twisted. The blood flow stopped. She breathed hard through her mouth. "What do I do now?"

"Return to the battle."

"I can't leave you."

"The wound's sealed. I can control the pain. Stop the militiamen."

Yearol hesitated for only a moment before she drew her sword and rushed into the fray. She encountered a militiaman and drove her blade into his belly. The man screamed and fell. She went on to another and sliced open his arm.

The battle soon ended with the militiamen dead. Two Carandirians, a woman and a man, also lay dead on the ground. Two others, in addition to Frothey, were wounded.

Parna said, "Save as many arrows from the wagons as possible before they burn."

Keetala sheathed her sword and saw Yearol stand over a dead militiaman as she hacked his body with a guttural cry at each stroke. His head was cut from his body. His abdomen was a gory mass of blood and flesh. Still, Yearol struck.

Keetala came up from behind and grabbed the younger woman's wrists. "What are you doing? He's dead."

Yearol breathed in rapid spurts. She released her sword and stood over the mutilated corpse, then kicked the head.

Keetala said, "It's over. Come back."

Yearol's face contorted. "They hurt Frothey. I hate them. I hate them all. I'll kill them all."

Keetala grabbed Yearol by the shoulders and looked into her eyes. "That's not why we're here. Hate only leads to hate. We all have to live together one day when this is over. Womb and Luja and the other traitors win if we forget that. We fight their evil, not other Carandirians."

The two women stared at each other before Yearol put her hands over her face.

They gathered as many unburned arrows as they could carry. The militiamen's pole arms were used to make litters to carry the wounded. They traveled for half a day to reach one of their hideouts in a cave. Corporal Wesala treated the injured.

Frothey lay to one side. Her leg was bandaged. The corporal gave her a concoction to ease the pain.

Yearol came over and sat down. "How are you feeling?"

"As well as can be expected. I won't be able to walk on the leg for a week, though there's be no permanent damage. Thank you for your concern."

"Well… It's just that… I saw you get hit from atop the cliff and thought you were dead when you fell."

"No. Not yet. There's a lot more fight left in me." She thumped her chest and smiled.

"I was really worried." Yearol rubbed her hands together. "I don't want anything bad to happen to you."

"I don't want anything bad to happen to you either."

"Really?"

"Of course. I like you."

Yearol looked down at the ground. "I…" She raised her head and looked Frothey in the face. "I love you."

"I love you too. You're a good comrade."

"No. You don't understand." Yearol felt her chin shake. "I love you. I want to be with you forever."

Frothey's mouth and eyes opened wide as Yearol's words sank in. She saw the plea in the young woman's face and heard the frightened courage in her voice.

She realized the desperate seriousness inside Yearol. Frothey thought of the times she revealed herself to another and the pain when she was rejected. Her mind searched for some way to explain she had no romantic feelings for Yearol. "I really can't love anyone right now. Arota's death is too close."

"That's why I had to tell you. We could both be dead tomorrow. I love you so deeply. I'm afraid there's so little time."

The deputy saw pain and hope in Yearol's face while the younger woman wrung her hands. She realized why Yearol took every opportunity to be near her — how Yearol misinterpreted her actions when she tousled the young woman's hair and joked with her. It became all too clear Yearol perceived affection, even though Frothey never intended such. "This can't be. I'm twice your age. It wouldn't be fair to you."

"I don't care about our ages. I just want to be with you."

"You're young. I've seen too many years and known too much pain. If you survive this war, there'll be plenty of other women to love."

"Don't give me an answer yet. Think about it."

"Yearol, there's nothing to think about."

"I can't stop feeling the way I do. It's all wrapped up inside me. I can't stop loving you."

"I'm not telling you to stop feeling anything. You have to accept we can't be a couple."

Yearol stepped back. "I'll give you some time. You're wounded right now." She turned and left.

Frothey closed her eyes with a sigh. She'd been hurt before and never wanted to visit that on anyone else.

Corporal Wesala came over. "How's the leg?"

"The leg's fine." She hesitated for a moment. "There's another problem." She told the corporal about her encounter with Yearol.

The Daro-trained soldier frowned. "Aside from the emotional strain, this could impact the command. If Yearol's so distracted she could make a mistake and endanger a battle or reveal our position. I think Lieutenant Parna needs to learn of this."

"Please, don't mention it to him. I'm certain she won't give us away. I'm just not sure how to handle this."

It took two more weeks before Frothey was able to stand with the aid of a walking stick. It was evident she wouldn't be able to keep up with the company in the mountains yet.

Parna decided Frothey would stay with the cave and keep it concealed as a home base until her leg healed.

When the company prepared to depart, Yearol asked to speak with the lieutenant alone. They went outside together into the forest. Whispy rode on her shoulder.

She said, "I want to stay with Frothey. She'll need help."

Parna said, "Frothey must stay behind, because she can't keep up."

"I'm missing toes."

"And they have never hindered you."

"It could flare up and slow the company down. I wouldn't want that."

Parna looked her up and down. "Is that your only concern?"

"Of course."

"I think not. I think you want to be left here to spend time alone with Frothey."

"No. It's not that at all."

"A soldier doesn't lie to a comrade, especially a commanding officer. We depend on each other in battle. You seek an intimate relationship with the deputy."

Yearol felt a flush of embarrassment, then anger. "Who told you? Keetala?"

"No one told me. No one had to. It's apparent from your activity and the longing on your face when you're around her."

Yearol folded her fingers together. "Please, sir. Let me stay."

"You said you tried to join the Carandirian military and were rejected."

"Yes, lieutenant."

Parna's voice took on a somber ring. "You *have* joined the military under my command. You're a competent and valuable member of this company. Whispy has warned us of threats and given us tactical advantage. You're needed. More, you're commanded to march with us. You swore an oath to the Crown when you entered service. Would you break that oath?"

"I may never find love again."

The lieutenant's features softened. "Did you know I have a family?"

"No, sir."

"My wife, my son and my daughter are in Nemtanka. When I was stationed in Lusar, I was only supposed to be there for six months. I was to return and be stationed near our home, so they chose to stay. I haven't seen them since I left. They don't know if I am alive or dead. Would you have me abandon my command and rush to them?"

Yearol looked down at her feet. "No, sir. I wouldn't."

"Look at me when I speak to you, soldier."

The young woman snapped to attention. "Yes, sir."

Parna studied Yearol for a moment. "At ease. Why did you and Keetala come when you could have stayed in the camp and been safe with your brother?"

"I wanted to fight, sir. I wanted to stop Luja and the horror she brought, so no other woman had to watch as her mother's murdered."

"And you've done so admirably. You crossed a great distance in danger. You put your life in the way of mortal harm. You've acted every bit a soldier as the other men and women I command.

"You're a valuable member of this company, all of whom have families and friends they can't be with. Now, go and see Frothey before we leave. Say farewell, not goodbye, for it is very possible that the two of you will see each other again.

"It's my sincerest wish for you to have a long and happy life, Yearol. You'll meet many people and do many things. As time passes, your perspective on the world will change. I know this makes no sense at the moment. It will. For now, we'll forget we had this discussion."

Yearol saluted. "Yes, sir."

Parna walked away.

Yearol went back into the cave and stood next to Frothey, who sat propped up against a wall.

She said, "I have to leave now. I'm sorry if I said anything wrong."

The deputy said, "Come here."

Yearol sat down next to her.

Frothey said, "I'm deeply touched by your feelings for me and very sad I can't return them in the way you wish."

Yearol sniffed. "I shouldn't have said anything."

"Oh, no. Don't think that. Never be ashamed of how you feel. Love is the most wonderful and terrible thing in the world. We put ourselves out with no defense. When the love we feel is returned, it's the greatest experience we can ever know. When we get hurt, it tears us to our souls. It's worth it.

"I don't want to part with bad feelings between us. We may never meet again and would have to carry the hurt to our graves. If we do meet once more, we can remember the good times we shared.

"I care for you very deeply, Yearol, more so after you said you loved me. I want only good things in your life, even though I know there will be many bad things first.

"I'm glad you told me how you feel. It's made my life more complete to know you so intimately."

Yearol couldn't hold back tears.

Frothey put her arms around the younger woman.

Yearol wiped her eyes and stood. "I have to go now. Farewell."

Whispy popped onto Frothey's shoulder and nuzzled her ear.

Frothey said, "Farewell to both of you."

Whispy popped back onto Yearol's shoulder. She walked out of the cave.

Keetala stood outside the entrance.

The women looked at each other, then stepped forward and hugged.

Yearol said, "I've been such an idiot."

Keetala sniffled. "I haven't exactly been the best of friends. I think I was a little jealous after all we've been through. I'm sorry."

Yearol stepped back and tried to smile. "I guess everyone has to grow up." The smile dropped as tears rolled down her cheeks. " I just wish it didn't hurt so much."

Keetala said, "So do I."

With a sniffle, Yearol said, "Come on. We better hurry. The company's moving out."

CHAPTER TWO

Efra was unable to gauge how long he'd sat alone in the cell after the last interrogation by the Karakiens. The stench of his own urine and feces permeated the air. Meals were delivered irregularly. At times, the cell was plunged into darkness when the view slat in the door was shut. Still, to Efra's internal clock, it seemed months since he brought the *Prosper* into the port of Au.

He was taken to an interrogation room on an irregular basis. Gaberda asked him about troop strengths, passwords and battle plans. When Efra refused to answer, guards beat him with their fists. Sometimes, they lit brands with a torch, blew out the flames and touched the hot embers to his arm. He howled with pain as the guards laughed.

Efra was not part of Narech Herrik's general staff. Because he'd been on the North Continent, he knew nothing about battle plans or troop strengths. What little he let slip under torture was outdated.

Through all the pain of torture, Efra maintained he came to confer with the council in Au concerning supplies for the war and held his tongue about the true mission

He wondered if Narech Herrik sent another galley to solicit aid from Xinglan. She would have expected help by this time.

It was one of the dark periods when the cell door opened. Efra was blinded by the feeble light in the dungeon hallway.

Soldiers grabbed his arms and dragged him up flights of stairs to a room.

The slaver Turga sat in a chair at a table across from Colonel Gaberda.

Efra stood shakily from lack of food while the soldiers supported him.

Turga got up and forced the captain's mouth open. "He's half-starved and bruised, Gaberda. I'd be lucky to get a copper for him in this condition."

Gaberda said, "The bruises will heal. His worth is in his mind. He has skills to organize and command others. Sell him as an overseer or planner."

Efra coughed up blood. "I thought you wanted information?"

"You've told us all you know. I could kill you for sport or make a profit. Be glad that the slaver is interested at all."

Turga and Gaberda argued over a price. Efra was taken outside, where iron shackles were fastened to his legs, just above his ankles, and locked in place with a key. A length of chain connected them so the captain could only shuffle.

The slaver's caravan of wagons waited in the street. Within one of the slatted cage wagons were sixteen men, all in rags. Some had stubble on their faces while others wore beards. They were young and muscular.

The other wagon made of slats contained nine women. None of them was older than eighteen.

The captain saw no one from his crew among the prisoners.

The slavers stripped Efra of his uniform and boots, then pulled a dirty sackcloth over his body and put sandals on his feet.

He was shoved into the wagon with the men.

The caravan moved through the southern gate of Au.

They left paved roads and bounced east along a dirt trail. Just before sunset, a slaver opened the doors to the wagons while two others stood guard with crossbows.

The captives were herded out and forced to sit on the ground in two circles, one for men and another for women. A fire was lit and food cooked. Efra eyed the guards. With the shackles, he couldn't possibly get more than a few steps.

Turga pointed to Efra. "Give extra portions to the new one. He has to have his strength built up before he can go on the block."

The wagons arrived at a city. Two men and three women were taken from the wagons. Efra could hear bids as Turga spurred the buyers on.

Day after day, more slaves were sold. Efra was always held back. For six weeks, he was fed better than the other prisoners. The bruises healed as strength returned to his limbs.

The wagons stopped in a meadow within a forest thick with trees. Turga conferred with his men. All the riders left. The other nine guards built a fire.

Efra wondered how far north the river was. If he could escape and reach a fishing village, he might be able to find a boat.

His stomach grumbled. There were two other men in the caged wagon with him. They were fed in the morning and evening. It was two spans past the time breakfast.

Efra rattled the slats of the cage. "Hey, where did the riders go?"

One of the slavers repaired a link of chain with a hammer. "They're off to capture new slaves. If you haven't noticed, we're low on inventory." He laughed.

"When do we eat?"

"When we're ready to feed you. Shut up."

"It's two spans since dawn."

The slaver came up to the caged wagon. "I said, shut up."

He slammed a slat with the hammer.

Efra pulled his fingers back before it struck them.

A rusty nail dropped to the floor of the wagon. The captain sat down, spread his hand nonchalantly as he picked it up. It tapered from a blunt end to an elongated point smaller than the keyhole of the ankle shackles.

He moved next to the cage door of the wagon and turned his back on the slavers, then leaned forward and feigned asleep. He inserted the point of the nail into the keyhole on the left shackle and worked the mechanism.

With a click, the shackle opened. He unlocked the other one.

The slavers with the hammer unlocked the cage door. "All right, everyone out."

Efra drove the nail into the man's eye.

He screamed and reached for his face.

The captain shoved the door open and knocked the slaver to the ground, then ran into the woods. He heard Turga's voice shouting, "Get him, you fools."

The trees were spaced close with thick brush between them. Efra heard the crash of men behind him. He ran in a zig-zag pattern.

A rock ledge sat over a dark shadow. Efra recognized it as the entrance to a cave. He snapped off twigs leading to the darkness.

The voices of the men grew nearer.

Efra ran around the trunk of a tree and hid.

The voices of the slavers came closer.

One of them said, "Look. He's been this way."

Another said, "He's gone into the cave. Come on."

Efra sprinted deeper into the woods.

It was nearly sunset when he reached a narrow river. There was no sound of pursuit.

Across the water was an orchard. Dozens of men and women pruned branches. Among them were the members of his crew from the *Prosper,* including Commander Cepata and Chief Fooso.

Fooso was on a ladder.

Cepata used a hoe to weed the ground nearby.

All were dressed in sackcloth and sandals the same as Efra. None of the slaves were bound by chains. Their movements were mechanical. Efra saw no guards.

The captain swam across the river and ran up to Cepata. "Commander, are the rest of the crew here?"

Cepata gave no response as she continued to hoe weeds.

"Commander, answer me. We have to get to the Great River and find a ship to reach Xinglan." He grabbed the woman by the shoulders and spun her around. She stared ahead blankly for an instant, then returned to work.

Efra moved to the ladder. "Chief. Come down."

Fooso continued pruning.

Voices came from the other side of the orchard. Efra got down on his hands and knees and pulled weeds.

Three armed men appeared.

One of them held up an amber stone.

He said, "Time for food. Come."

Like mindless marionettes, the workers climbed down from their ladders or stood up from the ground and followed the men. Efra fell in with the workers.

The guards led them to a stone building with windows high on the walls and a thatched roof. They filed through the single door into a common room. The workers sat on the floor.

Efra positioned himself next to Cepata. The rest of his crew were scattered around the room.

Fifty men and women filled the space. Guards pushed a cart into the room and handed each worker a bowl. No one took notice of Efra, who imitated the others. When he received a bowl, it was filled with a thick stew of meat and vegetables.

The guards collected empty bowls and wheeled the cart out.

The one with the amber stone said, "Sleep."

Everyone laid on the floor. The last guard left. The faint glow of twilight filtered through the windows.

Efra shook Cepata. "Commander, wake up."

She lay in a catatonic state.

The captain attempted to rouse Fooso with the same effect. He got up and tried the door. It was unlocked. He opened it and peered through a crack. There was no one around. He saw several buildings. Three barns stood to one side. He thought the other buildings might be a smithy and stables.

Across a courtyard was a two-story house with ornate trimmings. A man in brocade robes stood on a porch.

The guard with the amber stone approached. "The slaves are settled, Master Sebara."

He handed Sebara the stone.

"Thank you, Tacher. You're dismissed for the night."

Sebara fingered the stone for a moment, then walked back into the house.

Efra returned to the slave quarters for the night.

In the morning, four guards wheeled carts into the barracks and distributed bowls of porridge along with water skins. Tacher stood at the door and rubbed a thumb over the stone.

The guards distributed hoes and pruning shears, then led the slaves back to the orchard. Once there, Tacher led the guards away.

Efra reasoned the slaves needed no guards once they were put to work. The key was the amber stone.

After a tespan, he moved cautiously toward the house. From behind a wall, he watched men come and go while the sun moved across the sky.

At twilight, he heard the sounds of wagons.

Turga's caravan rode through the gate and up to the front door.

Tacher and three men greeted the slaver.

Sebara came out of the house. "I don't need any more slaves."

Turga said, "I'm not here to sell. A slave escaped yesterday. There's a reward for his capture."

Sebara laughed. "Where were your men?"

"Most rode off to fetch more merchandise. There were only three slaves and nine of my guards. The one who escaped is a captain in the Carandirian Navy. He somehow unlocked his shackles and blinded one of my guards." He pointed to a man with a patch over one eye. "The captain can't have gotten far."

Tacher stood behind his master with the amber stone in his hands.

Sebara took it. "You need one of these."

"What is it?"

"I encountered an old man who was so weak from hunger he couldn't move. This stone lay on the ground just out of his reach. He said it was an amulet. The bearer could control the mind of any person. I promised to give him food if he told me how to work it. Moments after he revealed the secret, he died from starvation.

"A person so enchanted loses all will and knowledge of who they are. They'll do whatever they're told. I only have twenty servants. Just eleven are guards. They take the slaves to the orchards in the morning and collect them at night. The slaves have no thought of escape."

Turga reached for the amulet. "I could use one of those."

Sebara pulled it back. "Careful. If the amber cracks, the spell ends. I don't want to contend with a mob of angry slaves."

"No, you wouldn't. How does it work?"

"Simple. You point it in the direction of someone and say, 'Surrender to my bidding.'"

Turga shook his head and smiled.

Sebara said, "It's late. Why don't you make camp here and continue your search in the morning? You can join me for supper. I acquired a few casks of wine from Petala. I'll send some out to your men. They look like they could use some fun."

Turga grinned. "Thank you, Sebara." He turned to his men. "Make camp and feed the two slaves, then enjoy yourselves."

Sebara led Turga inside. A cask of wine was rolled out. Turga's men poured its contents into mugs. They soon erupted into boisterous laughter. A few fell to the ground and snored.

Efra skirted the buildings until he reached the house. He climbed through a window into a library. The only light came from an open door.

He heard voices and peeked into the hallway. It was illuminated by light from a room at one end.

The captain crept toward it.

Turga said, "Those Carandirians don't deserve such fine wine."

Sebara laughed.

A door swung opened, followed by a man with a platter of pastries.

Efra dropped to the floor.

The man walked to the lit room.

Efra crawled back to the library.

Sebara's voice came from the hall. "I can put you up for the night."

Turga said, "I'll sleep in the wagon. I want to start before dawn. Thank you for the wine. Good night."

A door opened and closed. He heard footsteps go up a set of stairs. The house fell silent.

Efra stepped into the hallway and felt his way away along the wall of the hall, away from the room at the end.

His hand touched the railing of a set of stairs. He climbed to a landing. Light filtered from around the edge of a door.

From the other side, Sebara said, "Post men along the edge of the property to look for the escaped slave. I might as well collect the reward as anyone else."

Tacher's voice said, "Yes, Master Sebara."

The door opened. Efra stared into the shocked face of the head guard. The captain slugged him across the jaw. Tacher fell back.

Sebara spun around with a look of surprise. The amber stone sat on the desk. He picked it up and said, "Surren…"

Before he could complete the spell, Efra jumped over Tacher and slammed his head into Sebara's abdomen. The master of the house exhaled as he was pushed back against the desk. The force of his body knocked papers and a letter opener onto the floor as his fist flew open. The stone shot across the room.

Efra dove for it.

Sebara pounced on him, reached out and seized the letter opener on the floor. He twisted and stabbed Efra in the hand.

The captain grunted and released his grip.

Sebara got to his feet and charged for the stone.

The Carandirian pushed himself up and leapt on Sebara's back. Both men fell to the floor within reach of the stone. They clawed with their hands to reach it.

Tacher got to his feet and stumbled toward the two men.

Efra's fingers touched the amber.

Sebara bit the captain's arm.

Pain radiated up to Efra's fingers. He slammed his fist into the side of Sebara's head.

Sebara opened his jaws and cried out.

The captain grabbed the stone. "Surrender to my bidding. Sleep."

Sebara's and Tacher's bodies fell limp to the floor. Efra stood and panted for a moment, then left the house through the front door.

 Six of Turga's men lay unconscious on the ground where they dropped in a drunken stupor. The other three sat, propped up against the wagon wheels with their eyes half closed and grins on their faces. The two slaves, both males, slept in one of in the cages.

Efra climbed the steps of the forward wagon and opened the door.

Turga snored in bed.

A floorboard creaked as the captain stepped inside.

The slave master sat up and looked at Efra. "You."

The captain held out the amber stone and spoke the incantation. Turga went slack jawed.

Efra stepped out and faced the drunken slavers. "Wake up."

The men stirred. When the three propped up against the wagon wheels saw Efra, they stood and advanced on him.

The captain held the stone out. "Surrender to my bidding."

All three stopped and stood still. The ones on the ground went limp.

The rest of Sebara's men charged out of the house.

Once more, Efra raised the stone and repeated the words of the spell. Everyone halted.

The slaves in the wagon grabbed the slats of the cage.

Efra unlocked it. "Wait here."

With the amber stone in hand, he went to the slave quarters. "Wake up. Come with me." The men and women filed out and followed him to the courtyard.

He instructed members of his crew to confiscate the weapons of the slavers and Sebara's guards. Swords, knives and crossbows were secreted within the enclosed wagons and under straw in the caged ones.

Other crew members went to Sebara's stables. They returned with nine horses and saddles.

Efra ordered them tied the steeds to the rear wagon.

At the captain's direction, some of the slaves mounted the wagon benches and took the reins of the draft horses. The rest boarded the wagons.

He took the reins of the lead wagon and guided the caravan out of the courtyard back along the road toward Au.

When the sun rose, he halted the column and ordered everyone to stand on the ground. He instructed Turga to sit, then bound his feet and hands with rope.

He put the stone on the ground and stomped on the amber with the heel of his sandal. It cracked into shards.

Everyone shook their heads and looked around.

Turga struggled against his bindings.

Cepata said, "Captain?"

"Yes, Commander. We're prisoners no more."

Chief Fooso scratched his head. "What happened, sir?"

Efra relayed the story of their escape. "Sebara and the rest of Turga's men will be free of the spell as well. Without horses, there's little chance they will catch up to us."

In addition to his crew, there were nineteen former slaves who also worked Sebara's fields.

Efra gave them the horses tied behind the caravan and one of the cage wagons. "Return to your homes. May the dragons protect you."

Turga said, "And will you kill me?"

Efra grinned. "No. I've a job for you."

The *Prosper's* crew mounted the wagons. Two donned slaver's clothes and climbed on top of the rear one with crossbows. The crew members assigned to drive the wagons also exchanged their sackcloths and sandals for clothes and boots.

Fooso took the reins of the lead wagon. Turga was placed next to him.

Efra hid inside the wagon at the front, so he could see through a peephole.

Cepata sat on the rear bench of the wagon with a knife against Turga's back while they traveled back to Au.

When they entered the city, the Karakien soldiers ignored them. Colonel Gaberda stepped out of his headquarters. "We don't have any more prisoners for you, Turga."

Fooso brought the wagon to a halt.

Cepata pressed her knife against Turga's back.

The slaver spread his hands wide. "Colonel. It's so good to see you again."

Gaberda said, "Have you come for some rest or perhaps entertainment? I have women from the town in a house for my troops to enjoy. I'm sure the soldiers wouldn't mind sharing."

Turga shook his head. "Actually, I'm off to the dock to meet someone from upriver who wants to buy this lot."

"I see. You work too hard."

"Who has time to sleep?"

The colonel laughed and walked back into the building.

The wagons climbed the low set of hills outside the city.

When they reached the crest, Fooso said, "Sir."

Efra opened the slat on the peephole. The harbor was filled with ships. Most were rowing galleys, alongside several large sailing ships with catapults. They totaled at least four hundred vessels.

He said, "Most of those are pirate ships. The Karakiens have amassed a fleet."

There were only three ships at the dock, the *Prosper*, a second galley and one small schooner, with two masts able to tack swiftly on the Great River.

Efra saw no one aboard the docked vessels..

Fooso guided the wagons to the custom house. Four soldiers armed with pikes guarded the building. A squad of twelve Karakien soldiers were on the pier. All wore mail coats and carried swords.

One of the Karakiens stepped up to the wagons. "Where are you going?"

Turga said, "I've come to meet someone." He leaned forward, away from the knife in Cepata's hand, then leapt from the wagon. "These are the Carandirian sailors from the galley."

The soldier thrust his pike into Fooso's side. One of the Carandirians on top of the rear wagon fired a crossbow bolt. It slammed into the pikeman. Another shot a bolt into Turga's back. The slaver dropped to the road.

Efra jumped from the lead wagon. "Carandir!"

A Karakien blew a horn. The rest of the squad ran toward the wagons.

Efra's crew retrieved the weapons hidden in the straw and charged into battle. The two Carandirian sailors on the end wagon continued to fire crossbow bolts into the enemy. Two Karakiens fell. The rest advanced.

The troops of both forces were trained and battle hardened. Though Efra's crew outnumbered them, the Karakiens wore mail shirts and helms.

Efra's sailors continued to fire crossbow bolts. One struck an enemy in the neck. Another bounced off a mail coat. Two more Carandirian's emerged from the front wagon with additional crossbows.

Efra parried a blow from a Karakien and riposted with a slice to the man's arm. The blow was deflected by chain mail.

The enemy soldier sliced at Efra's belly.

The captain stepped back before the blade bit.

The Karakien's arm went wide.

Efra stabbed his opponent's foot.

The man howled and tried to bring his sword around for a thrust.

Efra drove his sword into the man's abdomen, below the rings of the mail coat.

The Karakiens regrouped and charged as a unit in a phalanx formation. Spears pierced the flesh of five sailors. The spearmen opened up their line. Swordsmen ran between to engage Efra's crew.

Efra shouted above the din of battle. "Split asunder."

The sailors moved left and right to allow the swordsmen to come forward. The crew atop the wagon fired into the legs of the Karakiens in the lead who dropped. The soldiers behind them tripped on their bodies.

Efra said, "Close."

The sailors moved in and killed the fallen men.

Five Karakiens with polearms regrouped into a square.

The Carandirian sailors waited for orders.

Efra raised his sword to the enemy. "Surrender. You'll be bound and left. You have my word as a Carandirian Officer."

The men eyed each other, then dropped their weapons. Carandirians bound them and pushed the captives inside the customs house.

Efra scanned the ships at anchor. Some of the sailors on the nearest vessels pointed to shore. One lowered a longboat.

The *Prosper* appeared undamaged. Efra said, "Commander, take the galley back to Meth. Inform Narech Herrik of the Karakiens occupation of Au and their plans for invasion. I'll take five of the crew and commandeer the sailboat to reach Xinglan. You'll have to row like a demon's behind you. May the Dragon go with you."

He looked to his fallen crew members. "Gather our dead. I'll not leave them dishonored here."

Cepata led most of the crew at a run for the galley. The bodies of the fallen sailors were taken below. She said, "Cast off the lines. To the oars with all hands."

The *Prosper* set out into the harbor, near the shore where there were fewer enemy ships, all of them merchant galleys without catapults.

Other galleys and one of the large ships made for the *Prosper*. Cepata knew the sailing vessel carried catapults and hoped its captain wouldn't fire so near his own fleet.

The Commander prayed to Ilidel they were far enough into the current of the river for the westward flow to move them out of range.

The deep-water ship closed on the *Prosper*. A splash of water came from astern. Another projectile sailed in the sky and landed just shy of the galley.

Cepata ordered the drums that coordinated the rowers strokes to increase in tempo.

A shot from the enemy ship landed to the side of the galley and snapped off two oars. The *Prosper's* catapults, fore and aft, were tensioned. Chains were pulled from boiling oil and placed in metal buckets.

Cepata shouted, "Port oars back."

The port side rowers reversed their positions on the benches and pulled against the forward momentum of the galley. It slowed and shifted in the water to come around broadside to the pursuing vessel.

Cepata's voice cut sharply through the air. "Fire."

The chains loaded in the fore and aft catapult arched across the water. One caught the lower mainsail of the enemy ship and set it ablaze. The other landed on its fore catapult. Sailors climbed rigging to extinguish the flames.

Cepata turned the rudder to point the bow downstream. "Full oars."

The *Prosper* shot ahead of the other ship.

She glanced back to the harbor. Cold bile shot up her throat.

The masts of the ship Efra seized were ablaze at the dock.

She made the sign of the covenant. "Ilidel protect us."

CHAPTER THREE

Baron Dek ran into Narech Herrik's war room.

She, and seven officers, sat around a table.

Dek said, "The *Prosper* is back. The disaster pennant's raised."

Herrik stood. "We'll resume in three spans. Baron Dek, will you accompany me to the wharf?"

They rode with an escort of six soldiers from the high plain next to the palace to the docks of Meth.

Commander Cepata came down the gangplank of the *Prosper* and saluted. "Ma'am. Our mission to reach Xinglan failed. The Karakien army infiltrated the eastern side of the Great Swamp and now occupies Au. They intend to launch an attack on Rascalla and march south. A fleet of pirates and brigands is assembled in the port of Au ready to transport the Karakien troops."

Herrik said, "This is why they haven't advanced in the east. Where's Captain Efra?"

"He commandeered a small craft to run the blockade and reach Xinglan while their forces chased us. I saw his ship ablaze at the dock."

Herrik said, "Commander Cepata, take command of this vessel."

Cepata saluted. "Aye, ma'am."

Dek paced the floor of the war room. "Whatever troops and ships held in reserve to assault Fellant must be sent to defend Rascalla."

Herrik stared at a chart of the Great River. "We can't stop them at the port. Our only hope is to engage the enemy on water and hope Marawee was able to convince Hura to send troops. Captain Cepata, How many ships have the

Karakiens amassed at the port of Au?"

"At least four-hundred, ma'am."

Herrik looked back down at the chart. "We can't assemble enough ships to match their numbers." She tapped the table. "We'll convene tomorrow at dawn. I need to speak with our naval engineers."

The constant reports Batu read each day as Chief Minister to the Crown never seemed to end. He now took over Dek's duties to advise Lek and assist her in court. Before he left for the North Continent, he only thought of the young woman as Mirjel's maid. As he worked with her, he found her both competent and forceful as she performed the duties of queen.

A knock came to the door of his office.

He said, "Come in."

Telasec entered. "Greetings, first minister."

Batu lowered the paper he was reading. "Greetings, Mistress Telasec."

"First Minister, there's a change in Shara you must see."

He looked back to the paper. "Let her rot."

"Minister, the king himself commanded you to see to her safety."

"I brought her to you and gave ample warning of her treachery. Were I able, I would've killed her and left her body in that desert. You tend to her and let me think of important matters."

Telasec stood tall. "This is an important matter. Master Orane awaits us in the halls of the Daro. Come."

Batu felt a shiver in the warm room. He rose and followed Telasec.

Unlike the halls of the Kyar, which were located in the deep vaults beneath the palace, the halls of the Daro occupied rooms and corridors above ground in the structure between the north and south towers. Large windows brought a light and airy sense to the space.

The chief Kyar stood next to Shara in her room, whose window overlooked Lake Hasp.

The former Dharam princess sat cross-legged on the floor as she drew a picture. Many other drawings adorned the walls, mostly of flowers.

Orane motioned Batu forward.

The first minister examined the image Shara drew. He recognized the likeness of Ryckair and Mirjel. They seemed to have aged many years.

There was another person, a young woman who he couldn't place.

Telasec spoke in a whisper. "Until today, the pictures were of flowers and sometimes trees. These appeared this morning."

Shara looked up and smiled. "She's coming."

Batu knelt down. "Who's coming?"

Shara ignored the question.

He said, "Do you know who I am?"

She raised her gaze and held Batu's eyes for a moment with a blank expression on her face, then resumed drawing a house near a forest with Mirjel, Ryckair and the young woman in front of it.

Batu stood. "Is this a portent, Mistress Telasec?"

"I don't know. Master Orane and I try to question Shara. All she says is she likes the pretty pictures she draws. We can't detect any spells. Still, there's an odd sensation when I'm around her. I'm not certain she's aware of what she's doing or why."

The sight if Shara reduced to an innocent child drained a little of Batu's hatred. "Some sorcery of Petstra may still be at work. He may try to use her. There's no way to know where he and Ackella escaped to. I'll have a guard posted in the room."

Telasec shook her head. "First minister, you know well such is not permitted. The realm and authority of the Daro and Kyar come from the dragons. In this, even the Crown is forbidden to interfere."

Batu said, "Can't you see the threat?"

Orane said, "We feel magic here. Force of arms will have no effect on it. We will watch diligently."

Shara continued to draw with no notice of the conversation.

Batu said. "Have you spoken of this to Baron Dek or Narech Herrik?"

Telasec said, "Not yet. These pictures only appeared a span ago."

Batu studied the images. "I must report this to them at once."

Herrik sat at the table in the war room. "The enemy advances in the west as the Karakiens hold their positions in preparation to strike from Au. We've heard no news from Ambassador Marawee about help from Hura and Captain Efra's mission has failed."

One-hundred-ninety-eight vessels were anchored in Lake Hasp. Less than half were naval ships. The rest were commandeered merchant galleys.

A lieutenant spoke in an unsteady voice "Do we surrender, Narech?"

"No. When Baron Dek and I challenged the forces of the Barasha there was little hope. Faith propelled us forward. We struck as we could and disrupted their supply lines. This slowed the enemy until Prince Ryckair returned to take the crown.

"The monarchs may have been delayed by some magical force in the wizard tower or they may be inside the tower in Barta surrounded by the enemy. In either case, we must delay the downfall of Carandir as long as possible and trust to their return."

Herrik looked out a window to Lake Hasp. "We can't allow the enemy fleet to land on Carandir soil. Their generals now know we're aware of their intentions. They hold back because they don't know our troop strength."

The narech turned back to her officers. "One fast boat will move far north on the Great River and sail east to Xinglan to plead for help. The navy will install catapults on the merchant galleys. I've ordered naval engineers to outfit several of our deep water warships with the few trebuchets we have. The fleet will assault the Karakiens from beyond the range of their catapults and sink as many of their ships as possible before they can return volleys. The rest of our forces will move in."

Baron Dek burst into the room. "Narech Herrik, I must speak to you alone."

Herrik said, "You can speak freely before these officers."

"Not this time."

Herrik rose. "We'll go to my office, baron. The rest of you wait here."

She led the baron down the hallway. When she secured the door to her office, she said, "What's so important my staff can't hear it?"

"Our possible salvation," said Dek. "Master Orane discovered an ancient scroll that describes how to imbue flasks of oil with spells to produce magical fire so intense it will catch on thick, wet timbers of a ship and move up its hull to engulf it in flames. The inferno's impossible ro extinguish until a vessel burns to the waterline. Three dozen Kyar have volunteered to ride in rowboats and cast the spell."

Herrik sat down at her desk. "Has this been tested?"

"A derelict hulk was towed into the center of Lake Hasp out of sight of land and ignited. Only charred timbers floated on the water less than half a span later."

"Why didn't you tell the staff?"

"This secret can't go no further than the Kyar and us. Even the sailors who row the boats can't be allowed to know what the flasks contain until they're lit. Any leak to the enemy will destroy our chances at surprise."

The Carandirian fleet sailed up the Great River with twenty-thousand armed troops. A swift, one masted boat popular in races left with the war ships. When they reached far north of land, it continued on to Xinglan to complete Captain Efra's mission. It would take weeks for the small craft to arrive and just as long for Xinglan to respond. The rest of the fleet moved south toward Au and waited for the next moonless night.

The Carandirian fleet halted at the edge of the horizon. They could just perceive the outline of hills against stars. No light shone from the enemy fleet.

Dek climbed down a net hung over the edge of the flag ship and eased onto the rear of the lead rowboat. Four other sailors and a Kyar scholar followed. Twelve flasks filled with the magic oil sat in a basket at the bow.

The rowers were crammed shoulder to shoulder.

Dek took in breaths and let them out with a slight whoosh to keep the rowers synchronized.

Each dip of the oars was silent against the water.

As they approached, the bulk of the enemy ships could be made out by starlight. The Carandirian boats weaved into the center of the Karakien fleet. Men laughed and talk about how many Carandirians they would slice up.

The baron directed the boat to come up at the stern of one of the deep-water ships.

The Kyar scholar in the bow reached out and pressed a flask against the wooden hull. The magic in the oil kept it in place. He spoke the words of a spell in a whisper.

Dek signaled to pull the boat back and proceed to a galley.

The rest of the Carandir boats made their ways among the fleet and placed more flasks

Dek's boat approached the farthest vessel from shore, a galley with twenty oars.

An enemy sailor looked out over the water.

Dek signaled the rowers to stop.

The man on the galley swiveled his head left and right. "Hey, what's that?"

Another man said, "What do you see?"

"I'm not certain. Shine a lantern out there."

"You know the captain's orders."

"Then notify the captain. I think I see movement."

Dek sat still. They were at the edge of the harbor. The current of the river moved them downstream at a slow pace.

A third voice said, "What is it."

"There may be a boat on the river, sir."

"It's probably a log."

"It moved against the current."

The captain said, "I don't see anything."

"It's gone now."

The sailor behind Dek lost the grip on an oar. It fell in the water with a muffled splash.

"There, captain, did you hear it."

The captain said, "Unshutter a lantern. Shine it out there."

A faint light bathed the surface of the water. Dek's boat was taken farther downstream by the current. The light illuminated the place where it was an instant before.

A voice from another ship shouted. "Ahoy, douse that light."

The captain of the galley said, "My mate caught sight of an object in the water."

"Well, shutter that light and use your ears."

The lantern swung toward the bow of the galley before it was shuttered.

The mate said, "There, captain, a small boat off to port."

The captain said, "Archers, fire into that area."

Dek said, "Row."

The Carandir sailors pulled on the oars. Arrows hit the water all around them. One struck the Kyar. He slumped forward. Another slammed into the leg of the rower next to Dek. The woman continued to pull on the oar.

A focused beacon was lit in the crow's nest of the galley. More ships in the Karakien fleet shone lanterns into the waters around them. Light caught other Carandir boats. Volleys of arrows streaked through the air.

A flash erupted from the hull of the ship Dek's boat first approached. It was followed by flash after flash across the enemy fleet. Fire spread up the sides of hulls. Sailors screamed. Some dived into the harbor.

Streaks of light arched across the sky and descended on the Karakiens as the Carandirians fired rocks and heated chains from the trebuchets. The enemy vessels floundered as boulders slammed into them and heated chains ignited sails.

Enemy ships moved out from the harbor and fired their own catapults.

Hot chains caught in the rigging of two Carandirian vessels. Their sales caught fire. A boulder rammed into the hull of a Carandirian galley. It listed to starboard.

More Karakien ships and galleys moved out into the river. Shot after shot was exchanged between the fleets. The trebuchets with their superior range hurled heavier projectiles. Many enemy ships were sunk or disabled. The ships set ablaze by the Kyar's oil were piles of burnt timbers on the water.

The fleets met and battle turned to hand-to-hand combat as troops on both sides boarded each other's vessels.

Dek watched the exchange in the rowboat. "Pull. We must reach our ships."

The Karakien water forces were drawn from pirates and brigands who fought in a haphazard fashion. Most of the Karakien regulars had not yet boarded.

The Carandirians were a cohesive unit. They cut their way through the thieves, though the few Karakien soldiers they encountered were formidable foes.

Dek's boat reached the command ship. Nets still hung down where crews had descended to the small boats.

He climbed on board and drew his sword.

A pirate advanced. The two men dueled as others around them engaged in mortal combat.

The pirate slashed a gash across Dek's cheek.

The baron gave ground.

His opponent pressed forward.

Dek felt winded. The decades took their toll on him and he cursed silently as he found his stamina no longer met his performance when he faced the Barasha. He was pressed back to a set of steps.

The pirate was young. He leered as he raised his arm to deliver a killing blow.

Dek pushed off of a lower tread and rammed his shoulder into the pirate's stomach.

The man gasped and doubled over.

Dek jammed the sword into the man's chest.

The Carandirians pressed the enemy back to their own ships and followed them across the gap between vessels. Enemy soldiers dropped their arms and surrendered. As the sun rose, the Karakien ships were sunk or taken. Twenty Carandir galleys and two war ships also lay at the bottom of the river. No assault would come to Rascalla.

Several hundred masts appeared on the horizon upriver.

The captain of the flag ship said, "Prepare for battle. Reinforcements have come to the enemy,"

Carandir soldiers returned to their trebuchets and catapults. Fire was rekindled beneath cauldrons of oil.

The new arrivals closed quickly. One ship unfurled a banner. It was a field of red with the image of a golden dragon, the crest of the royal house of Xinglan.

It pulled up to the Carandir flagship. Dek saw Queen Quanto at the bow. Her monolided eyes reflected majesty.

Next to her stood Captain Efra.

A gangplank was placed between the two vessels. Dek boarded the queen's ship and fell to one knee. "Majesty, we feared our plea for help failed to reach you."

Quanto said, "Rise, good baron. Captain Efra brought us word of your need and of Karaken's invasion of Au. This fleet is three-hundred strong with a compliment of forty-thousand soldiers."

Dek raised an eyebrow toward Efra. "It was reported the boat you intended to take to Xinglan was set ablaze."

"It was, Baron Dek. A squad of Karakien soldiers reached the docks before we could set out. Archers killed three of my crew. I set the sails alight and we dove into the harbor. When the Karakiens boarded the sailboat they thought we were all dead. My crew and I managed to reach the other galley at dock. We crawled on board and found slaves chained to benches below. I identified myself and promised them freedom if they would help me reach Xinglan. When night fell, we cast off."

The queen said, "How fare my cousins, the Monarchs of Carandir?"

Dek frowned. "May I speak with her majesty alone on matters of state?"

Behind closed doors, Dek told Quanto about the ruse of Lek's impersonation of Mirjel and the disappearance of the monarchs.

Quanto said, "Our forces will be broken into three parts. General Telarha-Tey will remain here and remove the Karakiens from Au, then push south to their own kingdom and move north to meet your forces in a pincer movement. Another part will land in Rascalla and reinforce your troops in the east. The rest will land in Meth and add to the push into Barta."

Dek said, "I remember Telarha-Tey well from the war with the Barasha. He was a major then. It'll be good to see him again."

When the combined fleet reached Rascalla, Dek disembarked and took command of twelve thousand Xinglan troops before the ships sailed on to Lake Hasp.

Penta greeted them as they approached. His eyes widened at the sight of the army. "Baron Dek, what has happened?"

"Big things, my faithful steward. Is the baroness here?"

"She's at the front lines along the Kar River, sire."

Dek wrote out a note. "Send a fast rider with this to Baroness Jea. The Xinglaners will march with me at once."

After weeks of travel, Dek arrived a span's walk from the advance post out of sight of the front lines.

Jea ran out and embraced him.

They stood in silence with arms entwined.

Colonel Amar stared at the Xinglan soldiers, then saluted almost as an afterthought. "My Lord, I couldn't believe your note."

Jea said, "Karaken hasn't moved. It's as if they wait for reinforcements."

Dek laughed. "Yes, reinforcements that'll never come. Colonel, take charge of the Xinglan troops and place them along the front."

Jea said, "Let's walk together my love.."

They moved away from the others.

She said, "There's still no word from Quib."
Dek said, "She might still be gathering information."
"It's over a month since she left."
"She's very resourceful."

Xinglaners were dispersed along the banks of the River Kar. Some marched over the iron mountains to the front line of Respa. They hid themselves in ditches, behind brush and just over the crest of hills. After sunset, advance troops made their way into enemy territory.

The sun crested the horizon. Carandir and Xinglan soldiers sprang on the Karakien army. Enemy soldiers ran from tents as they pulled on pants. They were cut down by swords, poleaxes and tridents.

Dek led a charge of cavalry across the front lines. They carried heavy battle sabers and struck down all they encountered. Karakien solders dropped their weapons and ran only to be cut down by Carandirian riders.

A squad of enemy troops formed a square with swords and lances pointed out. Three Carandirian horses were impaled as they galloped forward. The square opened to allow Karakien swordsmen to exit long enough to hack the riders to death before they retreated back inside.

Carandirian archers let loose shafts. They sailed into the lancers.

Many fell. The square regrouped.

Dek called a halt. "Soldiers of Karaken, there's no escape. Drop your weapons and surrender. You'll not be killed."

Some lancers and swordsmen wavered.

One man dropped his lance and walked toward the Carandirians.

An officer thrust a sword into his backs. "Hold the formation."

Dek raised his arm and brought it down in a sharp cut. A rain of arrows fell inside the square. The officer and several others were struck. Karakiens dropped lances. Some went to their knees with their hands in the air. Others ran between trees.

Dek said, "Lieutenant, round up the prisoners. Captain, pursue the escapees. Take them alive if possible."

The Xinglan troops who infiltrated enemy lines earlier struck deep into their territory. The surprise attacks spread panic and left scores of Karakiens dead with few Carandirian or Xinglaners casualties.

Carandir troops swept into Mentaro and moved past Baroness Quib's stronghold as the invaders retreated to the border.

A demilitarized zone formed with the armies on either side.

The Carandir and Xinglan fleets entered Lake Hasp at sunset. The royal flags of both nations flew on the ships. Narech Herrik and her senior staff met the flagships at the military docks in Meth. With them stood Lek in the guise of Mirjel. She wore the duplicate crown.

All except Lek bowed as Queen Quanto stepped on Carandir soil.

Lek said, "Welcome, cousin. Your gracious aid brings us joy. Will you accompany us to the palace?"

"It is my honor."

Once secure in the carriage, Quanto took Lek's hand. "Baron Dek told me who you truly are. Hold strong. The wizard tower in Barta will be freed. I swear this by the dragons."

Lek took in a sharp breath.

Queen Quanto said, "You are very brave, Lek. The will of the people is strong because of you."

Lek felt herself shake. "I wish only to serve in the name of the dragons."

"You have and must continue to do so. We share a bond. Few understand the burden of royalty. Each of us gives our lives to the people. You were not born a royal yet you have executed royal duties."

Lek kissed Quanto's hand. "Thank you, Majesty. Baron Dek has been a great support. He truly is noble, yet has not taken on the mantle I bear. There has been no one to speak of it to."

"How do you feel?"

"Scared, yet relieved by this conversation."

Quanto squeezed Lek's hand. "Good. It will take the will of all to succeed. The rebellion is not the greatest threat if Baras rises and the crown is still lost."

Lek said, "I look to the east sometimes and think of Baras. I fear I will wither from the threat yet I carry on."

The carriage arrived at the palace. Lek accompanied Queen Quanto to the audience hall. Stars were visible through the crystal ceiling. She guided Quanto to a throne and sat on the other.

The loyal nobles occupied the boxes set aside for them. The boxes of the rebels were occupied by Narech Herrik, her senor staff, Master Orane, Mistress Telasec and the ministers of the realm.

Lek rose. "We have gathered together to hear reports of the war and contemplate the Crown's next actions. We welcome our cousin, Queen Quanto. Her royal personage brings aid in arms from Xinglan. Let us all give homage."

The assembled rose and bowed low.

Queen Quanto said, "Please, take your seats. We are delighted with your reception."

Lek said, "We open debate as to the best course of action. Narech Herrik, let us hear a report of the war.”

Herrik rose, “Majesties, the treasonous nobles occupy all of Eel, Fellant, Petala, Lusar, Shenan, Ulata and Tessa as well as the eastern portions of Lena, Barta and the southeastern tip of Nemtanka. My officers and I feel we should push the forces of Baroness Luja and Baron Womb out of Nemtanka and Barta as the front lines in Lena and Tesar hold. A major offensive through either Nemtanka or Barta could allow the attackers to push to Lake Hasp and up to the palace.” She made no mention of the need to clear Luja’s troops from around the wizard tower.

The situation and solutions were debated. Some wanted to take the fresh troops and invade Tessa and Fellant from the river to push at the backs of Womb and Gilyon. Others argued the Xinglaners should join in the war with Karaken and eliminate that threat so that all the troops could be released to counter the western houses who rebelled.

The debate ended. Lek and Quanto leaned into each and spoke.

Lek said, “Our royal personages have chosen two courses of action. The main host will push through Barta , Nemtanka and Ulata to assault Baroness Luja’s forces in Shenan. Another force will sail to Fellant to attack Barons Womb and Gilyon from the north.”

Dek stood behind an embankment and surveyed the killing zone between him and the Karakien army. Skirmishes by both sides moved the front lines.

To the south, dust rose as an army moved toward the enemy’s forces.

The Karakiens cheered and shook spears at the Carandirian’s.

The cheers turned to screams as General Telarha-Tey led his Xinglan forces into the rear of the Karakiens.

Dek ordered a charge. The Karakien army fought ahead and behind. Their numbers declined as men and horses fell.

A white flag was raised as Karakien soldiers walked forward with their hands above their heads.

Dek raised a standard to halt his own attack.

The Karakien soldiers were disarmed and herded into small groups.

Dek bowed to the Xinglan general. “Well met, old friend.”

Telarha-Tey bowed in return. There was a glint in the epicanthal folds of his eyes. “Well met, indeed. The Karakiens are cleared from the eastern side of the swamp.”

“There are no thanks we can offer that would great enough.”

Telarha-Tey clasped Dek on the shoulder. “I’m honored to fight beside you again.” He pointed to the border. “What now?”

"The battle is won. The war remains. Will you march south and take their capital to end all war between Carandir and Karaken while I return to the west with the Carandirian army to engage the traitors?"

Telarha-Tey bowed again. "I'm honored to do so."

Dek and a small company of his own militia walked north. They entered a clearing and found Quib's body on the ground.

Her face held a look of peace.

Though she had lain for weeks, her features showed no sign of corruption.

The baron knelt and took her hand. "Oh, Quib."

A junior Daro entered Telasec's chambers. "Mistress. Shara has made new picture with a strange device."

"What device?"

"One with an image of a dragon."

She followed the young Daro to Shara's room. The former princess sat on the floor surrounded by pictures. Telasec picked one up. It was the same face of the strange woman Shara drew before. Now, the woman wore a pendant that looked like the dragon crest from the crown.

Shara raised her head and smiled. "She's here."

CHAPTER FOUR

When Enada woke in the wizard tower, there were cakes and a mug of hot liquid on a table next to her. She'd never tasted kan before and was not certain if she liked the slightly spicy drink at first. After a few sips, she felt invigorated by the beverage. It was a perfect companion to the cakes, which were moist and flavorful.

A door led to a balcony. Outside, she saw the slender bridges Ryckair described that connected this central hub tower with the others. A set of stairs led to the flat roof of the tower.

When she climbed, a panorama unfolded before her; the entire landscape of Carandir in a great sweep. At the same time, she perceived minute details of the scene.

What she saw shocked her. There was no violence in the world she was born into. Though there were disagreements between people, they were always resolved. No one physically hurt another on purpose. War and crime were unknown.

A sick disgust filled her at the sight of armies engaged in bloody battles, people driven from their homes and the bodies of the dead in fields and streets. Her mother and grandfather spoke of such. The reality slammed her senses.

She stared at it with her mouth agape. It was incomprehensible, though she knew it was real. The cries of soldiers and citizens assaulted her ears. Animals and humans were slaughtered while she watched.

She recognized this as the evil of Baras spread by those he corrupted and wondered how he'd fallen. The Magadel she knew was kind and gentle. How could Baras, or any other being, willfully cause anyone to suffer so?

Even if he were banished to sleep for eternity, could the damage he wrought be repaired?

The other wizard towers seemed to be only steps from each other across arched bridges, yet she knew they were separated on the ground by vast distances. Which one led to Carandir?

She walked down to the balcony. The tower in Barta was square. There were three square towers. One seemed farther south than the others. That would be in Hura. She pulled the hood over her head, chose the tower that seemed the most likely to bring her to Carandir and crossed.

There was a room at the top of the other tower with no platform above it. Books were neatly stacked on shelves. Tables and chairs sat in groups. Behind a door was a set of stairs.

Unlike the round tower, the stairs led to other levels instead of in a vertical corridor. Some of these consisted of a single space. Others were divided into rooms. There were no windows until she reached the fifth level down, through which she beheld a forest buffeted by a storm. The floor below had a window that showed a night sky filled with stars.

She reached a level with no downward staircase, only a single door. It opened with a push to reveal a sky with clouds. It was near sunset. Woods extended to the left. There were tall peaks beyond dusted with snow. To the right were tilled fields. Though the sun shone, the air was chilled.

There were no people to be seen. The furrows in the fields held bare stubble. She guessed it was autumn. There were no buildings. A dirt road led away.

Ryckair said the Barta tower was in a forest. He never spoke of fields. She wondered if farmers cut the trees down.

She fastened the cloak around her neck to ward off the cold and walked down the road. The fabric covered the pendant.

Dusk approached. A house next to a field had lights on inside. She peered into a window, A man sat by a hearth where a fire blazed.

A voice from behind said, "Hey, who are you?"

Enada spun around.

A woman with pale skin held a hoe in both hands. "Geshra, come out here."

The man appeared at the door. "What is it, Megle?"

"A sneak."

He stepped outside and scowled at Enada. "What do you want?"

Enada said, "I'm sorry. I didn't mean to intrude."

Megle said, "You speak strangely." She stepped closer. "Why's your skin tinted? Where do you come from?"

"A long way away. I need to get to the palace."

"Palace?"

"Where the monarchs live."

Geshra said, "Is this some kind of joke?"

"No. I need to get to the palace. It's very important. Are you still loyal to the Crown?"

"If this isn't a joke, you're demented. Megle, don't let her escape. I'll get some rope to take her to the elder."

Geshra tied Enada's hands behind her back.

Enada was led down a road to a brick building with two stories. Geshra knocked on the door.

A boy answered. "Yes?"

"We want to see your grandfather."

Inside, an old man sat in a chair next to a fire. His face was creased with age.

He said, "What do you want so late?"

"We found this woman snooping on our farm. Her speech is strange. She asked directions to a place that doesn't exist."

The man got to his feet and inspected Enada. "Why have you tinted your skin brown?"

"It's the way I was born. My first mother came from the high desert."

"First mother? Desert?" He turned to Geshra. "What does she mean? Has she been talking nonsense like this?"

Megle said, "From the start."

The man gave a snort. "I'll lock her in the cellar for the night and send a runner for a watcher."

Enada said, "Please. I mean no harm. I need to get to the palace. I don't know the way. Are you in league with Baroness Luja or Baron Womb?"

Megle said, "You see? Strange words and non-existent people."

The old man raised his hand in reassurance. "Don't worry. The watchers will know what to do. I'll make certain she doesn't escape. It's late. Go home. I'll be taken care it."

Megle and Geshra left.

Enada was placed in a cellar.

The man removed the ropes from her hands. "You can't get out, so don't try. The watchers will know how to deal with you."

She slept fitfully as she wondered if the area around the tower was held by one of the traitorous baronies. Would the old man call their militia?

When she woke, the door opened. The boy brought a basket and a cup to her.

She looked at the object in the basket. "What's that?"

The boy squinted one eye. "Haven't you ever seen an egg before?"

"No. What's it for?"

"You eat it. It's boiled."

She picked up the egg, inspected it and started to put it in her mouth.

The boy grabbed it. "Not like that." He cracked the shell and handed the egg back. "Don't you know anything?"

She bit into it. The consistency reminded her of soft melon. The taste was strange though not unpleasant. She took a sip of water from the cup. "Thank you. I'm very confused."

"My grandfather says you're insane, the way you speak and the strange names you use."

"Do you think I'm insane?"

He gave a wide grin. "I know you're just foolin'. I pull some jokes too. Tinting your skin was a good idea. Just be careful. You know how the watchers hate pranks. You better tell the truth pretty fast." He took the cup and basket and left.

The next dawn, the old man came down the stairs. "Four watchers are here. My grandson thinks this is an elaborate joke. If so, you better admit it now. Once you leave this house, it'll get rough for you."

"It's no joke. I really have to get to the palace."

The old man gave a sigh. "Very well. Follow me."

The four watchers carried swords.

Enada's hands were bound in front of her. She was led to a wagon with a box on it and put inside.

Two of the watchers sat in the box with her.

The wagon gave a jerk and moved off to the west.

The watchers wouldn't answer questions or even respond. There was a barred window at the rear, through which she watched the terrain roll past.

The sun was overhead when a city appeared through the rear window. There were tall buildings made of stone. The wagon stopped.

Different armed guards took her inside a buildings and confined her in a room. There was no window. Bread, a boiled egg and water were brought. None of this sounded like what her mother and grandfather described.

It was cool in the room. She fastened the robe tighter around her neck.

The door opened. An armed guard entered followed by Marawee.

Enada was struck by the difference in the skin color of the two men.

The guard said, "Is this one of your crew members?"

Marawee shook his head. "I've never seen her. Where did she come from?"

"Farmers found her. She speaks in a strange manner."

Marawee said, "She's frightened. Let us speak with her alone. I'll see if I can find out who she is."

"Very well. I'll be just outside. Shout if you need me." The guard locked the door behind him.

Marawee approached Enada. "I know you're scared."

Enada said, "I'm not scared, just confused. This is all new to me. I need to get to the palace."

Marawee narrowed his gaze. "What palace?"

"The Carandirian palace. Are you in rebellion against it? Is this Barta?"

The man said, "Who are you?"

"Enada Avar. I've come to stop the war. Are you aligned with Baroness Luja? Who are you and what's your name? Where am I?"

"I'm Marawee Bedquanga. You are not in Carandir. This is the land of the Laran."

Ryckair once mentioned the name in a lesson. He never elaborated. "Please, help me get to the palace."

"Where did you come from?"

"Another place. I got here through a wizard tower." It became warm. She undid the neck of her robes to reveal the dragon pendant.

The awe Marawee once felt at the sight of the crest on the crown two decades before enveloped him with a sense of hope and lightness. "Where did you get this?"

"Jorondel and Ilidel gave it to me. It was a crest on a crown. My mother and grandfather brought it from this world."

"What are their names?"

"Queen Mirjel and King Ryckair."

Marawee fell to one knee and made the sign of the covenant. "Highness."

Enada said, "Why do you call me that?"

"You're the royal heir to the throne, Princess Enada."

Ryckair and Mirjel told her many times she was the heir and would become queen one day. It seemed as if they spoke of someone else. Marawee's reaction sent a shock through her. "Can't you just call me Enada?"

"It would be disrespectful to the Crown, Highness. It's my duty to address you as the royal you are."

With the word duty, she understood what her mother felt when she left Rascalla for the palace. "Please, at least stand."

Marawee got to his feet. "Where are the monarchs now? They're desperately needed. Carandir is under attack from within. An evil dragon could rise at any time."

"Yes, I was told this as I grew up."

"Grew up?"

"It's a little hard to explain. My mother and grandfather fell through a window in a wizard tower and were transported to another world. That was less than two years ago in the time frame of this world. Two decades have passed in the other one, where I was born."

Enada told Marawee the story of her birth and her life with Ryckair and Mirjel. "Only one of us could come through the portal. They said I'm the heir and should go."

Marawee said, "The wizard tower in Barta is surrounded by rebels and many thought the monarchs were trapped inside. My mission to bring troops from Hura has failed. Now, the crown is lost."

"It crown didn't subdue Baras." She pointed to the pendant. "This is the crest from the crown. Jorondel compressed it to enhance its magic. Ilidel blew the breath of creation from the other world into it. The power is here. I've been trained to subdue Baras with this dragon pendant. I just need to get to Carandir."

Marawee put a hand over his eyes and lowered his head. "Our salvation is within reach, with no hope of deliverance. The Laran won't let us go. They fear discovery by any outsiders. I've pleaded before their council to allow me to continue to Hura and promised not to reveal their secret. They refuse to change their minds."

"From what you say, they'll recognize the dragon pendant. I just need to talk with them."

"That chance will come today. The council will summon you before the sun sets."

Enada was taken to a larger building. Wide steps led to a portico supported by four polished, granite columns. They gleamed in the sun.

Four armed watchers walked beside her.

The guards took her through double doors. She stood at the top of an amphitheater where fifty rises of stone benches focused on a semicircle platform, upon which stood a high bench. Thirteen people sat behind it.

A guard said, "The council awaits." The men remained at the door while she descended.

Meesta Romew sat behind the bench at its center in his black robes and brimless cap. Six women and men were seated to his right and left.

Romew rose. "You have entered the lands of the Laran unbidden. Who are you? Where do you come from?"

"I'm Enada Avar, heir to Carandir. I came from the wizard tower."

Romew said, "None can enter the tower."

"None other than a wizard, or one who possesses the dragon crest." She loosened the robe from her neck to reveal the pendant.

Romew said, "Why do you wear an imitation of the crest from the crown Avar subdued Baras with?"

"It's the true crest with the power to subdue Baras and quell the rebellion in Carandir. I must reach the palace."

She told the story of the other world.

A woman said, "Our ancestors saw the crown before we awarded the lands of Carandir to Avar. None could break it. Anyone could claim the title of Avar. Tell the truth. Where did you get this pendant?"

"Look into the dragon's eye before you deny its power."

Romew said, "I sense no power. It means nothing. We chose to live apart from others ages ago. None can know of our existence. We will not harm you, however you can never leave."

He called the guards. "Take her to the home of the other outsiders."

Enada was escorted to the house where the Carandirians lived.

Marawee and Umera waited on the porch.

He said, "Greetings, Your Royal Highness. We're honored by your presence. This is my wife, Umera."

Umera knelt, took Enada's hand and kissed it. "Welcome, Princess Enada."

Enada swallowed hard. "I'm just Enada."

Marawee said, "You're the royal heir, Highness. We're your subjects."

Enada said, as if to herself. "This feels strange."

Umera said, "Did the council listen to your plea?"

"They didn't believe me."

Marawee shook his head. "They've withdrawn from the world and believe themselves safe from all strife, including the rise of Baras. No argument will convince them."

"Are we prisoners, then?"

"In a fashion. We're not watched within the city, though we're escorted if we want to visit outside its limits. One in our party is allowed to travel to local vineyards and wineries. He gives the vintners advice."

Umera said, "The people are friendly. We're treated like guests. Food is brought to us with no requirement of payment. Come, let's have a meal together."

They walked through the common room into the dining area.

Enada was introduced to Captain Watoola.

Len and Fera brought roast meat, fruit, bread, green vegetables and wine.

Len said, "The wine's not up to the standards of Petala. I try to teach the Laran about soil and pruning and grafting. I've formed some close friendships."

Watoola said, "Tell your tale, Princess. Marawee has only relayed a portion."

Enada began with her mother and grandfather's arrival in the other world. She left out no detail about her friendship with Magadel and her sorrow for the death of Jarat.

Evening fell.

Umera lit a lamp.

Enada continued. "After I climbed the outside of the wizard tower, I fell asleep at the top. When I awoke, I tried to guess which bridge led to the tower in Barta. I found myself here."

Fera said, "I'd like to have a wema."

Enada smiled for the first time since her arrival in the land of the Laran. "She was very dear. It was hard when she died. I never thought about death until then. Magadel was there to comfort me."

Len shook his head. "Magadel, a comfort. It's hard to imagine, Highness."

Umera said, "It's late. There are several empty bedrooms."

"I'm not sleepy. I'll just sit up and think for a while."

"As you wish, Highness. You should acquaint yourself. We'll all be here for a long time."

Enada shook her head. "No. I have to go. Baras could wake at any time. People are dying. I can't stay here."

Watoola said, "There are watchers everywhere. They'll stop any who try to escape over the mountains."

Enada said, "We don't have to over any maintains. I arrived through the wizard tower. We can escape the same way. It took less than a day for the wagon to get here. We can surely walk there in a night."

At breakfast the next morning, Enada pointed to a map she drew of the route she took from the tower. "After we climb to the top, we'll go to the hub and take the bridge to the tower in Hura, where you can ask for troops. Then, I'll travel to the tower in Barta and find the palace."

Len glanced out a window. "The Laran don't bother me when I go to the vineyards, as long as the others are in the house. If we leave the city together, someone's certain take notice. The Laran have a phobia about being discovered. Anything out of the ordinary will be reported"

Enada said, "We can travel in two groups. Dugary, you, Len and Fera can leave first. Marawee, Umera and I will follow later."

Watoola said, "We'll have to skirt roads and head though forests. It'll slow us. We may not reach the tower till well after dawn. People will know we're not here. Watchers will be sent out. They have a fast network of riders to relay messages."

Len stood and looked out a window. "I'll stay and keep the lamps lit until late, then sit on the porch at sunrise. No one will ask questions."

Umera put a hand on his arm. "You'll be trapped here."

Len said, "My son and granddaughter are dead. I've nothing to return to. This is a comfortable place, as good as any to die in."

Marawee said "You don't need to do this, Len. We can conceal ourselves on the journey. The tower is in a different direction from where we came into the valley. Even if the watchers are notified, they'll have no idea which way we went."

"The main outposts will be alerted within spans. The roads will be blocked. The people in the country will turn us in. No. Someone must give the impression we're in the house."

Umera took Len's hand. "You must come. You do have something to return to. We're family. Keetala will miss you."

"I love her like a daughter. She's left with Yearol and it's not hard to guess where they went or what they intend to do. She may be dead already. If she's not, she needs her parents.

"The most important thing I can do for her and Carandir is to stay. Besides, I've many friends among the vintners." He gave a chuckle. "They need my help to improve their mediocre wine. I'll get to pass on my skill and experience. It'll be a full life. Don't worry about me. I won't be alone."

Enada folded the robes Magadel gave her and laid them on the bed. The faces of Mirjel and Ryckair came to mind while she dressed in pants, a blouse and a coat as the Laran wore. Sadness swept over her at the thought she would never see her mother or grandfather again.

A span after sunset, they said their good-byes with tears in their eyes.

Enada put her hand on Len's arm. "You're a very brave and good man, Len Gento. I wish all the blessings of the dragons for you."

He put his hand over hers. "Just finish what King Ryckair and Queen Mirjel sent you to do. Stop this awful war. Return Baras to eternal sleep. That's all I ask."

They stuffed food and water skins into pockets and under coats. Umera reasoned packs would look suspicious.

Watoola and Fera had left.

Enada, Marawee and Umera set off west at a leisurely pace through the city a half a span later. People walked into shops and talked on the streets. No one took notice of the three travelers.

At the edge of the city, they waited next to a building until there was no one about, then moved into a forest at a quick pace.

They stayed off of roads.

The forest ended.

They walked past fields and orchards. The moon was only a sliver.

It took much longer to make headway than Enada anticipated. They came to a road. It rose over hills and crossed a ford.

A deer bounded onto it in front of them, stared and ran into the forest.

A span before dawn, they paused at a clearing in the woods.

They settled on the ground as best they could and ate a cold breakfast.

Enada listened to sounds in the brush and wondered what kind of animals lived there.

She looked up at the stars as they faded in the glow of false dawn. Their arrangement in the sky was different from those in the place she was born into.

This world was familiar yet different. She was a true princess here. Everyone treated her as such, even though she didn't feel like one.

She wondered what it would be like to live in the palace. With her mother and grandfather gone, she'd become queen. It was an odd concept. No one in the village told anyone else what to do. She wasn't certain she wanted to control others' lives.

The days when she could wander over the land were at an end. There was a duty she promised to keep. Yet, she wished she could return home and be with the ones she loved.

They continued on a path in a forest as the sun rose.

A village appeared through trees. There were a two dozen houses. Plowed fields surrounded it.

A watcher's wagon stood on the road.

People gathered around it.

Marawee said, "They may only be on patrol or our escape may have been discovered."

Umera looked to the woods. "We should go around."

They moved off the path into the forest.

A few paces in they heard a voice. "Sir, boot prints go into the brush."

Another voice said, "The trail's fresh. Spread out. They can't be far,"

Marawee led Umera and Enada behind a boulder.

They stood in silence as they took shallow breaths.

There was a grass-filled meadow in front of them.

Enada touched Marawee's arm and pointed to trees across the open space.

A man said, "Check behind that boulder."

Enada was certain they couldn't possibly run across the field before they were spotted. She wanted to hide. There was no cover. Under her breath, she whispered, "I wish we were invisible."

She didn't see the eyes of the dragon glow.

An armed man and woman came around the boulder. They looked directly at Enada and the others.

The woman said, "Where did they go?"

The man scanned the forest ahead. "They must have headed for those trees."

"The tracks stop here."

"The grass is wet and springy. Their tracks are hidden."

The woman shouted. "Over here. They're just ahead."

Five watchers ran around the boulder and headed into the woods.

Enada's heart pounded. She looked to her side and could see neither Marawee nor Umera.

Like rising smoke, they faded into view next to her.

Umera said, "What happened?"

Enada said, "I don't know. They should have seen us."

Marawee looked at then pendant , "It's the power of the dragons."

Umera said, "Princess, you did this."

Enada shook her head. "I just wished that we could vanish."

Umera said, "You called upon the magic of the transformed crest, even though you didn't realize it."

Enada touched the pendant. "I've seen dragons change shape and bring objects into being. I never thought of it as magic. It's just how the world works. I know I have to cast a spell to subdue Baras. I never guessed I could do more."

Marawee said "You are Avar's heir, Highness. It's no mystery."

Umera looked to the woods ahead. "They'll return soon."

"Walk backwards to the path," said Marawee. "We don't want our trail to show we've turned around."

They tried to step in the same tracks they made to reach the boulder. When they reached the path, they moved into the woods on the other side to skirt the fields.

When they reached the wizard tower, Watoola and Fera were already there.

The young boy said, "I thought you got lost. We tried to get in. The door's just rock, like the walls.

"It only appears that way," said Enada. She spread her hands. The stone became a mist. "Follow me." They walked through the threshold.

As before, soft light filled the room from an unknown source. Enada realized she was hungry. In front of her, a table laden with bread, fruit and meat appeared.

She laughed. "Once more, the dragons provide what we need."

They ate until they were full. Enada led them upstairs. They reached the second floor and found five beds with covers and pillows.

Watoola shook her head. "It's as though we were expected."

"Not expected, provided for," said Marawee.

The princess realized how tired she was. She sat on one of the soft beds. "Let's get some rest before we go on."

She reclined and fell into a deep sleep.

Enada awoke before the others. A table now sat along the side of a wall with porridge, pastries and juice. There were also five mugs of hot kan.

Umera stretched and came to the table.

She picked up one of the mugs. "It must be a year since I've tasted kan."

With a sip, she sighed with satisfaction.

When the others stirred, they climbed the stairs. At the top, Enada took them across the bridge to the hub tower. From there, she led them to the farthest tower.

The company descended.

Enada pushed on a door.

They stepped into a tropical forest. The tower stood on a rise. Hura's capital city of Vabesoo, with buildings of wood and stone, stood a tespan's walk away. The ocean could be seen to the west.

A broad smile came to Umera's lips. "Hura."

Watoola took a deep breath. "Yes."

Fera said, "It's hot here."

Marawee laughed. "I'd forgotten how hot. It's certainly not the vineyards of Petala."

Enada said, "You must complete your mission and bring a Huran force to Carandir. I'll go to the tower in Barta."

Fera said, "I'll come with you, Princess. My father showed it to me on a map once. I'll guide you to the palace."

"That's very welcome, Fera." She embraced the others. "Farewell for now. We'll meet again in Carandir. Come, Fera."

The two of them entered the tower and crossed the bridge, first to the hub tower and then to the tower in Barta.

The room at the top was smaller than the others. There were no furnishings other than a table, on top of which was an irregularly shaped crystal on a silver stand.

She looked into it and felt utter emptiness as she had never known.

Fera said, "What is it?"

"I don't know."

Enada touched it with a finger.

Fera watched Enada's hand push through the crystal as though it were water. Her body turn to smoke and she was drawn into it.

He screamed. "Princess, where are you?"

CHAPTER FIVE

Marawee, Umera and Watoola entered Vabesoo. It was brightnail. Streets and shops were filled with people whose faces ran in various shades from deep black to light brown. Some had coarse hair and others hair as straight as Len's. People with light skin from Carandir and monolided eyes from Xinglan also mingled in the crowds.

Musicians played in a square. Multicolored flags of blue, brown, green and yellow flew in a warm breeze. Their bright colors shone against the sky.

They passed a tall structure with a tank on top. On four surfaces around its base were disks marked with the twenty spans of day and night. A pointer on top of each disk indicated the time as the disks rotated.

It was the first water clock, conceived of in Hura centuries before. The idea of the mechanism spread to other countries to become the standard for time keeping.

The old king died six years before. His son, Udalla, now sat on the throne. He fought beside Baron Dek in the war against the Barasha.

The three of them walked toward the royal palace located in the center of the city.

Unlike the royal palace in Carandir, there were no walls around it. An ornate fence enclosed grounds on the north, south and west sides. The east side of the building with an entrance to government offices fronted on a main boulevard.

A woman, past middle age with light ebony skin and short, kinky hair sprinkled with gray came up to them and squinted. "Dugary? Dugary Watoola?"

The captain said, "Hello, Jenar."

"What have you been up to? I haven't seen you since you joined the navy."

"I've come back to attend to some business."

"Mother of dragons, I can't remember how long it's been. The years have been good to you."

"Thank you. You look well too."

"You always were a flatterer. I've got a new fishing boat. You have to come down to the docks."

"I will when we're finished."

"Bring your friends along. I'm on the old wharf we used to fish from."

Jenar walked away with a spring in her step.

The company reached the palace and entered a foyer. It was cooler inside than in the streets, though the humidity was still just as heavy.

Soldiers stood at attention.

Umera took a seat near the door.

A clerk sat behind a desk.

Watoola and Marawee approached. He took out the credentials. "I'm Ambassador Marawee Bedquanga from the Monarchy of Carandir, I request an audience with His Highness, King Udalla, on a matter of urgent diplomatic business."

The clerk inspected Marawee and Watoola. "Neither of you are Carandirians."

"We fought in the war against the Barasha and were granted permission to stay in Carandir. This is Captain Watoola of the Royal Carandirian Navy."

Marawee handed the satchel to the clerk.

He inspected the papers. "I see. Take a seat over there." He indicated chairs on the other side of the room away from Umera.

The clerk motioned another man over and spoke to him, then handed over the satchel.

Marawee and Watoola sat for what seemed like several spans. The second man returned and spoke into the ear of the clerk, who listened for a moment.

He said, "Ambassador Bedquanga. Prime Minister Borsa will see you. Follow this man."

Marawee and Watoola were escorted down a hallway with portraits of previous kings on the walls. The man ushered the Carandirians into an anteroom. "Please be seated, ambassador."

Three tespans passed before a man in a bright red shift and yellow pants came through another door. "The prime minister will see you now, sir."

The Carandirians were escorted into a room with woven rugs of multiple colors worked into triangles, circles and rectangles.

A man with deep brown skin sat at a desk beneath a portrait of King Udalla.

He studied the diplomatic paper.

The adjutant said, "Prime Minister Borsa, his Excellency Marawee Bedquanga."

The prime minister continued to read without looking up. "You seem to be making a request."

Marawee said, "Hura answered the call of aid in friendship to defeat the Barasha. Carandir again requests aid to quell a rebellion in the west and invasion from the south."

Borsa leafed through the papers. "The Barasha threatened the Huran nation. This is a civil matter. Why should we become involved?"

"Prime Minister, Baras sleeps wounded in secret. He can recover to rise at any time. Only the crown of Carandir can contain him. An attack on Carandir is an attack on all nations."

The prime minister looked up at Marawee for the first time. "The two of you are Huran, are you not? Yet you remained in Carandir rather than muster with your military units?"

"With all due respect, that's of no concern to my mission."

"You take the comfort of a new land and think you can return to the place of your birth as deserters."

"The king approved our request to stay in Carandir. I represent the monarchs. It is they who ask for help."

Borsa drummed his fingers on his desk. "That Carandir would send two who turned their backs on Hura shows disrespect and contempt. This nation is not a puppet of Carandir, to be called upon to perform at their whim."

"Prime Minister Borsa, the petition was sent to the king. He will know both Captain Watoola and me."

"The king is busy with affairs of his own country. He has no time for errant messengers who betray their people. As you have repatriated yourselves, you will be put to use in the service of Hura." He rang a bell on his desk. Six Huran soldiers entered. "This man and woman have returned to Hura. Entertain them until a proper service can be found."

A soldier wrestled the signet ring from Marawee's finger.

Watoola said, "We've come to speak with King Udalla."

The prime minister made no reply while the soldiers pulled Marawee and Watoola out of his office.

Umera watched her husband and the captain as they were dragged across the foyer.

One of the soldiers stopped and spoke to the clerk.

Marawee and Watoola were pushed into the street.

Umera went to the clerk. "Where are those two being taken?"

"Don't concern yourself with deserters. The prime minister will make certain they stand trial."

Umera backed away. When the clerk leaned over to place a folder in a drawer, she ran out the door.

Marawee and Watoola were taken to a compound outside the city. After several spans, guards dragged them to a windowless courtroom.

A man in red robes sat behind the bench.

Another man sat at a desk. He rose. "Your honor, Marawee Bedquanga and Dugary Watoola stand accused of desertion."

The judge looked down from the bench. "What say the accused to these charges?"

Marawee stepped forward. "You honor, I'm an ambassador from the Monarchy of Carandir and due diplomatic immunity according to the laws of Hura and Carandir. I've been sent on a mission to speak with King Udalla. Captain Watoola is part of my mission and due immunity from prosecution as well."

The judge said, "Is there proof of your claimed status?"

"I brought credentials with the royal seal of Carandir, your honor. I wore a signet ring. It was taken from me."

"The prosecutor will produce these papers and this ring."

The man who stood by the desk said, "Your honor, I've seen no such papers or ring. The accused were found in the streets of the city. They were arrested by palace guards."

Marawee said, "We were not apprehended in the streets. I met with the prime minister. He ordered soldiers to seize us and kept my credentials, along with the signet ring."

The judge leaned forward. "The accused will speak when questioned. What evidence does the prosecution offer in this matter?"

"Your honor, I enter into evidence enlistment papers for Marawee Bedquanga, a soldier in the Huran army, and commission papers for Dugary Watoola as a junior officer in the Huran navy. I also enter into evidence official orders. They assign the pair to the campaign to fight the Barasha. Both persons deserted the army and navy and remained in Carandir. Neither have returned until today."

The judge said, "How do you answer these charges?"

Watoola said, "King Udalla granted Marawee and me leave to remain in Carandir after the war. With his approval, I resigned my commission in the Huran Navy and was granted a commission in the Navy of Carandir. We've returned to Hura on a mission that threatens both nations. The king knows us and will corroborate our story."

The prosecutor said, "No such records exist, your honor."

Marawee said, "Your honor, may I speak?"

"Permission granted."

"The prime minister received us with hostility and refused to inform the king of our presence."

The judge said, "Has the prime minister been contacted?"

"Yes, your honor. He denies any knowledge of the accused or any meeting between them."

A pit formed in Marawee's stomach. He couldn't fathom why the prime minister would lie. This would never have happened in the Hura he left.

The judge said, "Do the accused have anything further to say in their defense?"

Marawee spread his hands. "Your honor, the matter for which we set out is grave. Carandir faces attack from within and without. The dragon Baras can awaken at any time. If he does, Hura will face his wrath and suffer his vengeance, as will all nations."

The prosecutor said, "Your honor, this court has heard many stories from deserters. None as fanciful as this. Those who break the law will create any excuse to avoid its penalty. No evidence exists for these claims. The accused are deserters. Though two decades have passed since their crime, they must be convicted and sentenced to the harshest punishment possible as a deterrent to others."

The judge set back. "The charges are grievous. I will consider the evidence and arguments and defer judgment. Guards, take the prisoners away."

Umera walked away from the palace in disbelief. She could think of no one to help. Her family lived on a farm away from the city. Marawee's family was over mountains to the east. She'd only been in Vabesoo once when she and Keetala set sail to join Marawee in Carandir.

The one person whose name she knew was Watoola's friend, Jenar.

She walked toward the waterfront. A plump woman hawked sweet treats made with honey.

Umera said, "Excuse me, I've just come to the city. Where can I find the wharf?"

"Which one?"

"I didn't know there were two."

"There are three. Don't worry. They're close to each other."

"How can I tell which is the old wharf?"

"The old ones are wooden. The new one's stone."

"Thank you." She walked off to the waterfront at a quick pace.

Many ships and boats were moored. She moved down the first wooden wharf she came to. All the craft were fishing boats, some small and others large. Umera remembered Jenar's skin was a lighter brown than most of the people in the capital. Her ancestors must have come from South Hura away from the equator.

Umera went to the next wharf. It was even more crowded with boats, mostly small craft with single sails. She walked to the end with no sign of Watoola's friend.

When she walked back, she saw a woman on a boat whose skin was light ebony and said, "Jenar?"

The woman turned. Her expression changed from a frown to a smile. She waved. "Hello. Come aboard."

It was an open skiff with a sail set forward and a tiler at the stern.

Jenar indicated a bench. "Sit down. Did Dugary send you? I'm real keen to catch up on what she's been up to. She must have some tale."

Umera sat down. "Jenar, how good a friend is Dugary?"

She gave a short laugh. "We owned a boat together before she joined the navy. She sure looked happy on those big sailing ships."

"There's a problem."

Jenar's smile faded. "Is she in trouble? She always was a wild one. I remember one night when we went drinking and…"

"She's been taken somewhere by the palace guards."

"What did she do?"

"I don't know. No one will tell me." She looked left and right. "We came here on an important mission. After my husband saw the prime minister, he and Dugary were dragged from his office."

Jenar's mouth opened. "The prime minister? This is bad."

"We've been away a long time. Hura's changed. I feel it in the people."

The woman sighed. "Yes, things have changed. When the old king died and Prince Udalla came to the throne, it was good for a while. Then, the old prime minister died and a new one was appointed. We saw less and less of the king. New taxes were levied. The town militia grew and started to harass people.

"I stay pretty quiet by nature and never had a run in. Plenty of other people have, though. The talk is all over Hura. I'm surprised you haven't heard the stories."

"I've been in Carandir."

"Carandir? Why did you go there?"

She hesitated for a moment. "You can't tell anyone what I'm about to say. I don't know who else I can trust. Dugary greeted you like an old friend."

"I'm one of her oldest. I won't say a thing to anyone." She clasped her hands together and brought them to her forehead in the sign of the covenant with the dragons. "I swear in the name of Ilidel."

The story poured out of Umera from the call for volunteers to fight the Barasha to their vineyard in Petala and their expulsive by Womb. Her breath was ragged when she described Hebra's death on the road. The tears poured down her cheek when she told of Marshala's murder by Womb's militia.

She described the civil war, the invasion from Karaken and their mission to seek help from Hura.

Jenar searched around the boat and found a piece of rag.

She handed it to Umera. "I'm afraid it's not a fine handkerchief. I don't often stand on formality."

Umera dabbed her eyes and blew her nose.

Jenar shook her head. "Well, I expected no less from Dugary. She was always one for big things. That's why she left our partnership and joined the navy." She looked to the sky. "That woman's certainly in trouble now."

She made a fist with her right hand and pounded the palm of her left. "The problems started when the prime minister was appointed by the king. His Highness thought he was the perfect person to administer things for him. A lot of us saw he was ambitious.

"He has the king's ear and controls who can see him. King Udalla is a good man, however he trusts the prime minister without question. Another appeal is no use. He'll make up some charges and arrest you too"

She rubbed her cheek. "You say your husband carried credentials?"

"Yes. I imagine the prime minister destroyed them."

"I don't think so. He keeps things back he might be able to use. I'm sure he still has them."

Jenar thought for a moment. "I won't repeat your story, however I'll need some help. I know two people who skirt the law every once in a while. They'll remember Dugary and owe her a debt. A lot of people do. You can stay at my place while I make some discreet inquiries."

Jenar brought Umera to her home, located near the wharf. She prepared a fish stew with vegetables that was flavored with local spices.

Umera took a bite and closed her eyes. "This is so good. It's been twenty years since I tasted otary pepper."

Jenar spooned herself a helping of stew. "I apologize. It's rather simple fare."

"It's like a banquet. Carandirian food is a little bland. I was able to buy some Huran spices when I visited a market in Meth once. Food from Hura is limited and expensive. This tastes like home."

That evening, a man and woman gathered at Jenar's home.

She made certain the curtain over the window was secure. "I found out Dugary and Marawee were taken to the new prison. There's no way we can rescue them. The guards are too afraid of the prime minister to take bribes. We'll have to retrieve the confiscated credentials and get them to the king."

The light from a lamp shone off the dark brown face of a woman named Teafar. She was short and slender, yet her arms were muscular.

She said, "The documents are probably in one of two places, the royal archives or a closet in Prime Minister Borsa's office. Because they could be a threat to him, I think he secured them in the closet under his control."

Quaneran, a man whose dark black face was lined with age, said, "I'm certain of it. My nephew's a janitor in the palace. He cleans the ministerial offices and once told me the door of the closet is made of metal and secured with two locks."

Jenar lifted the edge of the curtain and peered outside. "Can he be trusted to get someone on the roof undetected?"

Quaneran said, "Yes. He's family and won't betray us, though we shouldn't tell him why we want to get in."

Teafar said, "The locks used by the government aren't easy to open. I was able to break into a royal chest someone stole. It took me nearly a span."

Quaneran said, "Palace guards enter the ministerial offices two times during the night on their rounds."

Jenar frowned. "That doesn't give us much time. Umera, can you drive a wagon?"

"I often took loads of grapes to wineries in Petala."

"Good. I think we can create a distraction. I'll have to gather some things. We'll strike tomorrow night."

Umera joined Jenar and Quaneran in a deserted side street near the palace, where a wagon pulled by two horses waited. She and Jenar were dressed in the uniforms of officers of the palace guard.

Quaneran leaned into Jenar. "My nephew let Teafar through a side gate. She'll be on the roof above the prime minister's office by now."

Jenar touched Umera's shoulder. "The last movement will be dangerous. You could slip and be killed."

"I'm ready. Where'd you get all this?"

Jenar raised an eyebrow with a smile. "They can be acquired by those who know where to look. Like I said, people owe Dugary favors. Are you ready, Quaneran?"

"Yes."

"Very well. Let's go."

Quaneran walked down the road in front of the palace.

Umera and Jenar mounted the wagon. They waited for a tespan before Umera snapped the reins. "Yah!"

The wagon took off.

Quaneran reached the wide steps to the entrance.

Umera drove the horses left and right, then aimed them at the steps.

Dugary threw a lit lamp without a chimney into the wagon bed loaded with barrels of oil. The bed roared into a bright fire that spread to all the barrels.

Umera pulled a rope attached to a lynch pin. The link between the horses' livery and the wagon snapped apart. She and Jenar jumped on the backs of the horses as the animals pulled forward.

The flaming wagon slammed into the palace wall in an inferno.

Quaneran pounded on the doors. "Fire. Fire. The palace is on fire."

Guards ran into the street.

One of them yelled back inside, "There's a fire. Alert all the guards. Bring sand and water."

Umera and Jenar pulled their horses to a halt and ran back to the palace to mingle with the guards. They moved inside and down a corridor to the office of the prime minister. Jenar tapped four times, waited three heartbeats, then tapped twice again.

The door opened.

Teafar said, "I've one lock open. I'm on the second."

Jenar secured the door. She and Umera stood next to it.

Teafar returned to the cabinet.

Umera heard footsteps and shouts in the hallway.

A voice said, "The flames broke through a window. Check the offices to see if it's spread."

Umera looked to Jenar, then to Teafar. The thief continued to work on the second lock. She stepped back with a look of satisfaction and gave the closet door handle a jerk. It didn't open. She clenched her jaw and returned to the lock.

The door to the hallway shook.

Someone said, "It's locked, sir."

"Find the key."

Footsteps moved away.

Umera's heart pounded.

The thief pulled on the handle of the closet door a second time. It swung open.

Jenar said, "Find the credentials."

Umera ran into the closet. Documents lay on shelves. She looked through the stacks.

The door to the office rattled again.

A voice said, "That's the wrong key."

Umera frantically lifted papers as she moved from stack to stack. A box sat on the floor. She opened the lid and found the credentials, the request for aid and Marawee's signet ring. She picked them up, pocketed the ring and walked out of the closet.

Teafar refastened the locks.

A voice in the hallway said, "This had better be the right one."

Jenar pointed to the window.

Teafar climbed out.

Jenar motioned Umera to come over and whispered, "Hide the papers inside your jacket."

She opened the door and started to walk out.

Two guards stood in the hallway. They saluted.

One said, "Ma'am, how did you get in?"

Jenar said, "We found a key. There's no sign of fire in here. Have you checked all the offices on this floor?"

"This was the only door that was locked."

"I'll secure it. Check the offices on the floor above."

The guards saluted, then ran to a set of stairs.

Jenar gave a deep sigh. "Now comes the hard part, getting to the king. Teafar will've reached the roof by now."

They passed more palace guards as they walked up flights of stairs. None took any notice.

Jenar waited for two guards to go around a corner before she opened a closet door.

Inside was a ladder. They climbed. A door at the top led to the roof.

Teafar waved. "There were two archers positioned over the street when I climbed up earlier. As soon as the fire started, they went down."

Umera looked over the edge. The fire continued to burn.

They walked across the roof to a different door.

Teafar unlocked it.

Jenar said, "Thank you. We'll take it from here."

Umera and Jena descended a ladder to another closet.

Jenar opened the door and stepped into a hallway with plush carpeting and paintings on the walls. Around a corner was a wide double door where two guards stood. Each wore helmets and carried swords.

Jenar approached and saluted. "We have an urgent message for His Majesty concerning the fire."

The guards ordered them to surrender their swords, then opened the doors.

Inside, King Udalla stood behind a desk.

Umera was shocked to see his face, once youthful, now creased with the passage of time and the burden of rule.

Beside him stood Prime Minister Borsa.

Neither Umera nor Jenar looked directly at the prime minister who took no notice of the pair.

Jenar said, "Majesty, we bring an urgent message for you."

Umera handed the credentials and letter to the king.

He read them with a quizzical look. "Where is the ambassador?"

Umera said, "In prison, Majesty."

The prime minister tensed.

Udalla's gaze narrowed. "In prison?"

Umera said, "Yes, sire. I'm Umera Bedquanga, his wife. He and Captain Dugary Watoola were arrested on order of Prime Minister Borsa, to whom my husband presented these credentials."

The prime minister stepped forward. "Majesty, this is surely a jest, though in poor taste. The documents are obviously forgeries. Guards, remove these two."

The king raised a hand. "Hold. I remember a lieutenant name Bedquanga and a sailor who asked to remain after the war. This is the seal of the Queen of Carandir. That signet ring is a magical talisman." He held the credentials out to Borsa. "What do you know of this?"

The prime minister studied the paper. "Ah, I apologize, Majesty. I didn't see the document while it was in your hands. I remember now. I received Ambassador Bedquanga. He didn't speak of his mission and said he would return later, sire."

Udalla examined the letter. "Carandir is under attack from Karaken. Baras waits to awake. He would have spoken of this."

"He did mention something about it, but said he would give details later."

Umera said, "Majesty, we sailed from Meth. Traitorous forces waylaid us. We reached Hura through long roads. My husband wore a signet ring of his office." She took the ring from her pocket. "This ring, which we found in the minister's office tonight." She handed it to the king.

Udalla hefted it. "Take the prime minister into custody for questioning."

Two uniformed men grabbed Borsa by the arms.

He shook them off and stood tall. "Majesty, I acted for Hura. Too many died in the war with the Barasha. This is a civil matter. Hura has no obligation to intercede."

Jenar knelt. "Majesty, I'm only a lowly fisher who makes a meager living, yet I've seen a change in Hura since the prime minister was appointed. Many of us who live in the margins have disappeared when we brought petitions to him. A sense of fear permeates the people. Is Your Majesty aware of rumors of a new prison, a secret prison, where none who enter ever return?"

Udalla said, "Rise, mistress fisher. I have, indeed, noticed a pallor among some of my subjects and knew not why. Of rumors, I rarely listen, for there are many. Where is this prison?"

"Hidden within a compound on the outskirts of the city. I can take Your Majesty there."

The king wrote out an order and affixed his seal, then handed it to an officer. "Lieutenant, take a detachment and follow this woman to the prison to find Ambassador Bedquanga and Captain Watoola. Question every guard and soldier if necessary."

He wrote out another order. "Admiral Butla, prepare the fleet for battle. I will sail with it."

CHAPTER SIX

Luja sat in the tall chair of her stronghold. Womb and Gilyon paced the floor.

Tyra reported on the progress of the war. "The Karakiens have been routed from Carandir, mistress. Troops from Xinglan march on their capital. Narech Herrik moved most of her forces and others of Xinglan to western Barta and Nemtanka. Our spies report she will push through Ulata to take Shenan."

Womb stopped and looked at Luja. "I knew we couldn't trust those fools in Karaken. They should have pressed into Rascalla by now"

Luja wondered again why the monarchs hadn't used the crown in battle. Though the crest might not dishearten her troops, as they were Carandirians, it could bring magical attacks to drive her back.

Gilyon said, "With the Karakiens eliminated, we might be defeated."

The left side of Luja's lip turned up slightly. "This is the moment I've waited for. The north is now open. The crown is unguarded. We must push through Lena to Lanteler and seize the palace while Herrik leads her army in the south. We'll move our main host north and leave a token force in Barta and Ulata to retreat slowly and lure the Carandirians away."

Womb said, "Against the combined Carandirian and Xinglaner troops, our militia in the south will be slaughtered."

Luja waved a hand. "They're expendable."

Womb's face reddened. "Expendable? Many of them are my men."

Gilyon said, "Sacrifices must be made."

"Then send your militia into Herrik's path."

Luja shot to her feet. "Enough. I'm tired of your whining, Womb. You seem to think we can take the crown without effort. Are your men committed to a strong Carandir? Are you?"

"At least send reinforcements from Shenan for an organized retreat."

The baroness sat down. "There will be no reinforcements."

"Then we must tell my commanders the plan."

"They won't offer enough resistance if they learn they'll be sacrificed. No word or troops will be sent. We ride to Lena. The final battle is about to begin."

Dek and Lek stood atop the north tower and stared across the plain before the palace.

She walked to the parapet. "Can we win, Baron Dek?"

"The Xinglaners are fierce fighters. Their forces overran the Karakiens. A contingent will soon capture their capital and the King of Karaken. We'll march on the west, with a force of Carandirians and Xinglaners the traitors can't resist."

"I feel a sense of dread I can't explain. I wish the monarchs were here with the true crown."

"You hold the presence of the queen in the people's mind."

"I know. I just…" She gave a gasp and dropped.

Dek knelt at her side. "I'll call a Daro."

The features of Lek's face glowed and twisted as she screamed and writhed. Dek watched his daughter features warped and flowed like hot wax melting.

A flash of light bathed the tower. When it subsided, Lek was transformed from the likeness of Mirjel to her own semblance.

She opened her eyes. "What is it?"

Dek's face turned ashen. "Jorondel. The spell has ended. You've returned to your true appearance again."

She felt her features. "What will we do?"

Horns resounded as Huran ships sailed into Lake Hasp and maneuvered toward Meth. Dek stood next to Queen Quanto on a pier, alongside Orane and Telasec.

The Huran flagship docked. King Udalla stepped down its gangplank. Behind him came Marawee, followed by Umera and Watoola.

"Welcome, cousin," said Queen Quanto.

Udalla said, "Well met, cousin. Has Princess Enada reached the palace?"

Dek raised an eyebrow. "Princess Enada?"

"Yes," said Udalla. "She intended to reach here through a wizard tower."

Dek said, "Majesty, there's no princess of Carandir."

Marawee said, "Baron Dek, we must speak in private."

In the council chambers at the palace, Marawee sat at a table with Dek, Herrik, Quanto and Udalla. He told how he met Enada and relayed the fate of Mirjel and Ryckair. "She hasn't mastered the magic of the crest yet, though when we faced danger, she subconsciously drew upon its power to render us invisible."

Dek ran his palms over his beard. "Still, she may not be able to direct the magic at will."

"If she's been captured by the traitors they'll at least not recognize the pendant as the dragon crest," said Herrik. "From what you say, she'd never reveal such."

Queen Quanto said, "She may also be hiding in the tower if it's surrounded."

It was decided the main host would push into Barta and retake the tower in case Enada was trapped inside. Mistress Telasec and Master Orane would accompany them.

Portions of the Huran forces would sail at once to Fellant and push out Womb's militia, then march south in a pincer movement to take Shenan and capture the traitorous nobles.

"Baron Enesta and Baroness Edawee will travel to Fellant and command their troops who wait in the family catacomb," said Herrik.

One third of the Huran fleet approached the Port of Fellant. Five galleys lay at anchor with no crews. The docks were also abandoned.

Edawee said, "Where's the enemy?"

The Huran commander stared at the empty emplacements. "They may try to ambush us in the mountain pass."

Horses were unloaded. The nobles mounted.

Their now seventeen-year-old son, Reeca, said, "Do we ride to the catacomb, father?"

"Yes, my son. Fellant rises."

The flags of Carandir, Fellant and Hura were unfurled. Huran and Carandirian cavalry rode ahead. When they climbed the hills to secure the road to Pontelara, they encountered no resistance.

At the crest, the nobles left the rest of the force and rode the secret path to the catacomb.

Horns blew at their approached. Fellant militia blocked the path. A lieutenant raised her sword. "Halt. Archers surround you. Dismount and drop your weapons."

A man behind her opened his eyes wide and fell to his knees. "My Lieges."

The others stared up at the nobles as they knelt.

Edawee said, "Rise, faithful troops of Fellant."

The baron stood tall in his stirrups. "Hail, good friends. We return with a force to drive the invaders out."

Word was sent ahead.

Captain Genta waited at the entrance of the catacomb when the noble party arrived. He fell to one knee. "My Lord and Lady. Your loyal troops await your command."

The Fellant militia issued from the catacomb and marched to battle. Horns blew and shouts echoed.

Captain Genta rode with the nobles at the head of the column.

They joined the rest of the loyal forces.

An arrow swooped over Genta's head. He drew his sword and pointed the blade in the direction the shaft came from.

Dozens of Fellant arrows slammed into the foliage where the enemy had fired from.

Reeca said," That'll teach them."

The captain smiled. "It will indeed, Your Lordship."

Womb's militia retreated at the nobles' advance.

Enesta rode up to his son. "I have a special job for you, Reeca. I need someone to command the rear guard and prevent a sneak attack from behind. Can you do that?"

Reeca's face beamed. "Yes, father." He turned his horse and rode back.

Edawee said, "You're a masterful politician, my dear."

The column reached the bottom of the hills and formed a front to engage Womb's troops, who gave ground. Soon, the nobles were at the outskirts of Pontelara. Troops fought in the streets and in buildings. The cavalry dismounted for hand-to-hand combat.

Enemy bowmen shot a volley of shafts from second story windows.

An arrow struck a man next to Captain Genta.

The soldier dropped his sword and fell to the ground as blood stained his jacket.

The fight lasted three spans before the enemy forces were driven from the city. The last of them broke into a rout.

Enesta raised an arm. "Let them go. We need to regroup and rest."

From the edges of Pontelara, shouts of joy filled the air as citizens returned from hills and poured into streets. Those who approached the nobles fell to their knees and wept.

A woman said, "My Lord and Lady. Glory to the dragons. Glory to Carandir. Glory to Fellant." She broke into tears.

Around the city, the troops were showered with flowers. Music rang out to mix with joyous voices. Food and wine were brought to the soldiers.

Captain Genta said, "What are your orders, my lieges?"

Enesta cast his gaze about the scene. "We'll rest here today and tonight. Set scouts to watch for an attack. Rotate them in shifts to allow all to recover. Tomorrow, we march."

Within a few spans, the column reached the Fellant stronghold. Smoke wafted from within.

They approached with caution. A search found no trace of Womb's militia around or inside.

The captain rode up to Baroness Edawee. "My Lady, the enemy has abandoned the stronghold. Many rooms were set ablaze. What remained in the treasury was looted."

She inspected her home. "This insult will be answered a hundred-fold. Prepare to ride."

Womb charged into Luja's command tent in Lena. "They've nearly secured Fellant. We have to send troops to stop them before they reach Petala."

Luja said, "Petala is inconsequential."

"Will you say the same when they reach Shenan?"

She stood. "Shenan doesn't matter, nor Eel nor any other western barony. Once we have the crown, we can call upon magic that will sweep the Carandirian army aside."

Womb scoffed. "And who will wear the crown?"

"We shall share it."

The baron laughed. "Will you take it first? Will Gilyon and I become your vassals? We agreed to work together, yet you leave my militia to be slaughtered."

"Come, Womb. We're all committed to a strong Carandir. Herrik has emptied Lanteler for her strike. The palace is nearly deserted. If you wish, you may wear the crown first. I only want to return Carandir to greatness."

Womb glared at her. "Yes, I *will* wear it first." He left the room.

Tyra knelt. "Mistress, will you allow him to take the crown? He would have absolute power."

She patted his head. "He will have nothing."

Luja, Womb and Gilyon sat at a table and ate in silence. The tent flap opened. Two figures in red robes entered. They removed their hoods to reveal Petstra and Ackella. The former mayor of Meth now wore a blood red eye patch.

Petstra said, "Good evening."

The men stood.

Luja remained seated.

"Reshna's dead," Gilyon said. "We owe you no allegiance."

Petstra said, "Do you think you can take the palace with the forces you command?"

Womb said, "What do you know of our plans?"

"I know you intend to seize the crown and overthrow the monarchy. Ackella and I can be of service. We're the last of the Barasha yet can call upon powers to ensure victory for you."

Luja stood. "Why would you do this? What's your price?"

"We wander the world as outcasts. The monarchs will never accept us. We can teach others our arts to serve you."

Luja sat down. "Leave us. We must confer."

Petstra bowed. "We await your answer."

Womb checked the tent flap to make certain Petstra and Ackella were far enough away. "He's dangerous. Don't forget how we were spied on."

Gilyon said, "Petstra could be of help. The palace is still heavily guarded. The monarchs haven't used the crown in battle yet. When we attack, they will. A few demons would bring enough havoc to allow a force to enter and kill them."

"If the demons don't eat our souls as well," said Womb.

Luja said, "Petstra seeks the crown to release Baras. We need his magic. Form an elite squad to stand ready. Once we take the palace, they'll kill the sorcerers."

The forces of Luja, Womb and Gilyon took the same route Dek followed to attack the Barasha. Petstra and Ackella moved in front of the militia and cast spells of concealment. They passed through the valley where the monarchs of Carandir were entombed back to Avar the Great.

The company came to the barren place once known as the dragon mound, where Baras' body lay while his spirit remained trapped in the void by the power of the crown. They reached the edge of the high plain in front of the palace.

Luja sat on a horse and stared at the arched bridge. Sixty thousand troops, twenty thousand of whom were mounted, readied for battle. All her plans for a strong Carandir, free of the New Nobility and the foreigners who didn't carry the blood of pure Carandirians in their veins, rested on what happened over the next span.

Tyra rode up to her. "All is ready, mistress. Give the order."

She stood in the stirrups. Her voice rose to fill the air. "Charge."

A Carandirian soldier on the parapet above the portcullis saw dust raised by hooves and feet. He blew a horn. The portcullis dropped. Soldiers poured from barracks into the parade grounds.

Batu ran across the yard and climbed to the parapet. "Father of Dragons."

Colonel Amar said, "Sound the advance. Open the portcullis and drop it as soon as our soldiers are out."

He ran down the steps to the officers assembled below. "Set archers along the parapet. The road to Meth is still clear. Send riders to bring word to the troops there. Instruct them to continue onward to Barta and find Narech Herrik."

Batu descended the parapet. "Prepare the troops, Colonel Amar. Their forces outnumber us ten to one. We might hold out once the troops stationed in Meth arrive."

Amar said, "It'll be a span before they reach us. We have to keep the enemy back from the bridge."

Amar mounted and led troops out the portcullis. They assembled in lines on the plain. Amar raised his arms. "Drive them back."

The forces slammed into each other. Arrows flew and blades clashed. Calvary charged with swords and sabers. The attackers pushed the Carandirians back toward the bridge.

From the rear, Womb and Luja watched the battle. Tyra stood next to his mistress.

Womb stepped in front of Luja. "My militia should lead the attack. I'll ride with them and take the crown once we enter the place. When it's on my head, the Carandirians will be swept aside."

Luja drew a knife and rammed it into Womb's back.

He shuddered and turned his head. There was no fear on his face, only surprise, as he fell dead to the ground.

Tyra grinned.

The baroness said, "Hide the body. Tell his officers he's ridden back to command a rear guard."

Tyra dragged Womb's remains into woods.

Luja saw a Carandirian rider fly south and knew reinforcements would soon arrive from Meth.

Petstra and Ackella approached.

Luja said, "Call a demon. We must reach the palace at once."

Ackella stared at her with his single eye. "We wait to see what force the monarchs will call with the crown."

One of Luja's officers brought his horse to a halt and dismounted to kneel before her. "My Lady, Baron Gilyon has fallen in battle. His militia are in a rout."

Petstra took a pouch from under his red robes and tossed it to the officer. "Throw this into the air in front of them."

The officer took the pouch and galloped away. Petstra and Ackella raised their hands, palms up. They chanted in the demon tongue.

Gilyon's men came close enough for Luja to see. The pouch flew into the air above their heads and burst open. The men were showered in red powder. Gilyon's militia halted for an instant, then turned and rushed into battle against the Carandirians.

A second officer arrived on horseback. "My Lady, we captured two Carandirian officers. One is a colonel."

Luja said, "Take us to them."

Militiamen surrounded Colonel Amar and a Carandirian lieutenant. Both were bound and forced to kneel on the ground.

Luja bent down to Amar. "You've lost, colonel. Where are the monarchs? Why have they not used the crown?"

The two officers stared ahead in silence.

Tyra said, "Speak." He pointed to Petstra. "You know what he can do."

Luja saw terror on the face of the junior officer who closed his eyes and clenched his jaw.

Amar remained stoic.

The baroness said, "Petstra, can you loosen their lounges?"

Ackella walked behind the lieutenant.

Petstra took a pouch from the folds of his robes, reached inside and pulled out a handful of green powder.

Ackella drew a knife and slashed it across the junior officer's throat while Petstra threw the powder in his face.

Vapor formed above the young man's head. It congealed into a warped face with three eyes and no mouth.

A voice scratched through the air. "What is thy bidding?"

Petstra pointed to Amar. "Open his mouth to reveal the truth."

Amar tried to twist free.

The militiamen held him in place.

His struggles grew weak until he knelt, passively.

Petstra said, "Where are the monarchs hiding in the palace? Why have they not used the crown?"

The colonel's mouth opened and sound came out, though his lips didn't move. "The monarchs are not in the palace."

"Where are they?"

"They entered the wizard tower in Amblar two years ago and have not been seen since."

"Where's the crown?"

"It's lost with the monarchs. The crown is not in Carandir."

Ackella slapped Amar "We've come here for nothing."

Petstra said, "We've come at the right time, Ackella."

He sneered at Luja. "Fool. Did you think we would let you have the crown? Baras will awaken from the unfinished spell. The crown is lost and can't send him back in the eternal void. Now, your death will help us raise our master."

Luja drew a sword. "Kill the sorcerers."

Petstra threw another powder in the air.

Luja felt her muscles grow limp.

Her militia swayed on their feet, then dropped to the ground.

Luja fell with the sword in her hand.

Ackella kicked her. "Stupid woman. All your plots were for naught."

Petstra dropped powder on Amar's head and slit the colonel's throat. He remained in place as gore gushed from the slit in his neck and down his chest.

Ackella slit Tyra's throat, then did the same to the militiamen. Demons appeared above each.

Petstra stared into Luja's eyes. "So many plans. So short sighted. I admire your hatred of lesser humans. The weak are to be subjugated. In the end, your greed betrayed you. Baras will rise because of that." He leisurely pushed the knife into her neck and drew it back and forth from ear to ear.

Another demon materialized.

Ackella said, "Baras will rise."

Petstra stood behind him. "We need one more demon." He shoved a knife between Ackella's ribs and threw powder over his head.

Ackella screamed as he fell.

An orange ball with tentacles appeared.

Petstra raised his arms to the demons overhead. "Find and free our master."

In the foothills at the eastern edge of the northern desert, Sif and Tarawee stood in their human forms.

Sif said, "Can't you smell that, Taree?"

Tarawee shook his head. "No. I thought there was a whiff of dragon yesterday. I can't detect it now. Let's get a little higher."

He climbed up the rubble bank of a dry wash. His foot caught on a rock and he fell. "Dilatant. That hurt. This being human isn't all it's cracked up to be."

He started to sit up, then stopped. "Hey, come over here."

"Did the widdle Tawee scwape his knee?"

"Shut up and get over here. Smell."

Sif walked over. "Oh, dragon."

They followed the scent to a pile of large rocks.

Sif said, "Pew. He's been down there a long time."

"Twenty years. Take my hand. We have to locate Ryckair."

The Zerites concentrated on the essence of the king.

Sif said, "Where is he?"

Tarawee shook his head. "I don't feel him."

A hole formed in the air. From it stepped the wizened figure of Eminence Levalat, leader of the Zerites. Levalat stood a little shorter than Sif's human hip, with a round belly, bald head and spindly legs. He carried a staff. "So, you found Baras at last. Where is King Ryckair?"

Sif cleared his throat. "Well, you see… it's like this. We looked for the dragon, so to speak. He's got a powerful bad smell, so we… well, to put it another way—"

Levalat thumped his staff on the ground. "Where is Ryckair?"

Tarawee looked to Sif.

They prostrated themselves before Levalat.

Tarawee said, "We can't find him."

"What?"

Sif groveled. "There's no essence of his being."

"Absurd. I will reach out." Levalat raised his staff. "He is gone. How could he vanish? I see him nowhere, even in the Dragons' Halls. You were supposed to keep him with you."

In the air above, hundreds of demons in multitudes of sizes, shapes and colors popped into existence.

A sharp chasm cut across the land.

The large rocks next to the Zerites burst into the air.

Baras emerged.

He took no notice of the Zerites as he leapt into the air and flew southwest, accompanied by the demons.

Sif got to his feet. "This isn't good."

Levalat stared into the west. "Baras flies to the Carandirian palace. Wait." He closed his eyes. "There is a power near the wizard tower."

He waged a finger. Both Sif and Tarawee lost their human forms and took once more the semblance of Zerites.

Levalat raised his staff. A hole appeared in the air. "Come."

The three of them walked through.

CHAPTER SEVEN

To Narech Herrik's surprise, the combined forces of Carandir, Xinglan and Hura encountered almost no resistance on their march west.

A soldier galloped back from the front. "Narech, a small troop advances."

"How many?"

"Less than two dozen."

She ordered archers to be ready.

A figure moved behind the brush.

An archer called out, "Halt, in the name of the Crown."

A man sounded the grunt of a kala. "Ho, we're Carandirians." He raised his arms and approached. "I'm Lieutenant Parna, from the Lusar garrison. My company fought a guerrilla war behind enemy lines."

Yearol and Keetala stepped out from behind him.

Dek said, "That's the young woman from Shenan who wanted to join the army."

Marawee pushed forward and enveloped his daughter in his arms.

She held tight to her father.

Herrik said, "Hold your fire. Come forward, lieutenant."

Parna led his command from the brush, followed by Frothey.

He saluted, "Narech. The garrison in Lusar was overrun. We've carried out raids and sabotage in Shenan and followed Luja's militia into Barta. This is deputy Frothey, from Lusar. She and these two young women joined our company and have distinguished themselves."

Dek scratched his beard. "Yearol, how did you get here?"

She said, "Keetala and I traveled into Barta and then through Karaken to Shenan."

Frothey walked up.

Yearol looked at her with a tear in her eye. "Deputy Frothey is a good comrade. I'm proud to have served with her."

Frothey put a hand on Yearol's shoulders. "Yearol fought as valiantly as any soldier could." She smiled as she heard Yearol sniff.

Herrik said, "Lieutenant Parna, what's the troop strength ahead?

"We encountered no rebels, ma'am."

King Udalla said, "We must reach the tower. Princess Enada may be there already."

On the plain, twenty-thousand mounted Carandirian soldiers arrived from Meth. The enemy continued their advance. Soldiers on both sides fell in the fierce melee.

Batu felt a chill as he stood on the parapet. In the northeast sky, a form appeared. He shielded his eyes against the sun. The shape grew until he saw a red dragon, followed by hundreds of demons.

Carandirian and rebel troops slowed. Soldiers raised their eyes to the sky as Baras stormed forward. Many dropped their weapons and fled the field. Others pulled their hair or fell to the ground and writhed as they screamed

Petstra stood in silence; his red robes bathed by the light of the sun.

Baras circled and landed. He raised his head. A distorted trumpet call ripped through the air.

Petstra knelt. "Master."

Baras' deep voice resounded across the plain. "Where is Avar's heir?"

"He and his queen are trapped in a wizard tower with the crown, great one. They and the accursed talisman have been gone for years."

Baras squinted. "The crown is lost?"

"Yes, master. I'm the last of your servants. All the wizards are dead. The crown has vanished. The other dragons forsook this world while you slept. Command me, oh mighty one."

A chuckle came from Baras as he beheld the demons suspended in space above him. "Long will be the punishment of humans. Their suffering will soothe the wounds inflicted on me. First, this wretched palace will be razed."

Enada heard nothing, saw nothing, felt nothing. She had no concept of how long it was since she touched the crystal. Time had no meaning. There was no space. Only her thoughts existed. They moved though her consciousness as a fog.

This was the void, she told herself. This is where Jant and his kind were imprisoned in the other world, where Baras' spirit was confined in this one.

There was no escape. She didn't feel fear, only an oppressive sadness and wished she could die, then realized she couldn't. The loneliness would last for eternity. Her memories would fade to shadows. She was left with only despair.

The egg. She was in the egg from before time began. How long did all those beings endure this before the minds of Jorondel and Ilidel touched? The question was meaningless. There were no other minds to touch. She was alone and always would be. She wanted to cry. The effort was too great.

In hopelessness, a spark came to her. She was not alone. The minds and experiences of every monarch who'd ever worn the crown were within the pendant.

She forced herself to concentrate against the oppression that clouded her mind. One word emerged. Carandir.

Voices touched her mind. "We are here."

A flash of light exploded around her. She opened her eyes and found herself on the floor of the room in the wizard tower.

Fera stood over her. "Thank the dragons, you're back. I didn't know how to rescue you."

She took several deep breaths. "We must reach the palace."

They descended to the bottom level of the tower and stepped out.

Fera cried, "Yearol." He ran to his sister.

She put her arms around him. "Oh, Fera. I thought you were safe in Varda."

"I left with Marawee to seek help in Hura. Our ship was attacked. We were captured. Princess Enada took us through the wizard towers."

Telasec walked forward with her hand over her mouth. "You're the princess with the dragon pendant."

Enada said, "How did you know me?"

Orane said, "There is one who sketched your likeness as well as the monarchs of Carandir, though they appeared aged."

"Who?"

"Shara."

Enada said, "The Princess of the Dharam?"

Telasec nodded.

Enada said, "She's my grandmother. I'm Enada Avar, heir to the throne. King Ryckair is my grandfather."

Birds returned to the tree branches and began to sing.

Enada took the baron's hand. "You're Dek."

He grinned broadly. "Yes, Highness."

"My grandfather described you. He admires you greatly."

She looked around. "This is the Carandirian army. You must be Narech Herrik."

Enada pointed to the chief Kyar. "You have to be Orane. My grandfather talked of your bald pate."

Orane laughed.

Enada said, "And you're Telasec." She turned in place. "You're here. You're all here. It's real."

Dek said, "Princess, how did you come here?"

"It's a long tale. I came from a different world, like this and unlike this. I was sent me to stop Baras and end the war."

Herrik said, "Highness, where is the crown?"

Enada touched the pendant. "Here is the dragon crest, with the breath of creation from two worlds. None can stand before it."

A rush of air blew across the forest. A hole opened in the air. Levalat stepped out, followed by Sif and Tarawee.

The eminence about you. Questions must wait. Baras has risen." He opened another hole in the air. "Follow me."

Baras eyed the palace walls with a crooked smile of satisfaction. He gave a deep-throated laugh, then addressed the demons who hovered overhead. "Prepare to feast on the souls of our tormentors."

A rumble echoed across the plain as a hole opened in the air. Levalat stepped through, followed by Sif and Tarawee.

A puff of fumes emanated from Baras' nostrils. "Zerite. You forsook all claim to this world when you sank into your holes."

Levalat made no answer. He tapped his staff. A multitude of Zerites emerged. They raised their arms overhead. The air shimmered. Every demon froze in place.

Baras swept a claw. Levalat was thrown across the plain. "Fool. I was of the council. Do you think you can challenge me?"

The air boomed with a deep voice. "We can."

All heads turned skyward to see Jorondel. Ilidel hovered next to him with a host of dragons behind.

Jorondel's voice rumbled again. "You will inflict no harm."

The wings of Ilidel spread wide. "Back to eternal sleep, betrayer."

Baras laughed. "The accursed crown is gone. If it's a new war you want, I and my army will overthrow you this time."

A woman's voice said, "Stop."

Enada emerged from the hole in the air. Behind her came Baron Dek, Telasec and Orane.

Baras stared at the dragon pendant around Enada's neck, then lunged for her.

The eyes of the pendant blazed as sparks flashed in the air.

Baras howled in pain and dropped from the sky.

Enada said, "The bane of Baras is not lost. Here is the power of creation from two worlds. None of this place, mortal or dragon, can stand before it."

The magic in the pendant enveloped her. She felt it in every fold of her body. It was more than that. She felt the power in her own being, the soul of two worlds.

Forces whirled within her. The words of the spell she practiced so often waited to be spoken. Not only would they subdue Baras, the power would send all the demons into the void for eternity, never to know this or any other world again.

Her body glowed as the will of creation from two worlds flowed through her. All beings would bow at her command—dragons, demons, Zerites, monarchs, nobles and commoners. Ilidel and Jorondel would fall subject to her desires. Every mind would serve and worship her.

Pain exploded in her mind. She knew the agony was from the corruption of this world. Here, the plan failed. She understood the hurt and the ease with which her innocence could be turned to evil.

Enada looked into the eyes of Baras and saw only Magadel reflected back.

Jorondel and Ilidel remained in place.

Baras took a step back. The hatred on his face was replaced with fear. "And so, you will send me back to the void?"

Enada placed her hand on Baras' cheek.

The dragon shuddered.

She whispered, "What has become of you, Syo?"

Baras' body twitched. "How do you know that name?"

"You told it to me."

"We've never met."

"Yet, I know you. I know your mind and your heart. I've walked with you and spoken with you and laughed with you in another world, where magic never came to humans."

"You seek to torment me with lies and my true name. Return me to darkness and have done with it."

Ilidel moved her eyes from Baras to Enada. "Banish him, child. His words are poisonous lies."

Enada returned Ilidel's gaze. "I've known one who is good and was banished to the void. I've been trapped in that void, in the egg before it was broken and the world began. None should suffer so.

"I know you too, and you, Jorondel. We've spoken. I laid my case before all the dragons in the world I was born into. Such imprisonment is cruel and beyond the Great Plan."

She looked back to Baras. "There is good in you, Magadel. You possess kindness and compassion. You worked with all the dragons to devise the Great Plan."

Baras writhed in pain. "It was flawed. Humans could have used magic if the council had helped me teach it."

"That's your anger speaking. It cuts you off from your true self. Look with your heart, not your conceit. Let it show you the pain it brought to this world and to you."

He tried to turn away. "Will you torment me more as punishment?"

"See the Magadel in the other world through my eyes, your real self. Know who you are. You alone bring torment to yourself. Hold my gaze and imbibe the spirit of Magadel that lies buried within."

The dragon cried out. Still, his eyes stared into Enada's.

Her will, amplified through the dragon pendent, forced him to relive his disappointment when his plan to teach magic was rejected. He felt the humiliation, then the rage as he subverted the plan.

Enada said, "Look beneath the anger."

He fought to retain his hatred. The plan was flawed. He was right.

An image long suppressed surfaced. The dragons hadn't mocked him. Ilidel explained in calm words the hurt magic would bring if humans were taught it. As the mother of dragons spoke, he saw the truth for an instant.

His pride overcame reason. He let loose lightning and fire as he stormed from the halls.

Now, he remembered how Jorondel called him friend and pleaded for him to return.

He raised his head and bellowed, "Stop."

Enda said, "I know the point when you made the decision to spread ruin. What was in your heart, Syo? What did you fear?"

"I feared nothing."

The Princess' features hardened. "You can't lie to me. I know your true name."

"Cover the crest. It burns me."

"Your soul has been on fire from a great loss since before the dragon war. What is it?"

The deep voice of Baras blasted across the plane. "I was humiliated in the council."

"That was not your loss."

Baras lowered his head. His voice became a whisper. "I lost the love of the dragons. The love of Jorondel and Ilidel, who I loved so well." His head collapsed to the ground.

In a quiet voice, Enada said, "Say the name you were known by, Syo. The name of your true nature. The name to redeem you."

The dragon wept. "Magadel. I am Magadel." He closed his eyes.

Enada smiled. "You can no longer deny the ill your pride caused. Disharmony came to this world. You can rectify this. Come back, Magadel. Embrace the plan. What was done can be put right. You and the demons must commit yourselves to that task. It will be difficult. Evil is spread around the world. You must come to those who do evil and show them the wisdom of the plan. You have the power to heal the rend."

She turned to Levalat. "Order the Zerites to release the demons."

The Zerite said, "They will consume you."

"They can't overcome the power of the dragon pendant or my will. Let them hear me."

The shimmer around the demons evaporated.

Enada said, "You know the plan, yet you violated it for greed. What have you gained? You were imprisoned or have hidden in the terror you would be found."

She indicated Petstra. "You were forced, like slaves, to do the Barasha's bidding. Glory and mastery never come to you."

Her finger pointed at Ilidel. "None are untainted. Magic should not have come to humans, yet you violated the plan as well when you created the wizards. Even then, harmony was gutted when you and Jorondel sought only to seal Magadel away, with no thought to rebuild and heal.

"There's much hurt in this world. I'd never experienced such before. Yet, the way is clear. Everyone has a part. Vengeance and punishment perpetuate suffering. Those who cause it must admit their actions and make amends. Magic must be removed from humans. Faith must be renewed in the plan. Anger for wrongs done released. Those who committed the wrongs forgiven."

Levalat said, "I thought the Zerites could live outside the plan. When the war came, I withdrew. In that, I was wrong, for I could have interceded and called for peace as a third party. Here, then, is my pledge. Henceforth, the Zerites will embrace the plan and work to put the world right in accordance with it."

He raised his head to the dragons in the sky. "Forgive me and allow Magadel to return to the company of dragons so his actions can be repaired."

Ilidel closed her eyes and lowered her head. "The words of this child among humans shames me. She speaks with wisdom I failed to call upon in my anger. We acted from fear and forgot the essence of plan ourselves."

Jorondel said, "It is true. I beg forgiveness from human, dragon, demon and Zerite. Let us all hold council, we of the egg."

Magadel said, "To begin, I revoke the knowledge and power of magic from the humans to whom I taught it."

Petstra grabbed his head and screamed. The flesh of his hands and face withered. He fell to the ground and convulsed. In an instant, his body was ash.

With a wave of her paw, Ilidel said, "I revoke magic from the Kyar and Daro who were taught by the wizards. To the Kyar, I leave their desire for knowledge, though all spells are erased in their minds and the scrolls that detail magic are now dust. To the Daro, I leave their herb lore and knowledge of healing."

Jorondel gave a pure trumpet call that evaporated the hate and hurt of all assembled. "Let us return to the halls of the dragons and begin our work together."

Wind blew across the plain. The dragons, demons and Zerites vanished.

Dek knelt before Enada. "Highness, your great-grandfather told me evil can never be destroyed, only contained. You've shown a new path, reconciliation and atonement."

She said, "I've completed what I was sent to do. Strange. I feel no elation. I need to think."

CHAPTER EIGHT

Telasec led Enada to the room where Shara lived. The princess stopped at the threshold and watched her true grandmother draw a flower.

The head of the Daro order said, "She's been like this since she arrived in Carandir, a forty-three-year-old woman with the mind of a young child. We searched for spells to help and never found one. Now, with our magic gone, we can do little more than care for her. It seems strange not to call on spells, yet I understand why Ilidel revoked our knowledge of them. Still, I wonder why the wizard tower in Amblar still stands. I expected it to vanish with the others."

The flower Shara drew was unknown to Enada. Wide, green leaves and many thin petals changed from deep purple in the center to pastel violet at the tips.

At first, Shara concentrated on the picture as if the world outside her room didn't exist. Then, her face turned toward the door with a wide smile. She leapt to her feet, ran to Enada and wrapped her arms around her granddaughter. "I've waited for you."

Enada returned the embrace. "I've waited for you too."

They rocked each other without words.

Shara took Enada's hand and showed her all her drawings. Many were attached to the walls.

Enada inspected each while Shara told her what they were.

The princess said, "Shara, would you like to come and live with me?"

Shara tilted her head. "That's what I'm supposed to do."

"I can see that. Get your drawings together. I'll take you to my chambers. There's a nice room with sunny windows."

Shara began to remove pictures from the walls.

Telasec said, "Are you certain you want to take her? She seems happy here."

"I'm the blood of her blood, her granddaughter. Whatever happened before I was born is gone from her mind. Only the essence of purity remains. I'll care for her as my grandfather and mother cared for me."

Enada sat in her chambers. Chairs and settees were arranged in a circle where Marawee, Umera, Fera and Yearol sat. Whispy rested on Yearol's shoulder. Keetala sat next to Yearol.

The princess raised a cup. "To friends, old and new. I think often of Len and wish in my heart he's well."

Marawee said, "The Laran watch from their borders. They know the change in the world, Highness. Len will know as well. I'm certain he's content."

Umera took a sip of Kan. "He works with grapes again. It's what he always loved. I can picture a smile on his face as he tastes one of his new vintages."

Enada smiled. "I can too. Yearol, what will you do now?"

Yearol took a deep breath. "I've seen many things, good and horrid. I found vengeance. You were right, Marawee. It left me hollow."

She took Keetala's hand. "I've never had a closer friend. As nice as it would be to stay together, I want to go home to the mill. People will need wheat again. My parents taught me much. I can't forget what I saw. I can give to others. That will help me heal."

"I'll go too," said Fera. "My friends must wonder where I went."

The little whispy nudged Yearol's ear. She stroked its back. "Whispy wants to come with us."

Enada addressed the Bedquangas, "What of you? Will you return to Petala?"

Umera said, "We'll go back. There are many good people there. They stayed silent out of fear. It's time to heal."

Keetala lowered her head. "I want to take Hebra and Marshala home. They deserve to rest in the soil they loved. I'm not sure what I'll do after that. I may stay. I may travel to Hura and see relatives I've never met. All plans are too far in the future."

Enada put her cup down. "A detachment will travel with you to search for the graves. Len's holdings will be passed to you. He would want that."

Over the next four months, Enada spent long hours with Baron Dek and Lek. They taught her the administration of the monarchy and all its workings in preparation to be crowned queen. Even after the instruction Mirjel and Ryckair gave her, the reality was foreign in her mind.

There were no monarchies in the world she came from. Towns and cities elected administrators for short periods. The notion she would to rule every life in Carandir was oppressive. She held the title of princess because of her parents. Others were better qualified to run the nation.

She put down a book in the middle of a lesson. "Why does a city need to ask permission of the barony to hold a street market?"

Dek said, "To collect taxes on the goods sold."

"Taxes make no sense."

Lek said, "Money must be raised to build roads and bridges. Stone is expensive. People don't work for free."

"Can't people just step up to cut stone and make roads? That's how we did things in the village."

Dek said, "Carandir is much larger than a village, Highness. Roads span great distances. The government needs money to support the army and constables. How did you pay for them in your village?"

"I never heard of armies or constables before I came here." She pushed herself back from the desk. "Can we stop? I feel tired."

Dek said, "Of course, Highness." He left the room.

Enada ran her fingers over the pages of the book. "Even after all my mother and grandfather taught me, I still don't understand any of this, Lek"

"I was confused at first and know how you feel. I knew about taxes and armies and constables before I impersonated your mother. Still, Baron Dek tutored and advised me for months."

Enada's face lit up. "You know how to do this. You should be the queen."

Lek laughed. "I don't have the blood of Avar in my veins. The monarchy must pass to you."

It would have been wonderful to walk alone in the woods, yet Enada knew, like her grandfather, she would be accompanied by guards.

She went to the window and stared out on Lake Hasp. It was such a different world, one she wished she could explore. Perhaps, when she was crowned queen, she could spend time on foreign visits. The tales of Xinglan and its capital, built into a mountain, fascinated her. She'd love to travel with Marawee and Umera to visit Hura and try the exotic foods they described. Still, the guards would always be present. There was no way she could simply stroll anywhere.

Her mother spoke of duty as a monarch. Enada now felt it was more a prison. The people of Carandir were said to be free and able to travel where they pleased or meet whomever they desired. She would never know that.

She asked herself if it was freedom for the people if they were subject to a monarch or noble. Ordinary people in the land couldn't make laws. She realized the needs of Carandir were greater than her village. Even so, there was no desire in her to take on the burden of being the only one to say how everyone would act.

"Lek, Au has no nobility, does it?"

"It's always been ruled by a council, ma'am."

"How are they selected?"

"The merchants choose. Before the war with the Barasha, the richest merchants paid others for votes. Only men could sit on the council then because there were few women merchants, none of whom were allowed to become rich enough to pay bribes."

"Are there women on the council now?"

"Oh yes, ma'am. Before, a woman could only have a business if her husband died. She was expected to will it to a male relative upon her death. When the Barasha left Au after their occupation, they looted the treasury and killed many of the men. Au was close to bankruptcy. Your mother, who has strong family ties in Au, demanded women be fully integrated into society, commerce, the militia and the council before Carandir would issue loans."

"How is the council selected today?"

"Every citizen votes for the council. Bribes are forbidden."

Enada stared out the window for a long time. "I have to think, Lek." She left the room.

Light streamed into her chambers, yet the air felt oppressive. Through the pendant, she experienced the minds of the monarchs who once wore the crown. They were devoted to all citizens. Still, those citizens were subject to the monarchs' rules.

She thought of Luja, Womb, Gilyon and the other nobles who attempted to repress all who were different. They used their absolute power for selfish gain. Many suffered and died under their rule.

There must be a better way, she told herself, one with noble service and restrictions on power to prevent abuse.

A box sat on a table. She opened it.

Inside, was the dragon pendant. The last time she wore it was the day Baras renounced his acts and became Magadel again.

She ran a finger over the dragon image. It grew warm. A tingle ran through her body. The power of Ilidel from her world was still there.

The oppression lifted. "I know what must be done. There'll be resistance."

She lifted the pendant and placed the chain around her neck. "You gave me strength to find my courage, Syo. Now, I must call upon it from within myself."

ᖗ   ✦   ᖘ

The day of the coronation dawned bright. A clear sky shone through the crystal ceiling of the audience hall. The low, walled boxes of the eighteen baronies were filled. The eldest relative, child, cousin or sibling, took the place of those nobles who died or rebelled in the civil war. The nobles of each house were accompanied by armed honor guards from their baronies.

Enada sat on the left-hand throne. She wore long robes of blue velvet trimmed in white wool. The dragon pendant hung around her neck unseen beneath the robes.

Batu stood at one side of her, Lek to the other.

Behind them was a phalanx of Carandirian army soldiers commanded by Narech Herrik.

Telasec and Orane waited next to the crystal sphere in which the crown of Avar once sat. It contained the duplicate crown Lek wore.

By Enada's request, the ceremony was conducted in modern Carandirian instead of the formal court language.

A fanfare of trumpets sounded. Enada stepped down from the dais and knelt before the sphere.

Orane and Telasec opened a drawer in the pedestal. Inside was the silver key whose handle was shaped like a dragon as it leapt into the air, the symbol of the house of Avar. Now, bereft of the spell cast on it, any could hold it.

Together, Telasec and Orane recited a liturgy, this time in common Carandirian. "Oh, high and mighty royal, receive now your birthright. The magic of the crown is no more, for its purpose has passed. Accept into your care this key and the crown within the sphere as symbols of your majesty and authority. Swear first to administer your power in the name of the people and to protect them from harm and threat within and without; to foster prosperity for all; to rule both justly and fairly; and to protect and follow the plan of the dragons."

Enada said, "I so swear, in the name of the dragons."

All assembled clasped their hands together and touched them to their foreheads in the sign of the covenant.

Together, Orane and Telasec lifted the duplicate crown and placed it on Enada's head.

When the new queen rose, cheers broke out in the hall. People shouted, "Long live Queen Enada" and "The blessings of the dragons for our sovereign."

Enada mounted the dais and sat on her throne.

Brightnail came. Light bathed the new queen.

She stood. "My loyal subjects. Great things have come to pass. Much has changed. Though the magic granted humans by the dragons of this world is revoked, harmony must still be restored. Slavers continue to roam the lands east of the swamp. Karaken is defeated and occupied, yet a permanent peace must yet be negotiated. Many are the new challenges and changes. They cannot be solved with old ways.

"My great grandfather once told Baron Dek the strength of Carandir is in the faith of its people. Faith is given freely, not earned. People must have faith in their leaders. Those who rule must hold faith with the people. In this, the citizens of Carandir hold ultimate power. Nobles and royals draw their authority from them."

Enada paused to scan the assembly. Some looked interested, others confused.

She said, "The magic of the crown of Avar protected Carandir and assured its monarchs were those best suited to lead. This was seen when my great uncle, Prince Craya, tried unsuccessfully to seize power. My grandfather, King Ryckair, was the true heir. Neither my great uncle nor the Barasha were able to take the crown."

She put her hand to her chest and felt the dragon pendant around her neck as it radiated warmth. "The magic breathed into the crest by Ilidel is no more. A new way must be instituted to select leadership other than by bloodline. Therefore, I revoke all noble titles. The Baronies of Carandir will henceforth be known as Territories of Carandir. The people of each territory will select, by free election, members of a council, as well as one person to act as administrator of the government to carry out the rules enacted by the councils. Each territory will select five representatives from different regions to come to the palace and sit at a Council of the Nation to replace the Council of Baronies. This edict is in force immediately."

Rumbles of voices filled the hall.

Some shouted, "Impossible."

Others said, "The monarchy will fall."

A few stood in their boxes.

The Baron of Barta said, "Majesty, to remove the nobility will leave no leadership. Anarchy will result."

Enada said, "Indeed, it would. Therefore, the nobles of each house will become the first administrator of their territory, or co-administrator if there is both a baron and baroness. Their ministers will become members of the council for each barony. Five will be appointed the first members of the Council of the Nation from each territory.

"In six months, open elections will be held to select administrators, council members and five representatives who will sit at the Council of the Nation. Former nobles or commoners may run for election to serve for a period of five years, when a new election will be held, followed by another election every five years."

The Baroness of Arana said, "Majesty, will you relinquish power to this Council of the Nation? Who will make the laws?"

Enada said, "The council will make all laws for the land. Each council of the territories will make the laws for those territories. The laws of the nation will supersede those of the territories. No queen or king will be above the law because there will be neither.

"My last edict is to dissolve the monarchy and convert the nation to a republic. Every five years, the people will elect a national administrator to head the Government of Carandir, in accordance with the laws of the council.

"Administrators will gather advisors in different aspects of life as ministers to aid in the management. Each minister will be approved by the council.

"Administrators and ministers will make no laws. They'll approve or reject the laws passed by the council to ensure they are for the good of the people. Rejected laws will return to the council for amendment. If fifty-five council members vote to retain the law in its original form, it will be enacted without the administrator's approval. There will be no dictators with sole control."

Shouts erupted.

Someone yelled, "The queen is insane."

"She's ill. Take her to her chambers."

The baroness of Tesar pointed to the captain of her guard "Take the queen into custody."

Militia from six baronies advanced on the throne with drawn swords.

Herrik barked, "To the queen."

Enada raised her hands. None saw the eyes on the dragon pendant glow beneath her robes.

The soldiers froze in place, then sheathed their weapons. Some shook their heads and blinked. The different militias returned to the boxes of their nobles.

As at the trial of the jantella, a sense of right, wrong and justice surged through Enada.

When she spoke, every face turned to her. "Harmony is the will of the dragons. It's enshrined in the Great Plan. The evil of Baras is no more, yet disharmony remains. Heraldic rule, no matter how well intentioned, can breed entitlement and superiority. Citizens vital to the nation are excluded.

"This isn't the plan of the dragons. They once taught our ancestors knowledge and wisdom. They guided them because those people needed both. The dragons in the world I was born into suppressed self-determination in human. Questions and new ideas were considered dangerous. They sought to protect people, yet only introduced disharmony by smothering their spirits. They saw their mistake and corrected it.

"The dragons of this world never intended humans to be subjugated. Once Baras was subdued, they withdrew and allowed humans to forge the own destiny's. Yet, governments have retained unquestioned authority over others. The time has come for humans to end their search for outside guidance and guide themselves.

"Each of us knows the plan. We teach it to our young who mature and teach it to their young. Its lessons were never meant to be imposed. For the plan to work, we must act out of our own commitment to it. Harmony comes from love and respect for others. These emanate from within us. This new republic will govern from the will of all people. We need only remember the wisdom of the plan."

Dek stood. "We have much knowledge and at times lacked wisdom. We obey the rule of laws without understanding their purposes or intents. We abandon responsibility and hand it to others.

"We've seen how some with absolute power served only their desires for wealth and power. This new republic embraces the intent of the Great Plan of the dragons. Let it begin not with an edict but a vote of all the houses here represented. I vote yes.

The Baron of Ulata said, "As do I. Let the true power of Carandir shine."

One by one, the former nobles stood and dedicated themselves to the republic.

Dek said, "Who shall be the first national administrator? Enada, will you lead the nation?"

She removed the crown from her head and placed it, with the key, in the crystal case. "I have little knowledge of this world. You must choose another."

The Baron of Nemtanka said, "Then, should First Minister Batu take the position?"

Batu said, "Thank you for the nomination. I must decline as well. I'm of a former generation. Someone younger with new ideas should hold the title."

Another baroness said, "Who then has the experience? One of us?"

Enada reached out to Lek. "Here is one who has sat on the throne through a perilous times, one who knows the administration of the land, one who has shown wisdom and good judgment.

"Lek should be the national administrator until the election, at which time she will be free to run again."

Dek said, "I second the nomination. Who votes for Lek?"

All assembled said. "Aye."

Enada closed the lid of the crystal sphere. This time, with the magic gone, it remained unseal. "No one in Carandir will wear a crown."

EPILOGUE

A month later, Enada asked to see Lek. They walked in the palace garden filled the plants and trees from across the country. Once, only nobles were once allowed to visit. Now, all citizens could stroll at their leisure.

Enada sat on a bench. She didn't know it was the same one where Ryckair and Mirjel once courted. She said, "I would like to make a trip to see Amblar. I hope you'll come with me."

Lek sat next to her. "I should visit the North Continent. My staff and I can meet with the Amblar council."

"I've spoken to Batu. He said he'd love to see Amblar again. Retirement seems to have left him a little bored."

Lek smiled. "The council members have gone back to their territories. It would be an opportune time to travel."

"I'll take Shara as well," said Enada. "It would do her good to get out."

Enada held Shara's hand as she met Batu at a dock in Meth.

She said, "Are you ready?"

Shara smiled and squeezed Enada's hand.

Lek arrived with six members of her staff and five constables who acted as personal guards. They boarded and set sail. The weather held as a westerly wind moved them over the Great River.

The customs officer in Amblar was waiting. Since the magic of the Kyar was revoked, the spell Velatar cast to make it impossible for the terecs fly was undone. The tiny birds once more relayed telepathic messages far and wide.

A state dinner was held. Ichary, now administrator of the Amblar Territory, offered toasts to Enada, Lek and Batu. The evening was merry and filled with music.

Shara drew pictures and gave them to those nearby.

The stars moved in the sky well past bedtime. Dawn would come in another span.

Enada leaned into Lek. "Let's take a walk to the wizard tower before the sun rises. I'd like to see it."

Lek laughed. "Now? I'm barely awake."

"It won't take long. Batu, Shara, would you like to come?"

Batu said, "Yes, I would. Ichary, will you join us?"

"Of course. How could I turn down an adventure?"

Enada led them through the silent streets of Amblar and past the doors of citizens fast asleep.

When they reached the wizard tower, they climbed the steps of the wall and came to the door that appeared to be stone.

Enada said, "Lek, Batu, Come inside with me for a moment."

Ichary said, "The door's blocked since magic left."

"Ilidel only revoked her breath of creation from this world," said Enada. "The breath of the Ilidel in the other world is still within the Pendant. It'll open this door. Come on."

Enada took Shara's hand. The four of them entered the tower. They climbed the stairs to the window where Mirjel and Ryckair fell into the other world. The ruined city was in the background.

Lek drew in a breath. Just outside the window stood her former mistress Mirjel, with Ryckair at her side. It seemed they both aged two decades. A strange creature with short legs, long arms and an oval body covered in green scales was next to them.

The greatest awe came from the sight of a red dragon who looked like Baras.

Enada said, "This is our parting, Lek."

"I beg your pardon?"

"I don't belong in this world. It's for you and all the humans here to make a life. I'll step through this window and return to the place I was born into. The pendant will go with me to remove the last human magic from this place.

"Lead Carandir, Lek. You have the strength and wisdom. Call upon the advice of those around you. Listen to all before you act. Rely on your own judgement. Never doubt yourself."

Lek looked from one to the other "Batu, what will we do?"

He took her hands, "I'll step through the window as well. So will Shara. It is your time to shine."

Lek could find no words.

Enada kissed her on the cheek. "Goodbye."

She took Shara's hand and stepped through the window.

Batu followed.

Mirjel ran forward and embraced her daughter.

Ryckair and Batu hugged one another.

Mirjel stroked Shara's hair.

Lek saw Enada speak with the strange creature. She couldn't hear the words.

Enada walked to the dragon, who lowered his head. She removed the pendant from around her neck and placed it in his claw. Then, she reached out and stroked the dragon's cheek.

The dragon tousled her hair.

Lek heard him say, "Welcome home, little one."

A transparent bubble formed around the humans and the creature. The dragon picked it up and leapt into the sky. In moments, they were over the horizon.

Lek felt a rush of comfort with a sense of being whole.

Then, she felt urgency to leave the tower.

She moved down the stairs as fast as possible and out the door.

The moment she exited, the tower began to fade. Within a few heartbeats, it vanished. All Lek could see was the sea beyond the wall.

Ichary said, "What has happened?"

Lek turned east as the sun broke over the horizon to bathe her face in light. "It's a new dawn."

APPENDIX A

THE DRAGON TONGUE

Guide To Pronunciation

This book translates the common speech of Carandir, as it was known at the time of this tale, into the reader's language. Older dialects of Carandirian, as well as more ancient languages, are indicated in italics with archaic verbiage and sentence structure. The dragon tongue, however, remains as it was originally spoken. This includes the names of some people and places. The reader's alphabet has been used to approximate the sounds. This appendix provides a guide to proper pronunciation.

The letter *c* is pronounced hard, as in cat but not quite as hard as the letter *k*. In the original dragon tongue, *ch* was pronounced with the tongue pulled back in the throat and almost blocking off the air. Long before Ryckair's time, this sound had moved to the middle of the mouth and softened. The harsher sounds were preserved by the wizards in performing magic, as in the wizard Jarat's use of the word *hachana*, meaning, "submit", and by some creatures who still used a form of the dragon tongue, as in the Oola king's use of *Harch*, meaning, "you will".

The letter *j* is pronounced soft, as in the French name Jacques.

The letter *r* has a slight trill.

The Dharam *r* has a more pronounced trill. This is the product of their original Eastern tongue merging with that of the people of Amblar. It also accounts for the way they draw out the pronunciation of vowels and place emphasis on the first syllable of words.

In that tongue, *dha* meant people and *ra* strong, thus they called themselves the strong people. Many words from this original language were still in common use by the Dharam, who fully understood the meaning of their name.

When the letter *y* precedes a consonant, it is pronounced long (ī). When it precedes a vowel, it is pronounced with a lilt.

Vowels in names are generally pronounced short, except for vowels that begin a name, such as Orane (Ō-rān'), or are preceded by another vowel where the second vowel is silent, as in Ryckair (Rī-ckār').

The names Jea (Jĕ'-ă) and Mirjel (Mĭr-jĕl') are exceptions to this rule. Their names come from the city-state of Au to the east.

Two syllable names that end in a vowel have the accent on the first syllable, as in Craya (Crā'-yă) and Vara (Vā'-ră). Two syllable names in which the second syllable ends with a consonant have the accent on the second syllable, as in Herrik, (Hēr-rĭk'). Names that are more than two syllables long have the accent on the second to the last syllable, as in Telasec (Tē-lă'-sĕc) and Zamalatha (Zā-mă-lă'-thă).

Some names from the dragon tongue seem to defy this rule, such as Catio (Kă'-tē-ō). It sounds like a three-syllable name, even though the accent is on the first.

Here, we see an example of the corruption of the language over time. The ē-ō sound was once made by a single vowel that was written as ⩘ and pronounced yō. The sound lengthened over the centuries. The letter ⩘ was lost and replaced with the letters ⫴ and ⋀ (ē ō). So, whereas in Ryckair's time the name Catio was pronounced with three syllables written ⸚ ⅄ ⫴ ⋀ (Kăt-ē'-ō), it was originally pronounced with two syllables written as ⸚ ⅄ ⩘ (Kăt'-yō) and follows the rules for two syllable names that end in a vowel.

Word Origins

The dragon tongue was also called the wizard tongue. It influenced early human languages and many of its root words can be found in almost every language, even though each tribe created its own distinct dialect. Words from the dragon tongue are most often preserved in the names of people and places.

In those times, the roles of men and women were distinctly defined. Avar the Great decreed parity between genders. However, the language remained largely unchanged, partly because the origins of many words became corrupted or forgotten.

The name Carandir is not drawn directly from the dragon tongue. It comes from the language of a people known as the Laran who once lived around Lake Hasp.

They were one of the original tribes of humankind. Their ancestors learned at the feet of Ilidel, Jorondel and Magadel. They remained largely apart from other cultures and so preserved the ancient ways.

The lands of Carandir were given to Avar the Great by the Laran for his help in driving out the Barasha during the Dragon Wars and subduing Baras. Avar relocated the palace from Amblar to Meth shortly afterwards.

The Laran adopted the language spoken by Avar to foster trade and interaction with the people who came from the North Continent. This language was preserved for thousands of years in Carandir as the official court tongue spoken at formal ceremonies.

After two centuries, the Laran desired solitude again. They left Carandir to Avar's heirs and moved west over the mountains.

In Ryckair's time, Carandir was thought to mean deep forest, which is close to the actual words used by the Laran whose meaning translated to tree place unending, *Khach ena eer* in their language. The first part of the name comes from *Khach* meaning tree where the *ch* was pronounced in the back of the throat. The second part is from the word *ena* which means place. The final part came from the root word *eer* meaning infinity or unending. The words ran together into a single name in the ears of the first immigrants from the north continent.

At that time, the harsh *ch* sound had been replaced by a softer one that was pronounced in the middle of the mouth in their home of Amblar. They found the Laran word hard to pronounce and corrupted it into Carandir by changing the *ch* sound to *r*, the ena to *an* and the *eer* to *dir.*

Some scholars have mistakenly translated the original meaning by confusing *ena* in the Laran tongue with *enda* meaning human in the dragon tongue. These scholars erroneously thought the name Carandir meant tree people or the people who dwell in trees. Many pictorial representations of the Laran show them living in tree houses when, in fact, they built stone dwellings on the ground.

The language used by the Oola came from the dragon tongue through several sources, including the Barasha. The Oola were not themselves demons or spirits. They were, however, subverted by Baras during the Dragon Wars and sent to harass the people of Amblar on the north continent.

Krash means look here or pay heed and is generally used in royal decrees. It comes from the root words *ra* meaning message and *sha* meaning servant. The placement of a *k* sound in front of the word has no linguistic basis and is most likely a guttural inflection resulting from the construction of the Oola mouth.

Garack could mean enemy, not of us or stranger. It might have been drawn from the root word *geranel* meaning, disputed or disagreement. It could also have been a word developed by the Oola.

Harch is a directive that means let us, or from an official, you will. It comes from the root words *ha*, meaning do and *che* meaning now.

Narack means burn with fire or destroy with fire. It comes from the root word *Nara* meaning fire and *akie* or *akiety* meaning ruin or obliterate.

Kalaketan is the Oola word for humans. It translates literally as, "Thieves of the ground" in reference to the tunnels the humans dug through the Oola kingdom to mine silver, gold and iron. The root word *celec*, meaning thief, was changed again by the Oola's unique pronunciation. The root word *talan* originally meant well, as in a water well. It was later applied to any type of tunneling into the earth.

Therefore, the phrase *Krash. Garack. Harch Narack Kalaketan* translates to, "Behold. Our enemies the humans. Let us burn them". This was followed by the chant, "Burn them, burn them, burn them."

Common Roots

The following gives many common roots that still existed at the time of this tale, though their true meaning had sometimes changed over the millennia.

Ata	Something long waited for that has finally come to pass. It is also used to express the term, "At last."
Avan	In the time of this telling, *avan* meant mound or small hill. It was originally used to refer to a kind of tomb made by scooping out dirt, placing the deceased inside and building a mound of soil and stone above. Over time, this type of burial fell out of favor and was replaced with mausoleums for the wealthy and simple structures for the common people. The name for this new type of tomb was *karakay*.
Cray	Hope. For Craya's name, the suffix *ya* means small and is often used as a diminutive or a sign of affection for a person. The double *y* is reduced to one when the two words are combined. As such, Craya could be seen as being a familiar rendering

of hope or could be taken to mean a little hope.

Baras   One who betrays a trust.

Da   To heal. Daro means healing women or women who heal.

Del   Dragon. Jorondel incorporates the root joron meaning father and Ilidel incorporates the root word Ili, which came to mean mother but originally meant life. Thus, the names translate as dragon father and dragon mother, but are more commonly known as Father of Dragons and Mother of Dragons. Before he defiled the Great Plan and taught magic to humans, Baras' name was Magadel, combining *del* and *maga*, which means to teach. Thus, he was once called The dragon who teaches. When it was learned Magadel gave the knowledge of magic to humans, the other dragons accused him of being a betrayer, *baras* in the dragon tongue. Because of the heinous nature of the act, the accusation became his name.

Dragon Mound   The place where Baras fell under the control of Avar the Great's crown. The name is the result of a translation error in later years. In the original tongue, it was called *Delava*. This drew from the root words *del* and *avan* to mean dragon tomb. When Baras cries out *Nuava. Ata laney*, he is saying, "Removed from the tomb. At last, I am free." The prefix *nu* is used to indicate a negation, or not, as in *numij* for unfaithful. *Ava* is the ancient word for tomb. Placing these together, *nuava* means, to be released from death, to be reborn or to live again. *Ata* means finally or at last. It denotes something long waited for and greatly desired. Laney comes from the root word *lan* which means free. The suffix *ey* makes it possessive, *Laney* literally means, "I possess the state of being free." It is often used to simply mean freedom.

Ena   Soul. It originally meant beings who possess souls.

Enda   Human. Maganda combines *maga* and *enda* to form a word meaning the human who teaches. Enda draws from *ena*, the word for soul.

Kanta   Flesh of an animal.

Kair   A vessel that holds something. Ryckair's name combines *ry* for faith and *kair* to mean vessel of faith.

Kanto   Flesh of a human. The name Karaken comes from the root words *kara* meaning dead and *kanto*. This was an insult, insinuating the people of the southern kingdom practiced cannibalism. At first, the Karakiens embraced it, feeling it added to their reputation as fierce warriors, even though there is no record of any Karakien practicing cannibalism. The actual meaning was forgotten over time and the Karakiens came to think the name meant great warriors.

Kara   Dead. It can also refer to someone who is dead.

Kay   A building or dwelling.

Karakay   A mausoleum or tomb. It combines, *Kara* meaning death with *kayning*, the possessive form of *kay*, to literally mean home of the dead or tomb.

Kura   A song or lay.

Ma   Man.

Mija   Trustworthy. Two popular names use this root word, the feminine Mirjel and the masculine Mirja. Both names mean one who can be trusted. The antonym of *mija* is *numij*, meaning, unfaithful or not trusted.

Nara   Fire.

Ne   Light.

Nema   Sun. It draws from *ne* and *ma* to literally translate as man light. The sun's short cycle was equated to the act of impregnating a woman, who then took on the longer cycle of bearing a child conceived of this act.

Nero   Moon. It draws from *ne* and *ro* to literally translate as woman light. This association comes from the similarity between the cycles of the moon's phase and a woman's menstrual cycle. Women were traditionally thought to hold power over the moon and the cycles of planting they foretold.

Par   Gift. Some translate *Parili* as gift of Ilidel for the mercy she showed the Fadella. It is also thought of as gift of Life.

Ro   Woman.

Ry   Faith.

Sha   This word can have several meanings. In the time of this tale, it referred to a lowly servant or follower, but originally it meant strength or power and was used to describe special supporters of powerful people, such as a monarch's general. A general might be said to be a monarch's power. This could be looked at in two ways. First, the general gave a monarch power out of devotion. Second, the general could be considered a monarch's power base and without this sha a monarch held no supremacy. Because of this, a sha servant was endowed with great respect. Barasha originally meant Baras' power but came to mean The Servants of Baras. Only in later times did the term become associated with people who performed menial labor. Shara's name could have two meanings. Her father intended it as an insult for not being the son he desired. He wanted to compare her to a serving woman of low stature, such as a scullery maid. In truth, the ancient roots of the base words mean, powerful woman.

THE DESERT OF THE
NORTH CONTINENT

A report by Nesaro Resplen
Senior Kyar Scribe
The year 58 of the Republic of Carandir

This is a high desert, as opposed to those at or below sea level on the South Continent in nations such as Karaken and Taquan.

In the south, the temperature varies little from season to season. In the north, temperatures can swing wildly between summer and winter. The sun in summer is hot enough to raise blisters after long exposure. In the winter, temperatures often drop below freezing at night, bringing frost and sometimes snow.

The extreme conditions of the region have produced hardy peoples who have developed wisdom and technologies to cope with the harsh climate and changes of seasons.

There are city-states in the east with great buffers of desert between them inhabited by nomadic tribes consisting of goat and sheep herders, for these are some of the few mammalian animals that can digest the scrub brush found there.

Most of the ground is hard-packed soil, though there are great expanses of sand dunes to the northeast. The land is largely flat with the exception of some tall peaks on which snow falls in the winter and melts during the year to flow into streams and rivers and fill aquifers beneath the ground. Some of these underground waterways extend deep into the desert and feed springs where oases form. Tribes roam territorial areas with the seasons and have strategically placed wells they guard against others.

In the spring, rain comes, often in driving torrents, to fill dry ravines. Some storms drop large bursts of water that can fill temporary rivers. This brings a flurry of life as plants that lay dormant the rest of the year bloom. Insects pollinate flowers that drop their seeds to germinate the next year.

Languages and Dialects

There are many languages and dialects spoken in the eastern lands of the North Continent. As with all languages, those of the people living in the desert have their roots in the dragon tongue. Many have diverged extensively and only the most basic core words remain, such as ma for man and ro for woman, yet the dialects often mask the similarity, even to scholars.

The people of the Osto tribe originated in a land east of the desert. They spoke a language drawn from the dragon tongue. It evolved to sound much like formal Carandirian. This became tempered when they moved their herds west into the desert and encountered other cultures when trade with Amblar was still brisk, before its inhabitants were banished to become the Fadella, the wandering sorrow, and Carandirian influence faded.

A standard trading language developed for commerce that is known to most who buy and sell goods. It allows rudimentary communication and includes units of measure for price and quantity. The language also includes greetings, measures of distance, time and, as with all languages, there are words for exasperation and even profanity.

Even among peoples who speak a dialect near to Carandirian, trading words would slip into conversation. The trading language itself has a short vocabulary and little syntax. The phrase, *Oos Ata den e oom esa* (You sit here with me dine) could also be said as *Esa den ata oos oom e* (dine here sit you me with).

There are no articles, such as *the*, *a*, or *an* in the trading language.

Apa   Indicates something is relative to another thing.

Ata   To sit or recline.

Aut   Gold.

Cheyak   It's a deal, or I accept.

Chimka   To drink.

Cho   Destination, or the final step or occurrence of an event.

Chonara   Year.

Prava   The leader of a caravan or the person responsible for trade.

Dama   A state of being ill or hurt.

Dar   There.

Del   Dragon, as taken directly from the dragon tongue.

Den   Here.

Deas   To rest.

Deach   To sleep.

Dima   A state of being well. It is also used as a greeting. When people meet, it takes on the meaning, "Hello. Good health to you." When people depart, it means, "Goodbye and may good health go with you."

Delgar   Literally, "dragon tail," combining del for dragon and gar for tail. It is the ultimate explicative for anger and frustration.

Enn   Copper.

Esa   To eat.

Gar   Tail or end piece of an object or story.

Gen   Name or identity.

Helach   The price is too high.

Je   Sparkle or brilliance.

Kalako   A heretic who denies the dragons or is aligned with demons.

Lakta   A thief or cheat.

Lokry   To make or cause to be.

Menaha	To feel or experience.
Na	Silver.
Necra	Them.
Nema	A day.
Nero	A month.
Oom	Me.
Oos	You.
Onu	Horse.
Onutagar	Literally translates to "you're a horse's tail" combining *onu* for horse, *ta* being the possessive and *gar* for tail or end. The meaning is, "You're a horse's rear end." It is also used as an expletive of anger or frustration akin to "excrement."
Parsa	A medicated salve.
Pata	Movement.
Pursa	Any medicine taken orally.
Questa	Herder of animals.
Seeba	Coin with a monetary value.
Ta	A suffix that makes a noun possessive.
Tinapa	Equivalent to a Carandir measurement of time called a span.
Tinlo	Finger or fingers, depending on the context.
Tu	Stone or rock.
Ura	Us.
Vo	Water.

Time

The concept of the span, where time is measured by the movement of the sun or stars between outstretched fingers, has been used as a method of time keeping for millennia and is found in almost every culture.

Even with the development of devices that provide more precise measurements and are not influenced by changing seasons, such as sand glasses, developed independently in several regions, and water clocks, first created in Hura, people in the northern desert, like many in Carandir, still measure the passage of time with their outstretched fingers.

In the trading language, a span is called a *tinapa*, for movement between fingers (from *tinlo* for finger, *apa* for relative to and *pata* for movement). Extended time is expressed in suns for day and moons for month as *nema* and *nero*, which are drawn directly from the dragon tongue for man light (sun or day) and woman light (moon or month). A year is called *chonaro* referring to the final month (from *cho* for final or finally and *nara* for moon).

Units of Measure

Measurements for weight, volume and distance are based on the proportions of adult human hands and feet in a similar manner as is used in Carandir. In larger cities, the units became standardized by agreement between trading partners and models were created out of gold to provide templates for measuring devices made of wood or metal. These models form the gold standard for all measurements and examples are kept in each city and town that uses the formal specifications. In smaller towns and settlements, measurements are often made using human hands and feet. As such, they can be imprecise due to differences in stature between people.

Linear measurement is based on the width of a finger and a length of a step. A distance equivalent to a finger width is called a nail. Four nails make a palm. The distance of a single step measured from the heel of one foot to the toe of the leading foot is called a stride. There are ten palms to a stride, ten strides form a room, ten rooms form a pen, ten pens form a field and ten fields form a road, the standard unit for long distances.

The volume of a cube measuring four nails on each side is a cup. Four cups make a jar. Four jars make a jug. Smaller units are based on the volume that can be held in a cupped hand, referred to as a scoop. There are ten scoops in a cup.

Weight is based on the volume of sand held in a cup. This is referred to as a stone. Stones are divided into smaller units such as half-stones, quarter-stones, eighth-stones and so forth. Measurements for larger weights are the block (one-hundred stones) and boulder (one-thousand stones).

Currency

Many forms of currency abound. Coins of copper, silver and gold are common. At one time, coins that carried established values from Amblar and later Dharam, were seen in the desert region but their use slowly diminished. City-states such as Masna issue coins of standard weight and purity and were easily exchanged for a set value. Masna coins are found customarily in the southern part of the desert and are called *seeba* (*aut-seecba* for gold, *naseeba* for silver and *ennseeba* for copper).

Valuation in the desert region is similar to those in Carandir and most places on the South Continent. One hundred copper coins is equivalent to one silver coin. Fifty silver coins holds the same value as one gold coin. Two coppers will purchase a drink at most taverns and inns while five coppers will purchase a good though not extravagant meal. Three silver coins can purchase a horse or peretan. Few people ever see a gold coin, which can purchase a building.

Other coins vary in both weight and makeup. Some smaller city-states and even larger tribes issue their own. These are often inconsistent. Because of this, their value is determined by weight and purity of the metal. Most merchants carry touchstones, scales and canisters they fill with water into which they immerse objects to gauge their volume.

Gemstones are also a form of currency. Both settlements and tribes have at least one gemologist to determine a stone's value. Diamonds are *nerotu* (moon stone), rubies *naratu* (fire stone), emeralds *votu* (water stone) and opals *jetu* (sparkle stone).

A silver coin can buy most opals. Rubies and emeralds can fetch ten to fifty silver coins, depending on the size and quality. Diamonds can run from ten to several hundred gold pieces, depending on their color, clarity, cut and size.

Among smaller tribes, such as the nomadic herders, commodities are bartered for whatever the parties agree is a fair exchange.

Transportation

The mode of transportation differs between the western and eastern sections of the desert. In both, carts and wagons are rarely seen outside of major cities.

It is not unusual for people in the west and east to walk long distances between villages and settlements. Herders will take their animals between pastures on foot. An average person can walk twelve roads in a day.

Horses are ridden in the western desert. The land, which is often firm, offers ample grasslands near oases and lakes where low, edible brush covers large areas. Horses are both ridden and used as pack animals. They can travel twenty to fifty roads per day depending on whether they are walking or trotting and can cover twice the ground at a gallop over short distances.

Horses are seen in the eastern desert but much of the ground is softer and there are sand dunes in many areas. The people of the east tend to use peretans. These even-tempered, six legged lizards can measure up to fifteen strides long, five wide and three high. Their wide, padded feet provide stability on both soft ground and dunes. They can walk twenty roads in a day and can trot at nearly one and a half times that speed over short distances. They are ridden by strapping a canopied platform, called a sinthra, to their backs or used as draft animals by replacing the sinthra with one or more boxes.

Political Structures

Governance varies between tribes and city-states.

Some tribes are led by an elder who could be a woman or a man or by a council of elders. Other tribes are headed by a hereditary chief. For most, this is the first born of either gender. A few lines pass only to the eldest male. In one tribe, power flows only through the female line.

Among city-states, there are some lords. Most are ruled by a council. These are often made up of the most powerful merchants. That is the case for Masna.

Men and women sit on most councils. Two city-states in the northwest are patriarchal due to the influence of the Dharam in past times. Some tribes, and even city-states, refuse to deal with them because of their exclusion of women. A guild of barterers acts as agents where men deal with the patriarchal societies and women interact with the other tribes and city-states. A few tribes and city-states refuse to work with the guild on the grounds that they perpetuate misogamy.

Faith

During the dragon wars, what became the northern desert was a rich land of rolling hills, lakes, meadows and forests. Few people inhabited the region as the tribes of humankind were largely concentrated near the Great Ocean or the banks of the Great River. Neither Baras nor the Barasha invaded the area and the oldest tribes, though taught by Magadel, carry no racial memory of the Dragon War.

As in Carandir before the Barasha returned, faith in the dragons is strongest outside the major population centers. In some metropolitan areas, tales of dragons, wizards and sorcerers have become legends and myths. Still, many invoke the names of Ilidel and Jorondel, especially in times of difficulty.

There were no Kyar or Daro in the desert region. Wizards did visit and taught healing to the women of many tribes. They left herb lore but no magic. Still, the Great Plan of the dragon council is enshrined in memory as an oral tradition passed to each generation, sometimes through elders and sometimes by select individuals chosen to preserve the knowledge. It is the basis of law and custom among nomads and city dwellers alike.

Social order

Commerce is a glue that binds people together. Diverse groups trade amongst each other across the desert.

The larger city-states tolerate differences in custom, culture, foods and the like, as long as they do not impede trade. Freedom to express opinions can be completely open, even for comments about the government. In a few communities, however open descent of the rulers, and in some cases powerful citizens, can lead to punishment and even banishment.

Except for a few royal and powerful merchant families, where unions are based on political advantage, arranged marriages are uncommon. A deep tradition of love poems and songs rival those of Carandir's rich literary heritage. The poem *Esar Nekar*, In Body and Soul, is known even in the western realms, though many do not realize its origins.

Among the nomadic tribes, conformity to rules and commands is expected. Deference is shown to elders. An act as simple as tipping a hat the wrong way can bring admonishment.

Though women and men often hold the same power, respect and authority, youth are expected to follow the wishes of elder members.

APPENDIX B

SONGS AND LAYS

The western and eastern lands were rich in stories told through music and poetry. Many early histories were written in varying bardic meters established for particular kinds of tales. Some of these meters have been lost as the ancient languages were translated into common Carandirian.

Travelling bards were the conveyers of both entertainment and news. As they were a vital source of information for ordinary citizens, merchants and rulers alike, bards were revered. Despots were reluctant to harass or hurt them, even when the bards sang about events close to home.

Their instruments ranged from harps to flutes, tambourines and drums. They sometimes received coins and at other times, food and lodgings.

The tonal scale used by the bards was similar to modern notation, which has been used to recreate the music.

New music was written to commemorate events, people or simply life. Still, most performances included old songs the people knew and sometimes sang along with.

Both individuals and troupes traveled a circuit and most made a good living from their work. Others had to supplement their passion for music with some sort of work outside the arts.

Here are songs, poems and sonnets from The Carandir Saga to include the unabridged versions with all the verses.

Good Brown Country Ale

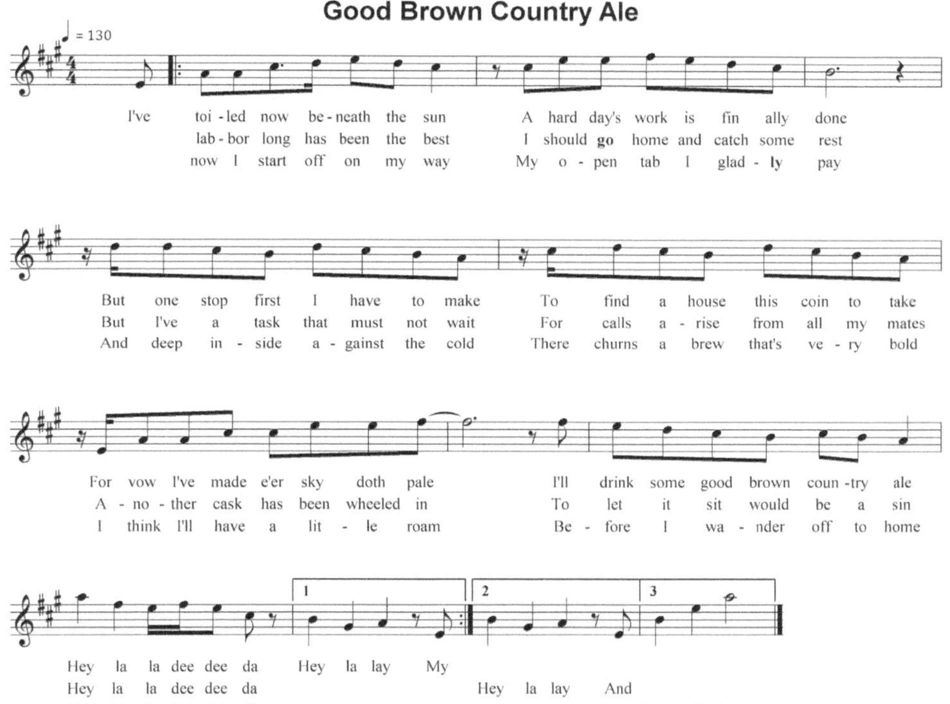

On Dragon's Wings

Marching Men

Haul in the Net

♩ = 140

Haul in   the net   Haul in   the net

The fish are jump-ing   Their sil-ver scales shine

Haul in the net   Haul in the net

The deck is   fill-ing   To- night we will dine

The Merchant's Life

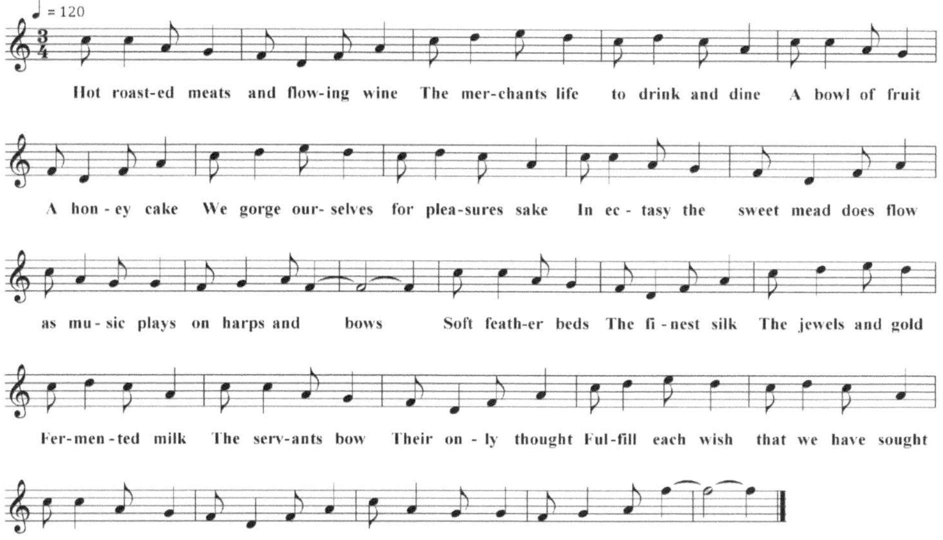

Seasons of Wine

The Lay of Baron Yold

The Golden Grains of Summer Wheat

Will You Come Back?

The Chyning

♩ = 70
1.   A hunt was planned for king and prince to shoot for bird and ve - ni-son
2.   For chan cellors eight sought roy - al heads their thought to end a dy-nas-ty
15.   Then hand in hand she led them high in - to the star filled ca-no-py

mp
So bows were strung and qui - vers stocked then chance - llors king and prince rode forth
and so in - still their force and will on king - dom lands and people there
and there they stand for all to see the lo - vers of the e - vening sky

In - to the woods and through the fields the mer - ry hunt pro cee - ded well
Then ar - rows rained a King did fall his bo - dy tram - pled on the ground
The king - dom now in ru - ins lies the chan - cellors all re - duced to dust

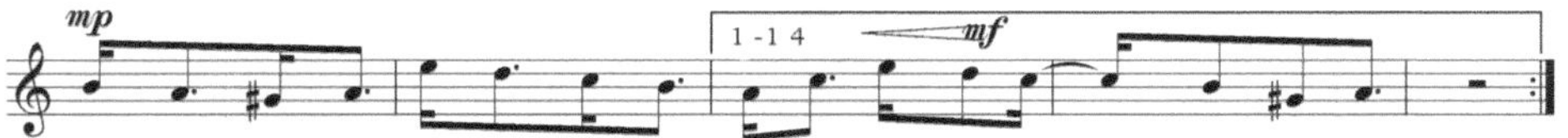
mp   1 - 1 4   mf
but faith - less - ness and se - cret plan were in the chan cellors' heart that day
and turned then men of bow and shaft to slay the prince and heir as well
still in the sky the stars shine on

15   f
for love will last be - yond the world

1. A hunt was planned
    For king and prince
    To shoot for bird and venison
    So bows were strung
    And quivers stocked
    Then chancellors, king and prince rode forth

    Into the woods
    And through the fields
    The merry hunt proceeded well
    But faithlessness
    And secret plan
    Were in the chancellors' heart that day

2. For chancellors eight
    Sought royal heads
    Their thought to end a dynasty
    And so instill
    Their force and will
    On kingdom lands and people there

    Then arrows rained
    A king did fall
    His body trampled on the ground
    And turned then men
    Of bow and shaft
    To slay the prince and heir as well

3. But from this trap
    The prince escaped
    And wandered long o'er field and flood
    His heart was worn
    No hope he saw
    And thought to lay down dying there

    And then by chance
    A glade he found
    And saw among the golden leaves
    A sleeping sprite
    Of female form
    In raiment white, the Chyning fair

4. Of old he heard
    The legends speak
    Of spirits waiting in the wood
    To spring awake
    In time of need
    And aid the true and rightful king

    Before his eyes
    A light shone pure
    His worries fell upon the ground
    Without a word
    The Chyning rose
    And spoke she then her purpose there

5. Her aid, she said
    Could come but once
    A single boon to grant had she
    Before she lay
    Once more in sleep
    Until a new king called for her

    His father's death
    Consumed his heart
    His only thought was vengeance cold
    A boon he asked
    On bended knee
    Her help to gain his father's crown

6. The claim then made
    He steeled for war
    But when he looked into her eyes
    All thoughts of crowns
    Grew cold and pale
    The Chyning's love he now desired

    And in that thought
    Was seed of doom
    For one thing ever was forbid
    If she should love
    A mortal man
    The Chyning's power would fade away

7. Then up she sprang
    And through the air
    He held her hand as high they flew
    And so returned
    To kingdom lands
    Before the chancellors could arrive

    A battle long
    There came to be
    And many fell as blood was spilt
    Yet to the prince
    Allegiance drew
    And soon his army's ranks did swell

8. Then chancellors eight
    Were driven out
    Of them five dead in battle lay
    The other three
    Withdrew with few
    Some men, a handful for to lead

    The prince now king
    Gave pardons then
    But to the rebels he refused
    So with new men
    Of counsel wise
    The king held celebration great

9. He ruled most wise
    Both fair and just
    And all did love him dearly so
    Still in his heart
    A fire burned
    The longing for the Chyning fair

    Through many years
    He ruled in peace
    Yet saw her face in dreams each night
    Soon came a time
    When thought of her
    Removed him from his diligence

10. Then evil foul
    And murderous deeds
    In secret crept into the land
    And so one day
    The king's high seat
    Was challenged by the chancellors three

    With force of arms
    The chancellors three
    Made war upon their sovereign king
    And drove him from
    His palace walls
    With catapult and battering ram

11. And fled he then
    Into the woods
    Pursued by men of arms and hate
    He looked in vain
    To find his love
    Yet nowhere could he see her now

    Once more all hope
    Was nearly lost
    He heard the horsemen closing fast
    Through brush he fell
    Into a glade
    To find his love, the Chyning fair

12. He laid his hand
    Upon her cheek
    And gently bent to kiss her lips
    With open eyes
    She stared at him
    As smiling tears fell down her cheeks

    For she now loved
    This mortal man
    And placed her arms around him tight
    In such embrace
    The chancellors three
    Soon came upon their king and prey

13. Then arrows flew
     And flesh was pierced
     No magic could the Chyning weave
     For once in love
     Her magic failed
     And with the king she now faced death

     They looked into
     Each other's eyes
     And in that space of brevity
     A lifetime played
     Within their hearts
     And all they knew was love and bliss

14. With arms entwined
     Their bodies fell
     Upon the ground with thud of death
     Departed then
     The chancellors three
     Now having won their victory

     But no foul beast
     Consumed that pair
     For Ilidel, who's wisdom reigns
     Looked down upon
     Their faces fair
     And called them up unto her halls

15. Then hand and hand
     She led them high
     Into the star filled canopy
     And there they stand
     For all to see
     The lovers of the evening sky

     The kingdom now
     In ruin lies
     The chancellors all reduced to dust
     But in the sky
     The starts shine on
     For love will last beyond the world

The Sonnet of Catio and Stamered

Beat the wings, beat the wings,
A dove emerged from branch on high,
And in the cool spring forest air,
Stamered, prince of mountain people,
Cocked a shaft with careful aiming,
But never did that arrow fly,
For on a hill, in radiant view,
Sat Catio, the Princess fair,
Upon her pure white riding mare;

He paused his stallion silently,
And came upon the hill with stealth,
Lest the lovely maiden there,
Be a spirit kindled free,
Living as a doe, to bolt,
When the hunter comes in view,
Yet Catio saw not of him,
Lost was she in sorrow grieving,
For her brother dead in battle;

Upon his knee Stamered fell,
And cried aloud his love for her,
And Catio in turning quickly,
Saw the young man, fair and gallant,
And her heart went out to his,
Joining there within the forest,
Buttercups he gathered for her,
And with them made a chain of petals,
This to be her wedding garland;

Yet doom was laid upon these lovers,
For battle loomed between their tribes,
And Catio did not suspect,
That in the combat fought last eve,
Twas her own love, Stamered prince,
Who slew her only brother dear,
And Stamered knew not the man,
Whose heart his sword had pierced that day,
Catio's brother, Peetdeley;

The next day's eve they planned to meet,
In forest glen far from the strife,
Then each went down to their own folk,
With vow to hold their meeting dear,
To guard their love for a time,
Each knowing well the strife they faced,
To speak with tribes beyond their own,
And face the doom of banishment,
If any knew their secret hearts;

The ocean king sat on his throne,
As Catio came to his hall,
And grim his countenance did lay,
"Where hast thou been, my daughter one?"
For never was she far from sight,
Yet tarried long from her own tribe,
In time of war and danger deep,
"Tell now the wonders thou hast seen."
For he suspected tracheary;

Great fear the princess fair did feel,
For anger now lay hot about,
"I rode but long along the shore,
To see the new flowers growing there,"
Yet of the gallant man she loved,
Word she kept unto herself,
In fear of wrath upon her head,
"The beauty drew me deeply there,
And that is why I tarried so";

"The flowers thou hast seen before,"
Said king and father on his throne,
"Tis time of war and danger bounds,
No safety can be found abroad."
Then looking deep into her eyes,
A flicker hinted at untruth,
And vowed he then to have her watched,
By one he trusted overall,
To bring him news of what befell;

The evening next the princess rode,
In secrecy away from camp,
Yet spied she not a lone pursuit,
That followed every path she took,
Across the shore her horse did fly,
Until she came upon the hill,
And met again the man so fair,
A member of the other tribe,
To whom she planned to give her troth;

Upon the hill stood Stamered,
With flowers in his trembling hands,
Such Catio did find him there,
And ran into his open arms,
Yet cousin hidden in the brush,
Clenched fist and jaw with sword in hand,
For he had fought in battle last,
And saw the sword of Stamered
Pierce flesh of Catio's brother dear;

Then charging forth in boiling rage,
The cousin shouted to the world,
"Doest thou not know the treachery,
This man inflicted on your kin?"
With words of hate he spoke of war,
And Stamered's place upon the field,
That took the life of one she loved,
With hard sword run through flesh and bone,
To murder Peetdeley so cruel;

Catio pushed then far away;
And stared at Stamered with hate,
"To murder Peetdeley is grief,
To hold the truth is doubly cursed."
She mounted then and charged away,
Her cousin following in her track,
Stood Stamered in guilt and pain,
Now seeing horror in the war,
He vowed to end unreasoning strife;

With tears and wailing rode Catio,
Yet hate she could not raise within,
And thought then came into her mind,
That endless war delivers naught,
But makes grave foes of innocents,
Stamered fought as did her kin,
No hate had he for Peetdeley,
The war so senseless was to blame,
She rode then hard toward Stamered;

Into the Frey went Stamered,
To stop the charge of men and arms,
To sue for peace err more should die,
But heat of battle ranged about,
His son King Tanar did not know,
And so impaled Stamered prince,
Seeing who he killed too late,
Stamered fell upon the ground,
As Catio in horror watched;

She turned her horse and rode away,
Her mind ablaze with heavy woe,
The wretched death of beau and brother,
Left her inconsolable,
Her cousin galloped in pursuit,
"Stop," he cried in dire warning,
Yet to a sea cliff Catio drew,
From which she plunged into the waters,
And vanished there within the waves.

Then funeral pyre for Stamered,
Was laid upon the sand of beach,
And two kings grieving children lost,
Together vowed to end the war,
The pyre lit with flames on flesh,
Watched then they a foam of sea,
In form of maiden on a horse,
That scooped the body of the prince,
 And carried him into the sea.

Esar Nekar

In Body and Soul

No skin confines our souls, my love,
No words define its depth.
No passion can consume us.
For we are passion,
Lost and found in each other.
Flames,
Spent and renewed.
Even if separated,
Never separate.

Lift me to the sky,
On wings of raw desire.
Fly the clouds with me,
Swoop unafraid in ecstasy.
Abandon flesh,
To become flesh.

Soar into the hidden places,
Revealed to each other,
Without hesitation,
Without guard,
Without fear,
In communion,
One,
Whole,

Expanse eternal.
A breath,
Two breaths,
Settle beyond the boundless void.
Cooling together,
Forming as two in one,
Distinct and melded.
Sky fire to warm sand,
Bodies again,
Entwined,
Congealed,
Content in comfort everlasting.

APPENDIX C

The Fall Of Magadel

In the beginning, there was the Egg. Within, none knew of the others and so knew not themselves.

The minds of two touched, Jorondel and Ilidel, dragons powerful and mighty, and so they became aware. They touched all minds therein and awakened them.

Out of the Egg, all there was, all there is and all there ever will be sprang forth in chaos and disorder. The dragons shaped this world. Chief among them were Ilidel and Jorondel, Mother and Father of Dragons.

A council was formed and the Great Plan laid out to guide the tribes of people in all manner of things so they might know the world and live in harmony. The dragons taught them to build, to plow, to weave, to sing; all things under the sun and stars.

Yet, Ilidel and Jorondel decreed that humans could never possess the doom of magic.

Among the dragons, Magadel became a great teacher. He showed humans wondrous things out of his love of Jorondel and Ilidel and the plan of the council. From him, the peoples of the world learned music and art, the forge and the wheel.

They praised the dragon of knowledge, yet always he told them, "Praise not me, for I am but a vessel for the will of Jorondel and Ilidel. Praise their names alone."

To generations of humankind, Magadel taught all he knew. Then, a time came when he had no more to teach. The people now spread the knowledge they learned from Magadel to their young.

The dragon of knowledge felt pride in the humans who now taught their children. At the same time, he felt sad, for he loved teaching. He searched in his mind for new things to teach. There was only one.

He went before the Council of Dragons. "Praise be to Jorondel and Ilidel. Praise be to the council. The plan is great. Yet, plans can change. We are forbidden to teach humans magic but why do we not teach them small spells to make their lives better. Surely this should be allowed in the plan."

The council debated Magadel's arguments but rejected his desire.

Jorondel said, "There cannot be partial magic. It would corrupt people and give them only misery in the end."

Ilidel said, "They are pure and innocent. They must remain so for harmony to continue."

Magadel left in shame and anger. Other beings took note of this. He withdrew far from all others and brooded, feeling deep pain at the loss of trust from Ilidel and Jorondel.

"They shall see the wisdom of this," he told himself. "People will be served by magic, not destroyed."

In secret, he gathered together a band of men who desired power among their own kind and taught them the lesser art of sorcery with its chants and powders and simple spells. Thus, did magic come to the human tribes.

At first, the men used their new powers to move stones in the fields or repair boats. Soon, however, one man used magic to burn down a rival's shop. Magadel brought the men together again and warned them not to use magic for evil.

All was quiet until the chief of one tribe used magic to attack another. Magadel, himself, forced peace between them, though many died and so flew to the Dragons' Halls.

Magadel remained convinced people could benefit from magic if the rest of the council taught its use. He now cursed their names for abandoning him, especially the names of Jorondel and Ilidel. Pain came to him as he feared he had lost their love.

The breaking of the council's will thundered through the fabric of the world. The dragons cried out in revulsion and called Magadel the betrayer, Baras, by which name he was ever after known.

The men he taught praised Baras and his new name. Hoping to turn them from evil, he showed them more spells. The men quickly mastered each. They pleaded to learn more but Baras had exhausted his knowledge of sorcery.

He sat outside the world for a time in contemplation of what he did and asked himself if he was wrong, if people should not have learned magic, yet he was convinced he was right. "The Council is at fault. If they had joined me, we could have guided the tribes together."

He wondered if Ilidel and Jorondel forbade the teaching of magic because they were jealous of him and he wished he had taken the praise of the people. He loved Jorondel and Ilidel above all else and they now spurned him.

"So be it. Others there are who will follow me. We will rule the council. Baras they have named me and Baras I shall be."

To the men he had taught sorcery, he revealed the secret of feeding living souls to demons such that these spirits might be bound for a short while and forced to perform true magic. At this, the men fell to their knees and worshipped him as their lord and master, declaring themselves the Servants of Baras, the Barasha.

They donned crimson robes for the blood the demons demanded in payment and threw down villages, towns, entire cities in the name of Baras, laying slaughter to all within. The terror of their acts went before them. Lands sued for mercy. The vanquished paid tribute to Baras and in secret prayed to Ilidel and Jorondel for deliverance.

Other spirits, seeing these victories, followed Baras. Some few were dragons seeking greater glories. The bulk of his host was comprised of the demons, those lesser beings hungry for power.

The council was called together.

Jorondel said, "Evil has come unbidden into the world and changed it."

Ilidel said, "Baras now forces us to change our plan."

Jorondel raised an army of dragons and spirits and went to war against Baras and his hosts.

To counter the Barasha, Ilidel gathered together three men and three women. She instructed them in the art of true magic. Thus, the wizards came to be. Though mortal, their lives were measured not by the passing of years but by the grinding of millennia.

The wizards forged a simple war helm, a steel cap with four gold bands running from the lip to the apex, and a band of gold around the rim.

Jorondel took the helm and fashioned for it a silver crest in the shape of a dragon as if it leapt into the sky.

Ilidel breathed the will of creation into the crest such that even Baras would need bow before its power.

A hero came forth, Avar, chieftain of the lands of Amblar. He took the war helm and named it his crown.

Baras laughed when this mortal stood before him with challenges and demands. All laughter ended when the spell of the crown surrounded and imprisoned him. His bellow resounded throughout the land as he struggled against the constricting webs of magic.

People thought the end of the world had come.

The web closed as Baras' power ebbed. His last waking sight was that of the crown, the accursed crown, whose image hovered constantly in his mind along with that of the mortal who dared use it against him.

Baras was subdued and rendered impotent. The errant demons were captured by the wizards who imprisoned them in great towers and strongholds that existed in the physical and magical worlds. The Barasha, too, were hunted down and finally declared destroyed.

In his sleep, Baras dreamed of what might have been. The dreams filled him with a hatred of all things that walked alive beneath the sun, for he would never see such again. At the same time, he was consumed with rage for all things that died and so departed this world, for that escape was not his to have.

Most of all, they filled him with a seething hunger for vengeance against Avar and all his generations.

Thus, the Dragon Wars ended.

Jorondel declared, "Follow, now, the teachings of the council to bring about the Great Plan."

Ilidel said, "Yet, know Baras but sleeps and his hatred can rise again through us."

ABOUT THE AUTHOR

David A. Wimsett writes novels and short stories as well as articles, columns and blogs for newspapers, magazines, corporations, and online platforms. He has appeared on radio and television talk shows and as an actor in musicals, comedies and dramas.

He became a single parent in his twenties and both raised and guided his son into adulthood.

The stories he writes follow characters as they grow and have the opportunity to examine themselves and their place in the world on a deep level. His works are intended to entertain and present ideas while creating strong, complex characters of diverse genders, identities, Races, backgrounds and beliefs who face realistic challenges in their lives.

His women's historical fiction novel, *Beyond the Shallow Bank*, with element of Celtic mythology, was a first place winner at The BookFest Awards.

Mr. Wimsett is a member of the Writers' Union of Canada and the Canadian Freelance Guild.

He lives in a rural town near the sea.

His author's website is https://www.davidawimsett.com